ONCE SHADOWS FALL

ONCE SHADOWS FALL

A THRILLER

ROBERT DANIELS

CROOKED LANE

NEW YORK

Copyright © 2015 by Robert M. Daniels Corp.

Published in the United States by Crooked Lane Books, an imprint of The Quick Brown Fox & Company LLC.

Crooked Lane Books and its logo are trademarks of The Quick Brown Fox & Company LLC.

The Library of Congress Cataloging-in-Publication Data is available upon request.

ISBN (hardcover): 978-1-62953-383-4
ISBN (paperback): 978-1-62953-484-8
ISBN (ePub): 978-1-62953-384-1
ISBN (Kindle): 978-1-62953-657-6
ISBN (ePDF): 978-1-62953-668-2

Cover design by Andy Ruggirello
Book design by Jennifer Canzone

Printed in the United States.

www.crookedlanebooks.com

Crooked Lane Books
2 Park Avenue, 10th Floor
New York, NY 10016

First Edition: December 2015

10 9 8 7 6 5 4 3 2 1

This book is dedicated to my mother, who gave me life and taught me the meaning of it through her boundless love, loyalty, and wisdom.

Prologue

Luck: hard to plan for it, impossible to predict when it might show up. Driving through the town of Jordan in search of a suitable subject for her class assignment, twenty-year-old Melissa Harris was almost ready to concede her luck had run out. Less than a week remained before she had to turn her class project in, and she'd come up with nothing for her photo study.

Romantic farmhouses and barns? Really?

Professor Micklenberg, however, was serious. Submit a portfolio or flunk the class. Landscape photography was supposed to be a spring semester cakewalk at the University of Georgia. Instead, it was turning out to be a major pain in the ass. College professors, she had found, took everything seriously, particularly themselves.

The first farm Melissa came to was nondescript and ordinary. Basically, a crashing bore. The second was worse. But just when she was about to give up, her luck changed. The first thing she noted about the last farm was that it was abandoned.

Romantic? Maybe not, but, well . . . interesting. At that point, she was willing to take interesting.

Melissa made a U-turn and pulled her Prius onto the shoulder. She got out and stood there, absorbing the details. Several hundred yards away, at the rise of an amber-colored hill dotted with wild flowers, sat a faded white-and-gray house. Something straight out of Wyeth's *Christina's World*. To the right of the house, perhaps a quarter mile from it, was an ancient barn, a silo, and a windmill, its blades turning slowly in the cool afternoon air. Farther to the right, a line of trees ran parallel to a set of railroad tracks that disappeared in the distance. The tracks were seemingly forgotten like the farm itself. Once this place had been filled with people. Sound. Movement.

Melissa nodded to herself. Search over.

The following day, armed with two cameras, a tripod, and a traveling mug of coffee, Melissa returned to Jordan. Located some forty miles north of Atlanta, the distance between the two had little to do with Jordan's historical distance from the twenty-first century. The town, like many southern towns, had a square, around which were a series of one- and two-story brick buildings and an old courthouse with white columns. In the middle of the square was a statue of a man she'd never heard of. Main Street, which was also State Road 21, connected to the highway five miles away. If anyone were inclined to visit Jordan, they'd find a bank at one end and a convenience store at the other end that doubled as a post office. On the way out of town was a gas station with pumps that were probably two or three generations old. The gas station attendant maintained that the Donneley farm had been abandoned for at least fifteen years.

For the second time in as many days, Melissa parked her car on the shoulder, retrieved her camera bag and tripod from the back seat, and started across the field. The sun had been up for nearly an hour, pushing the long shadows back toward the trees.

Partway across the field, Melissa slowed and stared at a scarecrow some distance away, its arms and head akimbo. A large, black bird was sitting on its shoulder pulling at something with its beak. Hearing her approach, the bird looked up, decided she was far enough away to present no threat, and went back to whatever it was pulling at. Melissa tried to recall if she'd seen it on her last visit.

Probably wasn't paying attention, she decided.

A moment later, a second bird glided in and landed at the scarecrow's feet.

"Not doing a very good job, are you?" she said under her breath and kept on walking. The scarecrow had no comment.

The barn's roofline was bowed in the middle, and the whole building seemed to be leaning slightly as if the passage of time was too much for it to bear. Its wood was gray and badly weathered. In the front was a pair of wide double doors faded to a barely recognizable shade of red.

Melissa placed her camera bag on the hood of a rusted Dodge Charger sitting up on concrete blocks near the entrance and proceeded to set up her tripod, breathing in the scent of jasmine in the air.

As she did on her first visit, she made a circuit around the barn, checking to see if there might be a better angle for her picture. There wasn't. As she rounded the corner, her eye came to rest on an irregular brown stain on the ground about three feet across. Odd. She didn't remember seeing that either. She looked around. There was nothing in the immediate area that could have caused it.

Guess I missed that, too.

The gas station attendant had assured her no one had been out there in years. Melissa shook her head and turned her attention to her camera and the task at hand.

One of the barn doors was closed, the other partially open, rocking back and forth in the morning breeze. Melissa approached the door and tentatively poked her head inside. Streaming through a broken window above the doors, sunlight lit portions of a dusty interior. A few insects buzzing around darted in and out of the diffuse light. Of course, nothing had changed. The barn was as empty as it had been a day ago. The stain continued to bother her, but she pushed it to the back of her mind because the light outside was changing rapidly. She tucked a strand of blond hair behind her ear and started back to the tripod.

Out of the corner of her eye, she saw another black bird land on the scarecrow's head.

"Jeez," she muttered. "You're supposed to scare them, not attract the stupid things."

A thought occurred to her. Why put a scarecrow in an abandoned field? Melissa stopped and considered the scarecrow more closely. Something wasn't right. For the first time, mixed in with the jasmine scent she'd smelled earlier was a foul odor unlike anything she'd ever smelled before.

Seemingly on their own, her feet began to move, drawing her toward the black figure.

No way those are crows, she thought. *They're too large.*

One of the birds swiveled its head in her direction and fixed a pair of malevolent eyes on her. It was holding something red in its beak. Her mind began to race, conjuring up ghost stories and movies with dark images that scared her as a child. As she came closer and the wind picked up, the more ubiquitous the smell became, seemingly coming from the ground and grass at the same time. Incongruously, around the scarecrow's neck was a thin, gold necklace. Without warning, the bird took off, startling her, its wings beating hard. Its companion let out a squawk of protest and followed suit. Melissa tracked their flight upward.

Four more birds were now circling overhead. She forced her feet to keep going.

Thirty feet from the macabre figure, she came to a halt, staring in horror at a deathly white face under the scarecrow's hat. A cry that tried to escape her throat turned into a croak as her voice deserted her. All the strength seemed to have drained from her legs. Rooted to the spot, she stood there.

"This is a joke," she whispered. "Someone's idea of a sick joke."

The scarecrow's hat, dislodged by the bird, finally slipped to the ground. It was no joke.

Melissa Harris began to scream.

Chapter 1

Detective Beth Sturgis leaned against the rear fender of her police cruiser and watched as the crime scene techs took the man's body down. Standing twenty yards away, Tony Colsart, Burton County's medical examiner, and his assistant waited to load the corpse into a body bag. Their van was parked close by. Two deputies, also present at the scene, stopped what they were doing to watch. No one spoke.

Once the body was properly secured, Colsart broke away and came toward them. Flashing blue lights from the other cruisers reflected off his face, making his movements appear staccato. Colsart's expression was grim.

Three months new to the Robbery-Homicide Division, thirty-four-year-old Beth Sturgis had worked a total of four murders during her brief tenure. The smell of death always got to her. It seemed to linger on her clothes and hair long after she was gone, a hazard of the profession. Being outdoors helped.

Next to Beth was Max Blaylock. Blaylock was a large man with a big stomach. He'd been Jordan's sheriff for the last twelve years. Without being asked, he poured Colsart a cup of coffee from a thermos resting on the trunk of his car and handed it to him. The ME accepted it gratefully, nodding his thanks.

"Tony, this is Beth Sturgis from Atlanta. I've asked them to step in and help. I'm thinking this one's too big for our little shop to handle."

Colsart and Beth shook hands. She was dressed in a gray pantsuit and a light-blue blouse. At five feet nine inches, her eyes were nearly level with his.

"Anything you can tell us?" Beth asked.

A wiry man with sandy hair, Colsart was in his early forties. "Apart from the obvious," he said, "not a helluva lot. There's a small-caliber gunshot wound to the face, just under the victim's left eye. Powder burns and ridging indicate it was made from close range."

"What about the time of death?" Beth asked.

"Judging from the way rigor's letting go, I'd estimate a little over thirty hours, give or take. We'll know more once I get him on the table."

"You think the bullet killed him?"

"Doubtful. It exited through the back of this neck and missed both the brain and spinal cord. I assume you noticed his pasty-white condition?"

"Hard to miss," Beth said.

"He appears to have died from blood loss," Colsart said. "Problem is, there's not enough at the base of the cross or the barn to account for it. This is really weird."

"You'll figure it out, Terrance," Blaylock reassured him. "Ain't no vampires in Jordan."

"I intend to," Colsart said. "Goddamn birds did a job on his body. What the hell are they?"

"Turkey buzzards," Blaylock said, looking up at the black shapes circling the field.

It was late in the afternoon, and the day had continued to brighten but without warmth. Yellow police tape declaring the area a crime scene had been stretched around the barn on stakes in a hundred-foot perimeter. The scarecrow and the house were similarly cordoned off. Five minutes after arriving on scene, Beth had called Ben Furman with Atlanta's crime lab to come out. He and a helper were at the moment painstakingly going over the ground for anything that might yield evidence.

Beth turned to the sheriff and asked, "Ever see him before?"

Blaylock shook his head. "I don't think he's local."

"Think you'll identify him?" Colsart asked.

"Ben told me he got a clean set of prints off his good hand," Beth said. "Assuming the vic's in the system, there shouldn't be a problem."

"Good hand?" Blaylock said.

"The left one's missing its ring finger."

"I missed that completely. I was concentrating on the gunshot."

"Not a problem," Beth said. "Maybe we'll catch a break and get some latents off the body."

"Not likely," Colsart said. "Your tech did a preliminary with the Polilight and didn't look happy."

"Sick bastard to do something like this," Blaylock muttered to no one in particular.

When Colsart finished his coffee, he handed the cup to the sheriff, who crumpled it and tossed it onto the back floorboard of his car.

Beth said, "Tony, I don't know your situation up here, but I'd like to move this to the top of the list if possible."

"Shouldn't be a problem," Colsart said. "We don't do as much business as Atlanta. You might want to have your boss give Dr. Andrews a call though. He's the one who can put a rush on it. I'm just a lowly assistant ME."

"Well, use your influence," Beth said.

"Right. My influence. Got it."

Blaylock turned to the medical examiner and asked, "You and the wife still attending that couple's class over at church?"

Colsart responded with a flat look. "Every Friday night, rain or shine."

"Is it any good?"

"It's what I live for."

The sheriff laughed to himself.

"Some fights I should get into," Colsart said, "Some I shouldn't. Diane thinks we need to communicate better, so we go." He inquired of Beth, "You married?"

"Not at the moment," she said. "The class is about communicating?"

"Basically. You learn how to talk to each other and hear what the other person's saying. Stuff like that. The instructor wrote a book."

"Yeah?" Blaylock said. "What's it called?"

"*The Power of Yes.*"

"And?"

Colsart shrugged.

"You read it?" the sheriff asked.

"Not yet. The wife did. She only got up to the power of *no*."

Beth and Blaylock both smiled. Like the air going out of a balloon, their smiles faded as the body was loaded into the van.

"I'll see what I can do about moving the autopsy up," Colsart said. "Call me tomorrow."

After he left, they watched the ME's van lurch over the field as it made its way back to the road.

"Got a mess here, Detective," Blaylock said. "You sure you want to take this on?"

"No, but I've got it now," Beth said. "You already turned the case over."

"I can turn it back," Blaylock said. "No disrespect, but I thought you city types worked with a partner."

"Usually," Beth said. "Mine's on medical leave at the moment. I was about to give him a call."

Blaylock nodded and moved away to watch the techs at work. Beth removed her cell phone from her jacket pocket and dialed her partner. After four rings, she was about to disconnect when Leonard Cass answered.

"Sorry, Beth," Cass said. "I'm still moving like molasses. What's up?"

"We caught a case in the town of Jordan. Interdepartmental request for assistance."

"Lovely. Someone up there steal a chicken?"

"A little worse than that. I'm standing in the middle of a field outside town. Someone shot a guy in the face and strung him up on a cross dressed as a scarecrow."

"Holy shit. Are you serious?"

"The ME just took him down and the techs are going over the scene now. On top of everything else, the sick bastard cut off one of his fingers. This is a nasty one, Lenny."

There was a silence on the phone as Cass processed the information. "Fuck. We got us a copycat," he said.

"Looks like it," Beth said. "I hope that's all there is."

"Meaning?"

"The sheriff also mentioned two women have gone missing. He doesn't think they're related. I'm praying he's right."

"Jesus," Cass said. "I need to get my ass back in the office."

"Come back when you're ready," Beth said. "I can hold down the fort till then. A few more weeks won't kill me."

More silence followed. "Is he sure about the women?"

"He just mentioned it in passing. You know, like when it rains, it pours."

"Yeah," Cass said. "Let's hope they're not related. Does the name Jackson Kale mean anything to you?"

Beth frowned as she watched the techs conferring with each other about something. "No. Should it?"

"Kale was the FBI's lead investigator on the Scarecrow case eight years ago."

"Before I joined the department," Beth said. "Is he still around?"

"He pulled the plug and took a teaching position somewhere."

"How come?"

"The official reason was medical, but I heard there were problems with Internal Affairs or whatever the feds call it. He might be worth talking to."

"What kind of medical problems?"

"Who knows? Like I said, it was just a rumor. Maybe the pressure got to him. Putting on a medical label might have been the Bureau's way of saying thanks for a job well done and bye. I mean, the guy was a hero."

"Too bad he's gone," Beth said. "I'll see if I can find him."

"You understand once the papers get hold of this, the shit'll hit the fan."

"Can't wait."

"Let's keep the missing finger out of the report for the time being. You understand why?"

"It's what you did on the Scarecrow case."

"Smart girl. I'm here if you need me."

"And I'm here if you need me," Beth said.

When they disconnected, she tried to recall the details of the Scarecrow murders. Sixteen deaths in all. Men and women. Bodies mutilated. The city of Atlanta and surrounding counties in a state of panic. The national media and lurid tabloids you find at checkout counters picked up the story and only made matters worse.

"Please don't let it be happening again," Beth whispered and then went to watch the forensic techs work.

Chapter 2

It wasn't hard to track down Jackson Kale. Beth looked in the white pages and found he was still listed. Following that, she sent a request to the FBI for his file. The file confirmed that Kale had voluntarily left the Bureau for "medical and personal reasons." Beth was aware she was reading an edited version, or at least as much as the FBI was willing to share.

Nolvia Borjas, the department secretary, who'd brought the fax to her, looked over her shoulder as she went through it and asked, "Who's that?"

"A former federal agent," Beth said.

Always curious, Nolvia turned her head to the side to get a better look. "Cute."

"Mmm," Beth said noncommittally.

"Is he involved in your case?"

"Not really. He worked on a similar one a few years ago. Would you run a DMV on him and see if they have anything more current? This address is pretty old."

"Sure," Nolvia said. "He looks familiar. Was he ever around here?"

"It's possible," Beth admitted.

"Give me five minutes," Nolvia said. "By the way, Lieutenant Fancher wants you to stop by her office before you sign out."

Beth looked at the glass-wall enclosure where Penny Fancher sat talking on the phone. Fancher was Beth's boss in the Northside Division. She didn't have much street experience and had gotten into management via administration. Her reputation around the department was that she was fair-minded and competent and would back you up if push came to shove. That, at least, was comforting to know until her partner returned from convalescence. Trying to learn the ropes had Beth feeling like a fish out of water. Unwritten rules and norms, which a partner typically passed on to the junior member, weren't the easiest to pick up. Cass was a longtime veteran in Homicide and a good teacher. She missed having him there.

The lieutenant chose that moment to look up and motioned for Beth to come in. It was close to four o'clock, and as it was on most Friday afternoons, the squad room was nearly empty. Many of the detectives would be at Winston's Pub just down the street before heading home for the weekend. She still wasn't completely comfortable socializing with them and generally avoided such gatherings.

Beth stood up and walked past a row of eight cubicles with gray metal desks that faced each other. She would have preferred they faced the opposite way, giving at least an illusion of privacy.

Most of the shades in the office were halfway down to block out Atlanta's late afternoon sun, which always seemed to be strongest at that time of day. Penelope Fancher was in her early forties and had short, brown hair. She was just under five foot six, slightly heavyset, and wore little makeup. Beth heard somewhere she'd been married once. There seemed to be a lot of that going around. The divorce rate among cops was ridiculous.

"Have a seat," the lieutenant said. "Coffee?"

"I'm good. Thanks."

"How're you settling in, Beth?"

"Slowly."

"Any problems?"

"A few sexist remarks now and then, but most of the guys have been pretty helpful."

"The remarks go with the territory," Fancher said. "Anything I need to address?"

"Nope."

"If there's anything I can do to smooth the transition, don't hesitate to give me a shout."

"I will, boss," Beth said. "I appreciate the offer."

"I see from the board you caught that homicide in Jordan," Fancher said. "Are you okay to work it alone until Lenny Cass gets back?"

"We've been talking on the phone. I'm good for now. If I need help, I'll send up a flare."

The lieutenant considered that for a moment and then asked, "What's your take on the case?"

"The autopsy's set for Monday," Beth said. "We'll know more about the cause of death after the cut and toxicology come back."

Beth hoped Fancher wouldn't push. She'd deliberately avoided mentioning her request for the FBI file on Jackson Kale. Feds and cops never mixed particularly well, and that went for former feds, too. Earlier, she'd pulled the book on the original Scarecrow murders and planned to study them over the weekend. The truth was she wanted this case, wanted the opportunity to show she belonged. It was hers and she was going to solve it. Simple as that.

Her statement seemed to satisfy the lieutenant, who said, "If you're sure you can stay on top of this solo, I'll go along. Otherwise, I can pull one of the guys off their assignment to work with you. The budget cuts are killing everyone."

"I'll be fine," Beth assured her.

She was about to continue when she saw Nolvia coming down the hall holding a sheet of paper with the results from the DMV search. Beth reached behind her and motioned with her hand for Nolvia to keep going. Nolvia's footsteps slowed momentarily as she reached the door and then picked up again. Fancher didn't notice.

"Have you developed any suspects yet?"

"It's way too soon to say. We just got an ID back on the victim," Beth said. "Jerome Haffner, forty-three years old, Vinings resident. I was about to head out and knock on some doors."

"That's good. The first forty-eight hours are critical," Fancher said, repeating the oft-quoted maxim in homicide investigations.

"Got it," Beth said.

"Sounds good. Keep me up to date on the developments. I'm trying to get our clearance rate above sixty percent."

Which, as Beth was coming to learn, was the bottom line. Fancher might be a good administrator, but she wasn't a street cop. From the memos that came across her desk weekly, it was obvious the lieutenant tended to focus on statistics.

Better her than me.

"I'll do my best," Beth said. "If it's okay with you, I'd like to keep my cruiser over the weekend. My car's warranty ran out last month, and it turned into a Ford."

Penny Fancher smiled. "I know the feeling. Go ahead. I'll authorize it."

That seemed to end the conversation. Beth got up and returned to her desk to find the DMV report she'd asked for. She located a phone number for Kale and dialed it. A woman with a distinct Scottish accent answered the phone.

"Kale residence."

"Is Jackson Kale available?"

"No, I'm sorry. He's not here right now. May I take a message, miss?"

"This is Detective Sturgis with the Atlanta Police Department. When do you expect him home?"

"I don't expect him at all. I'm his housekeeper. The man's probably teaching class, isn't he?"

"Do you know what school that would be, ma'am?"

"Of course I do. It's Georgia Tech. Kale's a professor, you know."

Beth didn't know if he was or wasn't, but there was no point pursuing the conversation further. She'd gotten what she needed. She thanked the housekeeper and left her name and number.

After disconnecting, she studied Jack Kale's folder again. The information sheet listed him as thirty-eight years old, six foot two, and 192 pounds with brown hair. He wasn't a bad-looking man, quite different from the blond, five-foot-eight actor who had portrayed him in the film. What stood out, even in the photocopy in front of her, were his eyes. According to his file, he studied psychology at Ohio State University but for some reason chose not to pursue that profession, joining the FBI instead. He'd served four years in the Marine Corps and had seen combat in Afghanistan, where he was awarded a Purple Heart and a Bronze Star.

Interesting man, she decided, glancing at the photo again.

It was nearly four thirty, and everyone was either gone or getting ready to leave. Beth shut down her computer, gathered the file together, and did the same.

Chapter 3

Along with the FBI and DMV reports, Beth placed the loose-leaf binder containing the Scarecrow file into her briefcase and headed for the elevator. Penelope Fancher waved good-bye from her office. She was probably trying to find a way to make the numbers look better.

The elevator arrived and the doors opened to reveal two men in conversation. Beth immediately recognized Deputy Chief Noah Ritson. The other man she didn't know.

"Afternoon, Chief," she said, stepping into the car.

"Detective Sturgis," Ritson said. "Nice to see you again. How are things in Homicide?"

Beth resisted the impulse to say, "Dead." Ritson wasn't known for his sense of humor. She was actually surprised he remembered her name at all. The only time they'd met was at her graduation from the academy some five years earlier.

"Busy, Chief," Beth said.

"Have you met Burt Wiggins?" Ritson asked. "Burt works with me up on seven."

"No, I haven't," Beth said, shaking hands with him.

Wiggins was the chief's administrative assistant. Both men were dressed in medium-blue suits and crisp white shirts. The only difference was the color of their ties: one red, and the other blue.

Wiggins smiled at her. "I remember now," he said. "All those transfer requests hit my desk first."

Beth immediately felt the color in her face rise. "Sorry about that. It's not that I didn't like Environment. It's just—"

"There's a little more action in Homicide, eh?" Ritson said, finishing the sentence for her.

"Something like that," Beth said as the elevator came to a halt. The men waited for her to exit before they got out.

"Off for the weekend?" Ritson asked.

"No, Chief. I need to talk with some neighbors about a man who was killed in Jordan. I'm trying to get a better line on who he was and what he was doing when the crime went down."

Ritson nodded. "A very disturbing situation. Sounds like we have a copycat on our hands."

"That's my take so far, sir," Beth said.

Beth wasn't surprised that Ritson knew about the case. Penny Fancher had probably talked to him earlier. For the last thirty years, the deputy chief had his finger on everything in the department. It was how he had survived so long when others fell by the wayside.

Ritson informed her, "This case has the potential to create a great deal of media attention, Detective, not to mention a public outcry. The crime sounds bizarre."

"No argument from me," Beth said.

"I'd like to be kept up to speed on your investigation. You'll have the full resources of the department at your disposal."

"I appreciate that, Chief."

The group slowed at the glass door leading to the parking lot. Ritson turned to her.

"Things are changing for us, Beth, but our basic mission remains the same—protect and serve the public. The obvious physical differences aside, I believe, with proper training, any woman can be the equal of a man."

"Well, I don't like to set my sights too low," Beth said.

As soon as the words were out of her mouth, she regretted them.

Ritson's attention sharpened. He studied her for a moment before his face creased into a smile and he chuckled.

"That's marvelous," he said. "Set your sights too low. May I tell that to my wife?"

"Oh . . . sure," Beth said. "I didn't mean any disrespect."

"None taken. Good luck with your investigation."

Both men nodded to her and headed out the door. The last look Wiggins threw in her direction fell somewhere between amusement and "Oh boy."

Muttering to herself about being an idiot, Beth hurried to her cruiser, got in, and started the engine. She had the distinct feeling their eyes were on her as she drove out of the lot.

Chapter 4

On impulse, Beth decided to head to the Georgia Tech campus rather than fight her way through Atlanta's rush-hour traffic to Vinings where Jerome Haffner lived. She reasoned there was a better chance of catching people at home later in the evening.

At the administration building's reception counter, she asked a matronly woman where she could find Jackson Kale.

"Professor Kale's office is at the College of Criminal Justice. Do you need a campus map?"

"I guess so," Beth said.

The woman reached beneath the counter and produced one showing the university's layout. Using a yellow highlighter, she circled a building and drew a path toward it.

"This is the Hayes Building," she said. "Unfortunately, his office hours are over."

"I thought you said he was in."

"I did. Professor Kale's teaching now. His class lets out in twenty minutes or so. If you hurry, you can just catch him."

Beth thanked her and departed. After a few wrong turns involving streets that weren't on the map, she came to a red brick building near the edge of campus with the name "Hayes" above the door. A young man in jeans and a T-shirt informed her Jack Kale's classroom was on the second floor. As Beth climbed the steps, memories of trudging up a similar staircase at Boston College drifted back to her. There were no pangs of nostalgia. It had been a turbulent, heady time in her life, marked by two long-term relationships, one of which had led to marriage. Twelve years older than she was and a published author with a national best seller to his credit, she wondered if William Camden was still charming the pants off nineteen-year-old co-eds. Probably. Leopards don't change their spots.

The classroom had two doors. Beth slipped in the back one and took a seat in the last row. The room was arranged in the style of an amphitheater with contemporary beige desks and chairs. Kale, wearing a vested gray herringbone suit and a white shirt with a bow tie, was at the bottom. Behind him was a whiteboard. He was in the midst of a lecture. The suit was an old-fashioned cut, like one of those her grandfather owned and refused to throw away. The bow tie was a surprise. It wasn't a bad look and sort of fit her image of what a professor should wear.

"The famous French criminologist Edmond Locard theorized that in every homicide, there's an exchange between the victim and the murderer or the murdered and the crime scene. Those of you who plan to pursue a career in law enforcement would do well to familiarize yourself with at least basic forensic technique. I know this class is about behavioral science, but you can't be a one-trick pony. The field is changing rapidly, daily it seems, and advances are coming at us all the time."

Beth studied the speaker. Funny how you form a mental picture of someone. She conceded his photo didn't do him justice. The FBI file only provided a sketch of his background and his career with them. What it didn't say was that he had a fine deep voice that easily carried to the back of the classroom. For one brief moment, his eyes settled on her and then moved on.

"Professor," a young woman in the first row said, "yesterday we talked about patterns and psychological profiles. Can I ask a question about that?"

"Have at it."

"Well, in today's newspaper, there was a story about the police in Virginia arresting a man in connection with five women who were strangled outside of Richmond. Did you read that?"

"As a matter of fact, I did."

The girl went on. "They're saying that he's probably a drug addict as well as schizophrenic and that he walked away from a mental hospital three months ago. I'm confused, because that kind of pathology doesn't really fit a serial killer's pattern, at least not the ones we've been studying."

"No, it doesn't," Kale agreed. "Schizophrenics as a group are no more dangerous than the rest of the population. Probably less so."

"Then how do we know about what type of profile to concentrate on? I mean, we have a midterm coming up."

Kale smiled, then said, "The answer is you don't. People are incredibly complex. Even twins raised under virtually identical circumstances can turn out quite differently. Certainly patterns exist, and some of them are predictive. But not every square peg fits in a square hole. Human beings have a perverse way of not sliding nicely into a mold. As an investigator, your job is to assemble as many facts as you can and use your intellect and experience to get the true picture.

"Does that help, Ms. Carmichael?"

"I guess," the girl said, though she still sounded perplexed.

"Let me put it this way. You have very little chance of learning the truth if you know in advance what the truth ought to be." Kale glanced around the room and continued, "As Ms. Carmichael said, we do have a midterm coming up on Monday, so I'll end class early and give you a little extra time to study. Don't stress over it, people."

There was a general shifting of chairs as students got up and began to file out. Beth noted 85 percent of them were women. One actually put an apple on his desk as she passed by.

"No way," Beth said to herself.

After a second, she realized she was the last person still seated.

Jackson Kale was standing there watching her. "Detective Sturgis, I presume?"

For a moment Beth was thrown off that he knew her name. Then she remembered her conversation with the housekeeper. She'd probably called him.

"Do I look that much like a cop?" she asked, starting down the aisle.

"Not in the least. My housekeeper left a message about your call. Jack Kale," he added, offering his hand.

"Elizabeth Sturgis."

His eyes were more hazel than brown, something that hadn't come across in the file photo. He released her hand and then folded his own in front of him, waiting for her to continue.

"Do you have a couple of minutes, Professor?"

"Jack."

"Jack," she repeated. "I was wondering if I could ask you a few questions."

"Sure. That was my last class. I have coffee in the office."

"We can talk right here."

"All right," he said, leaning back against his desk. "Would you care to have a seat?"

"Standing's fine."

"It is, but sitting makes it easier to take notes," Kale said, nodding toward the legal pad she was holding.

She immediately felt foolish. Like most cops, her tendency was to take control of an interview and direct the questions. The man had a disconcerting gaze . . . not leering or even intense, just sort of focused.

"I guess sitting's better," she conceded, smiling. "And maybe your office would be more comfortable."

Kale nodded and gathered his lecture notes, pausing momentarily when he noticed the apple sitting on the corner of his desk. He picked it up, tossed it in the air, and caught it as he headed for the door.

Chapter 5

Jack Kale's office was comfortable, though slightly messy, and definitely masculine. A dark-brown Chesterfield sofa sat along the right hand wall under a window. About a third of it was covered in blue test booklets. In front of his desk were two matching leather guest chairs. Behind the desk was a credenza with a keyboard and flat-screen monitor. The wall opposite the window contained the usual detritus of education.

Jack scooped up the test booklets and placed them in a stack at the end of the couch, clearing a place for Beth to sit.

While he was busy retrieving two white porcelain mugs from the top drawer of a metal file cabinet, Beth studied the office further. On the wall above the credenza was a renaissance print of St. Mark's Square in Venice. She recognized it from her visit to Italy on her honeymoon. The only other picture was a photo of a smiling preteen girl at the corner of his desk.

Jack returned with the coffee and took a seat opposite her in one of his guest chairs. She liked the fact that he didn't retreat behind his desk, putting a barrier between them.

"Your daughter?" she asked.

"Morgan," he said. "Age twelve going on twenty-eight. She's a handful."

"I remember what it was like being twelve," Beth said. "Does she get along with your wife?"

"Ex-wife. Katherine remarried a few years ago. They both live in California now."

Shit, Beth thought. *The damn file said he was married.*

"Did you read all those?" she asked, pointing at the books on his shelves.

"Not all. Some are reference materials," he said. "But you didn't come here to talk about me. Most of my background is probably in that file in your briefcase."

Beth stared down at her lap for a moment and smiled. The hardest people to interview were cops, and that included ex-cops.

"Just making conversation," she said.

"To put the subject at ease. I understand. How's the coffee?"

"Terrible"

Jack blinked and sat back in his chair, then sniffed his mug and took a tentative sip. The expression on his face confirmed it.

"Jesus," he said, taking the cup from her. "You're right. Give me a minute and I'll make us a new pot. Or would you prefer tea instead?"

"Honestly, don't go to any trouble. I appreciate the offer."

His getting flustered was kind of funny. One minute a calm professor lecturing about schizophrenia and investigative techniques, the next, a man fumbling to make coffee.

"Sorry," Jack said. "How about a rain check?"

"Uh . . . that would be fine," Beth said.

"So, what can I do for you, Ms. Sturgis?"

"Well, for starters, you can call me Beth."

"Fair enough, Beth."

The follow-up question she was about to ask remained on the tip of her tongue when she noticed a book on Jack's desk titled *Psychoanalysis*.

"You're a psychiatrist?"

"Psychologist," he said.

"I was an anthropology major," Beth told him. "I don't get all that stuff about the subconscious."

"Neither do I," Jack said.

"Really?"

"No."

She responded with a flat look.

"Sorry," Jack said. There was an amused expression playing at the corners of his mouth.

"I dated a psychologist once. They always answer a question with a question."

"How should we answer them?"

Beth opened her mouth to reply, then closed it again and informed him, "You're aware I carry a gun."

He smiled and held up his hands in surrender. "All right, what brings you here today, Beth?"

"I have a few questions about a case you worked on some years ago. Do you recall a man named Howard Lincoln Pell?"

The pleasant smile faded from Jack's face. It wasn't much of a change, but it was noticeable. "I do."

"You were with the FBI then—their senior profiler."

Kale nodded and didn't reply.

Beth continued, "It's hard to read between the lines, but it looks like you basically took over the role of lead investigator."

"Sometimes a case turns out that way," Jack said. "Your department remained involved."

"Isn't that a little unusual for a psychologist?"

"Before I joined the Bureau, I was assigned to the Marine Corps Criminal Investigation Division. They had a program that let me work and pursue my doctoral degree."

"So you became . . . what, a behaviorist?"

"Behaviorist, psychologist. It's pretty much the same thing. Criminalist is probably the closest description."

"I didn't know that," Beth said.

"No reason for you to."

"I haven't had time to track down the other detectives who worked the case with you. Mike Dibella's retired and living someplace in Florida. His partner left the department and works security for a casino in Atlantic City."

"Why?"

"Why what?" Beth asked.

"Why do you need to track them down and talk with me?"

"A case just fell into my lap yesterday," she told him. "A man was murdered several days ago in Jordan. He was found shot in the face and dressed as a scarecrow in the middle of a field. Local law enforcement called us in to assist."

Jack nodded his understanding but offered nothing in return. The only reaction, if it was one, was that the color in his face seemed to have risen a shade.

"I'm hoping you can give me some insight into Howard Pell," Beth said. "Not everything gets in the book."

"What is it you need to know?"

"It's pretty obvious we're dealing with a copycat."

"I'm familiar with the term, Beth," Jack said. "Unfortunately, I've been out of police work for quite a while now. I doubt I'd be of much help."

"But you remember the case."

"Vividly."

"Then talk to me."

"There's nothing to talk about. The Scarecrow was a monster—literally. An aberration that shouldn't exist in this world. Somehow, Dr. Pell slipped through the cracks and went on for years before he snapped. It seems to me the murder book should contain everything you need."

"It might," Beth said. "But you knew Pell better than anyone."

Jack laughed to himself without humor and looked out the window for several seconds. "I'm not sure how to respond." The last words were spoken more to himself than to her.

"Every detective forms impressions and feelings about a case," Beth said. "All I'm asking for is a few minutes of your time."

Jack continued to stare out the window.

"Jack?"

"Yes. You want a few minutes. I heard." He took a deep breath and turned back to her. "The cause of death was the gunshot?"

"We don't know yet," Beth said. "When I examined the body, it was nothing obvious. There was certainly a gunshot wound, but the ME didn't think that would be fatal. The odd thing is the victim was as white as a sheet as if all the blood had been drained out of him. Even more interesting: the ring finger on his left hand was missing. The autopsy's set for Monday. Would you be interested in attending?"

Jack looked at her sharply at the mention of the body's condition. After several seconds, he said, "No. I'm not with the FBI anymore."

"I understand," Beth said. "But you're still more or less in the field."

"As I've said, I'm pretty backed up at the moment. I'm sorry."

Perplexed at his attitude, she decided to ignore his last comment and push harder. She took the crime scene photos from her briefcase and spread them out on the middle section of his couch.

"Would you at least look at the preliminary report? I made an extra copy for you."

"I . . . sure."

For the next several minutes, he studied the gruesome pictures, shaking his head. The rise and fall of his chest had been noticeable a moment ago, but now he seemed to have calmed himself. When he finished with the last one, he held his hand out for the accompanying notes. She passed them to him and waited, feeling very much like a student again.

Jack finally inquired, "Sheriff Blaylock was the responding officer?"

"Right."

"And he's the one who spotted the two sets of shoeprints in this photo?"

"He pointed them out to me. I had electrostats made."

"And from them, you concluded there were two men present at the scene, apart from the victim."

"Correct," Beth said. "It makes sense. Jerome Haffner was a big man. It would've taken more than one person to carry him and hoist him up on that cross."

"Not if the killer tied him to it while he was lying on the ground and then lifted it."

"They still had to get him there," Beth said.

"From where?"

"That we don't know. There's a farmhouse about a quarter mile from where the victim was found, and the road is at least a five-minute hike. Unfortunately, there were no tracks coming or going. The barn looked good, but it was empty. I went through it and forensics followed behind me. It was clean. Since there was so little blood present, we figured they killed him someplace else and brought him there for some sick reason."

"And carried him across the field at the risk of being seen?"

"The place is deserted. Even the railroad tracks are abandoned. I read that Pell had a helper in the beginning, before he killed him. It fits the pattern."

"Did you check outside the barn?"

"Outside?"

"That's what I said."

"Well, I walked around it with Sheriff Blaylock and two deputies. We didn't see anything."

"Four people walked the crime scene?"

Beth was beginning to regret having asked for his help, but said, "More eyes to search."

"Ideally, you want no more than two people. With every additional person, the odds of contamination go up. What about the house?"

"We looked, of course, but it was clean."

Jack picked up the electrostatic images of the shoeprints and examined them again.

"First off, you're dealing with one killer, not two. Granted, the shoe-prints are different, but sometimes a clever criminal will use different shoes to throw you off. I think that's what's happened here. If you look at the depth of the prints, they're the same. If something heavy was being carried in one direction, there would be a difference."

Beth tentatively said, "Okay . . . that makes sense."

"You see this close-up picture of the locket and chain around the victim's neck?"

"Sure."

"Obviously that's not the kind of jewelry a man wears. According to your notes, the sheriff mentioned two women are missing, right?"

"Um-hm."

"If I had to speculate, I'd say their disappearance and this man's death are both related. The locket probably belongs to one of them. Whoever did this is sending you a message. He's got one or both women and doesn't care if you know it. In fact, he wants you to know it."

"Damn," Beth said, as the implications began to dawn on her.

"It's also clear this isn't the entire murder scene. You should check the area again for a basement or maybe a root cellar. You're probably right about the victim being killed someplace else. I just don't think it's that far away or that the killer would risk driving around with a body."

"How can you be so sure?"

"I'm not. It's just a reasonable hypothesis," Jack said. "Your bigger problem is the missing women. I don't believe in coincidences. Something's either happened to them or it's about to—something bad, I'm afraid."

"Then help us," Beth said.

"I'm sorry. I'm not in a position to."

It was an odd choice of words. She was frustrated and wanted to shake him. All her instincts told her he was interested, but something was holding him back. Beth tried a different approach.

"Tell me this: if we're dealing with a copycat, what's driving him psychologically?"

"If?" Jack said.

"Obviously," Beth said. "I checked with Meadowbrook before I came out. Pell is still there. He's had almost no visitors and very little contact with the outside world. What else could there be?"

"What else, indeed?" Jack said absently. "To answer your question, if someone is out there modeling after Howard Pell, you'd look for a person with sociopathic tendencies, a loner who possesses higher-than-average intelligence. The crime scene tells us that much. Mind you, those are just broad categories. There are a lot of factors to consider."

"Not all square pegs fit in square holes," Beth said.

Jack smiled. "Right."

"Would you at least be willing to come out and look at the crime scene?"

Jack was holding one of the coffee cups in both his hands. He rotated it first one way and then the other for several seconds. "I wish I could be more help. I'm sorry, Beth."

With that he stood, indicating the meeting was over.

"So am I," she said.

Chapter 6

Beth Sturgis was confused and fuming as she marched across campus. In one minute, Jack Kale had gone from open and charming to uncommunicative and detached for no reason she could see.

Beth fished around in her purse, found her cell phone, and called Max Blaylock. He answered on the second ring.

"Sheriff, is the scene still secure?"

"Yep. I've got one of my guys out there. He claims he's dying of boredom."

"I want him to check the barn and the house and look for either a basement or a root cellar."

"How come?"

"I just came from a meeting with a man named Jackson Kale who used to work with the FBI. He thinks the victim was killed there or someplace close by. If you do locate a basement, I want you to seal it immediately and call me. I'll have forensics come out and go over the area with a fine-tooth comb."

"No problem," Blaylock said. "Why do I know that name?"

"He was the one who ran the fed's Scarecrow investigation a few years back."

"Right. The guy who chased Pell to Cloudland Canyon. They made a TV movie, if I remember right. Is he coming aboard?"

"No, Kale's out of law enforcement now. He's teaching at Georgia Tech," Beth said.

"Too bad. I heard he was a bright guy. I'll give Avilles a call and get him started. Did Kale think they killed Haffner in a cellar then hauled him up top?"

"He didn't say Haffner was killed there, only that there's a second scene. He also doesn't think there are two killers."

"Has to be. You saw the victim. He'd be a handful for one man to lift."

Beth explained Jack's theory.

The sheriff processed that for a moment. "Like I said, bright guy."

"The bigger problem is your two missing women," Beth said.

"How do you mean?"

"That locket and chain around Haffner's neck might belong to one of them. Kale thinks it was left deliberately. If that's true, we're probably dealing with a short time frame."

"Oh, Jesus," Blaylock said. "I know both families. This ain't good."

"No, it's not," she said. "Ask your other deputy to talk to the families and see if someone recognizes it."

"I'll do it myself."

After they disconnected, Beth placed a second call.

Chapter 7

From his window, Jack Kale watched Beth head toward the parking lot. Even her walk was mad. She was a beautiful woman with a sharp mind, and he'd been enjoying her company, a luxury he hadn't allowed himself for a long time. Funny how chemistry works. One minute it's there, and the next someone says, "I'm really into astrology," and it's gone.

Her news about the killing in Jordan had rocked him, though he managed to conceal it well. He was good at that. When you're in law enforcement, you learn to put on a cop face.

Sooner or later, he knew they would come. But he was in no position to help anyone anymore. He reached into his desk, took two pills from a bottle, and swallowed them dry. Jack turned away from the window and looked at the picture of his daughter for several seconds. Protecting her was paramount.

When Morgan and her mother moved to California, it nearly killed him. After hearing the news, he'd gotten drunk and stayed that way for two days. The void of their absence made him feel like his insides had been torn out. But there was no choice. They talked on the phone frequently, and a couple of times a year, he flew out to visit. It was a poor substitute for having a family close by. The telephone company likes to say long distance is the next best thing to being there. It's not. If everything went well, she would spend the summer with him. He was still nervous about that. Nevertheless, it was a start.

Disturbed by his conversation with Beth, Jack let his mind wander. In time, his eye came to rest on the stack of test booklets on his couch. Next to them was the crime scene report Ms. Sturgis had "accidentally" left. Nice touch. With a sigh, he picked up both, stuffed them in his briefcase, and headed for the door.

Chapter 8

Special Agent Paul Hilderbrand made his way through the restaurant to where Beth Sturgis was sitting. She was wearing a green dress that ended well above her knees. Two businessmen at the next table, nursing their after-work drinks, were checking out her legs. Not surprising. The tall brunette had been an associate editor on a popular travel magazine before going into police work. It was an odd career change and one that Hilderbrand never fully understood.

Kaleidoscope was an upscale bistro in Brookhaven that didn't get crowded until after eight at night. Until then, it was mostly neighborhood families. When the families drifted back to their homes, they were replaced by young women in little black dresses and young men in designer jeans with labels on the back pockets. Conversations took place at the bar and around a long common table that ran down the center of the room. Hilderbrand, thirty-eight years old, had come straight from work and was wearing charcoal-gray slacks and a blue blazer. His shirt was white and his tie was a maroon stripe.

Beth looked up from her drink, spotted him, and waved. A little more than two years had passed since their relationship ended. It had been by mutual consent, prompted by Hilderbrand's transfer to the FBI's field office in Phoenix, Arizona. He'd recently returned to Atlanta and they'd run into each other several times, mostly at law enforcement functions. Though the magic was gone, they'd remained friends.

Hilderbrand bent down and gave Beth a quick kiss before taking a chair opposite her.

"You look great," he said.

"So do you."

"I was surprised to get your call. Pleasantly surprised. It's been a while."

"It has. Thanks for coming, Paul. I need to pick your brain about a few things."

"What about the rest of me?"

"I'm trying to be strong," Beth said. "Can I buy you a drink?"

Hilderbrand sighed. "I suppose," he said, throwing a hard look at the businessman at the next table who was staring again. The man returned to his conversation.

"I'll have a beer. They sell twenty different kinds here, you know."

"I didn't," Beth said. "Ever try Blue Moon Ale?"

"Not really."

Beth caught the waitress's attention and ordered him a beer. It arrived in a tall frosted glass a minute later, complete with an orange slice.

"What's this?" Hilderbrand asked.

"An orange slice," she said.

"I can see that. What's it doing in my drink?"

"That's the way it's served," Beth said.

Hilderbrand made a face. "Seems a little gay," he grumbled.

"If any guys make a move on you, I'll protect you," Beth said.

Hilderbrand shrugged, took a sip, and nodded his approval. "Everything still the same?"

"I'm still single if that's what you mean," Beth said.

"You still have Peekaboo?"

"Peekachu," Beth said, referring to her cat. "And yes, we're still together."

"That's great," he said. "Give him my regards."

"I will," Beth said. "Nobody really owns a cat. It's more like they have staff."

"I remember."

In point of fact, he hated the stupid beast. And as far as he could tell, the feeling was mutual. He still had scars on his hand from its claws. Under the best of circumstances, it was an ill-tempered monster that only let Beth hold it.

"So, why the call?" he asked.

"Like I said, I need some information."

"On what?"

"More like on who," Beth said. "Do you remember Jackson Kale?"

"Sure," Hilderbrand said. "Jack left the Bureau a few years ago. I heard he's still in Atlanta, teaching someplace."

"Georgia Tech," Beth said. "I met him today."

"Did you? Casual or business?"

"Business."

"What sort of business?"

"Earlier this morning, a man was found murdered in the town of Jordan. Whoever did it dressed him up as a scarecrow and hung his body up in the middle of a field."

Hilderbrand's glass paused halfway to his lips. He slowly put it back down, his expression suddenly full of interest.

Beth continued. "Obviously, the first thing that came to my mind was, copycat. The whole situation's pretty creepy."

"Sounds like it."

"You were part of the task force who worked the Scarecrow case."

Hilderbrand nodded. "Not a fun assignment."

"And Jack Kale was, too."

"That's right. He was our profiler."

"From everything in the file, it looks like he took over," Beth said.

"I wouldn't argue with that. We were at a complete dead end. Bodies were piling up. The newspapers were going nuts. Christ, even the governor and director were calling daily."

"Tell me about him," Beth said. "As soon as I mentioned the Scarecrow, he shut down on me. His reaction didn't make sense."

"Not so odd if you know the case."

"Explain."

"I can't."

"Why?"

"Because the bosses won't like it."

"What?"

"Seven years ago, they announced the case was closed and the killer was caught. People got promoted. Careers were made. Everybody was happy the monster was safely tucked away in a mental asylum. But there were whispers."

"What do you mean?"

"Something wasn't kosher. Word came down from above to leave matters rest and not to talk about it. Nothing's changed."

"That's crazy."

"There are just some subjects that are off limits," Hilderbrand said. "Better to let sleeping dogs lie."

"I can't, Paul. I'm working a murder case."

Hilderbrand nodded and took a sip of his drink.

For the first time she could remember, he looked uncomfortable. Whatever else he was, he was a good cop and a straight shooter. This was the second time she was being stonewalled, and she didn't like it. Eventually, the silence grew awkward.

"This is a completely new case," Beth said. "Pell is still in Mayfield. I checked."

"Good. He can stay there and rot."

"There's no question we're dealing with an imitator. If some nut's out there modeling his career after a serial killer, I need all the details I can get to stop him."

"You said Kale refused to help you?"

"I said he shut down. One minute he was friendly and pleasant, the next he practically tossed me out of his office. I don't get it."

"Everything about that freakin' case was ugly," Hilderbrand said, lowering his voice. "Beyond ugly. Absolutely the worst I've ever seen."

"That still doesn't explain Jack's reaction," Beth said.

"He had a partner."

"Right. I saw that in the file. Pell killed a female agent—Constance somebody."

"Connie Belasco," Paul said after a pause. "Nine months out of Quantico."

"What happened to her?"

"Dr. Pell caught her at home one night and amputated her arms and legs. When he was through torturing her, he put a bullet in her head."

Beth gasped. None of this had been in the file. The only mention she'd seen regarding Belasco's injuries was that an agent had been shot to death and her body mutilated. Losing a partner was nearly the equivalent of losing a spouse. She could see why no one wanted to talk about it. She wondered whether the notation about Jack's *medical reason* for leaving was somehow related. Confused, she raised the question to Hilderbrand.

He shrugged. "Medical . . . emotional. What's the difference? Sometimes one size fits all. If you were in charge, would you want to advertise one of your agents went to pieces?"

"No, but—"

"Jack Kale was a helluva cop. Something inside him went south after it happened. That's all I'm gonna say. His separation was best for everyone concerned."

"I don't understand," Beth said.

"I know you don't. I'm not sure anyone does except Jack Kale."

"C'mon. This is important. I can't be stumbling around in the dark on this."

"I'm not saying don't investigate," Hilderbrand said. "Go out and catch the bastard who killed that man. If he's a copycat, great. Just tread lightly before you start drawing comparisons. And don't expect a lot of help from the Bureau."

"Why?"

Hilderbrand lapsed into silence again. He seemed to be struggling to find the right words. The silence grew longer. The din of conversations in the room began to blend together into white noise.

"Paul?"

Hilderbrand finished his drink and stood. "Thanks for the drink, Beth. It was good to see you again."

Beth Sturgis watched him walk out of the restaurant and into the street. "I'll be damned," she said shaking her head.

Chapter 9

When she returned home, Beth hung her dress in the closet, changed into a pair of worn sweats and a T-shirt, and climbed into bed with the Scarecrow file. She was still shaken by what Paul had told her. Imitator or not, they were dealing with an extremely dangerous individual who had to be caught before more people died. As much as she didn't want to, in the morning, she would approach Penny Fancher and request additional help.

While she was musing over what to say, Peekachu jumped lightly onto the bed and joined her. Beth kept reading. Tired of being ignored, the cat butted her with his head to get her attention. She responded by scratching him behind the ears. The large tabby began to purr and stretched out in the middle of the bed, closing his eyes. Beth moved closer to the edge to give herself more room.

Outside her bedroom window, the accent lights came on in her small patio garden. They were a minor extravagance she'd installed shortly after buying the house. The town house was a major extravagance and a stretch to manage each month on her salary. After moving out of her boyfriend's home nine months earlier, she couldn't see returning to an apartment. So she gathered her financial papers and approached a bank without much hope of success. To her surprise, they gave her a loan. Now she was a homeowner with all the headaches that entailed. But it was all hers, and that made a difference.

In the corner of the patio was a standing fountain with a lion's head. It was nearly six feet tall and looked like an old friend. She'd run across it one day while wandering through Scott's Antique Market in nearby Jonesboro and bought it on the spot. Water poured from the lion's mouth into a deep bowl. At the bottom of the bowl, a small light projected shadows created by the moving water upward onto a vine-covered pergola. When the weather was nice, she'd leave the windows open and let the sound of the water and the scent from her gardenias lull her to sleep.

The Scarecrow file contained a photo of Howard Lincoln Pell. Nothing about the man seemed extraordinary except his eyes. They reminded her of dark, fathomless marbles, lacking in pity, remorse, or regard for human life. Maybe she was projecting, making him fit her preconceptions as Jack Kale had told his class.

Pell had actually consulted with the detectives early on in the case. According to neighbors interviewed after his arrest, he'd led a quiet life, something newspapers always seemed to point out. Psychologists at Meadowbrook Hospital for the Criminally Insane tested him and found his IQ was at genius level. Try as they might, they could never get Pell to offer any reason for his actions.

According to D. H. Felton, the detective who wrote the case summary, Pell's assistance turned out to be bogus. The clues he planted at the various murder scenes were designed to mislead. His plan was working quite well, until Jackson Kale entered the picture. As she read further, Beth was astounded by Kale's leaps of insight, which seemed to defy logic.

In the end, a two-day chase took place across the state of Georgia ending at Cloudland Canyon, a picturesque gorge in the northern part of the state. Locked in a death struggle with each other, Jack Kale and Howard Pell went over the cliff together. Somehow, both men had survived.

The report only made vague references to their injuries. Kale's had been serious but not life threatening, making his medical discharge all the more puzzling. Those sustained by Pell were apparently extensive. At least that's what the report's author implied. Police reports had a funny way of ending up in court, so cops were cautious about what they wrote down. All the narrative said was, "Subject's injuries prevented this investigator from speaking with him for sixteen weeks while he was in the hospital. After that, access to him was restricted by his legal counsel."

Internal Affairs from both the APD and the FBI followed up and concluded there was no wrongdoing on Kale's part. They found Howard Pell's injuries "were suffered during an assault on the arresting officer."

Predictably, a lawsuit followed in which the APD, Kale, and the FBI were all sued. The file included a newspaper clipping where Pell's lawyer claimed Kale had "eviscerated his client." Beth blinked and read that part again. A search party had found Pell with his intestines sitting on top of his chest. The image caused her shoulders to tighten. Somehow, she couldn't connect the man she'd met earlier with that type of violence. Neither could the jury, who had little sympathy for Pell. They found for the defendants and dismissed the case.

Other photographs followed, horrific, dark images that projected the unspeakable anguish Pell's victims had suffered. Edward Chastain, the third victim, age forty-one, and a father of four, had been abducted and brutally murdered. The ME was uncertain whether the skin had been stripped off his hand before or after he was dead. Little by little, the crime scene photos showed earth being removed from the grave where Chastain's body was recovered. Like Jerome Haffner, one of his fingers was missing, and burst capillaries indicated the man had been buried alive. Beth fought down her revulsion and kept reading. Kale was right. There were monsters in the world, and some of them walked on two legs.

It was nearly one o'clock in the morning when she finished, and for the first time since she'd moved into the house, Beth got up, shut and locked the windows, and turned on her burglar alarm before returning to bed.

Chapter 10

Beth was at her desk at seven forty-five the next morning going over the last section of the murder book. She'd already downed a full cup of coffee hoping it would wake her up. Her eyes felt scratchy and dry and she was having trouble getting started. The phone rang.

"Sturgis."

"He was right," Max Blaylock said. "We found a tunnel about twenty minutes ago."

"A tunnel?"

"I started asking around and spoke to old Judge Etheridge, who grew up around here. He told me a number of farms in the area were once part of a larger plantation dating back to the Civil War. Turns out some of the slaves weren't crazy about the way things were being run and decided to make a break for freedom using tunnels to escape."

"Where was it found?"

"The barn."

"We looked there. It was empty," Beth said.

"Not completely. Remember those moldy hay bales stacked in the corner in front of the work bench?"

"Sure."

"After we spoke, I told Avilles to start poking around. Anyway, he got to figuring, who stacks hay in front of a place they work? He moved the bales and saw the bench was sitting on a trap door."

"Did he—?"

"No. He lifted the door to see what was under it but didn't go down. All he did was shine his Maglite into the hole. Looks like there's a small room underneath and a tunnel that runs toward the railroad tracks."

"I'll leave here in thirty minutes," Beth said, now fully awake.

As soon as they disconnected, she checked Penelope Fancher's office to see if the lieutenant was in. She was there, studying something on her computer screen.

A few detectives had drifted into the squad room and were already at their desks working the phones; one or two were typing or reviewing reports. Beth walked past the row of cubicles. Each one was reserved for a set of partners. Their desks faced each other.

At Fancher's door, she tapped and waited for her to look up.

"Come in, Beth," Fancher said. "You're here nice and early."

"Thought I'd get a jump on the day, LT."

Fancher smiled. "Nothing makes the boss happier than seeing people who work for her busy. What's up?"

"I'm about to head back to Jordan. The sheriff just called and said they found a tunnel in the barn."

"Why is that important?"

"I don't know yet," Beth said. "But I think it will be. Yesterday I spoke with a former FBI agent who worked the original Scarecrow case. It was his idea. He thinks there's a second crime scene nearby. This could be it."

"You're making another trip to Jordan because this man thought there could be another scene?"

"I am," Beth said. "It merits another look. I'll want forensics again, too."

Lieutenant Fancher leaned back in her seat and considered this. She then informed Beth, "Our unit has a major backlog of uncleareds. We're also understaffed. Are you certain this trip is necessary?"

"Tell me you're kidding."

"I'm not. I was just going over the numbers, and we're way behind where we should be. It doesn't help that the city council cut our budget by thirteen percent, Detective."

"I still have to work the case."

Fancher drew a long breath. "This is an interdepartmental referral. That means we're assisting as a courtesy, not taking it over. Can't you get by with one of their people?"

Penelope Fancher was a number cruncher, and the bottom line mattered to her because it was scrutinized by the bosses. Add to that the fact that the crime happened outside the city limits and the town of Jordan was getting the short end of the stick.

"I'll try," Beth said evenly. "The problem is they're not equipped to handle what we're dealing with here."

"And what's that? Yesterday you told me the killer's a copycat."

"I still feel that way," Beth said. "My partner thinks there's bad mojo in the air on this one."

"How so?"

"The way that man was killed, the missing finger, the lack of blood, the locket around his neck, the missing women, and now we find a tunnel. Take your pick. Whoever did this is following the Scarecrow's playbook."

"Tell me about the locket," Fancher said.

"According to the sheriff, there are two missing women in Jordan. The man I spoke with yesterday, Jack Kale, thinks the killer's sending us a message he has one of them. That means we can expect another victim. If there's any chance of preventing it, we need to move and move quickly."

Penny Fancher reached forward and nudged her computer mouse. She studied the screen for several seconds, then said, "Dusty Shelton's tied up on the south side until later this afternoon. Head up there and see what you can do with one of the locals. I'll have a uniform meet you in the garage as backup. If you think you'll need more help, I'll spring Shelton loose as soon as he's done and send him your way."

She'd been with Robbery-Homicide a whole three months and had a single week-long course in forensic training. Hopefully her five years' experience working environmental crimes would do. Every detective knew the rudiments of investigative techniques. She hoped Max Blaylock wouldn't realize he was getting shortchanged.

*

On the way back to her desk, she ran into Dan Pappas. He was a no-nonsense cop with fifteen years in Homicide.

"Enjoy your talk with Penny Pincher?" he said, using the lieutenant's nickname around the squad.

"The best," Beth said.

"Got something cookin'?"

"I landed a murder case up in Jordan."

"Jordan?"

"Interdepartmental request for assistance."

"On your way up there now?"

"Yep."

"Who's your backup?" Pappas asked.

"Fancher's giving me a uniform. She told me to use one of the locals," Beth said.

"Figures," Pappas said. "How 'bout I take a ride with you? I need to stretch my legs. The fresh air'll do me good."

"It might get you in trouble, Dan," Beth said, looking toward Fancher's office.

"Lenny Cass is still flat of his back," Pappas said. "If he finds out I let you go solo, I'll be in more trouble with him."

"You sure?"

"Assisting another detective in a dangerous situation is what we do. Pincher has a problem with that, she can file a beef."

Pappas got up and put on his jacket. The man was built like a defensive tackle, probably six foot four and close to 250 pounds. His face carried the scars of childhood acne. If he gave any thought to his clothes, it didn't show. He always reminded her of a walking unmade bed. If they had to go into a tunnel together, she hoped it wouldn't be too narrow for his shoulders. Though she was grateful for his offer, she couldn't bring herself to say so, other than to thank him.

"Tell me a little about the case," he said.

"Let's get rolling before Fancher waylays you. I'll bring you up to speed on the way."

Chapter 11

The uniform was waiting for them in the garage. Beth told him he was off the hook and free to carry on. He gave them a half salute and headed back to the elevators. During the ride, she filled Pappas in on the murder details and her meeting with Jack Kale.

"I met him during the original investigation," Pappas said when she had finished. "Quiet and kinda intense."

"Well, he's a jerk," Beth said. "I asked for his help—nicely, mind you—and he about tossed me out of his office."

"That's odd."

"You should have been there. Any idea what's the matter with him?"

Pappas shrugged. "There were some rumors floating around."

"What sort of rumors?" Beth asked.

"The feds were especially tight-mouthed, but about a year after we caught Pell, I ran into an agent who worked the taskforce with us and asked how Kale was doing. The guy said physically fine."

"*Physically?*"

"Yeah. It was a strange response. Anyway, we talked some more and he let on Kale had left the Bureau. That really floored me. I mean, he was their fair-haired boy, particularly with all the publicity after nailing Pell."

"Sounds that way," Beth said. "You ever find out why he left?"

"Sometimes you have to read between the lines."

"Okay, give."

"We chitchatted for a while, and I eventually asked how Kale was keeping busy in his retirement. I figured maybe he had a book deal going or something. The guy just shook his head and told me no one had seen him for months. 'Vacation?' I said. 'Nah,' he says. He never comes out of his house. The guy turned into a recluse."

"Maybe all the publicity got to him."

"Maybe," Pappas said. "But that's not the vibe I picked up. It was like he collapsed emotionally."

"Jeez," Beth said.

"Yeah. Jeez."

Chapter 12

A light rain was falling when they arrived in Jordan. The cross still stood in the middle of the field, a stark reminder of what happened there. Beth and Pappas found a couple of yellow ponchos in the trunk and put them on, then made their way through the tall grass. Sheriff Max Blaylock and Juan Avilles, the deputy who found the tunnel, were waiting for them in the barn. Beth made the introductions.

"I spoke with the families of both women," the sheriff informed them. "Sandra Goldner and Betsy Ann Tinsley are still missing. The locket belongs to Betsy Ann. Her mother identified it as her birthday present."

Beth asked, "Were they together when they disappeared?"

"According to Sandra's brother, they went into Atlanta Thursday night to meet Betsy's new boyfriend, Jerome Haffner, the gentleman we found in the field."

"Who is he?" Pappas asked.

"Was," Blaylock said. "Some bigwig with a brokerage firm. That's all we know so far."

"Any ransom demand yet?" Pappas asked.

"Nothing," Blaylock said. "The families haven't heard a word."

Beth made a note of that in a little book she carried and then looked over to where Avilles was standing nearby. The deputy was a tall, skinny young man with close-cropped brown hair and an overbite.

"Good work finding that trap door."

"Appreciate it, ma'am."

Without looking up, she added, "It's Beth or Detective Sturgis. I'm not that much older than you."

"Yes, ma'am."

"Any idea where the tunnel comes out?" Pappas asked.

"Not yet," Blaylock said. "Avilles and I walked the tracks some but didn't see anything."

"Guess we're about to find out," Beth said. "Show me the door."

Avilles led them to the corner of the barn where the workbench had sat the day before. It was now pushed off to one side.

"I used gloves when I moved it," he said. "Same for the door handle."

"You did right," Beth said, feeling a little tick of excitement growing inside her. She glanced down and saw the floor had been swept. Hay was spread over it to disguise the broom marks. The straw on top was clearly fresher.

"Prick cleaned up after himself," Pappas observed.

The detective placed the crime scene kit on one of the hay bales and removed a digital camera from the box. He took a few pictures while Beth ran the Polilight over the workbench and the trap door handle.

"Got a partial print here, Dan," she said. "Looks like a good one."

"Is your tech coming out?" the sheriff asked.

"He'll be here. We're just doing the preliminaries."

Near the bench was a window covered with an elaborate spider web, where a white moth was struggling to free itself. Making its way slowly along one of the diagonal strands was a white spider about the size of a quarter. Transfixed, Beth stared at it. After a moment, she snapped out of her trance and used the end of her Maglite to destroy the web. The moth fluttered off.

"Wasn't in the way," Avilles observed.

"I don't like predators," Beth muttered slowly and turned her attention to the trap door.

The deputy and Pappas exchanged glances. Pappas snapped a picture of the handle as Beth held her pen next to the print to mark its location and provide some perspective. He then dusted the area while she kept the Polilight in place. Once that was done, he lifted the print off with tape and attached it to a card.

"Slender," Pappas observed. "Could belong to a woman."

He deposited the card with the print in a plastic bag and sealed it. They then returned to the trap door and shined their Maglites into the hole while the sheriff and his deputy looked on. A black beetle skittered across the top rung of the ladder and disappeared into a crack in the shaft. Conscious the men were watching her, Beth clenched her jaw. She'd never cared for tight places, and the thought of going down there made her stomach clench. A queasy stomach, however, was better than dying of embarrassment because she froze and couldn't do her job. Being a woman in a men's club only made matters worse.

Lesser of two evils, her inner voice whispered.

After what seemed like an eternity, she forced herself to move, dropped down into a crouch, and examined the first few rungs of the ladder closely. There were markings in the dust. Someone had clearly been there.

Pappas saw them as well and asked, "How do you want to play this?"

Beth pulled the poncho over her head and tossed it onto the hay. "We'll never find that girl standing here," she said, drawing her weapon. "Me first. You follow."

"I'll come, too," Avilles said.

Beth liked him better for that.

"Let's keep it at two," she said, remembering Jack Kale's comment about the number of people walking a crime scene. "Any more and we risk contamination. You okay with that?"

Avilles nodded.

"Sheriff?" Beth asked.

"Makes sense," Blaylock said. "We'll guard the front door. I don't know if you'll have reception down there, but try to stay in touch with your cell phone so we know you're all right."

Beth pulled her phone out and examined the screen. "Two bars," she said. "I'll keep going as long as I can." She turned to Pappas and asked, "Ready?"

"Ready."

"As soon as I clear the area, you follow."

Pappas nodded.

Grateful she'd worn slacks that day, Beth lowered herself down the ladder rung by rung. Pappas and Avilles used their flashlights to light the way. At the midpoint, Beth paused and looked closer at the rung level with her eyes.

"Got a blue thread here," she announced, placing it in an evidence bag.

"Betsy Ann's mom told me she was wearing a blue blouse when she left home," Avilles said.

The lower she got, the more she became conscious of a dank smell hovering in the darkness. Her heart was beating faster, so much so that she had to force herself to take several breaths to slow her respiration down.

The room they'd seen from above was nothing more than an irregular opening at the bottom of the ladder. It couldn't have been more than six feet square. She assumed a combat stance and swept her light and gun back and forth until she was satisfied there were no threats. The light revealed a series of wooden two-by-eight boards jammed into the walls for support. They were frail with age and did nothing to increase her comfort level. Ahead, the tunnel's blackness swallowed her flashlight beam. The roof was only an inch or two above her head and supported by more of the beams.

Pappas won't be happy.

"Clear, Dan," she called up. "Watch your head when you come down. It's pretty tight."

The big detective began his descent. When he reached the bottom, there was barely enough room for them to stand shoulder to shoulder.

"Nice place you got here," he grumbled.

"Yeah."

"Any idea how far it runs?" he said, squinting down the tunnel.

Beth shook her head. Although it was cooler below the barn, her face was bathed in perspiration.

"You okay?" Pappas asked.

"Fine. Let's—"

Pappas put a meaty hand on her shoulder and said, "My wife hates basements, too. Let's take it slow and easy, okay?"

"Slow and easy," Beth repeated.

"Check the ground every few feet for trip wires."

"Trip wires?" Beth said.

Pappas explained further. "I was in Desert Storm. The Taliban loved to booby-trap homes we were trying to clear."

"That's wonderful, Dan. I feel loads better now."

"It pays to be cautious."

Beth nodded her agreement. "Ready?"

"Still want the lead?" Pappas asked.

"No, but I got it," Beth said.

Widthwise, the tunnel was uncomfortably narrow with barely enough clearance for her shoulders. It was worse for Pappas. In order to negotiate his way, the detective had to turn sideways. He called the sheriff on his cell phone to let him know they were moving out. After a hundred feet, the air began to feel heavy, making breathing difficult.

"Fuck," Pappas said, startling her.

She spun around and leveled her flashlight at him. "What?"

"Just tore my goddamn jacket on an exposed nail," he said. "Monica's gonna kill me."

"You scared the hell out of me," Beth said. "Are you hurt?"

"It's just a scratch. I'll live."

With that, they started forward again as the darkness closed around them. After another fifty feet, Pappas's phone lost reception. He stuck it in his pocket. Beth gradually came to a halt and listened. Somewhere, not far off, water was dripping.

"You hear that?" she said.

"Yep. Keep movin'," Pappas said.

It took thirty yards to identify the source. The tunnel suddenly widened into a second room. Rainwater was dripping from the roof onto the top of a cast-iron stove.

"What the hell?" Pappas said.

"It's an old stove."

"Great detective work. What's the fuck's a stove doing down here?"

Beth raised her shoulders and ran the beam from her Maglite across the surface and sides, checking for a trap. At first she thought the slender, white object sticking out of the burner was a twig. When the realization that she was looking at a finger hit her, she recoiled, taking a step backward into Pappas.

"Oh my God," she said.

Pappas saw the grisly object at the same time. "Sonofabitch," he said. "I think we just found the source of your print."

Beth fought down a wave of nausea and forced herself to move closer. Her legs suddenly felt like lead.

"Get a picture," she told Pappas, pulling another plastic bag from her back pocket.

The camera's built-in flash momentarily lit the room, revealing another ladder in the corner. At the top was a second trap door. She and Pappas spent several minutes examining the stove, floor, and ladder hoping to find more clues. There was nothing.

When Pappas took the bag from her and put the severed finger inside, she didn't protest. It was slender and the nail was coated with red lacquer—clearly that of a woman.

Once they were satisfied the room had given up all its secrets, Pappas said, "Let's get the hell outta here. I'll go first. That door looks heavy."

The detective started to climb but stopped three-quarters of the way up and shined his light near where his left hand was grasping.

"What is it?" Beth called up.

"Looks like a drop of blood," he said. "I think I can dig it out with my knife."

Pappas reached into his pants pocket and produced a small folding Buck knife and began to work the wood, eventually breaking off a piece. He bagged it.

"Maybe it's the killer's and we'll catch a break with a DNA match," Beth said.

"We should be so lucky," Pappas said. "This bastard is playing some kind of game with these clues and the footprints."

"He might have missed it," Beth said without conviction.

The trap door was heavy, and it took an effort to lift it. A layer of sod covered the top, placed there for camouflage. They emerged, blinking into the gray daylight to find themselves only about fifty yards from the barn. The railroad tracks were no more than thirty feet away. As light flooded into the hole they'd just climbed out of, they saw what had not been apparent in the darkness: the dirt at the base of the ladder was dark brown, a different color from what was in the tunnel.

Beth and Pappas looked at each other and then at the soles of their shoes.

"Goddamnit," Pappas said.

"Got to be the victim's blood."

Pappas pulled out his cell phone and called the sheriff again.

As Blaylock and Avilles made their way to them, Beth began to examine the area. The rain was coming down harder now, soaking her clothes and hair and running down the back of her neck.

"Dan, tell them to stay back. I need to work this area."

Pappas nodded and moved off to intercept them.

Remembering as much as she could from her forensics class and watching techs over the years, Beth set up a ten-yard grid in her mind and began walking it, first one way and then the other. The killer and at least one of the victims had likely been in the tunnel. Hopefully one or both had left a clue behind.

On her third pass, something caught Beth's eye. Another set of footprints she missed the first time was now visible, angling toward the woods. She knew the train tracks crossed the road about a quarter mile from where she was standing because she'd driven over them on her way to the farm. More broken stalks of grass confirmed her suspicions.

This is how the bastard left.

Beth placed a call to Ben Furman at the crime lab.

"Ben? Beth Sturgis. I need you back out at the Donneley farm in Jordan. We found the second crime scene."

Chapter 13

Jack Kale was in his front yard watering a white azalea bush when a Crown Victoria pulled into his driveway. Beth Sturgis got out.

After their meeting, he had a feeling she'd be back. For a moment, he couldn't decide whether he was annoyed or pleased at her appearance. Jack shut the hose and watched her walk across the lawn to him.

"Hi," she said.

"Detective Sturgis."

"I was in your neighborhood and thought I'd stop by."

"Were you?" Jack asked doubtfully.

"No, I just drove in from Jordan," she said. "You were right. We found a tunnel."

Jack nodded. "What about the women?"

"Nothing so far. What we did find wasn't good. There was a great deal of blood down there."

Jack nodded. "Don't be surprised if you turn up roofies or Seconal when you get it analyzed. The combination of blood loss and tranquilizers would make your original victim compliant and easy for the killer to manage."

"I'll tell the ME," Beth said. "We found other things at the scene, but we're not sure what to make of them."

"What things?"

"Take a ride with me and see for yourself."

"I can't, Beth. I've been out of the game too long."

She ignored his comment and continued, "You were right about the missing women being victims."

"That's not good."

"No, it's not," Beth agreed. "I have a bad feeling about them."

51

"Understood."

"Are you interested in hearing more?"

Jack looked up at the second story of his house for a few seconds and then nodded.

"The killer severed a woman's finger and left it for us to find on an old stove in the tunnel."

The more bits and pieces she doled out, the more she began to dislike herself. For reasons she couldn't understand, he was struggling with the news. She compounded that by leaving her statements open ended, hoping to keep his curiosity up. He refused to take the bait.

"Well," Jack said, "I'm sure you and your partner will figure it out. The case sounds like an interesting one."

"My partner's flat on his back recuperating from a hernia operation. Another detective's backing me. You know each other."

"Really?"

"Dan Pappas," Beth said. "He worked with you on the original case."

Jack nodded slowly. "I remember Pappas. He's a good man."

"So how about it?" Beth said. "Take a ride with me and give the scene a look."

"Your department has any number of qualified people. You don't need me."

"No one has your experience with Pell and his methods. It won't take long. I promise."

"Time isn't the issue," Jack said. "It's just that I have a lot going on right now."

"I know. You said that yesterday."

"Nothing's changed, Beth," Jack said patiently.

"Right. Your bush would miss you," she said, finally giving in to her frustration.

"I'm sorry," Jack said.

"So am I. You really disappoint me."

Jack had no response to that. He simply looked down at his shoes.

She turned and started back to her car, then stopped.

"You owe me a cup of coffee."

"Excuse me?"

"A cup of coffee. You said you'd give me a rain check when I was at your office."

"Well, yes, but—"

"I'm ready," Beth said.

"I'm afraid I don't have any in the house," Jack said. "I planned on going shopping later."

"Not a problem," Beth said. "We can dine out."

Jack hesitated and then said, "All right. Give me a few minutes to change clothes. Would you care to come in?"

"Sure," Beth said.

*

As soon as she stepped through the front door, she was greeted by an enormous German shepherd.

"This is Marta," Jack said.

"MARTA? Like the train?"

Jack smiled. "She's a rescue dog. Someone left her on the elevated platform at the Dunwoody station a few years ago. Hold your hand out and let her sniff you. She's quite friendly."

Beth made a loose fist and extended it to the dog and watched her nostrils take in her scent. A moment later, Marta's tail wagged and she moved closer. Beth scratched her head. The shepherd then lowered her nose to check out her shoes.

"She's probably smelling my cat."

"Marty likes cats."

"To eat them or play with them?"

Jack stifled a laugh and headed for his bedroom to change, leaving Beth and Marta alone in the living room.

"Just us girls, huh?" Beth said.

Marta's tail wagged in response.

Curiosity got the better of her and Beth began to explore. Unlike Jack's office at the university, his living room was surprisingly neat. A worn oriental rug with muted reds and yellows dominated the middle of the room. At one end was a couch, two club chairs, and a low coffee table with a half-empty bottle of Scotch on it. Next to the bottle were the blue test booklets she'd seen the day before. Beth laughed to herself.

Guess he's making progress.

To the right of the couch was a fireplace with a very old-looking limestone mantel. Above that hung a large, rectangular impressionist painting of a man and a woman in dated evening clothes like people in an F. Scott Fitzgerald story. The man was facing away from his companion, holding a cigarette in one hand and a drink in the other. She was looking at him, arms folded in front of her, grasping her elbows.

Beth couldn't decide what her expression meant, which was probably the point the artist was trying to make.

"What do you think?" she asked Marta, who was sitting there watching her.

Across from the fireplace, one entire wall was taken up with built-in shelves filled with books. Between the books were a few photographs in silver frames. One was of a young girl and a woman. From the resemblance, she was sure the woman was the girl's mother. Both had the same facial shape and skin tone. She recognized the girl from the photograph in Jack's office. The woman, like herself, was a brunette.

"Former lady of the house?" she asked Marta.

Marta's tail thumped against the couch a couple of times.

Beth turned back to the books and read a few of the titles, something detectives did out of habit. *Group Psychology, Abnormal Psychology, Cognitive-Behavioral Techniques, The Rise of Theodore Roosevelt*, and Robert Parker's *Thin Air*.

Wandering around the room, she came to a pair of French double doors that looked out onto a patio, a backyard with two cherry trees, and a doghouse.

"Your place?"

Thump. Thump.

Jack finally reappeared. He'd changed into dark-blue jeans, and a white golf shirt with a small polo player logo on the left side. Yuck, she thought.

"Ready when you are," he said.

"We can take my car," Beth said. "I'm blocking you in."

Marta looked from one to the other and decided the invitation didn't include her. She walked back to the Oriental rug, turned around three times, and settled in front of the couch again with a sigh.

As they pulled out of the driveway, Jack asked, "Are you familiar with this neighborhood?"

"Enough," Beth said.

"Where are we going?"

"Jordan. They have a great coffee shop on the square."

The rest of the ride passed in silence.

Chapter 14

When she reached the town, Beth pulled up to the bakery she'd spotted on her first trip, praying they sold coffee. Jack didn't look happy.

"How do you take it?" she asked.

He turned and stared at her.

"Look, I'm sorry," Beth said. "It was a mean trick. If you give me thirty minutes at the scene, I'll make it up to you. I promise."

Silence.

"I'll get you home right away so you can do . . . whatever. Thirty minutes, that's all."

There was still no response. Jack's finger began to tap a rhythm on his knee.

"Okay," Beth said. "This was a bad idea. But I'm out of my depth here and I can use the help."

When more seconds ticked by and he still didn't respond, she was ready to conclude her strategy might not have been effective. Beth reluctantly reached for the ignition key and started the engine.

"Black," Jack said, "with one of those blue sweetener things."

Beth nearly smiled with relief but managed to stop herself in time, or rather the expression on Jack's face did. She hurriedly left the car. When she returned she informed him, "I bought you a cappuccino."

Jack opened his mouth to reply, then decided against it. He simply nodded his thanks.

She explained further. "I saw the machine in your kitchen and figured you liked them better."

Jack made a noise deep in his throat, which she interpreted as gratitude.

"Are we good?" Beth asked.

"Thirty minutes."

*

The other cars were parked along the road's shoulder. Ben Furman's van from the crime lab was there along with a second deputy's vehicle. As they crossed the field, Beth began a running commentary on the house, the barn, and what they'd found in the tunnel. Jack appeared to be half listening. His eyes were focused on the cross.

Max Blaylock and Dan Pappas were waiting for them at the barn. The sky was leaden and the air heavy with humidity. Swarms of gnats hovered over the tall grass. An absence of bird and insect noise had settled over the place as if even they were avoiding it. The sheriff introduced himself and shook Jack's hand. Pappas nodded to him.

"Good to see you, Jack. It's been a few years."

"Dan."

Max Blaylock said, "Detective Pappas tells me you handled the original investigation."

"I did."

"It's pretty obvious we've got a copycat," Blaylock said.

Jack didn't respond to that directly. "I understand you recovered blood samples from the ladder and tunnel."

Pappas informed him, "There was a good amount down there, Jack. Beth and I walked through the middle of it while we were stumbling about in the dark."

"Regardless of who it belongs, to that shouldn't affect the DNA," Jack said.

"They also found an old stove," Blaylock said. "Hell of an odd thing to run across in a slave tunnel you ask me."

"Most likely it's a prohibition tunnel," Jack said. "The stove's presence makes brewing moonshine a safe bet. It would have been a simple matter to load barrels onto a northbound freightliner."

The sheriff hooked his thumbs in his belt and extended his lower lip. "Detectives Sturgis and Pappas found some other items not far from the end of the tunnel. You wanna take a look at them?"

Jack didn't respond. His eyes had strayed again to the cross in the field.

"Professor?" Blaylock said.

"Did that yield anything?" Jack said, motioning with his chin.

"It yielded Jerome Haffner," Blaylock said. "Some blood of course— not a lot, as I'm sure Beth told you. Most of it was in the tunnel. There were also a couple of threads, like the ones they found down there."

"Was the victim wearing blue?" Jack asked over his shoulder.

"Yeah, Betsy Ann Tinsley, one of the missing women," Blaylock said. "According to her mother, that's what she had on when she left home."

"Was the cross like that when you took him down?"

"I think so," Beth said, pulling a photo out of the file. She examined it for a moment and was about to pass the picture to Jack, but he was already making his way through the grass toward it.

Beth and the others exchanged glances and hurried to catch up.

As they walked, the sheriff speculated, "Maybe Haffner's weight caused it to lean. He was a big guy. That's why I figured the killer had help."

Jack nodded absently and kept going.

"Be tough for one man to put him up there, Jack," Pappas said.

"Not if the killer staked him out on the ground first," Jack said. "Has anyone looked under it?"

"Under what? The cross?" Blaylock said.

"Exactly."

"We checked the area," Beth said. "But no one's moved it."

Jack turned to her. "Do you remember showing me the electrostats of the shoeprints?"

"You thought the killer made both because the depth was the same."

"I also said the crime scene was staged. That cross is perpendicular to the field, not facing it as you'd expect. Let's take a closer look."

Pappas looked at the sheriff and shrugged. When they were about ten feet away, Jack came to a halt and folded his arms across his chest. He stared silently at the cross as if he were trying to solve some complicated mathematical problem.

Nearly a minute ticked by before he spoke again. "Dan, help me take this down."

"Why?" Beth asked.

"You said the body had been drained of blood, right?"

"Most of it," Beth said.

"Was there enough in the tunnel to account for the difference?"

Beth considered his question for a moment, then answered, "I'd say no."

"The ground at the base of the stake has been turned—recently, from the look of it."

"Yeah, maybe," Blaylock said. "But why so big an area if the guy was just putting the cross up? This has gotta be six feet wide."

The same thought occurred to everyone at once.

"Shit," Pappas said.

*

Avilles and the second deputy returned from town with two shovels and began to dig. At Jack's direction, the earth was removed and placed onto a tarp they'd brought along. Beth and Ben Furman sifted through the growing mound looking for clues. At one point, Pappas's cell phone rang. He took it out, checked the screen, and then returned it to his pocket.

"Everything okay?" Beth asked, noting his expression.

"Text message from the lieutenant to call in."

"Maybe you should."

Pappas lifted his shoulders. "Reception's lousy out here. I'll wait till I get—"

The detective broke off what he was saying to look at Jack, who had dropped into a crouch and was collecting a soil sample. He'd donned a pair of blue latex gloves he borrowed from Beth earlier and was using a small pocket knife to scoop dirt and place it into a plastic evidence bag.

"Whatcha got, Jack?" Pappas asked.

"A possible outlier."

"A what?"

"An outlier—something that shouldn't be here. The coloration and texture of this soil is different from the rest. It also contains some shiny particles. I can't tell what they are by looking."

He turned to Ben Furman. "Your lab has a gas chromatograph mass spectrometer, don't you?"

"We sure do," Furman said.

"And an electron microscope?"

"Yep."

"You should analyze this as soon as possible," Jack said. "They almost look like bits of shell."

A curse from the second deputy interrupted the rest of Jack's comments. Everyone turned toward the hole. Sticking out of the loose soil was a woman's hand. One of the fingers was missing.

Chapter 15

It was nearly seven o'clock by the time Beth pulled into Jack's driveway. "I'm sorry about keeping you so long," she said. "You were really helpful. Thanks."

"You're welcome."

During the ride, Beth wanted to get Jack's thoughts on what they found, but he had lapsed into a moody silence shortly after they left the farm, making the trip back seem even longer than the one there.

Betsy Ann Tinsley's body was removed from the shallow grave and turned over to the medical examiner. A pall had settled over the farm. Conversations were few, and when someone did speak, it was in a whisper. No one could recall anything like the gruesome picture taking shape before them. More bizarre still were the page from an old almanac buried with her and the oxidized portion of a brass plate bearing the name "McKeachern, M." None of it made any sense. Pieces of a puzzle.

"Would you like to grab a bite to eat?" Beth asked. "I owe you."

"It's been a long day," Jack said. "I need to feed Marta."

"Sure. Maybe another time."

Jack gave her a tight-lipped smile that seemed rather sad and left the vehicle without another word. She sat there watching him until he disappeared into the house. When the lights came on, she started her car and pulled out of the driveway.

Maybe my cat'll be happy to see me.

*

The fog surrounding Sandra Goldner slowly lifted as she regained consciousness. Her head was throbbing and her vision was still blurry. She tried moving her arms and found she couldn't. They were secured above her head by a pair of handcuffs looped over a metal pipe. Before passing out for the third time, she'd yelled for help until her voice was hoarse in the desperate hope someone would come.

The murky darkness enveloping her was terrifying. There was barely enough light seeping through the opening of a huge iron door to see by. It was nearly twenty feet across and at least that much in height. Behind her was another door identical to the first. The floor she was sitting on was cement and incredibly uncomfortable. She tried shaking the pipe. It was firmly anchored and wouldn't budge. All she managed to do was rub the skin around her wrists raw.

Calm, she told herself. *Stay calm. Panic is the enemy now.* As the assistant general manager of a bank with fifteen employees, Sandra considered herself someone who didn't panic easily. You had to be.

Think. There's a way out of this mess. Use your intelligence. Even the most challenging situation has a solution. But intelligence didn't cover being kidnapped from a public parking lot. The last thing she remembered was walking to her car before a searing pain hit. Her shoulder still bore the mark where the electrodes had attached themselves. After that—blackness.

Sandra screamed as a tiny animal skittered across her legs, drawing them back out of reflex. In the deathly silence, her hearing had become acute. Though she could barely see it, the sound of the little rodent's nails running across the floor were clear enough. At first her mind refused to accept this was happening. Now that she had time to think, she was completely focused on survival. It was the only consideration.

Six weeks had passed since her divorce from Chad, a womanizing, cheating, low-life drunk. She was just beginning to feel human again. With some trepidation, she accepted Betsy Ann's invitation to come with her to Atlanta and meet her new boyfriend and his buddy. She'd known Betsy Ann since middle school and her friend assured her the guy was all right, a respectable stock broker.

On the whole, the evening had been a success, but it was too soon. She needed more time to recover from the breakup of her marriage. Even friendly divorces, and hers would hardly qualify as that, took their toll. It was like hitting yourself in the head with a hammer. The only good thing was that eventually you stopped. Jerome's friend was divorced himself and seemed to sense her discomfort. He told her he hoped they could get together again but didn't ask for her phone number when they said good night. Hopefully, there'd be a lot of nice guys in her future.

When this nightmare's over, she told herself, *I'm taking that vacation to Italy I've been promising myself.*

She gave the pipe another shake. Nothing.

Occasionally, there were other noises in the strange room. She considered it further and decided it was really more like a cylindrical space that reminded her of the inside of a grain silo. Creaks and groans came from beyond the back door, as if something was pressing against it. The door was so massive Sandra couldn't imagine what that could be.

She gathered herself once more and tried yelling for help. The only response was the echo of her voice bouncing off the walls.

Does anyone know I'm here? Are they even looking for me? Sooner or later, someone will come and take me away from this terrible place. She clung to that thought like a drowning person clings to a piece of driftwood. Someone had to come.

Chapter 16

The following morning found Jack Kale sitting in a comfortable leather club chair in the home office of Dr. Morris Shottner.

"Thanks for seeing me," Jack said. "Hope I'm not ruining your weekend."

"Forty years of practice hasn't helped my golf game," Shottner said. "One more day won't make a difference. I was surprised by your call. It's been, what, almost a year?" The doctor consulted his notes and corrected himself. "Sixteen months."

Shottner was a bearded man of middle height in his early sixties. He was wearing a pair of glasses with silver rims that made his eyes seem larger than they were. His office smelled vaguely of pipe tobacco. Two large jars of the stuff sat on the corner of his desk.

"When did it happen?" Shottner asked.

"Around one in the morning," Jack said.

"Any different from the others?"

"About the same. Shortness of breath, pressure in my chest, dry mouth, profuse sweating. I thought I was having a heart attack."

"But you weren't."

"No."

"I don't need to tell you PTSD symptoms can masquerade as heart attacks. Their reappearance is what concerns me."

Jack nodded and looked out the window at two squirrels chasing each other around the trunk of an old oak tree on Shottner's lawn. When they were through, they continued jumping from branch to branch in a constant state of motion. One of them paused and looked in the window at him, tilting its head to one side.

Perhaps he considers me sluggish, sitting here like this, Jack thought.

He turned back to the doctor who was waiting for him to continue.

"The timing concerns me, too," Jack said. "That's why I called."

"You think your trip to Jordan precipitated it?"

"Don't you?"

"Possibly," Shottner said. "How are you doing with the—?"

"Taking them once in a while."

"How do you define once in a while?"

"More than I should but less than before."

"That's progress," the doctor said, "as long as you're not upping the medication on your own again. What are those papers on the seat next to you?"

"The detective I met sent me a fax with the crime report and findings from the murder scene."

"And the photo?"

"A color image of a plaque they found in the woman's grave," Jack said.

"Ah."

"Ah?"

"That's what therapists say to make themselves sound smart. Didn't they teach you that in graduate school?"

"I never say 'Ah,'" Jack said.

"I rest my case." Shottner paused to take a polished briarwood pipe with a curved black stem from a rack on his credenza. He filled it with tobacco from one of the jars. When the pipe was full, Shottner used a slender metal tool to tamp the tobacco down but didn't light it.

"There were two bodies found in Jordan," Jack said. "A man and a woman."

"Terrible," Shottner said.

"And another woman is still missing."

"So you went there to help with their investigation. That was kind."

"I was basically kidnapped by one of the detectives."

"Unusual technique."

Jack shrugged. "Unusual woman."

"You could have said no."

"It was a little difficult. I was already in the car and she was driving."

"I've never known you to be at a loss for words, Jack."

Jack considered this for several seconds, then said, "So you think I wanted to go?"

"What do you think?" Shottner said.

"Definitely not."

"Okay."

"You don't agree?" Jack said.

"I neither agree nor disagree. I merely find it interesting after so many years." Shottner asked, "Did a nightmare follow last night's attack?"

"Not this time," Jack said, annoyed at the noncommittal answer. "Maybe that's progress."

"Possibly. What are your feelings?"

Jack took a weary breath and let it out. "The detective on the case told me psychiatrists always answer questions with questions."

"She may have a point," the doctor said and lit his pipe.

"You know Morgan's coming to visit this summer," Jack said. "I'm really looking forward to seeing her again. Seems she grows six inches each time we're apart."

"I'm told children do that," Shottner said, blowing a stream of blue smoke into the air. "You don't mind, do you?"

"What?" Jack said.

"I asked if the smoke bothers you."

"Uh . . . no," Jack mumbled. He'd been looking at Beth Sturgis's fax.

"You feel comfortable with Morgan in the house now?"

"I can't keep her away forever," Jack said. "She insisted. The girl has a mind of her . . ."

Jack's voice trailed away as his eye fell on a photocopy of the almanac page they'd recovered from the grave. It made no sense. Yet he knew there had to be a reason for its presence. Page 403 talked about ocean currents and had been torn from the middle of a book.

"What were you saying?" Shottner asked.

"Huh? Oh, I said she has a mind of her own—like her mother."

"Do you and Katherine still speak?"

"Generally about Morgan. Katherine's married now. I'm not part of her life anymore."

"Maybe we should explore that," Shottner suggested.

"Perhaps another time would be better," Jack said.

Page 403.

"That's what you say whenever the subject comes up," Shottner said.

"Resistance to therapy." Jack smiled.

"Possibly."

"To what end?"

"That, my dear professor, is what we're here to find out."

No salinity was noted on the mollusk fragments.

"The subconscious is extremely logical, Jack. It accepts whatever we put in without judgment."

Jack took another breath. "You'd think after eight years we'd be able to figure it out."

"Psychotherapy doesn't operate on a timetable," Shottner said.

"I know that. It's just frustrating."

"Do you still feel the same way about hypnosis? That's still an option, you know."

The brass plaque bearing the name "McKeachern, M." shows signs of oxidation on only one side.

Jack stood up so abruptly it startled the doctor, causing him to drop the match he was using to relight his pipe. He used his hand to extinguish it against the desktop.

"I've got to go," Jack said.

"Obviously," Shottner said. "I take it something's occurred to you?"

"I think I know what he's doing."

"Who?"

"The UNSUB."

"UNSUB?"

"Unknown subject. It's police slang."

"Well, always glad to help," Shottner said.

Jack was already halfway out the door and called over his shoulder, "Thanks, Moe. Sorry to screw up your weekend. I'll phone later."

Chapter 17

Jack's cell phone was out by the time he reached his car. He fumbled around in his pockets for a few seconds trying to find Beth Sturgis's business card and finally dialed her number.

"Sturgis."

"Jack Kale. Where are you?"

"Uh . . . I'm here at the crime lab. We've been trying to pin down some of the particles in that soil sample you found. They look like—"

"That broken plaque we recovered—do you still have it?"

"Of course. Why?"

"The composition's brass, right?"

"Just a moment," Beth said, putting him on speaker.

A muffled conversation took place in the background with a male voice. A moment later, Ben Furman came on the line.

"Hey, Jack," the tech said. "Yeah, it's definitely brass. There were no prints—"

"You won't find any," Jack said. "The killer's too smart for that, or thinks he is. Only one side was oxidized, correct?"

"Yep."

"Which means the other side was protected from the elements."

"Makes sense," Furman said.

"Have you traced the name yet?"

"I'm working on that now," Beth said. "The problem is there are fifty McKeacherns in the book. It's gonna take some time."

"We don't have any time," Jack said.

"Why?"

"The other woman. He's got her and he's going to kill her. That's what the page in the almanac means. It has nothing to do with ocean

66

currents. Four-oh-three is a date—April third. I don't know why I didn't see it before."

"That's today," Beth said.

"We may already be too late."

"Oh, Christ."

Jack started his engine and backed out of the driveway.

"There's a common thread running through what we found," he said.

"What?"

"Where do you find sand and shell?" he snapped.

"The ocean," Beth and Furman both said at the same time.

"Or river beds, if the conditions are right," Jack said. "I'm about thirty minutes from you. Keep working on McKeachern. Narrow it down to anything having to do with the water. If we find who or what they are, I have a feeling it'll tie the other pieces together."

Chapter 18

Jack came through the crime lab door and spotted Dan Pappas and two other men standing off to one side.

"Thought you were temporary help," he said.

"Thought you were, too," Pappas replied.

Beth was seated across the room speaking to someone on the phone, while Ben Furman was hunched over a microscope peering through the lens at something. Neither looked up. Before Jack could say anything further, the two men with Pappas approached him.

"Professor Kale, I'm Burt Wiggins. I work with Deputy Chief Ritson. This is Captain Kostner, who heads our Robbery-Homicide Division. I believe you know each other."

"We do," Jack said, shaking hands with both men in turn. "Good to see you again, Art."

"You, too, Jack," Kostner said.

Wiggins continued, "I understand you've been assisting Detectives Pappas and Sturgis with their investigation."

"Not really. I—"

"We've been following the developments and wanted to say thanks for your contributions."

"Glad to help," Jack said.

"Detective Sturgis has been quite complimentary," Wiggins added.

Jack glanced at Beth, who was still involved in her conversation and scribbling notes furiously. He didn't think Wiggins and Kostner had just dropped by but decided to see where the conversation was going.

"My pleasure," he said noncommittally.

"We'd like you to continue with us," Wiggins informed him.

"I beg your pardon?"

"We're saying we need your help, Jack," Kostner said. "There's a madman running around killing people."

"I know that, but I'm not in a position to get involved with anything at the moment. Actually, I'm in the middle of an important academic research project right now."

"Professor," Wiggins said, "a woman's life may be hanging in the balance."

"I'm sorry. I really can't—"

"Then what are you doing here?" Wiggins asked.

Jack was in the middle of formulating an answer when his eyes drifted to a poster on the wall with the Atlanta Police Department's symbol—a badge bearing the words "Protect and Serve" at the bottom. Allowing himself to be pulled into this investigation had been a mistake. If he left now, he could say everything he wanted in an e-mail and the cops could take it from there.

"I'm not sure I can answer that," Jack said. "I suppose I thought I could be of some help."

"Got 'em," Beth called out from across the room. "McKeachern Manufacturing out of Cleveland, Ohio. They make water pumps and hydraulic control systems."

Everyone turned back to Jack at the same time, expecting an answer to leap from his lips. He was still drawing a blank. *Shells, sand, water.* Somehow it was all connected.

"Beth," he said. "Get on the phone and see if they can give you a list of their customers in the state of Georgia."

"It's Saturday, Jack. They're probably closed."

"How bout I call the Cleveland Police?" Pappas suggested. "They probably have an emergency contact number. If they don't, their Fire and Rescue will."

"Go," Jack said, walking to where Furman was sitting. "Have you identified what type of sand we recovered?"

"Type?"

"Sand has all kinds of different consistencies and can vary widely from place to place. In Hawaii, where they've had volcanic activity, it's black on some beaches. In Destin, Florida, it's lighter in color and more powdery."

"These grains look pretty coarse to me, Jack. We need a geologist," Furman said.

"Then let's find one quick. Call Georgia State University and see if they have someone there who can help."

"Hopefully that woman's still alive," Pappas said.

Jack's mouth tightened at the comment. Against his own instincts, he was getting deeper and deeper into something that he should be backing away from, but he didn't know how to get out. It felt like the investigation's vortex was sucking him along. Wiggins and Kostner both stepped back to allow him space. Quite suddenly, the atmosphere in the lab had intensified into a measured sort of frenzy.

Beth announced, "I'm talking with Arnold Pulaski, the weekend shift supervisor at McKeachern. He has no idea who the customers are. He called someone from the main office who's on the way in."

Pappas's voice abruptly carried across the room. "Yeah, yeah, yeah, I know it's Saturday, lady. This is a matter of life and death. We're trying to find a kidnapped woman, so get off your ass and dig me up a geologist."

"Dig me up a geologist?" Jack repeated, mouthing the words to him.

Pappas shrugged and continued with his conversation. "No, I'm not being funny. This is on the level. A woman's about to die, and . . . yeah, I'll hold."

He gave Jack a thumbs up. Nearly four excruciating minutes crawled by before someone came back on the line.

Pappas listened for a moment and then said, "Hold on, Dr. Maynard. I'm gonna put you on speaker." The detective pointed to Jack and nodded.

"Dr. Maynard, this is Jack Kale at the Atlanta crime lab. Are you up to speed on what we're dealing with?"

"Yes. Something about a kidnapped woman. I'm at home at the moment. How can I help you?"

"I assume you have a computer in your house and a monitor with good quality resolution."

"Of course."

"If you'll give me your e-mail address, I'll have Ben Furman send you a photo of some evidence we found at the crime scene. I'm hoping you can help identify where it came from."

"Certainly," Maynard said. "I'll do my best."

Two more minutes passed as they fidgeted and waited for the transmission to complete. Still on the line, Maynard confirmed he'd opened the file and was examining the photo. He asked, "Was there any salinity in the sample?"

"Salinity?" Pappas said.

"Salt."

"None," Furman answered. "I noted that in my report."

"Good," Maynard said. "That eliminates beach and ocean environments. From the color and coarseness of the sand, I'd say this comes from a river someplace. It's the bits of shell that are confusing me. I can give Cheryl Angstrom with our zoology department a call and run this by her. If we pin down the type of shell, we can match the precise location."

"Wonderful," Jack said. "Please try to get a hold of her."

As they disconnected, Beth looked at Jack and shook her head as if to say, How do you know this stuff?

He smiled at her, turned to Furman, and asked if he had a map of the state of Georgia and the Southeast. One was found and placed on a whiteboard that took up nearly one whole side of the room. While Jack was in the process of studying it, the phone rang again. Beth Sturgis answered and had a rapid conversation with a harried supervisor from McKeachern Manufacturing.

"No, sir, we don't need a search warrant for this information. We're asking for your cooperation to save a young woman's life."

She hit the speaker button so they all could hear.

"I'm sympathetic, of course," the supervisor said. "But I'm afraid it would be against company policy. Here at McKeachern, we value our customers' privacy and do our best to protect it."

"Protect this," Beth said, the color in her face rising. "If that woman dies because you sit on your ass and insist on following company policy, I'll make sure every freakin' newspaper, television, and radio station in the country knows you and your company are responsible. You'll be lucky to find a job shoveling dog shit."

"I, uh—"

"We're talking about water pumps and pipes," Beth snapped, "not goddamn state secrets."

Pappas, who was standing near Jack, inched a little closer and whispered sotto voce, "Got a full head of steam goin'."

"Scary," Jack whispered back.

There was a pause on the phone as the supervisor digested this.

"Well, I suppose, given the emergency, I could make an exception, if you'll agree not to publically disclose our customers' names. We don't wish to appear uncooperative."

"Agreed," Beth said. "Thank you very much."

"Do you have an e-mail address?"

Within thirty seconds, the e-mail arrived. The list contained six names.

"I'll take the first three," Beth said. "Dan, you take the second three."

"Not necessary. It's this one," Jack said, pointing to the fifth name.

"How do you know?" Beth asked.

"According to the 'Sold To' column, the first four are new pipes purchased by Buckner, Elsworth, and Fannin Counties for different school and park projects. The sixth is replacement piping for the Department of Transportation," Jack said, reading the invoice. "None of these have anything even remotely connected to a river or a lake. The fifth does."

"That leaves the Army Corps of Engineers," Beth said.

Jack asked, "Is your man still on the line?"

"Sir, are you still there?" Beth said to the speakerphone.

"Yes, ma'am."

"Ask him what a Model 250FCG is," Jack said.

"I heard the gentleman," the supervisor said. "Tell him it's a flood control gate. The Corps of Engineers bought it to replace an older model about three years ago."

"How big is it?" Jack asked.

"Huge. They use it to adjust a river's water level."

"Adjust the water level," Jack reiterated half to himself. He was staring at the state map on the opposite side of the room.

Why change how much water is flowing? Navigation was possible, but that didn't apply to the Chattahoochee River. It wasn't a navigable river. That leaves industry. Better still, it fit.

"Buford Dam!" Jack said. "It releases water from Lake Lanier."

"So what?" Furman said.

Jack crossed the room to the map and used his finger to trace the course of the Chattahoochee River. It followed the state line between Georgia and Alabama, eventually emptying into the gulf.

"The mussel beds," Jack said. "They're a large industry in Alabama. That's what those bits and pieces of shell are, mussel shells. Our killer left a puzzle for us to solve. If Sandra Goldner's alive, that's where we'll find her." He turned to Ben Furman. "Ben, get on the horn with the Army and find out where the control gate is located at the dam."

Beth and Pappas were already in motion, heading for the door. Jack started to follow when Wiggins's voice stopped him.

"Where are you going, Professor?"

"With them. I may be able to help—"

"I'm afraid I can't allow that. You're a civilian." He turned to Pappas and said, "Go."

"But—"

"Go," Wiggins repeated. "I'm sorry, Dr. Kale. We need to finish our talk."

Beth and Pappas threw apologetic looks at Jack and disappeared through the crime lab door.

Chapter 19

Jack watched them leave. When he turned back, his eye fell on the poster again. "Protect and Serve," he whispered to himself. Captain Kostner put a sympathetic hand on his shoulder.

"I'm sorry, Jack. Burt's right. If we let you go and you get hurt or that girl gets hurt, the city's ass would be in a sling. There's no choice."

"Actually, there is," Burt Wiggins said. "That's why we're here. Both the deputy chief and Public Safety Director Cartwright would like you to consult on the case with us. We're prepared to pay you four hundred dollars a day, plus expenses."

"A consultant," Jack said.

"Exactly."

"It won't cure the problem. I'd still be a civilian." Jack turned to Kostner. "You can't run this investigation from behind a desk, Art. You know that."

"I do," the captain said. "You'd be assigned to Robbery-Homicide with a temporary rank of detective lieutenant. That way it's all nice and legal."

Furman interrupted their conversation to say, "I've got Lieutenant Shaffer with the Corps of Engineers on the phone."

Jack motioned for Furman to put the call on speaker.

"This is Jack Kale, Lieutenant. I'm, ah . . . consulting with the Atlanta Police Department. Has Ben told you what's going on?"

"He has."

"Three years ago, the Corps bought a hydraulic control system from McKeachern Manufacturing in Cleveland."

"Before my time," Shaffer said. "But it sounds right. We've been replacing the old units on dams throughout the Southeast."

"Would Buford Dam and Lake Lanier be on that list?"

"Those records are kept in South Carolina, Mr. Kale. I can check for you."

"That's not important right now. Am I correct in assuming the unit controls water flowing out of Lake Lanier for users downstream?"

"You are."

"As far as the mussel beds in Mobile, Alabama?"

"That's where the river empties."

"Can you describe what your system looks like?"

"Basically, it consists of two portal doors and a motorized assembly to move them. They're quite large, as you can imagine. Once they're opened, water enters the spillway—"

"At the base of the dam?"

"Right. The water flows along the spillway and into the Chatta-hoochee River via a culvert."

Jack asked, "Do you plan any releases over the next few days?"

"Just a moment."

He waited while Shaffer flipped through some papers in the background.

"As a matter of fact, we have a twenty-six-minute pour scheduled for one o'clock today."

"I need you to stop it," Jack said. It was 12:18.

"That would be a little hard," Shaffer said. "The entire operation's governed by computer. Water levels are constantly monitored. If we have a weather event, such as too much rainfall, two engineers are dispatched to confirm it and override the system. My nearest crew's three hours away."

Jack fought down a rising sense of urgency and forced himself to speak calmly. "Pull the plug. There has to be an emergency cutoff switch."

"We have safeguards, of course," Shaffer said, "but they're operated locally. If you're suggesting someone has tampered with—"

"I'm saying there's a good chance a woman is about to die if that flood gate opens. You've *got* to stop it."

"Mr. Kale, I understand your concern, but I can't change the laws of physics. I assure you the facility's secure. A person can't just waltz in there."

"I don't know what kind of security you have," Jack said, glancing at the clock on the wall. "Two detectives are en route right now. I need to know exactly where that control gate is and how they get to it."

There was a pause on the phone as the lieutenant considered his options. "Let me see if I can get hold of Colonel Zucker. I'm gonna need his authorization."

It was at that point that Captain Kostner got on the phone and identified himself. "Lieutenant, I appreciate the position you're in. But you just heard Dr. Kale tell you we'll have two people on site in about thirty minutes. That means that *three* lives are now at risk. We don't have time to go up the chain of command. This one's on you, son. We need that info ten minutes ago."

"Shit," Shaffer said. There was another pause. "I'm scrambling our Emergency Response Team. This is what your officers need to look for."

*

12:44

Sandra Goldner couldn't shout anymore. Her voice was gone. Her lips were cracked and dry. She'd lost all feeling in her hands and arms. She thought about the two little finches she owned. They needed food and fresh water. So did she.

To distract herself, Sandra tried thinking about the upcoming bank audit next week and what she needed to do to get ready for it. But no matter how hard she concentrated, her mind always came back to the terrible room. No one had come.

Earlier, exhausted and weak, she'd fallen into a fitful sleep. The short rest was welcome, but even that didn't last as a series of noises pulled her awake. At first it sounded like someone was moving heavy deadbolts. Then it happened again—metal sliding against metal. Finally, a heavy thunk came from the door in front of her. She knew it. They were coming. Maybe she'd get her finches that new bird cage she'd been looking at in Petco.

Seconds after the last thunk had died away, it was replaced by another sound. At first Sandra couldn't identify the source. It seemed to be coming from all around her. Then the enormous door in front of her began to move. Little by little, it slid along a track until it disappeared into a wall.

Sandra squinted against the bright sunlight pouring into the room. As her eyes adjusted, she found herself looking at an odd cement street with high slanted walls on both sides. It reminded her of the bayous in Houston her sister had pointed out when she visited.

What in God's name is this place?

She glanced behind her at the other door. It was still locked in place. More creaks and groans reached her ears as if something was pressing on it. For the first time she noticed water trickling in from beneath the door.

Chapter 20

12:55

Beth's cruiser fishtailed as she shot around a corner and onto the gravel access road that led to Buford Dam. Beth tore up the highway doing more than a hundred miles an hour, horn blasting and weaving in and out of traffic like a madwoman. Every few seconds her eyes flicked to the dashboard clock.

Please, God, let us be in time. She wanted to scream at the clock to tell it to stop. *Just a couple minutes more. That's all we need.*

Pappas eyed the speedometer and gripped the hand rest a little tighter. He'd been speaking with Jack on his cell phone.

"You still there?" Jack asked.

"Yeah," Pappas said. "Danica Patrick here just took a turn at a hundred and eighty. The dam's right in front of us. How do we find her?"

"There'll be a security gate in about a half mile. It's nothing more than a chain link fence, but it's locked. Beyond that, the road continues to the top of the dam and then across to the opposite side."

"I see it," Beth said.

"Holy shit," Pappas said.

"What is it?" Jack asked.

"The gate ain't locked anymore," Pappas told him. "What happens when we reach the top?"

"Look for a staircase where the road meets the dam. You should see it at the extreme right corner. That leads down to the spill control gates and the culvert."

"Gotcha," Pappas said. "We're almost there."

"The spill control is nothing more than a couple of big doors at the bottom."

"Okay," Pappas said. "We're out of the car. I see the staircase. Starting down now. Christ, this dam is huge."

"Listen close, Dan. You've got about two minutes before the water's released. The whole thing's controlled by a computer. Before that happens, a siren'll sound three blasts. There'll be a thirty-second gap before the final siren starts. You'll recognize it by the one-second intervals. If that happens, get your asses out of there."

"Got it."

*

12:58

Beth sprinted ahead of the big detective, who was talking on the phone as he ran. Drawing her gun, she started down the metal stairs. Far below her, the cement spillway stretched stark and white against the landscape. Beyond that in the distance, the Chattahoochee River flowed through the green countryside. Halfway down the stairs, the sound of three siren blasts split the air. Pappas came close behind her, breathing heavily.

"That's the one-minute warning," he said. "After that, some gate opens and water comes pouring out, and it's gonna be coming hard. Jack says we don't enter the gate system or the culvert once the final siren starts."

Beth nodded and started forward once more. At the bottom of the stairs, she came to a second chain link fence with an access door secured by a sizable padlock. Leveling her gun, she fired two shots into it, blowing the lock apart, then kicked the door open. *Jack'll have a fit*, she thought. After another step, she froze.

"Listen!" Beth shouted.

A banging sound was coming from inside the room behind the spillway door.

"Sandra! Sandra Goldner, are you there?" Beth yelled. "This is the police. We're coming to get you out."

More banging.

"Hang on, lady," Pappas yelled. "We'll be—"

The rest of the detective's words were lost as the last siren went off. Above the gaping doorway, a red light began to flash. With a vast roar, water came rushing out of the opening. Pappas grabbed for Beth.

"No!" she screamed.

Pappas tightened his grip as she fought to break free. In seconds, water pouring from Lake Lanier flooded the culvert, moving higher and higher at an incredible speed toward a pipe at the opposite end. The two detectives stood there watching helplessly. Pappas finally released her, sick to his stomach. Twenty-six minutes later, the red light stopped flashing and the siren ceased its relentless blasts. The only sound now came from the wind and water moving beneath them.

Chapter 21

Jack Kale realized he was holding his breath. He slowly let it out. He'd been gripping the phone so tightly, his hand hurt. When the siren finally went off, no one in the room spoke. Burt Wiggins slumped into a chair, shaking his head. Jack felt like all the energy had been drained from his body.

Captain Kostner was the first to recover and took the phone from him. "Dan, you still there?" he asked.

"Yeah," Pappas said. "Still here."

"Any chance Ms. Goldner—"

"None. I saw her when the door opened. Bastard had her chained to a pipe."

"What about Detective Sturgis?"

"She's fine."

"I'll call the ME and get him rolling," Kostner said. "Will you need forensics?"

"There won't be anything left," Pappas informed him. "That water came out of that hole like a freakin' rocket."

Kostner's face lost a good deal of its color. He turned to Jack. "You agree?"

It took an effort for Jack to collect his thoughts and get the words out. "Someone still has to work the scene."

Pappas apparently heard the comment and said, "I'm standing twenty yards away looking at it, and I'm telling you it's a waste of time. Nothing could've survived that. Whatever was in there got blown away by the water."

"I understand," Jack said, "but—"

"Jack, it was strong enough to tear her clothes off."

Jack explained, "There's still the chain or whatever he used to secure her."

"Beth and I can handle that."

"You need to locate the killer's entry and exit points and maybe a vantage point as well. One provides cover; the other searches." His voice sounded tired even to him.

Beth Sturgis came on the line. "What do you mean vantage point?"

"Exactly what I said. First, do *not* assume you're alone. The killer could easily have set a trap. Second, there's been no ransom demand, so there's a good chance he's the type of freak to hang around and watch the show."

"Crap," Beth said, looking around her.

"In fact, I'd say it's more likely than not," Jack said. "Remember, he left clues for us to find at the farm. There was no reason for that."

Beth said, "I'll go down, Dan. You stay up here and make sure we don't have company."

"I don't know," Pappas said uneasily.

"I'll be fine. What Jack's saying makes sense. I need to get the tech kit out of my car. Give me a minute."

Jack added, "You'll need to move quickly. The lieutenant I spoke with told me he scrambled their tactical team. They should be there shortly, and more people—"

"Contaminate the scene," Beth said. "I know."

*

A short while later, Beth found herself standing in front of the control gate, frustrated. The first portal had shut, sealing the chamber off once again. She called Jack to report that. He decided to stay on the phone with her.

"When the engineers arrive, they can reopen it," he said, "but you need to keep them back until you finish processing everything."

"There won't be much to do until then," Beth said.

"Try to locate the killer's point of egress."

"Jack, the spillway walls are angled and at least twenty feet high. He didn't come down or leave from them. In all likelihood, he used the stairs."

"In all likelihood?"

"What else is there?"

"Could he have come from the river using the spillway?"

"Not really."

ONCE SHADOWS FALL

"The water's got to get to the river somehow. Can people walk in the spillway?"

Beth squinted against the glare, using her hand to shield her eyes. "It's possible," she said. "The spillway drops in elevation to funnel the water into a large pipe. Beyond that is the river."

"Understood," Jack said. "Could the killer have gotten in that way?"

"No—wait a minute, yes. I see a ladder. There's another chain link fence at the top. Pretty crummy security, if you ask me."

"What about the pipe itself?" Jack asked. "Could he and the woman have walked through it to gain access?"

"Possibly," Beth said. "It's about ten feet high. How far does it go?"

"According to Lieutenant Shaffer, a little over seventeen hundred feet. After that, it intersects the Chattahoochee. It might be worth checking out."

"Great, another tunnel," Beth muttered. "It would be incredibly tough for the killer to get in that way. He'd have to carry the victim."

"Not really. Remember I mentioned roofies at the farm? He could have walked her in."

"Good point," Beth conceded.

"Wait for backup," Jack said. "You shouldn't go in there alone."

"I'm a big girl, Jack. Pappas'll be with me. At least this time he won't have to bend down."

*

For the second time in as many days, Beth and Pappas found themselves walking down a tunnel. Unlike the first, this one had light at both ends. It was hot, humid, and damp smelling. A third of the way through, they came upon a woman's shoe and a portion of what appeared to be an orange cocktail dress.

Pappas asked, "Do we know what Sandra was wearing when she left home?"

"An orange print dress."

She took a photograph and then bagged both items. Their trip to the opposite end yielded no clues. The pipe itself was surrounded by another chain link enclosure to keep people out, along with an access door where it emerged.

"Looks like you were right," Beth told Jack. "The killer came this way. The lock's been cut."

"Bring it with you," Jack said.

"I know that," Beth said, annoyed.

"Footprints over here," Pappas said. "A man and woman, by the look of 'em. Better tell Ben to come out and make some casts."

Beth said, "I can see a single-track path going up the hill. I'll bet that's where he parked his car."

"Let's go find out," Pappas said.

As they made their way along the path, Beth was suddenly seized by the feeling they were being watched. Pappas must have felt it, too, because he kept scanning the woods on each side of them. The trees and underbrush were just beginning to grow in, which made matters worse. Here and there a few wild dogwoods were blooming. As the slope steepened, the forest around them grew denser. In minutes they found themselves breathing heavily.

Eventually, the path let them out at the top of a hill with a road running perpendicular to it. A short distance away was a gravel clearing. Below, the Chattahoochee River, now several inches higher, flowed placidly on through the countryside. In the distance through an opening in the trees was an unrestricted view of the dam, the spillway, and the control gate they'd just come from. Beth knew in an instant Jack had guessed right.

How does he do that?

Without speaking, Pappas tapped her on the shoulder and pointed at the ground. Just off the road in the red clay where the gravel ended was a partial tire tread mark and more footprints.

Beth laid out a grid in her mind and began to walk it while Pappas checked the area out.

"Dan, take a look at this," she said, pointing to a black spot on the ground.

"Some fluid drip. Oil, maybe," Pappas said, dropping down and rubbing the substance between his thumb and forefinger.

Chapter 22

Jack disconnected and was sitting in the crime lab with Captain Kostner and Burt Wiggins. Ben Furman and his assistant had left to meet Beth and Pappas.

"Thanks for the offer, Burt. I think your people can handle it from here," Jack said.

"Just not as quickly or efficiently as they could with you on board," Kostner said.

"It's just that I'm pretty tied up at the moment with my classes and this research paper I'm writing."

"Demanding job," Kostner said.

Jack's eyes locked on the captain, who returned the look calmly. He then turned to Burt Wiggins and said, "I'm not sure I'd be a good fit. I left the FBI under—"

"We know all about the IA investigation," said Kostner. "Anyone might have lost it under the circumstances. If it were me, I'm not sure I would have let Pell live. You did, and that says something about you. It's ancient history. Do you really think the killer is going to stop now?"

A long pause ensued before Jack answered. "No . . . he's just getting started."

He glanced away and looked at the equipment scattered around the room. He didn't want to be there. So why, as Wiggins asked, was he? Oddly, he felt composed. Breathing normal. No tightness in his chest. Mouth's not dry. No desire to escape. So far, so good.

"So you just gonna walk away?" Kostner asked.

"It's not that simple, Art," Jack said. "I've been out of the profession for a long time."

"Sure," Kostner said. "It took you a whole five minutes to figure out the clues that prick left. Give it a while; your timing'll come back."

I'll get you for that, Art. Nice move.

Jack laughed to himself and was about to offer up a different argument when his eye fell once again on the department's poster.

"Protect and Serve."

He pushed the sleeves of his sport coat back, picked up Beth's file, and sat down to read it.

*

It took the Emergency Response Team more than forty minutes to arrive on site via helicopter. They were led by a Sergeant Kowalski, who was big enough to be a pro wrestler. His head was shaven and his biceps filled his black shirt sleeves to the point of straining. The body armor he was wearing only made his chest seem larger.

Pappas explained the situation while the remaining six men in Kowalski's squad spread out to make sure the dam was secure. The process took another half hour. When it was done, a corporal came back and reported.

"Everything's good except for the front gate and the padlock down below. Someone blew 'em to hell."

"I'm afraid that was me," Beth said.

"Yes, ma'am. We sorta figured that. I called the base and told 'em to get a repair unit out here."

Beth asked the sergeant, "Can you have one of your men open the outer door? I need to process the scene."

Kowalski turned to the corporal and jerked his head toward a small concrete bunker at the end of the road where the computer control was located.

"Nasty business," Kowalski said. "Both of you going in?"

"No choice," Beth said.

"Yeah," Kowalski said. "Give us a few minutes. You got some ear protection?"

"Why?"

"Once the door's open, the siren goes off. It's gonna be loud in that chamber."

"We didn't bring anything," Beth said.

"Let me see what I can do." Kowalski keyed the hand mic on his shoulder. "Brentano, go back to the chopper and bring me two com sets."

*

86

Several minutes later, the warning siren began to blare, once again shattering the relative tranquility around them as the massive door slid open. It left a gaping maw that reminded Beth of a painting she'd once seen depicting the mouth of hell. Thanks to Sergeant Kowalski and the Corps of Engineers, she and Pappas were now wearing two headsets and were able to speak with each other. The units were effective at shutting out most but not all the noise.

As they entered the chamber, she saw there were still several inches of water present in the room. Muttering to herself about ruining a good pair of shoes, Beth nodded to Pappas and stepped in. The shock of cold hit her immediately, but she gritted her teeth and kept going.

Why didn't I stay in anthropology?

Pappas's voice came over the headset.

"You still want in first?"

"Yeah," Beth said. "I can see her hanging from the pipe. I'll take the vic, then walk the grid. You check the entrance to see if anything might have hung up."

"Fat chance," Pappas said.

"I know."

With the siren continuing its mournful blasts, Beth looked around and took several photographs of the victim. She wanted to cover Sandra, but there was nothing to do it with. Inside, the noise was magnified tremendously, bouncing off the walls, making even thinking difficult.

Sandra Goldner hung by her arms from a pair of old-style handcuffs.

She was a tall woman with limp blonde hair. The worst part were her eyes. Beth's mind began to play tricks thinking that they were following her. She shook off the feeling and continued a methodical inspection. Pappas was right. The rising water had swept away anything useful. All she wanted to do was finish her search and get the hell out of there before she threw up. Taking a deep breath, she steeled herself and approached Sandra Goldner, gently shutting the woman's eyes. At nearly the same time, the siren ceased its dirge, startling both her and Pappas.

Kowalski's voice came over her headset. "Hope that helps. One of my guys figured out how to kill the noise."

"It does," Beth said. "Thanks."

"Your ME and crime tech just showed up. Want me to send 'em down?"

"Give us five minutes," Beth said. "I'm about to examine the body."

"Jeez," Kowalski said. "Will do."

Now that the noise was gone, she and Pappas pulled off their com units and draped them around their necks. Beth then carefully checked under the victim's fingernails and then moved on to her hair, combing it for any trace evidence that might have survived the water.

Pappas commented on the scorch marks on Sandra Goldner's shoulder. "The fucker Tasered her."

Beth nodded. She took a photograph and continued examining the body. Without warning, a deep groan coming from under the rear door froze both detectives. Beth and Pappas looked at each other.

"I know," he said. "Place gives me the creeps, too. You finished?"

"Pretty much."

"Let's get outta here."

"What about the cuffs?" Beth said. "I don't want to leave her like this."

"Neither do I, but my key won't work and neither will yours. The cuffs are too old. We'll have to cut 'em."

"Wonderful," Beth said.

Chapter 23

The killer closed the book he was reading, shut his eyes, and leaned back in his chair. The Mayans had it right. At least this particular sect of their society did. They were called the Eaters of Souls. When a vanquished enemy fell into their hands, the body was dismembered and the pieces passed around to be eaten. The heart was saved for the shaman and the chief. Not really a novel concept. Religions around the world practiced simulated rituals like it every week. Of course, he would never dream of eating anyone. That would be barbaric. Still, the name intrigued him.

The real key was to be in complete control of another human being. To decree whether they would live or die and how. That, he decided, was a rough equivalent of owning their soul.

"Eater of Souls," he whispered, savoring the phrase, as he ran his fingers over the book. *"Eater of Souls."*

Still too long. He needed a better name. Something catchy.

The killer smiled.

Soul Eater. Now that had a nice ring to it.

The killer picked up a little bottle of medicine from the end table next to him and tilted the clear liquid first one way and then the other. Alongside it lay two hypodermic needles and his favorite toy. The Taser was quick, quiet, and efficient. Also on the table were two scalpels. He would have preferred an obsidian flake knife. It was far sharper than any of the new instruments, but sad to say, they were not readily available and their edge began to degrade in the air after twenty minutes or so. It would be nice to try it one day. Traditions were important.

*

"We were so close," Beth said. "So close. I could see her."

"Don't beat yourself up," Pappas said. "There was nothing we could have done."

Beth shook her head and took a sip of the rum and Coke in front of her.

Han Lo's wasn't crowded at that hour. Sooner or later the little Chinese restaurant on Buford Highway would fill up with cops. It was Jack's first visit and he liked it, though no one would ever accuse the owner of putting in too much atmosphere. According to Pappas, the décor hadn't changed in thirty years and was basically straight out of the seventies. At most there were twenty tables. No tablecloths. Paper napkins. The menu was written on a chalkboard that sat on a chair near the cash register and was basically whatever Mrs. Lo decided to cook that day. A pupu platter consisting of egg rolls, satay chicken strips coated with peanut sauce, and some tempura shrimp and vegetables occupied the middle of their table.

On returning to the office earlier, Captain Kostner informed them Jack would be joining the investigation and that Pappas had been reassigned as Beth's partner until Leonard Cass was off medical leave. They both received the news well. At least Pappas did. As a detective lieutenant, Jack now technically outranked each of them, which may have accounted for Beth's cool attitude toward him at the moment. She was pleasant enough, though somewhat distant. It was obvious she wasn't happy with the situation. Jack wasn't sure why. Hadn't she asked him to help? Pappas didn't seem to care one way or the other.

Beth met his eyes across the table and responded with a perfunctory smile. There were few things, he thought, colder than the icy smile of a beautiful woman.

Beth said, "I'm going out to Mayfield tomorrow to interview Howard Pell, if that's all right with you."

"You don't need my permission," Jack said. "It's still your case."

"Not according to Captain Kostner."

Time to fix this, Jack decided.

"Beth, it'll be your case and your collar," he assured her. "I'm just here to help."

"Probably work to your benefit," Pappas added.

"How's that?" Beth asked. "One minute I'm in charge of an investigation, my first as a lead since I joined the department, the next I'm taking orders from our new consultant."

Pappas took a long breath and let it out. "You've got a lot to learn, rookie."

"Is that so?"

"Yeah, that's so," Pappas said. "Kostner isn't operating alone. There's a reason Burt Wiggins showed up with him."

"I don't get it," Beth said.

"Think it through. Kale comes out of retirement to help nail this asshole. If he succeeds, great. He's still a consultant and the department takes the credit for their brilliant move. If we fall flat on our faces, he gets it in the neck."

Beth looked at Jack, who sat there silently.

Pappas continued, "That's one reason Chief Ritson wants him to be our front man with the press. It's a sure bet the story'll hit the papers sooner or later."

"I know, but—"

"Ritson's protecting the department," Jack said. "He knows it. I know it. And he knows that I know it."

"But you took the job anyway," Beth said.

"The killer's just warming up. If we don't stop him, more people will die."

Beth stared at him for a long moment and then at Pappas who raised his eyebrows.

"Shit," she said. "You must think I'm a bitch."

"The thought crossed my mind," Jack said and took a sip of his club soda.

Beth responded by slowly raising her middle finger then excused herself to go to the ladies' room.

"Well, that went well," Jack said.

"She wants to prove herself," Pappas said.

Jack nodded. Both men sipped their drinks quietly for a time and then turned to watch a waitress in a short, black skirt lean across a table to collect some glasses.

Jack said, "Leering is frowned upon in a man of your position."

"Yeah? So what were you doing?"

"Checking for concealed weapons."

Pappas chuckled and clinked his bottle against Jack's glass. "You gonna be able to manage the investigation with your teaching?"

"I took a leave of absence," Jack said. "Our dean thinks it will bring credit to the university."

"Let's hope." Pappas paused for a beat, then asked, "Mind if I ask you a question?"

"Go ahead."

91

"I'm pretty sure you're not in this for the money. And I'm pretty sure it wasn't the glamour of the job that brought you back."

"Hardly," Jack said.

"So, just between us, why are you here?"

Jack took a small sip of his soda and then set the glass carefully down on his coaster and centered it.

"The easy answer is I don't like not knowing."

"Not knowing what?" Pappas said.

"Who the killer is. Why he's killing people. Why he's leaving clues. Why he decided to imitate Howard Pell. The more I think about it, the longer the list gets."

Pappas digested this for a moment.

"All right," he said, "that makes sense. How 'bout the hard answer?"

Jack ran the tip of his forefinger around the rim of his glass and didn't reply immediately. The pause seemed to stretch before he continued.

"When you were in uniform, you ever work an accident?"

"A few."

"What's the first thing you did if there was a crowd?"

"Told everyone to keep back. Sometimes I'd have one of them run for a blanket. Maybe call for a doctor if they could get there before the EMTs."

"In other words, you followed your training and took control of the situation."

"Sure."

"You directed people to do certain things, because if you didn't, they would just stand around believing someone else was taking care of the problems."

"I guess so."

"That's human nature. Psychologists have a fancy name for it, *diffusion of responsibility*, but it comes down to this: people always assume the other guy is doing what needs to be done. That's rarely the case."

"No argument from me," Pappas said.

"And if someone doesn't take responsibility, things start to unravel," Jack said.

"Like how?"

"How we choose to live," Jack said. "Society has a structure—some of it good, some of it bad. The bottom line is what you see when you look in the mirror each morning—one of the crowd, or someone who's there to stop a predator. When people ignore who they are, they're just fooling themselves. Most of the time it doesn't work out. You do what you're put here to do."

Pappas nodded and didn't interrupt.

"A doctor pal of mine asked why I didn't tell Beth no when she shanghaied me up to the farm. I didn't answer him at the time, but I gave it some thought and concluded that's what I was doing—trying to ignore who I am."

"Mirror's a tough critic," Pappas said.

"Very," Jack replied.

"Glad you're in," Pappas said, holding out his hand.

"Thank you," Jack said as they shook.

The detective's next question wasn't entirely unexpected. Jack was tempted to tell him he said only one question when they began.

"Are there any . . . ah, issues I should know about?"

"Not really," Jack said.

"There was some stuff in your file about separating from the feds for medical reasons."

When he got no response, Pappas held his hands up in a peace gesture and said, "I'm not tryin' to get in your business. It's just I don't need you droppin' dead of a heart attack or something in the middle of the case."

"You can rest easy. It's nothing to worry about. You have my word." He then shifted the topic and asked, "What's the story with Detective Sturgis?"

"Everybody in the department had the same question. You ever hear of William Camden?"

"The author?"

"She was married to him. Normally, she doesn't say much about herself."

"Understandable. She seems like a private person."

"She worked for some fancy travel magazine up in New York as an editor or something. I don't know. Her dad's a cop up in Charlotte and a real decent guy. I've met him a couple of times. So no big deal for a kid to follow in her father's footsteps, right?"

"Sure."

Pappas took a sip of his drink.

Jack said, "That's the official version, right?"

Pappas glanced around before he continued. "I hear she had a baby sister who hanged herself. Apparently, the kid was bullied in school pretty bad. Beth was the one who found her. She was like fourteen at the time. I figure that had something to do with it."

An image of what that must have been like flashed into Jack's mind. He shook his head to clear it.

"She told you that?"

"She told Lenny Cass. That's her regular partner. Poor schmuck's laid up recovering from a hernia operation. Sometimes you tell your partner stuff you don't tell anyone else. Keep it quiet, okay?"

Jack told him he would.

"Bottom line is she's a little rigid in her views but she comes down on the right side of things," Pappas said.

"How do you know it's the right side?" Jack asked.

"That's the side I'm on."

Jack nodded. "So she became a cop."

"Did real good at the academy, I'm told. Smart as a whip."

"I can see that. We'll need all the help we can get. She mentioned she's new to Robbery-Homicide."

"Also true," Pappas said. "You're on probation for six months after you transfer. Before landing here, she was making cases against polluters and toxic dumping in Environmental Enforcement."

Jack screwed up his face.

"Right," Pappas said. "That's why she's so hot to prove herself."

"And right out of the box, she gets stuck with me as the APD's poster boy. I can see why it doesn't sit well."

Pappas lifted his beer bottle in a toast.

"Crap," Jack said. "I'll make sure she gets credit for everything."

"Proving you belong to the bosses is one thing. Proving you belong to yourself is something else."

"For a big dumb jock, you're pretty insightful."

"I have my moments."

They broke off their conversation as Beth returned. Several men at the bar tracked her progress.

"You boys have a nice talk?" she said.

"Yeah," Pappas said. "We bonded."

Puzzled, Beth frowned and looked at Jack.

"There's something I'd like to ask you," he said.

"Okay."

"What were you feeling when you were at the scene?"

"Feeling?"

"Right. What was going through your mind?"

Beth glanced at Pappas to make sure she wasn't the subject of a joke. The detective raised his shoulders. Around them, the murmur of conversations and restaurant sounds blended into a white noise.

A long moment passed before she said, "I remember feeling sad."

"Why sad?"

"That piece of dress we found in the pipe. It was a cocktail dress. I thought it was so sad that she went out hoping to have a nice time and it ended like this."

"And what else?"

Beth frowned. "There's nothing to base this on other than your comment that we might not be alone, but that just brought it together for me. As soon as you said it, I definitely had the feeling we were being watched."

The seconds seemed to stretch as Jack held her eyes.

"I need you to keep right on thinking that way every minute until this case is over. We're dealing with an incredibly dangerous individual. Do not let your guard down even for an instant."

Beth and Pappas looked at each other.

"Are you trying to scare me?" Beth asked.

"Absolutely." There wasn't the slightest trace of humor in his face when he said it.

Chapter 24

On Monday morning, three uniform officers and two men dressed in suits were in the conference room when Jack arrived. They were talking among themselves. Rather than interrupt, he moved to the end of the room where a large urn of coffee and a plate of pastries had been set up. He poured himself a cup and picked out a chocolate-glazed donut and dropped a dollar into a shoebox someone had set up for honor payments. His self-imposed ration was two cups in the morning, which he had at his house. Of course, they were small cups, so he decided to risk a third.

Outside the window, a light rain had begun falling. On the wet pavement below, a scattering of brightly colored umbrellas glided across the sidewalk. Waltz of the gumdrops.

Beth was in the middle of writing notes about the murders on a whiteboard. Jack checked his watch. It was three minutes to eight. The voice mail he received from her the night before indicated they would meet at eight o'clock.

Eager to prove herself, he thought.

Dan Pappas appeared alongside him and picked out a donut covered in sprinkles.

"Sprinkles?"

"The best," Pappas said, keeping his voice down so as not to interrupt Beth.

"You have no taste in donuts," Jack said.

"I must, I'm a cop."

"Who are the suits?" Jack asked.

"Frick and Frack."

"Excuse me?"

"That's just what we call them. The tall one's Ed Mundas. His partner's Dwayne Stafford."

"I take it they're joining us."

Pappas nodded. "They're good men. Beth asked the lieutenant for more help. With three murders, we need to put some people on the street."

"Agreed," Jack said as four more detectives entered the room. Two he recalled meeting during the Scarecrow case. The other two weren't familiar to him. He turned to Pappas. "My message last night said the autopsies have been moved up."

"She also called the deputy chief at home on Saturday night and asked him to intercede with the ME. He phoned Dr. Andrews himself and voila: more troops, instant autopsies."

"Anything special so far?" Jack asked.

"Two of the three were Tasered," Pappas said, "plus all of 'em had Seconal in their blood, so you were right about that. Two were missing the ring finger on the left hand. The vics at the farm both died of asphyxiation; the lady at Lake Lanier, drowning."

Jack was quiet for a moment, then said, "Lady at the lake," half to himself.

When Beth finished, she introduced Jack to the others. Stafford and Mundas were both tall, slender, and spoke with noticeable southern accents. It was hard to tell them apart. Jack tried to associate their names with their faces but, after a moment, wasn't sure which was which.

"What I'd like," he said, "is for you two to start interviewing the victims' neighbors. It's possible the killer simply happened on them by chance, but it would be nice to know if any of them were connected, beyond just being friends or knowing Jerome Haffner."

Frick, or maybe it was Frack, took notes while the other listened.

"Yes, sir. Will do. Ms. Sturgis already told us that. We'll also be checking to see if the neighbors noticed any strange folk hangin' around."

"Good."

"Vehicles, too," his partner added.

Jack turned to Beth and asked, "You got a tire print?"

"It's a Goodyear 275-16, with noticeable wear on the inside. They're commonly found on vans. About a grillion were sold last year."

"A grillion?" Jack said.

"It's a technical term," Beth said. "You've been out of the business for a while."

Jack smiled. "What about the fluid drip?"

"The vehicle probably belongs to our killer," Beth said. "The drip is transmission fluid. If we find the vehicle, we can get a match and place it at the scene."

She'd been busy and was looking very pleased with herself. *As well she should*, Jack thought.

"And the footprints on the hill?" he asked.

"I'm assuming one was from Sarah Goldner. The sheriff's checking the size against her other shoes with the family. The man's shoe is a size twelve and different from what we saw at the farm. The sole is made of something called Vibram. It's manufactured in China for Rockmart Footwear. There was nothing distinctive about the wear pattern. This one could be the real deal instead of a plant."

Pappas asked, "Where's it sold?"

"Everywhere," Beth said. "There are about thirty thousand retail outlets across the U.S. You can also buy them online."

Pappas informed him, "We do have one piece of good news, Jack."

"Oh?"

"Sheriff Blaylock had his deputies canvas the neighbors. Two of them down the road from the Donneley farm noticed a white panel van driving around before the killings. Seems everybody knows everybody up there."

"Excellent," Jack said. "Let's see if there are any reports of stolen vehicles matching that description. The killer probably wouldn't risk using his own transportation."

"Will do," Pappas said.

"We should also see if any rental agencies have one out. If that's the case, the killer might have acquired it near his own home, which would give us an area to concentrate on. Wouldn't you agree, Beth?"

"Oh . . . uh, sure. I'll get on it."

As soon as the words were out, Jack realized he'd made a mistake. Despite running through what he viewed as the routine and sensible steps they should take, he was conscious of an elephant in the room— the unspoken question about who was in charge. The meeting's focus was beginning to shift to him. Despite their discussion the previous night, Beth's expression spoke volumes. She was putting up a good front but appeared awkward and uneasy. His comments were inadvertently undercutting her authority.

He needed to correct the problem.

"As most of you know, Chief Ritson asked me to consult with the department. Obviously, we have a serious situation on our hands.

Detective Sturgis is still the lead on this case, so if there are any command decisions to be made, check with her. I'll be around to offer assistance where needed."

Several of the uniforms nodded. As long as there was a clear chain of command, with one of their own running the show, they were happy. The bottom line was, no one liked being told how to do their job, particularly by a former fed like him. Word would filter through the department quickly.

Jack took a sip of coffee and made a face. He'd forgotten to add sweetener. He took stock of the room they were in and couldn't recall if he'd ever been there before. It was about thirty by fifteen and had a long conference table with eight blue upholstered chairs and a window that looked out over the parking lot. From the window, through a thin line of trees, was I-285 or the "Perimeter," as Atlantans called it. Cars moved in a steady stream at speeds that indicated the posted speed limit was more a suggestion than the law. Overhead were a series of fluorescent lights he associated with unpleasant places. Despite his being used to speaking with groups, he realized he was nervous. It had been a long time since he was around other cops. A brief sense of loss for his office at school and the comfort of his daily routine swept over him. There wasn't much help for it now.

Beth Sturgis resumed her talk with the uniforms. At one point, she looked up at him and then continued her conversation. He read nothing in her expression. What was she thinking? Had his speech worked? Was she still resentful? Well, he'd done his best. Maybe she was unsure what to do next. He often was. In the end, it came down to instinct. An investigation is like building a house of cards. You construct it level by level and hope it doesn't come crashing down. This one had gotten off to a miserable start.

*

The meeting eventually broke up and people drifted back to their desks or to whatever they had been working on. Jack spent some time on the computer searching the FBI's database for similar crimes and patterns and came up empty. He wasn't surprised. It was nearly eleven o'clock before he closed the screen and went to the break room for a second cup of coffee.

When Jack entered the room, the conversations abruptly died away. With the exception of Beth Sturgis, all the detectives who had been at the meeting earlier were there. Some averted their eyes. Others occupied themselves by fixing coffee or looking at the interesting things in the parking lot. He didn't need to be a psychologist to know they had been talking about him.

"Am I interrupting anything?"

"Nah," Pappas said, "we were just jawing about the case. You remember Dave Childers and Jimmy Spruell, don't you? They were part of the original Scarecrow task force way back when."

"Of course," Jack said, shaking hands with both men. "Glad to be working with you again."

Childers's handshake seemed genuine enough, but Spruell's was perfunctory. Moreover, he seemed to find Jack's comment about working together again funny. Confused, Jack looked at him for an explanation.

"Nothing personal, Professor, but we haven't had great luck working with the feds in the past."

"I'm not a fed anymore. I'm part of the department now."

"Right, right, our special consultant. I heard Beth Sturgis earlier."

"Jimmy," Dave Childers said.

"No offense meant, man. I just remember our consultant doing a lot of running around on his own the last time. Generally, we found out what was going on after the fact."

"I'll try to share more," Jack said. "Things were pretty crazy back then."

"Of course they were. Unfortunately, that TV movie made us look like a bunch of idiots. You know, poor dumb Keystone Cops wouldn't recognize a clue if they tripped over it."

Jack looked down at his feet for a moment. "I didn't have much to do with that movie, and I apologize if it came out that way. I promise it wasn't due to anything I said."

"Artistic license, right?"

"Knock it off, Jimmy," Pappas said.

"I'm only saying what everyone thinks."

Jack held Spruell's eye for a moment and nodded slowly, then said, "I think I'll get my coffee another time. Good seeing you both again."

He was partway to the door when Spruell asked, "Hey, whatever happened to that partner of yours? I heard she got cut up pretty bad."

As soon as the words were out, the atmosphere in the room changed. Everyone felt it. Jack stopped and turned around, the smile fading from his face.

"She died, Detective," he said and started walking toward Spruell.

Pappas immediately stepped between them. "I ain't gonna tell you again, Jimmy. That's enough."

*

When Jack was gone, Spruell shook his head and muttered, "Fuckin' showboater."

"You're a goddamn idiot, Spruell. You know that?" Pappas said and followed Jack out.

With the smirk still on his face, Spruell turned to his partner for support. The older detective shook his head.

"What?" Spruell asked.

"Jack Kale's no showboater, Jimmy."

"Is that right?"

"Yeah, it's right. Pappas probably just saved you a trip to the hospital. Kale would have taken your head off."

Chapter 25

The Soul Eater sat in a cafe reading the *Atlanta Journal* over his morning coffee. Because the deaths had occurred out of town, the story had been relegated to page three. That was disappointing. In time, he'd merit page one. It was simply a matter of being patient. And if there was one thing he prided himself on, it was his patience.

His cup was nearly empty when the waitress glided over to refresh it. Doubtful she recognized him. That was one of his strengths. Ordinary was good. The ability to blend in, to disappear into the public flotsam, was priceless. Most of his victims never knew he was there until it was too late.

He had done his homework. The woman he'd been observing, Donna Christine Camp, was forty-three, divorced, and the mother of two children presently living with their father in Tampa, Florida. Very sad. Her apartment was three blocks away from the cafe, which allowed her to walk to work. That fit nicely into his plans. She looked five years older than her Facebook photo and wore too much makeup. As a rule, he didn't care for excess makeup on women. Tattoos were worse. Why do women do that?

He watched Ms. Camp out of the corner of his eye as she moved to another table, wondering how she would look wrapped in white linen bandages. She gave a customer a perfunctory smile. Clearly, she didn't like her job. After further reflection, he decided the makeup made her look cheap. Makeup needed to be applied carefully, exotically.

He'd been up all night studying the diary. Brilliant. It was as if Albert was speaking directly to him from the grave. His own museum. Why hadn't it occurred to him before? He couldn't wait until he and Ms. Camp got together.

*

Thanks to Lieutenant Fancher, who had apparently spoken to the deputy chief, the conference room they'd been using was converted into a command center and temporary office for Jack. All things considered, he'd have been happier working out of his home. Ironically, his own words came back to haunt him. You can't run an investigation from the sidelines.

Beth Sturgis stopped in the doorway and watched as Jack turned a complete circle in his desk chair. She was carrying a copy of the murder book.

"What are you doing?" she asked.

"Two times," he said, making one final rotation. "That's the best I can manage. My chair at school can do three."

Beth started to respond but changed her mind. She put the book on his desk and left, shaking her head. Jack shrugged and picked up the loose-leaf notebook and began to study it. That he could do so dispassionately was slightly surprising. All his instincts told him it was only a matter of time before the killer struck again. There had been no ransom demands, so this one got his kicks from the death itself and possibly from watching the cops fumble around for clues. If a generalization could be made about serial killers, they tended to operate on their own timetable. Howard Pell did, and if the copycat was following him, there was a good chance he might use a similar pattern.

He went through the book slowly trying to find a unique signature in the new killer's method but saw nothing that stood out. Like Pell, the only common threads were the crimes had been committed underground and two of the victims had a missing finger.

What confused him were the clues being left behind. Pell had done so with the intent of misleading the police. But he'd also left other clues inadvertently, which proved to be his undoing. So they were dealing with a mimic, but Jack had a feeling this killer was different. Try as he might, he couldn't shake the feeling that something else was at work beneath the surface. Unfortunately, at this stage, he had no idea what that could be. Whatever perverse logic was operating inside the killer's head, he needed to understand it quickly.

Beth returned with photos of the victims and put them up on the whiteboard. On one side she started a list of what they knew about the killer, which was precious little. She stood there concentrating on it, absently chewing on the end of a pencil. There was another stuck in her hair.

Probably forgot she put it there, Jack thought.

Since his speech earlier, much of the tension building between them had eased. He continued to watch her, forgetting that women have a kind of built-in radar about such things. Beth chose that moment to turn around and caught him staring.

"Sorry," he said. "I was just . . . ah, studying—"

"My legs?"

"Well, close enough," he said.

Her response was a raised eyebrow. Thankfully, she didn't take offense or get angry. In fact, she smiled, and this time there was no frost in it.

"I appreciate what you did earlier," she said.

Jack nodded. "I meant it."

"I know you did."

"You were doing fine without my help."

"I appreciate that," Beth said. "Were you like that with your partner?"

"Some," Jack answered, stiffening slightly. "Let's change the subject."

"Okay," Beth said. "Didn't mean to intrude. I heard you had some words earlier with Jimmy Spruell."

"It was nothing."

"Do I need to talk to him?"

"Not at all," Jack said. "I'm a big boy and I can fight my own battles. It's over."

That seemed to satisfy her. Beth then informed him, "I'm going to Mayfield later to interview Howard Pell. Would you like to tag along?"

"You can handle it. I'd be a distraction."

There was a pause before she asked, "To Pell or me?"

This time it was Jack's turn to be surprised. Was there was another meaning behind her words?

When he didn't respond, Beth said, "I'll let you know how it turns out," and stood up.

"One word of advice," Jack said. "Don't discuss your personal life with him no matter how hard Pell pushes."

*

There was something different about the parking lot. Donna Camp couldn't put her finger on it. Her apartment was only a few blocks away. Though the neighborhood wasn't the greatest, she felt safe enough. In her purse was a compact canister of pepper spray attached to a keychain she'd bought for self-defense. She gave it a few more seconds of thought then pushed it away. There were more pressing things on her mind.

After a quick stop to change, it was off to Georgia State for her evening class and hopefully a better life. Things were finally beginning to look up. It was spring and she loved this time of year. Every day it would stay light a little longer. Soon the dogwoods and azaleas would be out, along with the flowering crab trees she thought were so beautiful. She missed her garden and the home she'd been forced to sell after the divorce. For the time being, she took pleasure in the world coming back to life again. So would she. With some hard work she'd get everything back and send for her kids. Yes, things were definitely looking better. It was just a matter of time.

Only a few cars remained in the parking lot. At the far end, sitting by itself near the exit, was a white van. She'd seen it several times before and decided it belonged to a customer, though she didn't know which one.

She noted the lot's security light was out and made a mental note to mention it to the manager, who'd probably tell her it wasn't his job. Donna scanned the immediate area and decided she was just being silly. Nevertheless, she opened her purse and made sure the pepper spray was within easy reach.

Across the street, three teenage boys bopped along listening to whatever was playing on their iPods, pants hanging below their butts and baseball caps on sideways—not exactly slaves to fashion.

Thank God her boys hadn't gone through that phase.

Near a hole in the fence, a cat silently watched as she passed. The smell of ethnic cooking drifted through an open window in a nearby building and made its way to the asphalt below. What little color the street possessed came from the graffiti on the walls. Working a double shift at the cafe was hard, but there were bills to pay and promises to keep.

"And miles to go before I sleep," she whispered to herself.

The bearded man who stepped out from in front of the van startled her. He was tall, well-dressed, and seemed as surprised to see her as she was to see him.

"Excuse me," he said, swallowing. "I hope I didn't frighten you."

"I think we frightened each other," Donna said.

"My apologies. Can you tell me if this is Butler Street? I've gotten a little turned around."

"Butler is two blocks west," Donna said, pointing back toward the cafe.

As soon as she turned, a sudden movement caught the corner of her eye. Her hand immediately went to the pepper spray in her purse. Too late. A blinding pain shot through her body. She tried to scream, but nothing came out.

The tall man caught her as she fell and pulled her back to the van. She was dimly aware her hands and feet were being bound. As hard as she tried to struggle, it was no use. She was paralyzed. Panic set in. *My God, no. This can't be happening.*

A piece of tape was placed over her mouth, followed by a stinging sensation in her thigh. Consciousness slipped further and further away. The last thing she remembered was looking up at the dark security light and the graffiti.

Chapter 26

A uniformed patrolman's appearance in the doorway interrupted the balance of Jack and Beth's conversation. He had just been telling her he wasn't convinced the killer was a complete Pell imitator. The officer was holding an old-fashioned satchel similar to what carpetbaggers used to carry after the Civil War. Jack noticed the blue latex glove on his hand immediately.

The officer said, "Lieutenant, this was found at the Atlanta Historical Society. I thought I'd better bring it to you."

It took Jack a moment to process that the man was speaking to him. The newly acquired and largely honorary rank he'd been given hadn't sunk in yet.

"Why me?"

"It has your name on it, sir."

Jack and Beth exchanged puzzled glances. He pushed away from his desk, donned a pair of latex gloves himself, and took the bag from the cop.

"Anything ticking inside?" Jack asked.

The cop smiled. "No, sir. The bomb squad was called out first. Sergeant Mahan gave it the once-over and said it's clean."

"That's a relief. You say it was just sitting out in the open?"

"More or less. It was in a flower bed near the entrance. I checked with the staff to see if anyone saw who put it there."

"I take it no one did."

"No, sir. Probably placed there last night after the museum closed according to the gift shop lady. She was one of the last to leave and was sure she'd have noticed it."

Jack read the nametag on the cop's chest: "C. Harrison."

"Good work, Harrison. What's the *C* stand for?"

"Corey."

"Have a seat, Corey. Maybe we can figure out why someone's leaving me presents."

Inside the satchel was a woman's shoe, a blouse, a bolt cutter, and a bag of dirt.

Jack asked, "Is this everything?"

"Far as I know," Harrison said. "The soil was my idea—at least partially."

"Oh?"

"I noticed a footprint in the flower bed right near where the satchel was sitting. The dirt was a different color, so I figured maybe it belonged to whoever put it there. I scooped some out and bagged it, then taped off the area in case you wanted to see it for yourself."

"Excellent," Jack said. "What did you mean, it was partially your idea?"

"I attended one of your lectures a few years ago. I guess some of it stuck."

Grabbing a metal tray off a workbench that had been brought in for him, Jack emptied the contents out, then put on a pair of magnifying goggles and used a slender probe to separate some of the particles mixed in with the sample.

"You're right," he said. "The color and content are clearly different. If I had to guess, I'd say this red stuff is brick dust of some sort. Maybe Ben Furman can pin it down."

"What do bolt cutters have to do with brick dust?" Harrison asked.

"Hard to say at this point," Jack said. He considered the question further, then turned to Beth. "Would you hand me that lock you brought back from the lake? I have an idea."

She did and then removed the woman's blouse from the satchel and began examining it while Jack continued what he was doing. After thirty seconds or so, he announced, "It matches."

"What does?" Harrison asked.

"See here," Jack said, taking off his goggles and handing them to the patrolman. He then pointed to a small nick in the blade.

"Okay," Harrison said.

"Now look here," Jack said, pushing the lock toward him.

"Got it," Harrison said. "This bolt cutter snapped the lock. But why leave it for you?"

"Because he's sending a message that he has another woman," Jack said.

"Sick bastard," Harrison said. "What are you—?"

"There are two messages," Beth said, without looking up from the blouse.

Both men turned to her. She continued, "The first is obvious. He definitely wants us to know he's snatched someone else. The second is more subtle—he's not talking to us, Jack. He's talking to you."

Jack frowned but chose not to reply.

"The bag has your name on it. If you don't find this new woman in time, he's saying it'll be your fault if she dies. Sick, I know, but I'd bet anything I'm right."

Jack took a deep breath and asked Harrison, "Would you mind taking this over to Ben Furman at the crime lab? Tell him I need it analyzed ASAP."

"Sure thing, Lieutenant."

"Hold on," Beth said. "Jack, take a look at this and tell me what you think?"

Jack and Harrison crossed the room to where Beth was working. She turned the collar of the blouse up and was peering at a small bit of fiber.

"I think I found one of your outliers," Beth said.

"Maybe so," Jack said. Taking a pair of tweezers, he removed the material and placed it in a plastic bag. He handed it to Harrison and added, "Have Ben scope this and let us know the composition."

The officer shook hands with both of them and left the room, passing Dan Pappas on the way in with a half salute.

"What's up?" the detective asked.

"Nothing good," Beth said. "The killer left a package for Jack last night. He's taken another woman."

"Whaddya mean he left a package for Jack?"

"That uniform you just passed found a satchel with a woman's shoe and blouse and a bolt cutter sitting in a flower bed this morning at the Historical Society. It had Jack's name on it."

Pappas blinked And looked at Jack, who lifted his shoulders.

"Sonofabitch," Pappas said.

"There was also a soil sample the cop picked up," Beth said. "We sent it over to the lab."

When she was through filling him in on the other details, Pappas said, "I'll make your morning complete. On the ride in, I was listening to the radio. The murders are all over the news."

"And the hits just keep on coming," Jack muttered.

"The talk show guy was saying the Scarecrow's returned. Guess no one told him Pell is still locked up in Mayfield."

"So much for keeping this under wraps," Beth said. "Have we issued a statement?"

"Chief Ritson went on the air and said the murders are most likely the work of a deranged copycat."

"That's it?" Beth asked.

"No, he also said the department is being proactive and brought in Professor Jackson Kale to work with us because he's familiar with the original case and the psychology of the criminal mind."

Beth glanced at Jack, who didn't appear particularly surprised. There was a wry smile on his face. She felt herself growing angry at the tactics being used. First rule of thumb—cover your ass. From the expression on Pappas's face, she didn't need to voice her opinion.

Pappas further informed them, "I just got back from speaking with Jerome Haffner's neighbors."

"Anything useful?" Beth asked.

"Not really. The guy was well liked, divorced about five years ago, and has two kids who visit every other weekend. They were all shocked, of course. I'll be getting a search warrant for his condo later."

"Good," Beth said. "What about his employer? We need to speak with them."

"Haffner worked at Lane-Custis in Atlantic Center as a financial planner. If I can convince his company to cooperate and turn over his client records, I'd like to go through them and see if anyone lost a pile of money. If that happened, could be someone was pissed at him."

They both agreed that was a good idea.

Pappas shrugged. "We gotta start someplace. We've got squat so far."

"Any criminal history on Haffner?" Beth asked.

"Clean, apart from a couple of speeding tickets."

"Not very helpful," Jack said.

"This might be," Pappas said. "One lady I interviewed remembers a white van being parked across from Haffner's place a few days before the murder. She thought it might have been a repair man."

"Any writing on the van?"

"Not that Mrs. Abramowitz could recall. I checked with the building manager and Haffner didn't have any maintenance work scheduled. According to their policy, he'll let repair people in provided the owner clears it with him first."

"That's the second time we have a white van," Jack said.

"Third. Stafford and Mundas spoke with Sandra Goldner's brother, who shared a house with her. He definitely remembers seeing one two days before Sandra went missing. That makes three people in Jordan."

"All right," Jack said, "let's review what we know about the killer."

"He wears a size twelve shoe, so he's probably tall," Beth said.

"Possibly," Jack said. "Shoe size doesn't always correlate to height."

"The fucker's smart," Pappas said. "He plans things out."

"Agreed," Jack said. "So are we."

"If that hair we found on Betsy Anne's clothes belongs to him, he's Caucasian," Beth said.

Jack looked at Pappas, who nodded his agreement. He walked over to the board and added the note.

"Anyone think he knows computers?" Pappas asked.

"Why?" Beth asked.

"He had to open those flood gates to stash Sandra inside," Pappas said.

Jack informed him, "According to the Army, yesterday was the second of two water releases this week. They post the schedule on the Internet."

"Brilliant," Pappas said.

"Could he have entered the chamber after the inner gate holding the river back had shut?" Jack asked. "The outer door would still be open to allow for drainage."

"Maybe," Pappas said. "There's a gap of about two minutes."

"That might be enough time," Beth said.

"Let's say that's a possibility," Jack said, adding another note to the whiteboard. When he was done, he picked up the phone and called Ben Furman at the crime lab.

"Ben? Jack Kale here. Looks like we have a fourth kidnapping. I just sent you a satchel and some other evidence to look at."

"Got it. I was just about to get started."

"I'll be over in a few minutes," Jack said and disconnected.

He asked Beth, "Want to see what Ben comes up with? Or are you still on your way to interview Pell?"

Beth checked her watch. "I'm running late now. Call me if you find anything interesting."

Chapter 27

Two exits past Jordan, Beth pulled off the highway and followed the signs to the Mayfield State Mental Health Institute, a distance of two miles from the town. It was just starting to rain. Within minutes, the pleasant spring shower turned into a full-blown downpour with large, heavy drops the windshield wipers were having a hard time staying ahead of. The sky continued to grow ominous, split by flashes of lightning. Thanks to the local weather forecaster, who promised the day would be a "nine" on his Channel Eleven Weather Meter, she hadn't bothered with a raincoat that morning.

Mayfield's innocuous name belied its appearance. The cream-colored building, consisting of three floors, was a tribute to government design: utterly without character or charm. Around the perimeter of the property was a fence topped by interlooping coils of razor wire, which did nothing to soften the atmosphere. The place seemed to press down on you almost as soon as you entered the grounds. All the windows had bars.

At the front gate, a guard in a yellow rain slicker informed Beth the director wanted to speak with her before she saw Howard Pell.

"No problem," she said, deciding it was better not to rock the boat.

"I'll let him know you're here. Is this about those people who were murdered over the weekend?"

"We don't know yet," Beth said. "I'm still in the fact-gathering stage."

"Good luck," the guard told her.

A moment later, the security gate rumbled to life, crawling sideways on rollers across the cement drive. Beth parked directly in front of the main entrance and went in.

*

The Soul Eater added the last brick to the course he was working, tapping it into place with the handle of a trowel. In a few hours, the alcove would be completely sealed. To his left were a similar series of arches that had been bricked up.

No one had been in this part of the city for years. Beneath the streets and out of sight, Atlanta had simply grown over the crumbling old neighborhood. Even the railroad spur that once served the building he was in had been abandoned, broken apart by union soldiers as the city burned more than a hundred and sixty years ago.

The Soul Eater closed his eyes and let his mind drift to the account of the fire he'd read and reread. He could practically hear the shouts and cries as flames consumed everything in their path. He imagined the searing heat. What a spectacle it must have been. He picked up another brick.

*

Inside the alcove, Donna Camp had been awake for nearly fifteen minutes watching her captor with mounting horror as she realized what was happening. Her blouse and one shoe were missing, but that, thank God, was all. She could tell she hadn't been raped. Near him lay a roll of white linen cloth about eight inches wide.

Sealing me in. He's sealing me in.

The brick wall he was building was nearly three feet high. Very carefully, she moved her legs and confirmed the rope had been cut. She could vaguely remember being led into the dungeon, but it was like trying to recall a dream. She tested her arms and discovered her wrists were still bound. Two wide metal dishes held aloft by a tripod were positioned at either side of the opening, giving the room a templelike appearance.

As the effects of the drug she'd been given began to wear off, her mind turned to thoughts of escape. In the corner was her purse with the pepper spray. If she could just get her hands free.

Unfortunately, she had no idea where she was. Someplace dark and musty. Nor did she know why this madman had taken her. Donna's thoughts shifted to her children, strengthening her resolve to free herself. Little by little, she rotated her wrists, testing the bonds, first one way, and then the other. Yes, there was a little play in the rope. Nearly an hour went by before she worked a hand free.

The Soul Eater started on the next row of bricks.

"You're doing it wrong," she said, drawing herself into a sitting position.

The bearded man stopped and looked curiously at her. He didn't reply. It was as if he was looking at a bug.

"My husband was a contractor," Donna said. "You're doing it all wrong."

"Sufficient for my purpose."

"That's what all the losers say before the wall collapses."

The Soul Eater frowned and considered the bricks. It was more work than he thought. Still, any job worth doing was worth doing well. Who said that? Franklin? Probably.

"Why are you doing this?" Donna said.

The man gave no indication he heard her. He simply went back to building the wall.

"I don't have any money," she said. "Nobody in my family does, if you're hoping for a ransom."

"Pity."

"Tell me what you want."

"A little quiet would be appreciated," he said, tapping another brick into place.

"I get it," Donna said, drawing out the words. "You're one of those guys who're mad at women. Didn't your mommy breastfeed you? No? Wife left you? C'mon, you can tell me."

The Soul Eater took some mortar off the pallet he was holding and added it to the wall.

"Cat got your tongue?" Donna asked.

Unfazed, he continued his work until her laughter stopped him again.

"It's really not wise to make me mad," he said. "Not wise at all."

"You don't frighten me," Donna said.

"I should," he answered quietly.

The truth was he did scare Donna. Quite a lot. But she could see from the little tick that had started under his right eye that her comments were getting to him. What she was attempting was dangerous. For all she knew, he might change his mind and kill her on the spot.

"Now I understand," she said. "That wall's the only thing you can get up. There are medicines for that, you know."

The Soul Eater glanced at her. He took the next brick, jammed it into place, and kept working.

Donna continued with the only weapon she had. "It's pretty obvious. You couldn't do it with me, so you erect something as a substitute. We learned that in psychology."

The last comment did it. Donna watched him toss the trowel down and grab a roll of duct tape lying on the floor. He started for her.

As soon as he bent down to put the tape over her mouth, Donna threw the dirt she'd been holding into his face and lashed out with her foot, catching him squarely in the jaw. With her captor temporarily disabled, she dashed across the room for her purse and the pepper spray.

*

Pain exploded across the killer's face as he fought to clear his vision. He was in agony and could barely see. He stumbled across the room to a water bottle he'd brought with him and splashed it in his eyes. It felt like there was gravel in them. When his vision began to clear, he saw that Donna was gone. He kept still and listened. Outside, he could hear her scrambling over the rubble in the dim building. A smile slowly appeared on his face. She was going the wrong way.

With a sigh, the Soul Eater bent down and picked up his trowel and went to find her.

Chapter 28

The desk in Dr. Charles Raymond's office was large and impressively free of clutter. In fact, it was free of everything, save for a phone and a yellow legal pad with blue lines. On the wall were framed diplomas from Piedmont College and the University of Guatemala School of Medicine. He managed to keep Beth waiting for more than fifteen minutes before he swept into the room and introduced himself.

"I'm terribly sorry, Ms. Sturgis. I was tied up on an important conference call to Los Angeles."

Beth wondered if he would have mentioned the call if he'd been speaking with someone in Macon, Georgia.

"It's quite all right," she said. "Thank you for arranging the visit."

"Not at all. We're more than happy to work with the authorities. Terrible business about those people who were murdered. I take it that's why you're here."

"Our investigation's just getting started," she replied automatically.

"That's essentially what I told the reporters."

"Oh?"

"They're quite an aggressive lot. Still, the similarities to Pell are intriguing, wouldn't you agree?"

"They are, Doctor."

Her use of his title seemed to please him. Raymond tented his fingers importantly and informed her. "Both my staff and I are at your disposal. In fact, we, or should I say I, may be able to save you a great deal of time."

"How's that?"

"Well, obviously, I've had a great deal of contact with Pell over the years, which puts me in a unique position. I know the man's mind and the way he thinks. Believe me, he'll try to mislead you if he can."

"Why?"

"Because it's all a game to him—a sick game, I grant you."

"I see."

"Pell is what we call a classic sociopath, a person utterly without conscience. On top of that, he's extremely bright. He may or may not help you."

Beth already had a good idea what to expect from studying the file and newspaper accounts about Howard Pell. Nevertheless, she thanked Raymond for his advice and said she'd be careful. It seemed the fastest way to get her interview started.

Dr. Raymond further advised her, "Caution probably won't be enough. Trust me, you need a professional to guide you."

As he was talking, the doctor's eyes took in Beth's legs and then made their way back to her face. She bit her tongue and decided not to comment.

"That's very generous of you."

Raymond smiled benignly. "What I'm saying is, I'm offering my services, Beth. May I call you Beth?"

Only if I can call you a pig, she thought.

"Of course, Doctor," she smiled.

"And I'd like it if you would call me Charles."

"I'll certainly discuss your offer with Chief Ritson, Charles."

"Do you know, I've called him twice since the story broke, but he hasn't returned my calls yet."

"I'm so sorry. I'll be sure to mention it," Beth said.

That seemed to mollify him. He nodded, then noticed some lint on his sleeve and flicked it off. Despite the office being cool, he had a sheen of sweat on his forehead. Raymond was in his late fifties, and somewhat overweight. The beard he wore was reminiscent of Freud, as was his pattern baldness.

"I'd love to give you a tour of our little facility," he said, "if you have the time."

"Thank you, Charles. Unfortunately, I'm somewhat pressed at the moment. Perhaps on my next visit. May I see Pell's visitor list?"

Raymond was disappointed but said he understood. He then surprised her by asking, "How long do you think we'll need for the session?"

"I'm sorry, *we*?"

"Well, naturally I assumed you'd want me present. As Pell's doctor, the therapeutic relationship I've developed with him over the years will save you scads of time."

"Again, that's very kind, but I prefer to conduct interviews one on one."

"I must warn you, the man's into mind games. Something I can easily see through. It's a matter of experience, really."

"If I get confused, I'll call you in," Beth said, glancing at a clock on the wall. "Or I can consult with Jackson Kale later."

"Kale? Yes, I heard his name mentioned on the radio. No disrespect to a colleague, but he's only a psychologist. I'm a clinically trained physician."

"I'll keep it in mind," Beth said. "Now if you could take me to him, I'd like to get started. We can pick up the visitor list later."

A brief look of annoyance crossed Raymond's face, but he managed to conceal it and shifted topics. "Very well," he said, shaking his head. "Perhaps you could join me later for a glass of wine. We'll go over what you've learned."

Why me? Beth thought. Like any attractive woman, she had long experience in dealing with persistent men. The best way to deflect them was to smile pleasantly and say how lovely that would be if she could find the time. Which she did.

Dr. Raymond led her down a long olive-green corridor to a room with a metal table that was bolted to the floor. At opposite ends of the ceiling were two small cameras. The far wall was taken up by a mirror, which Beth guessed was used for observation.

Two men were waiting for them. One was a short, powerfully built man in black hospital scrubs, while the other was tall and wore a brown sport coat.

"This is Dr. Cairo," Raymond said, introducing the sport coat. "He's worked with Pell quite a bit. I asked him to be present in case you have any questions. And this is Ron Curry, our psychiatric nurse."

Dr. Cairo was probably in his early forties and had brown hair and blue eyes that rarely blinked, something she found disconcerting.

"We'll be bringing Pell in in just a minute," Cairo said. "Here are the rules: Stay in your chair at all times and do not get close to him. Ron will have to lock your gun in the safe until your interview is over."

"That's fine," Beth said, handing over her weapon to the nurse.

"Also, if you have anything sharp, like a knife or a pen, please give it to him," Cairo said.

Beth did as asked.

Cairo continued, "I assume you've brought a tape recorder."

"I have."

"It's fine to use it. We have recording equipment that will pick up everything being said in the room along with cameras for video."

"I saw them."

"We'll try to give you as much privacy as possible, but one of us will be in there at all times."

Beth started to protest, then changed her mind when he quickly added, "It's for your own safety."

"Agreed."

"Very good," Cairo said. He nodded to the nurse, who relayed the order over his walkie-talkie.

In the room, Beth took a seat facing the door and watched as two uniform officers, each holding one of Howard Pell's arms, led him in. He was shorter than she imagined and not physically imposing in any way. Both wrists were manacled and secured to a chain that ran around his waist. Once seated, a second chain was attached from his waist to the floor. One of the uniforms checked to make sure it was properly bolted and then both exited the room. She noticed they both exercised a great deal of caution around the man sitting across from her.

"Dr. Pell, my name is Elizabeth Sturgis. I'm a detective with the Atlanta Police. Thank you for seeing me."

"Obsession."

"Excuse me?"

"You're wearing Obsession. Not the perfume. The cologne, I suspect. My wife was partial to it. Am I right?"

Beth kept her expression neutral. According to the file, Pell had decapitated his wife and kept her head in a jar.

"You're very perceptive, Doctor," she said.

Pell inclined his head at the compliment.

"Are you comfortable?" Beth asked.

He responded by lifting the chain securing his arms. "As comfortable as circumstances permit."

"May I get you something to drink?"

"A soft drink, if you please."

Beth turned to the nurse. "Is that possible? If there's a charge, I'll pay."

"I'm not permitted to leave the room, Detective."

"Would you call someone, please?"

Curry didn't seem happy but used his walkie-talkie to relay the request. Beth turned back to Pell.

"Doctor, I'm here investigating three murders that occurred several days ago."

"Yes. A terrible situation," Pell said. "I heard about it on the news."

"I was hoping that—"

"I could help you?"

"Yes."

"Do tell me what happened. It sounds ghastly."

Beth reconstructed the scene in the field, finding the tunnel, and the discovery of Betsy Ann Tinsley's body in a shallow grave.

Pell listened attentively, nodding occasionally as Beth spoke, and then said, "You took photographs, of course? May I see them, please?"

Beth opened her briefcase and removed the crime scene photos. She was about to hand them to him when Curry instructed, "Please don't lean any closer, Ms. Sturgis. Just spread them out so he can see them."

A thin smile appeared on Pell's face.

"The staff here tends to be alarmist."

"I understand," Beth said. "Can you see the photographs all right?"

"You haven't been a detective very long, have you, Elizabeth?"

"Excuse me?"

"A detective. A crime fighter. A caped crusader for law and order, without the cape."

"Five years, Doctor."

"And what were you before that?"

"That's not really relevant, Dr. Pell. If you'd just take a look—"

"You want my help, don't you?"

"That's why I came," Beth said. "If you're not going to—"

"Then kindly answer my question. It's not complex. Whatever did you do before you were a police officer?"

Jack Kale's warning about not revealing personal information came back to her. Pell sat there calmly waiting for an answer, the half smile still on his face.

She made her decision. "I worked for a travel magazine."

"As?"

"An associate editor, Dr. Pell."

Pell shut his eyes and took a deep breath before pointedly looking at the fourth finger on her right hand for a wedding ring.

"Why did you leave, may I ask?"

"I was ready for a change."

"Was the work too mundane?"

"It was interesting enough."

"A change," he repeated.

"Something like that," Beth said. "I've seen *Silence of the Lambs* and read the book. Your Lector impersonation's excellent. Very impressive. If I'm wasting my time, please tell me now."

Pell raised an eyebrow and studied her. Seconds ticked by. Beth finally had enough and reached for the photographs.

"The scarecrow's cross is facing the wrong way," Pell said.

Beth's hand froze. "That's what Jack Kale said."

"Ah, clever Jack Kale. The television mentioned him. To tell the truth, it was actually him I was expecting."

"Dr. Kale's consulting with our department," Beth said.

"He's quite a terrible man, you know," Pell said. He was about to say more but stopped when the door opened and Charles Raymond came in carrying a Coca-Cola. The timing couldn't have been worse. Raymond managed to look both petulant and annoyed at the same time. Pell didn't bother to turn around.

"Good morning, Dr. Raymond. Your aftershave precedes you. You really must do something about that."

Raymond glanced at Beth and then handed the drink to Curry and left again. The nurse cautiously placed it on the table within Pell's reach.

"Thank you," Pell said softly.

Curry didn't respond. He resumed his place at the door.

Beth waited until he finished drinking and then asked, "Why is Jack Kale terrible, Dr. Pell?"

"Because he tried to eviscerate me. Did, actually."

"What do you mean?"

"He sliced my stomach open and pulled my intestines out." Pell unbuttoned the top of his jumpsuit and opened it up, revealing a lateral scar going all the way across his stomach.

Beth stared at it for a moment. "I'm sorry," she said.

"As if that wasn't enough, he tried to frame me for that poor agent's murder," Pell said.

"His partner, Constance Belasco," Beth said.

Pell smiled thinly again. "You've done your homework. Wasn't this in the file?"

"Some of it."

"That's what keeps you ahead of the men in your department. You have to work harder than they do. Am I right?"

"Another woman's been kidnapped, Doctor. I was hoping you could give me some insight about the killer, since he seems to be imitating you."

"Why should I?"

"Because it might save her life."

"Is that what drives you, Elizabeth? You want to save the life of a woman you've never met? What is she to you?"

"A human being who needs help."

"Most people need help," Pell said.

She was aware of his attempt to manipulate her. But as long as he kept talking and believed it was working, that was fine. The main thing she needed was information and to understand the mind of whomever was out there killing people. She was willing to put up with the games for as long as it took.

"I can't help most people," she told him. "But I may be able to save this one."

Pell took another sip of his drink, watching her over the cup he held. He'd changed since his file photo. He was thinner now and his hair was completely gray and close-cropped. Pell finally spoke.

"How is it you know your killer has another woman?"

"Because he left clues for us to find," Beth said.

"Tell me about them."

Beth did, leaving nothing out. When she was finished, he said, "You and your associates believe the murders were done by someone imitating me, correct?"

"Yes."

"But Jack Kale doesn't subscribe to that theory, does he?"

"He hasn't said so directly," Beth said.

Pell seemed to find that amusing. His smile was as substantial as a wisp of fog.

When nothing more was forthcoming, Beth prompted, "Can you help me, Doctor?"

Pell turned the cup of soda first one way and then the other, arranging it on the table as if its position was important to him. She was ready to conclude the trip had been a waste of time when Pell continued, "Have you asked yourself why the killer left his clues at the Historical Society?"

"What do you mean?"

"A bright ambitious girl like yourself should be able to figure that out . . . an old satchel left at a museum. Do let me know what you find."

"But—"

"Good day, Elizabeth. I've enjoyed our chat."

Beth was about to press him for an answer when Dr. Raymond chose that exact moment to enter the room again.

"I have that information you requested, Ms. Sturgis," he said, holding up a blue file folder.

Idiot. It was a good thing she didn't have her gun. Pell leaned back in his chair and closed his eyes.

"I've grown quite fatigued by all these questions. Please take me back now."

Raymond gave her a sympathetic look and said, "Perhaps it would be best to keep this session short."

"I'm not finished," Beth told him.

"Do come and visit me again," Pell said. "I'm afraid that poor woman doesn't have much time left."

Chapter 29

It was obvious Pell hated Jack Kale. Only natural since Jack was the one who caught him. Driving through the last remnants of the storm, Beth reviewed her conversation with the killer. Why had he said Jack had framed him for his partner's murder? He didn't deny any of the other murders or that he had performed that gruesome surgery on her. It was probably the product of a sick mind and another attempt to manipulate her. Not a very subtle one at that. He obviously knew they were working together. She'd said as much herself. What better way to undermine her confidence in a partner than to create doubt?

Pell was convinced he was smarter than everyone else. Maybe he was, but look where it got him. Jack was right not to come. Howard Pell was a perverted individual, playing mental games, as Raymond said, and exerting what little control he could still exercise by dropping obsequious hints here and there. The only consideration now was finding that missing woman. And the clock was ticking. Of that she had no doubt. It might have been the one true thing Pell had said.

By the time Beth reached Atlanta, the sun was creating oil-slick rainbows in sidewalk puddles. Her cell phone beeped with a message from Jack asking that she join him at the crime lab.

She found him hunched over a microscope peering at something. Ben Furman was at the opposite end of the room adjusting the dials on an odd-looking device.

Jack informed her, "The fiber you found is asbestos. We've also broken down the soil sample and have some interesting results."

"Like what?"

"First, that soil definitely comes from someplace other than the Historical Society grounds."

"Where?"

"That's the sixty-four-thousand-dollar question," Jack said. "Ben is about to burn a sample in the gas chromatograph spectrometer. We're getting close."

Furman muttered under his breath, which caused them both to look at him.

"The damn thing must be out of whack," he said. "The nitrogen content in the soil is off the chart."

"Run it again," Jack said.

They waited while the tech cleared out and reset the machine.

"Same results," he said.

"Okay," Jack said. "Anything distinctive about the brick chips?"

"Other than being old and crumbling, they're probably handmade as opposed to machine made."

"And the mortar?" Jack asked.

"It contains a very high lime content, which indicates age."

"Why?" Beth asked.

"More lime was incorporated into mortar used in the older buildings because it's breathable and moves as the structure settles. You don't see that much with modern stuff."

Beth informed them, "Pell said the satchel and the Historical Society were the key."

"He's partially right," Jack said. "Let's take a ride."

"To where?"

"The Historical Society. I need an old map of the city."

Within minutes they were traveling down Peachtree Road. Eventually, they turned off at West Paces Ferry. Jack used his cell phone to call ahead and spoke with the director of the museum.

"What are you looking for?" Beth asked as they entered the building.

"I'm not sure. Possibly a company that manufactured fertilizer," Jack said.

"Here in Atlanta?"

"Obviously not for many years. If they existed at all, it was a long time ago. Everything points to it—a carpetbag, brick and mortar from an ancient building, the Historical Society itself. They all indicate age. All we have to do is find out where they intersect."

"There are a lot of old buildings in Atlanta," Beth said.

"Not that many, thanks to General Sherman. Much of the city was burned toward the end of the Civil War."

The director of the Historical Society was waiting for them in the lobby. Ellen Amblin was in her early sixties, stylishly dressed, and confined to a wheelchair. She possessed an intelligent face and gray hair that was swept back from her head and held in place by a clip.

"It's good to see you again, Jack," she said.

"Ma'am?"

"You don't remember me, do you?"

"No, I'm afraid I don't."

"Well, I really can't blame you. It's been quite a few years. Your mother used to bring you to my parent's store. They owned a little antique shop in the Peachtree Battle Center."

"My goodness," Jack said, shaking her hand. "It's good to see you as well. Forgive me for not remembering. This is Detective Sturgis."

The women shook hands. Beth seemed delighted.

She said, "I'd love to hear what Jack was like as a little boy."

"Oh, he was quite precocious. Always touching things and getting into mischief. His mother had an awful time keeping up with him. In fact, I remember—"

"Miss Ellen, as I mentioned on the phone, we're in a bit of a hurry. This is police business."

"Yes, of course. I've pulled out several maps from our library that show Atlanta's early development all the way back to when it was called Marthasville."

"I thought it was always called Atlanta," Beth said as they started down a long hallway. She glanced at Jack with an amused smile playing at the corners of her mouth. He continued to look straight ahead.

"Officially, we've had three names," Ellen Amblin informed them. "Terminus was the other. Atlanta came last."

Jack asked, "Are you familiar with any companies that manufactured fertilizer, say from the Civil War period to around the turn of the century?"

"I'm afraid not."

"What about stockyards or places where animals were kept? This was a major stopping point for the railroad in the South," Jack said.

"*The* major stopping point," the director agreed. "At one time, sheep and cattle were herded through the middle of downtown, but I'm afraid whatever was here is long gone now."

They arrived in the library where three maps were hanging on easels. The stockyards shown on the first map, dated 1840, were gone by the time the second map was published in 1885. A third map, produced in

1901, showed three feed and fertilizer companies. Two were well north of the city. The third was now the site of Lenox Mall.

"It has to be here," Jack said, staring at the maps. All of Pell's murders were subterranean. He believed the killer was following that pattern.

"I'm sorry. So much of the city has been rebuilt in the last hundred years. Very little of the old town is left."

"Obviously it has something to do with the Civil War," Beth said. "Otherwise, why leave the carpetbag?"

The director said, "Except for a church at Peachtree and North Avenue, I'm not familiar with any brick buildings that old. After the war, when Reconstruction began, everything was more or less plowed under."

Jack's head came up. "What did you say?"

"You mean about Reconstruction?"

"No, after that. Plowed under—everything was plowed under," he repeated. He turned to Beth. "The killer used a tunnel to move one victim, buried another, and locked a third in a vault under the dam."

They held each other's eyes for a moment, the same thought occurring to both simultaneously.

Jack moved to the oldest map and pointed to an area across from the present courthouse.

"There," he said.

"Underground Atlanta," Beth said. "It's part of an entertainment complex now."

"Not all of it," Ellen Amblin said. "Only the first section was rebuilt. The back is sealed off. At one time, it was part of Atlanta's downtown. They had streets and shops, and—"

"The Beckworth Munitions Company," Jack said, stabbing the map with his finger. "I should have made the nitrogen connection sooner. That's where he's got her."

Chapter 30

Beth called dispatch and asked them to alert the SWAT team as they sped through the streets. Jack was driving.

"They'll be onsite in five minutes," Beth said. "I told them to get all civilians out of the area."

Jack nodded, slowed at an intersection slightly, then ran the red light.

"How did you know about the arms company?" Beth asked.

"I didn't," Jack said. "The part about nitrogen threw me off. It kept going around in my head. Then I saw the name and remembered nitrogen is a principal component in the manufacture of explosives—you know, like nitroglycerin."

"You just know this stuff?"

Jack shrugged and kept driving. "I read a lot."

*

The only sound Donna could hear was her own breathing. The linen cloth covering her mouth and face was just woven loosely enough to breathe and see through. But even the little light filtering through the alcove opening disappeared as the last brick was set into place. She had been so close to getting away. Making her way through the crumbling building, she could see people walking on an odd street between openings in a fence. She had no idea where she was, and the street only confused her further. It was like something out of an old-time movie, paved with cobblestones and unusually dark like it was night. She never heard the Soul Eater coming until it was too late. Now she was surrounded by the ominous blackness again.

Her jaw still ached from where he'd hit her. When she awoke, she'd found herself completely bound in the wrapping and back in the alcove. As the last brick went into place, everything became muffled. She tried shouting for help, but there was no one to hear her cries. Eventually, she gave up. It was becoming harder and harder to think. Some part of her brain realized the air inside the little room was slowly disappearing. Panic tried to take control of her mind. *You have to do something!*

The choices were simple. Use up more air calling for help or lay here and die for lack of oxygen. Her eyes were growing steadily heavier. False images began to float in front of her—colors generated by her brain. Is this how it feels?

Maybe if she slept for a bit, just a few minutes to gather herself. More shapes swam before her along with those little stars you see when you stand up too quickly. Shooting stars. She remembered pasting them on the ceiling of her boys' room when they were little. Shooting stars that continued to glow after the lights were out. Slowly, inexorably, the stars began to recede in the distance, growing fainter and fainter. Donna Camp closed her eyes and went to sleep.

*

A uniform officer responding to the emergency call was already at the parking lot keeping more people from entering the Underground Atlanta complex. Jack recognized Corey Harrison immediately.

"Nice to see you again, Harrison," he said.

"I was on my way to court when your alert went out. What's up?"

"We think our killer has the woman somewhere in there," Jack said, pointing.

"Really?"

"It's a reasonable guess. That evidence you brought in was crucial. Are you familiar with the layout here?"

"A little," Harrison said. "My girlfriend and I visited after the renovations were complete. Basically, it's just a couple of streets with restaurants and souvenir shops."

Beth said, "There's supposed to be a closed section they haven't started on yet."

"It's probably at the north end of Old Alabama Street," Harrison said. "I remember seeing some broken-down old buildings there but never paid much attention to them."

Beth nodded and went to the trunk of her car and removed two body armor vests and handed one to Jack. They both put them on. She explained to Harrison, "Tactical should be here any minute. Let them know we're on scene."

She then turned to Jack. "Are you armed?"

"Uh . . . no, I didn't think I'd need to carry a gun."

"Jack, you can't go into a dangerous situation without a weapon."

"He can have my backup," Harrison said. He knelt down, removed a compact revolver from his ankle holster, and handed it to him.

Jack looked at the gun and frowned. It was a five-shot .22-caliber Smith & Wesson the cops referred to as pop guns.

"Better than using harsh language," Harrison said.

Jack managed a smile and thanked him.

"How about I come with you guys?" Harrison said. "I can have radio advise tactical we're in."

Beth looked at Jack and then back to Harrison and nodded.

"Let's go."

As soon as they cleared the entrance, the three found themselves in the midst of Underground Atlanta. Beth wasn't sure what was above them, but she could hear the rumble of traffic. Around her old-fashioned lampposts spilled light onto the cobblestones.

The street they were on ended at a sidewalk restaurant flanked by a gift shop and a store called Ye Olde Printing Company—Stationers. Perhaps a hundred yards away, at the opposite end, was a gray, wooden fence blocking off further access. Beyond it she could see three or four brick buildings, or rather what was left of them. Their front and sides were blackened and none looked particularly safe. Portions of one had already collapsed. The roof and top floor of the building across from it were completely gone.

Without speaking, they spread out. Beth took one side of the street, Jack the other, and Harrison moved to the middle. As they drew closer, she could see the area beyond the fence had once been used to house construction materials. Large mounds of sand and concrete blocks still remained. Atlanta's city fathers had hoped to turn Underground Atlanta into a tourist attraction, similar to Boston's Faneuil Hall or New York's South Street Seaport. The fact that Beth had never visited there or knew anyone who did said something about how the public had received it. Harrison finished speaking with radio dispatch and stopped in front of the gate.

"Looks like the lock's been snapped off," he said, drawing his gun. "Someone probably used a crowbar on it."

Jack and Beth joined him as he pushed the right half of the door open. It was large enough to drive a truck through. The door swung back on its hinges to reveal a narrow street.

The buildings were no more than piles of rubble. Whatever was left was now sealed in by the road overhead and a wall at the very end that cast them into perpetual night.

"SWAT's here," Harrison said, listening over his earpiece. "They're clearing out the last civilians now."

"Where do you think he has her?" Beth asked.

"If he's consistent, it'll probably be in a basement. That's where Pell's last victim was found," Jack said, coming to a halt at a ruined brick structure.

Boards and debris were blocking the building's entrance. They searched for another way in and found nothing.

"Commander Sheeley's on his way," Harrison said. "He says to stay put until he's secured the area."

"We don't have time to stay put," Beth said, "and neither does that woman."

"I'm just telling you what he . . ."

Harrison's words went to Jack and Beth's backs. They were already in the process of negotiating their way over the rubble. Harrison cursed under his breath and followed.

All that was left of the Beckworth Munitions Company was a faded sign that hung above an interior courtyard. Its four sides were surrounded by the building's shell. Above them, only the framework of the roof remained. Portions of two walls had collapsed as had a wooden balcony that ran along the inside of the second floor. Sections were still intact, but the majority now lay in the courtyard, its timbers charred by fire.

Low light glinted off broken windows high up in the remaining brick walls. It was a desolate, abandoned place that had once been filled with activity. No one had been here for years. The echo of wagons moving and men shouting, laughing, and cursing long ago reverberated within these walls. Now the only sound was wind passing through the shattered beams.

"This ain't smart," a voice behind them said.

All three turned to see the SWAT team commander making his way across the entrance.

"We think there's a woman somewhere in this building," Beth said.

"I know, but you don't go stumbling into an unsecured situation unless you're tired of living."

Sheeley was dressed completely in black body armor with the word SWAT and a gold badge emblazoned over his right breast.

"She may be dying as we speak," Beth said. "Let us help and—"

"Just give me a few minutes to make sure there are no surprises waiting for us. It won't take long."

"But—"

"We'll move as quickly as we can. I promise. In the meantime, I want you to fall back outside."

Beth opened her mouth to protest and stopped. Sheeley was right. Barging into an uncontrolled area without making sure it was safe was foolish and against department policy. Conscious the clock was ticking, she told him to have his men look for a basement.

Six of Sheeley's squad, dressed as he was, entered the courtyard and began to check different portions of the structure, splitting into two-man teams. Within minutes each team called in advising the area was clear. The last to report was team two.

"Myers here, boss. We found the basement, but it's empty."

"You sure?"

"There's an inch of dust on the steps going down. It's the same with the floor. I promise you, no one's been on them for years. This is a dead end."

"She has to be here," Jack said. "Everything fits."

"Fine. Tell us where to look," Sheeley said.

Jack shook his head. "I don't know. All indications are—"

"Why are those arches sealed?" Beth asked.

The men turned to see what she was looking at. Across the courtyard, a small group of arches under a section of the balcony had been bricked over. The arches on either side were open.

Beth asked Jack, "Didn't you say you found old mortar mixed in with the brick chips—lime or something?"

"Absolutely," Jack said, staring at the arches.

Sheeley understood immediately. He snatched the hand mic off his shoulder and snapped, "Antonelli, Johnson, grab the battering ram and meet us here on the double."

Chapter 31

There was no need to guess which arch Donna camp was entombed behind. In the dim light, it had not been possible to see the color difference between the old and new mortar or the joint discrepancy in the courses of brick. Once they were close, both became apparent. The recently constructed wall gave way after only two blows with the battering ram. Jack, Harrison, and Beth stood off to one side and watched with a cold dread building in them at what they might find inside.

Two SWAT officers climbed over the pile of brick and disappeared into the shadows. A moment later Antonelli yelled, "She's alive! I saw her move. He's got her wrapped up like a mummy. We need oxygen ASAP! Someone call the medics!"

The EMT unit arrived within minutes and transferred Donna Camp to a stretcher, cautiously carrying her out of the alcove. One of the technicians started an IV drip to combat her dehydration.

"Is she able to talk?" Jack asked.

"Yeah. She's pretty banged up, but she should be okay."

"I need a few minutes with her."

"Jack, they need to get this woman to a hospital," Beth said.

Jack ignored her and moved to the stretcher. "Ma'am, are you well enough to speak with me?"

"I think so," Donna said.

"Did you see the man who did this to you?"

"Yes."

"Can you describe him?"

"He's tall with brown hair and blue eyes. He had a beard, but it didn't look real."

"Did you speak with him?"

"Uh-huh. I asked him if the wall was the only thing he could get up. He didn't like that."

Jack stifled a laugh. "No, I don't imagine he did. How did he react?"

"He tried to put tape over my mouth. When he got close, I kicked him and ran. But he caught me again." Donna tentatively touched her left eye and winced.

"He hit you?"

"Uh-huh."

"Do you recall which hand he used?"

Donna thought for a second and then said, "His left one."

"You're doing great," Jack reassured. "Did he do anything else besides hit you?"

"Nothing sexual, if that's what you mean," Donna said.

Jack glanced at Beth. She already had a plastic evidence bag in one hand and was in the process of filling out a description card. Quick learner.

"I'm very glad to hear that," Jack said to Donna, putting a hand on her shoulder. "You're a brave woman. You said you kicked him?"

"Correct."

"Which foot?"

"This one," Donna answered, lifting her right leg. "You can have my shoe if you need it."

"We do," Jack said. "When we're done, I'd like you to spend a little time with Detective Sturgis, so she can check the rest of your clothes."

"For fibers and fingerprints?"

Jack smiled, "Been watching *CSI* on television?"

"I don't mind. I want to help."

"You already have. Tell me what else you remember about him."

"He might have been wearing a wig, too, but it was hard to tell because it was dark."

"I understand. And you're sure his eye color was blue?"

"Probably more gray now that I think of it."

"After he hit you, did he put his hands anywhere else on your body?"

"Around my throat, but he was wearing gloves—brown leather gloves."

Jack nodded. No surprise there. "What about you? Did you put your hands on him?"

"I tried to fight, but he was too strong," Donna said. She seemed to sag a little with the last statement.

Jack caught Beth's warning look and thanked her. He nodded to her and stood back while she ran a sticky roller over the woman's clothes to pick up trace evidence.

After the EMTs left for the hospital, they went back to the alcove and began searching the area for clues. Forensics arrived and set up two portable lights, which helped a great deal. Their work was methodical and painstaking and yielded a good set of footprints. Whether these were left by the killer or by someone else, Jack didn't know. He ordered comparison prints from each of the SWAT officers to eliminate them. The unspoken question on everyone's mind was what would they find behind the other alcoves.

Rather than knock down the wall as they did the first one, Sheeley sent one of his men for a hammer and cold chisel. Little by little, the mortar was chipped away and a brick was removed. The officer then used his Maglite to peer into the room, sweeping the beam from side to side slowly. Everyone's attention was riveted on him.

Suddenly, the man's hand stopped moving. He pulled his head back and said, "Holy shit."

Most of the color seemed to have left his face. He turned back to Sheeley and announced, "There's another body in here."

Chapter 32

It took the rest of the day and into the night before the other walls came down. One by one, the bricks were removed and placed into separate piles. Ben Furman and two assistants arrived on the scene and worked tirelessly. Dan Pappas, back from interviewing witnesses, showed up along with Deputy Chief Noah Ritson and Burt Wiggins. They watched from the sidelines without comment. Sheeley and his men also stayed to see the developing nightmare. They had the expression of people who had just discovered their training would be of no value. The atmosphere in the courtyard took on a surreal quality. Police and technicians moved in and out of the lights going about their tasks without speaking. A group of uniforms were assigned to keep the crowd back, which was growing in size with every passing hour. Among the onlookers were reporters from the newspaper, CNN, Fox News, and all three major networks.

After the last body was removed and turned over to the medical examiner, Noah Ritson motioned the detectives away from the cameras now set up behind the police barricade.

Ritson addressed Jack first. "I noticed you speaking with the crime scene photographer a minute ago. What was that about?"

"I asked her to get some pictures of the crowd."

"You think our man is here?"

"It's possible," Jack said. "Detectives Sturgis and Pappas found what looks like an observation point near the dam. Sometimes these nuts like to hang around and see our reactions."

"Nuts?"

"It captures the spirit, Chief," Jack said.

Ritson smiled. "We'll need to make a statement to the media. What can you tell me?"

Jack noted his use of the term *we* rather than *I* when he mentioned making a statement.

"Five of the victims are female; one is male. Judging from the clothing and the state of decomposition on the first woman we took out, I'd say her body has been here for quite a while. Years, probably. The ME or maybe a forensic anthropologist can give us a better idea."

"What about the others?" Ritson asked.

"Thanks to the lack of moisture and the alcove being sealed, the bodies are in surprisingly good condition. The style of clothes indicates they were here even longer than the first victim. Since around the early nineteen hundreds, I imagine."

"How can you be sure?"

"Best guess, Chief, unless they attended a costume party before they were murdered."

"You're telling me we've had a serial killer running around since the turn of the last century?" Ritson said.

Jack took a deep breath and looked through the gate to where the crowd was congregating. "I'm only telling you what I observed. It's too soon to reach any conclusions."

Ritson took a moment to digest the implications. "Okay. Get cleaned up and think over what you want to say. We don't need to set off a general panic." He turned to Beth and Pappas. "I want both of you at the press conference. I'll handle the broad strokes and then Professor Kale will take over."

Pappas waited until the chief was out of earshot and leaned around Jack to look at him from the back.

"What are you doing?" Beth asked.

"Checking to see if there's a bull's-eye strapped to his ass."

A short distance away, reporters jockeyed for position.

"Showtime," Jack mumbled as they started forward.

The reporters began shouting questions almost before Chief Ritson was in position. He held his hands up for quiet.

"As some of you know, another woman was recently abducted. Thanks to some quick thinking on the part of our investigative team, I'm pleased to announce she was rescued several hours ago. She's now resting comfortably at Grady Hospital."

"What's her name, Chief?" a reporter from WXIA called out.

"We'd prefer to keep that confidential for the time being until she's had a chance to speak with her family."

"Was she hurt in any way?"

"Some bruises and scrapes, I'm told, but otherwise she appears to be in good health—badly shaken, but all right."

"Was she sexually assaulted?" a reporter from Fox News asked.

Ritson squinted against the glare and shielded his eyes to see who had spoken. "She advised us there was nothing like that."

The reporter followed up with another question. "How about ransom demands?"

"At this time we're not aware of any demands for money, but we're still investigating."

An attractive blonde woman who Jack recognized from a TV news special about the zoo's new panda asked the inevitable next question. This was probably a juicier story than what the panda was up to. "If this woman was rescued hours ago, what were you doing in there so long?"

The chief, used to dealing with the media, answered calmly. "Gail, in any crime scene, it's important that we examine the area for clues carefully and methodically. We wouldn't want to miss something significant."

One reporter's voice rose above the others. "Is that why Jackson Kale is here?"

Earlier, Jack had seen Burt Wiggins talking with her and had no doubt the question was preplanned. It fit Ritson's style of managing the flow of information. Not a bad idea, when he thought about it.

"Professor Kale and the rest of our team were the ones who pieced the clues together and figured out where the kidnapper had her hidden. They were assisted by a uniform officer who initially recovered a number of evidentiary items near the Historical Society and realized their importance. Their efforts were central in her rescue. As you might imagine, we're justifiably proud."

Several reporters broke into a round of applause.

"So this is unrelated to the recent deaths in Jordan and at Lake Lanier?" the same reporter asked.

"This may be a good time to turn this over to Professor Kale, who can fill you in on the details," the chief said.

Despite his new rank as a lieutenant, Jack took note that Ritson continued to refer to him as "professor," thereby reinforcing his separate status from the department. As he stepped up to the microphone, he felt his heart rate and respiration start to climb. As unobtrusively as he could, he took several breaths and tried to relax.

A reporter for the *Atlanta Journal* asked, "Dr. Kale, was this woman's abduction related to the other deaths?"

"Yes."

"I'm confused. Don't kidnappers generally abduct people because they want money or something in return?"

"Generally," Jack said. "I should clarify. This was an attempted murder, not a kidnapping."

A murmur ran through the crowd before the same reporter continued, "What was the motive?"

"I don't know."

"There was a report she was wrapped up like a mummy."

"It's true that the victim was bound," Jack said, keeping the information to a minimum.

"Do you have any suspects at this time?"

"Suspects, no. But we're making progress."

"What does that mean?" the reporter asked.

"Just what I said. We know, for example, the killer is a white male, tall, with light-blue or gray eyes."

A reporter who had once interviewed Jack jumped in with his own question. "Jack, given your previous experience with Howard Pell and the similarities to the murders in Jordan, do you think you're dealing with a copycat?"

Jack considered the question and then said, "No, I don't believe that. The killer wants it to appear that way, but he's operating under a different agenda."

"We've seen what looked like a number of bodies being carried out. Did the same man kill them all?"

"It's too soon to say what the causes of death were. Suffice to say, they don't appear to be from natural reasons. As soon as we know more, we'll make an announcement. By tomorrow morning, a tip line will be set up. We're asking for the public's help. If you know anything about these deaths, please give us a call. You can do it in confidence."

"Are you saying the public is at risk?" Patterson asked.

"I'm not supposed to instill panic, but until the killer's caught, I'd say everyone's at risk. That's why we need your help."

*

The Soul Eater drove slowly listening to the press conference on his car radio. He was surprised Kale had put the clues together so quickly. By all rights, it should have taken longer. *So they discovered my little mausoleum. What of it? They were meant to be found . . . eventually.* He touched the book lying on the seat next to him. It was old, covered in black leather, and bent from years of use. Kale's quick discoveries simply meant he would have to move his schedule up as well, which was annoying but not fatal to his plan.

Kale was a bright man, and sooner or later, he'd figure the puzzle out. But by then it would be too late. The Soul Eater calmed his mind and used his turn signal to change lanes. Wouldn't want to give the police an excuse to pull him over.

He thought about the two detectives standing dutifully behind Clever Jack, the tall brunette and her cumbersome partner with the scarred face. They were there to show support. How touching.

At Fourteenth Street, the killer turned east and then turned again on Peachtree Road and proceeded north through Buckhead, past Lenox Mall and Phipps Plaza, marveling how the two shopping centers had managed to avoid any regional identity over the years. Eventually, he came to Brookhaven and found the street where Jack Kale lived. He pulled over to the curb and shut off his engine.

Chapter 33

It took a moment before Jack realized the scream that had woken him was his.

Light from a streetlamp glinted through the curtains of his bedroom. He was lying on the floor, still wearing the same clothes he wore at Underground Atlanta. His head was throbbing. The ceiling and walls seemed to be spinning. A clammy film of sweat covered his face. His clothes were damp.

It was the same old nightmare. The same ship that appeared in those dreams, the one that he could never explain. Same cobblestone street. Same gaslight. Connie Belasco's face, or what was left of it, was contorted in unimaginable pain. Her large, dark eyes stared back at him in mute accusation.

Jack lay there, looking out the window at the houses along his street. Through the parted curtains, he could see his neighbor asleep in an arm chair with a book on her lap. His eyes eventually drifted back to the streetlamp. Painful to look at. Maybe if he stared long enough, it would burn away the image of Connie, reduced to a limbless freak by a monster.

Jack lifted his head and let it sink back down to the rug. Marta was lying next to him. He rolled over, rubbed his face against Marta's neck, and told her everything would be all right, wondering if dogs could tell when people were lying.

He had no idea what time it was. Late probably. The prospect of going back to sleep was unattractive. One drink to steady himself wouldn't hurt. He had a vague recollection of the panic attack striking just before he fell asleep. It was all a jumble.

When he was sufficiently recovered, he rose and staggered over to the liquor cabinet, only to find the bottle of Macallan Scotch was gone. He'd hidden it someplace. Where?

Didn't matter. Wellington's Bar was only a short drive away. They'd be open until three o'clock in the morning. He found his bottle of pills in the bedroom and took several.

The murder book, containing the crime scene, forensic, and medical examiner's reports, was on the floor where he'd dropped it. The book also contained investigative notes, witness statements, evidence descriptions, and photos of the victims. In short, everything relating to their deaths. Jack bent down, straightened the pages, and then shut the binder and left the house.

Getting to Wellington's meant he had to drive past the cemetery where Connie Belasco was buried. He owed her a visit, even if it was late. Several months had passed since the last time he was there. It was nearly one in the morning. She'd understand.

Jack turned onto Mt. Vernon Road, the street that ran alongside the cemetery, with its awful crematorium, and parked. The night was still. The only things moving were moths hovering around a street light. Serenity Park, as they called it, was lit by a pale half-moon. He couldn't see Connie's grave but was able to pick out the large oak he used for a landmark. She'd be about fifty feet to the left. Leaning back against the headrest, Jack shut his eyes and let the cool early morning air wash over him.

Before the panic attack hit, he'd been thinking about time. Or, to be more specific, the passage of it. The time his daughter was born. The time he spent in the Marines. His years with the FBI. And what the last seven years had been like.

Life or merely existence, he wasn't sure which.

Eventually, his mind turned to that day at Cloudland Canyon, as it so often did. Burt Wiggins pointed out that he'd pulled back before killing Pell. Maybe that counted for something. But he'd looked into the pit and saw his own reflection staring back at him. That's when time froze for Jack Kale.

Beth Sturgis, in all her naiveté, wanted to fight evil, a losing proposition if ever he'd heard one. Like energy, true evil couldn't be destroyed. It merely changed form and reappeared someplace else. Einstein had once said, "The definition of insanity is doing the same thing over and over and expecting a different result." That might mean he was insane, because he was following the same path again. Perhaps he should call Mayfield and see if they had a spare room available. One with a view. What times he and Pell could have together. Doing the same thing over and over until nothing remained of either of them. All gone. No one home. Like Connie.

Jack looked again at the old oak. Its branches formed a canopy against the sky. Was he doing the right thing, letting circumstances drag him along? Hard to say. At some signal beyond his understanding, a hundred birds nesting in the tree chose that moment to take flight, startling him. He watched them soar into the air, silhouettes against the pale moonlight. Then his eye moved to the left where Connie's grave was. Did she just whisper something? Or was he imagining it?

"Maybe you're right," he whispered back and started the engine.

*

One of Wellington's chief attractions was that it stayed open late, or early depending on your point of view. Its patrons were laborers and people who went to work without a tie. They sat at the bar or at tables drinking quietly. An old-style television hung on the wall above the liquor bottles perpetually tuned to one of the ESPN channels. There were no twenty- or thirtysomethings in chic clothes. Nobody struck up idle conversations. People were there to drink, as he was.

The pills had long since kicked in.

Jack finished his Scotch and held his glass up to the waitress for a refill.

"You want to go easy on that stuff," she said.

"No," Jack said. "I don't."

His tongue felt thick and the words came out slightly slurred.

"Last one, honey. We're closing in ten minutes."

"All the more reason to hurry."

"Sure," she said, taking his glass.

The murder book was open on the table next to him to the forensics section. He tried concentrating on Furman's findings, but the words swam on the page. The bar's low lighting only made things worse. Eventually, he gave up and concentrated on the Scotch.

The waitress reappeared with his drink.

"You want me to call you a cab?" she asked.

Jack downed the contents in one shot and handed her a twenty.

"It's a nice night," he said. "I think I'll walk for a bit."

"The hotel usually has a few taxis waiting out front," she said. "It's about four blocks down the street."

"Thank you," Jack said.

"You gonna be all right?"

"In what sense do you ask?"

"To get home," she said. "You don't look so great."

"Rough day at the office," Jack said.

"Yeah. Well, take it slow, okay?"

With the binder under his arm, Jack left the bar and began walking along Peachtree Road. Atlanta had thirty-eight separate streets named Peachtree. Made sense. After all, Georgia was the Peach State. Wherever you looked, it was peaches. Peach this. Peach that. So how come they called it the Dogwood City?

For some reason, that struck him as funny. Jack slowed to a halt and looked around, trying to decide where he was. Surely he should have reached the hotel by now. He'd been walking for nearly twenty minutes. He stepped out into the middle of the street for a better look and realized he'd gone the wrong way. Without checking the traffic, he started back for the sidewalk and found himself in the headlights of a car bearing down on him at high speed. The driver swerved at the last moment and sped by, horn blaring. Jack lost his balance, crashed into a pair of garbage cans, and fell to the ground. Head and pavement made contact, stunning him. The murder book went flying.

Fifteen minutes later, Jack was sitting on the curb trying to collect his wits when the short blast of a siren got his attention. Another pair of headlights lit up his immediate area. They were accompanied by flashing blue lights.

Jack put his hand up, squinting against the glare. Two uniform cops exited their cruiser and approached him.

"You all right, buddy?" one of the cops asked.

"Just resting for a minute," Jack said.

"You picked a helluva place to do it," the cop said, eyeing the overturned trash cans. "Pull your feet in so they don't get run over."

Jack pulled his feet in.

"You need medical attention? That's a nasty scrape on your forehead."

"I'll be fine," Jack said.

"Glad to hear it. If you're okay, why don't you run along home?"

Jack stared at the officer without responding.

"You hear what I said, pal?"

"I have a theory that the world revolves," Jack said.

"Yeah?"

"I'm waiting for my house to pass."

The cop exchanged a glance with his partner, then asked to see some ID.

Chapter 34

Dan Pappas entered the lobby of the adult detention center and flashed his badge to the receptionist at the window. He asked for the sergeant on duty and was directed to a door at the far side of the room marked "Personnel Only."

Each time he'd been there, it seemed like the same people were in the lobby. Some were on pay phones calling bondsmen. Others were talking in low tones to family members, trying to raise bail for those on the other side of the wall. Several years ago, some genius decided that "detention center" was politically correct, so the county changed the name. Supposedly, it played better than "jail." Call it what you want; both had bars.

The sergeant he asked for was waiting on the inside. William Cludder was a gray-haired, twenty-four-year veteran with the sheriff's department. They'd known each other professionally for quite some time.

"Sorry to get you up so early," Cludder said. "He had your card in his wallet."

Pappas glanced at a wall clock. It was just after seven.

"Not a problem. Appreciate you calling."

"Guy says he's a lieutenant with RHD."

"He is," Pappas said.

Cludder looked out the window and muttered a curse under his breath.

"He had no ID, only his driver's license. There's no record of him in the system. What's the deal?"

"New acquisition," Pappas said. "You process him yet?"

"Naw. I decided to wait for you. You bein' straight with me?"

"Completely," Pappas said.

Cludder informed him, "I got eight months to retirement. I don't need any headaches."

"There won't be any," Pappas said. "Can you lose the paperwork?"

The sergeant searched Pappas's face for a moment and then handed him the arrest report he'd been holding. "What paperwork?"

"Thanks, Bill. What about the uniforms?"

"They're good. They said he was a bit of a wiseass but didn't give them any trouble. Where do I know this guy from?"

"It ain't important," Pappas said. "All you need to know is he's on our side."

"If you say so," Cludder said.

"I say so," Pappas said.

Cludder didn't push the point. He'd been in the system long enough to know how it operated. "He's not drunk, but he's on something. These pills maybe."

The sergeant pulled a bottle of Paxil out of his pocket and tossed them to Pappas.

"They're prescription," Pappas said, examining the bottle.

"Don't mean he's not abusing."

"Where is he?"

"Number six on the A wing."

Pappas found cell six without any trouble. The door was already open, having been electronically released on the sergeant's order. Jack was sitting on a metal bench with his head in his hands, the only one in the room. Except for a metal toilet in the corner and two unmade bunk beds, it was completely empty. The floor was gray cement.

"Morning, Jack," Pappas said.

Jack looked up. Medical intake had applied a butterfly bandage to his forehead. His eyes were bloodshot.

When Jack didn't respond or make a move to get up, Pappas asked, "You ready to leave, or you planning to move in?"

"That's it?" Jack said.

"C'mon, before they change their minds," Pappas said.

*

Once they were in the car, Pappas asked for directions to Jack's house.

"I need to pick up my ride first."

Pappas nodded. Jack told him where it was located.

"What happened to your head?" Pappas asked.

"Close encounter with a curb."

"The cops who picked you up thought you were out of it."

"Trained observers."

"Is this a one-time thing, or do we have a problem here?" Pappas said.

"We?" Jack said.

"Consultant or not, you're working for the APD now. People need to rely on you and vice versa. You get my meaning?"

"Sure."

"I don't need to be worrying about you going off the deep end if push comes to shove."

"Understood."

"You told me the other day your medical situation wasn't an issue. This have anything to do with it?"

"They're separate," Jack said.

"So what gives?" Pappas said.

"Sometimes I drink too much," Jack said. "It's not a big deal."

"Me, too," Pappas said. "I'm asking again: is this a one-time thing?"

"I can control it," Jack said.

Pappas shook his head. "Kale, it ain't real good to mix pills and liquor. You know that."

"I won't let it interfere with what we're doing."

Pappas studied the man sitting next to him staring out the window. Book smart didn't necessarily mean overall smart.

Jack tightened his lips and continued to look out the window.

"How long's this been going on?"

"A few years," Jack said.

Pappas wondered if a few years coincided with his leaving the FBI. One plus one didn't necessarily equal two. Things were rarely as simple as that.

They eventually reached Wellington's Bar. Jack's car was still in the parking lot where he left it. He thanked Pappas and started to get out. The detective put a hand on his shoulder and stopped him.

"You remember how this works, right? Partners watch each other's backs. We even look out for consultants."

"Sure," Jack said.

"If you need the meds, great, but it's nuts washing them down with Scotch. I need to have your word that won't happen again."

"You have it."

"All right," Pappas said. "I'm taking what you say at face value. I'll look out for you. So will Sturgis. She's trying so hard to impress you.

She's been staying until ten o'clock every night hoping to get up to speed on all that forensic stuff you seem to know. That's a good woman."

"I know," Jack said.

"You run into trouble, you can call me. It don't matter what time."

"I appreciate that, Dan."

"This stays between us," Pappas said.

"I ain't gonna mention it to her. But there's only so much covering we can do before the genie gets out of the bottle. The paperwork's history. As far as everyone's concerned, it never happened."

Pappas stayed there until Jack started his car and pulled out of the lot.

Chapter 35

Dr. Morris Shottner looked over the rim of his glasses and waited for Jack to continue. This time Jack had chosen to sit on the couch instead of the chair he normally used. He didn't think that was significant. Jack's eyes, Shottner noted, were bloodshot, and it looked like he hadn't shaved in at least a day.

"When did it happen?" Shottner asked.

"As soon as I got home," Jack said.

"Any specific trigger?"

Jack shook his head. "There never is, Moe."

"We simply haven't found it yet."

Jack's smile was meaningless.

Shottner continued, "I saw your interview on the news this morning. I take it you haven't been to bed yet?"

"No, I was too busy having a heart attack."

"Panic attack," Shottner said. "You look like hell."

"Thank you for noticing."

"Would you care for some coffee?"

"Please."

Shottner went into the kitchen and returned with a china cup and saucer. After Jack had taken a sip, Shottner inquired, "Was the woman standing behind you one of the investigators?"

"She was."

"The same lady who kidnapped you?"

"The same. Her name's Beth Sturgis. She's the lead in the case."

"Really? Then why did you do all the talking?" Shottner asked.

"Sacrificial lamb," Jack said. "In case things go south. The department can always say their consultant didn't work out."

"I see. And she's fine with you taking over?"

"I don't think it sits well, but she's new and is going along with the program. She thinks she needs to prove herself."

"She picked quite a case to do it."

"Not much choice," Jack said. "The orders come from the top. I'm the official spokesman until further notice."

"You appeared to handle the situation well," Shottner said.

"Think so?"

"That was my impression. Can you recall what you were feeling while you were addressing the reporters?"

"Not much of anything. I was there to do damage control."

Shottner was hoping to gain some insight into what kicked off the latest panic attack, but that could only come from Jack, who seemed to have no idea at all. It was no use forcing the issue. Instead he asked, "The woman you rescued, is she all right?"

"She appears to be," Jack said. "I called the hospital to check on her. She'll be discharged later today. I've arranged for police protection in case the killer decides to try again."

"Wonderful. Is it true she was wrapped as a mummy?"

"Yes. That was something Pell never did. The killings started off the same, but this one is trying to separate himself."

"Individuating."

"I just said that."

"But not as artfully," the doctor said. "Having police protection sounds very sensible. Out of curiosity, why do you suppose this man chose her?"

"I've been asking myself the same question."

"You think you'll find out?"

"Yes," Jack said without hesitation.

"Just like that?" Shottner said. "You can understand what makes a person tick?"

"I'm afraid so," Jack said.

It was an odd choice of words. Shottner sat back in the seat, observing Jack for a moment. He waited once again for him to continue, but nothing more was forthcoming. The doctor reached forward and made a note on his pad.

Chapter 36

The Soul Eater wandered through Piedmont Park. It was dusk and most of the visitors had gone home to their families or whatever such people do. In the lake, a single toy sailboat remained. A sandy-haired boy of about eight stood on the shore working the levers on a radio control device for the boat while his mother looked on from a bench.

A young couple walking hand in hand along the path passed close by him with no more than a glance. Why should they do otherwise? He was dressed as a cop and cops were safe. He smiled to himself and kept going. *We're here to protect you.* It was all part of being invisible.

This time it would be more complicated . . . and riskier. But there was no choice. The pressure in him was building.

Just over the treetops, the sun threw long shadows onto the water, illuminating parts of it like jewels. On Tenth Street, a few cars already had their lights on. He glanced around to make sure no one was watching. The conditions weren't optimal, but they'd do.

He stopped to watch the toy sailboat. The boy noticed him and explained what kind of boat it was. The Soul Eater pretended to be interested. After a few minutes, the boy's mother decided it was time to go and called to her son. The child's shoulders slumped, but he didn't argue. He adjusted the control levers causing the sailboat to begin a lazy turn back to shore.

The mother was plump and wearing jeans that were about a size too small when she bought them. She got up and walked to where they were standing.

"Aaron couldn't wait to try out his birthday present," she said.

"At that age, neither could I," he said. "Haven't changed much over the years."

"Boys and their toys," she sighed, smiling.

The Soul Eater smiled too, just to show what a regular guy he was. Of course they were safe with him. He explained to the boy, "Your mom's right, son. It's getting dark."

The mother felt obliged to explain they normally didn't stay out late, but she had made an exception because it was a special occasion.

"Understandable," said the killer, ruffling the boy's hair. "Do you live nearby?"

"On Barksdale Drive," she said.

"That's not too far. I'll walk with you to your car."

"Oh, please don't go to any trouble."

"No trouble at all, ma'am. Nothing like a police escort."

As they walked, the woman kept up an incessant stream of conversation. In five minutes she managed to talk about the weather, clothes, her job, and being a mother. He found himself getting annoyed. Would she ever shut up? Her son said nothing. Perhaps he was intimidated by the presence of a policeman. More likely, he wanted to get home and play with his XBox or PlayStation.

After crossing Tenth Street onto Taft, the woman pointed and told him her car was at the end of the street. Of course, he knew that. He'd watched her park. His van, stolen earlier that day, was in the driveway directly behind her. It was too risky using the same vehicle again.

The Soul Eater's hand moved to the Taser on his utility belt. He wasn't certain if a young child would survive the jolt of electricity, so he'd taken the extra precaution of bringing along a cloth soaked in chloroform. It was now in a plastic bag in his back pocket.

There were lights on in several houses along the street. It was possible someone would see them walking together, which made the risk even more delicious. Wouldn't the newspapers have a field day with that? He could just see the headlines: "Is the Scarecrow a Cop?"

As they neared the woman's car, she reached into her purse, removed a remote-entry fob, and pressed a button. A polite beep of the horn and flash of the headlights followed.

"Looks like we made it safe and sound," she said.

"Not quite."

Chapter 37

Detectives Stafford and Mundas were speaking with Beth and Pappas when Jack returned to the office. He searched his memory trying to remember which was which and gave up.

Beth informed him, "We have a possible lead. Mundas spoke with Betsy Ann Tinsley's neighbor. She told him Betsy Ann and Sandra Goldner recently joined the Parkwood Health Club."

Jack turned to Mundas and asked, "Why is that important?"

"I'm Mundas, sir. He's Stafford," the other detective said.

"Sorry."

The real Mundas continued, "Because Jerome Haffner and Donna Camp are also members of that club."

"Tinsley and Goldner lived in Jordan. You're telling me they drove forty-five minutes to Atlanta to get a workout?" Jack said.

"The Atlanta club runs a mixed doubles tennis league," Beth said. "That's where Betsy Ann met Haffner. According to Goldner's brother, she talked Sandra into a trial membership. Apparently, it's a good way to meet single guys."

"Interesting," Jack said.

"Four people at the same club's a helluva coincidence," Pappas said.

"I agree," Jack said. "Any chance a judge will issue a subpoena for their list of members? I'm reluctant to ask the club management at this point. If the killer is there, it might spook him."

Pappas commented, "We can always sic Beth on them. She can terrorize them the way she did that guy at McKeachern."

Beth gave her partner a flat look and asked, "If they won't cooperate, do we have enough as it stands now?"

"Dicey," Jack said. "Maybe you could kidnap the manager and force him to ride around with you until he cracks."

"It's a she," Beth informed him, taking the ribbing in stride. "There has to be some way around this. We need that list. If it's not a member, it may be an employee."

"Let's start with the state licensing board," Pappas suggested.

"Explain," Beth said.

"Parkwood has a cafe where they sell sandwiches, salads, and cock-tails. If you work in a place that sells alcohol, you have to go through a background check. We make nice to the board secretary, I'll bet we can get their employee list in a few minutes."

"How do you know they have a cafe?" Beth asked.

"I used to play tennis a few years ago," Pappas said. "They have eight courts."

The surprise must have shown on Jack's face because Pappas added, "Pretty good at it, too."

*

Beth made the call. In under an hour, an e-mail arrived from the Georgia State Licensing Board. Jack was just finishing his first cup of coffee. The list contained all of Parkwood's employees.

She handed it to Stafford and told him to start running criminal background checks. Mundas was assigned the DMV records in the hope that one of them might own a white van like the one seen in the town of Jordan before the first killings.

Jack watched Beth as she was speaking. She was becoming more comfortable with her role as the case lead. If she was nervous or uncer-tain, she was covering it nicely.

When she was through, she turned to him and asked, "Can you see any kind of a pattern emerging?"

"Not really," Jack said candidly.

"Even with the bodies we found?"

"I asked a colleague at school to look at the clothes," Jack said. "He called me on the way in this morning from the ME's office to say two of them are approximately a hundred years old. Another dates from around 1930 or so. After that there's a gap of nearly eighty years before we see the next two. I was told they also recovered a quarter in the pocket of the most recent victim dated 2006. That gives us a baseline to work from."

"About the time Howard Pell got started," Beth said.

"It's consistent. I've never believed he revealed all his victims or where they were buried. This could be his work."

"Well, it's obvious it ain't the same guy running around since 1900," Pappas said. "I'll jump on the missing persons. By the way, Fancher said the chief wants daily reports."

Beth said, "Jack, could you handle that? I want to take Dan with me to Mayfield and speak to Pell again."

"Why?"

"Because I think he knows more than he's saying. We should also take a closer look at his visitors list."

Before Jack could respond, Ed Mundas came back in the room holding a piece of paper. He was followed by Dwayne Stafford, who was grinning like the Cheshire Cat.

"What?" Beth asked.

"George Merkle, personal trainer," Stafford said. "Hired a little over two years ago. He has a record for assault and was a guest at Mayfield for twenty-four months."

Stafford turned to his partner, who appeared equally smug. Beth gave in and said, "And?"

"I called Parkwood and pretended to be interested in joining. Seems ol' Mr. Merkle runs their introductory health and fitness program. They use it to entice new members into signing up for lessons. I'd say there's a pretty good chance that brought him into contact with each of the victims."

"That's great," Beth said. She turned to Pappas. "Mayfield can wait. Let's go have a talk with Merkle."

Pappas stayed put and gestured toward Dwayne Stafford with his chin.

"Was there something you wanted to add?" Beth asked.

"Not if you don't consider that he drives a white van important."

Beth blinked. "Fantastic. Is he working now?"

"Day off," Stafford said. "The gal at the front desk told me he doesn't come in until tomorrow. According to the DMV, his address is still current."

"Let me see his photo," Beth said.

Stafford handed it to her.

"Light blue eyes," Beth said, showing it to Jack and Pappas.

"Interesting," Jack said.

Pappas suggested, "Why don't you and the professor go? I still need to work up a search warrant for Jerome Haffner's employer."

"Wanna take a ride?" Beth asked Jack.

Chapter 38

After some discussion, it was decided they would take Beth's personal car to attract less attention. Jack told her he had to call his housekeeper and ask her to feed and walk Marta. They agreed to meet in the parking lot.

Beth had the car running when he arrived. She glanced at him sideways as he got in and then pulled up to the exit, waiting for a gap to open in the stream of cars. Fortunately, rush hour was beginning to die down, but at the ramp to I-285, she had to wait again before sliding into the traffic. Jack quickly learned that she liked to drive fast. Worse, she insisted on looking at him when she spoke, which raised both his blood pressure and his anxiety level. Every once in a while, she would change lanes for no apparent reason. But having a partner meant trusting them, so he held his breath and remained hopeful they would arrive in one piece.

"Did you reach Mrs. Dougherty?" Beth asked.

"Yep. I also called my daughter. Her junior high class is in New York on a field trip."

"New York? I used to go to the zoo when I was in middle school."

"Different times," Jack said. "I wanted to give her some tips."

"Such as?"

"Where the best shopping is. Take the subway instead of cabs—with a friend, of course. Go for a ride on the Staten Island Ferry."

"How'd it go?"

"Her mother already covered the shopping. The rest was accepted tolerantly. At least she managed to keep any annoyance out of her voice."

"I knew everything there was to know at that age, too," Beth said. "Is her summer visit still on?"

"Sure is," Jack said.

"You must be excited."

"Nervous. She has a number of friends in the neighborhood, which helps. Getting reacquainted after a gap's always a little difficult."

"Must be tough being separated," Beth said.

"It is. What about you? Any family close by?"

"My folks and my brother live in Charlotte."

From his conversations with Pappas, he knew Beth was divorced and she didn't date cops. It was possible her decision also included consultants. While Jack was speculating on the subject, he noticed something on the back seat that caught his attention, a pair of men's tennis shoes. Curiosity finally won out. "Your boyfriend forget his shoes?"

Beth glanced over her shoulder then back at the road. They were getting dangerously close to a car crawling along at the posted speed limit.

"Those are my brother's."

"He has big feet," Jack blurted out. The comment sounded idiotic as soon as the words left his mouth. He fought the urge to pound his head on the dashboard.

"They're a deterrent."

"Against what?"

"Cops asking me out."

"Is that a problem?"

"Only if I let it become one. It's not a good idea to mix social with business. What about you?"

"I wasn't mixing anything until you kidnapped me," Jack said.

Beth smiled. "So there's no one special in your life right now?"

"Just me and Marta," Jack said.

"She's beautiful, but not much of a conversationalist," Beth said.

"You'd be surprised how well she makes her feelings known."

"Most women do," Beth said. "Speech isn't necessarily a requirement."

"So I've learned."

"How does Morgan feel about you being single?"

"Like all kids, she wanted her mother and me to get back together in the beginning. She realizes that won't happen now. Basically, she's fine with it, but I think she'd like me to find someone."

"Did she actually say that?"

"Not in so many words," Jack said. "I think you'd like each other."

"Why?" Beth asked.

Jack shrugged. "Well, you're both intelligent. You both have a good sense of humor. The word *headstrong* also comes to mind. That sort of thing. Just a feeling."

"Tell me more," Beth said. "I'm all about feelings."

"Uh . . . your exit's coming up," Jack said.

Beth took in a breath through her nostrils and let it out.

Chapter 39

They passed the next few miles listening to the radio and didn't speak. Beth reviewed the exchange in her mind, something she had a tendency to do. For all Jack's wit and charm—yes, he could be charming—there was a melancholy about him she sensed but didn't understand. The way his brain worked fascinated her. The man could concentrate hard enough to light a match. But there was something beneath the surface she couldn't put her finger on.

She was still thinking about this when they pulled into George Merkle's neighborhood.

*

The house was a one-story ranch with a red shingle roof that looked like it had been built in the early fifties. Several of the shingles had recently been replaced with a color that didn't quite match. More needed replacing.

In front of a two-car garage sat a lawn mower. Inside the garage was a white van. The lawn was about half finished. Merkle had either run out of gas or decided to take a break.

Once they exited the car, Beth asked if Jack was still carrying a gun.

"I gave Harrison back his revolver," Jack said.

Beth rolled her eyes, opened the passenger door, and retrieved her backup weapon from the glove compartment.

"Didn't they teach you anything in the FBI?" she asked.

"I didn't think I'd be needing a gun today."

"Jack."

He held his hands up in mock surrender. "I have an HK at home. I'll bring it tomorrow. I promise."

She almost smiled because he sounded like a chastised boy.

"It's for your own good," she said. "And mine, too. It's also department policy."

"Even for consultants?"

"Especially for consultants."

"Are you sure you don't want to wait and maybe put a tail on this man to see if his behavior is suspicious or erratic?" Jack asked.

"Everything fits, Jack. I want to look him in the face and gauge his reactions."

At Merkle's door, Beth knocked loudly and waited. A minute went by before they heard footsteps coming toward them from within. Both moved to opposite sides of the door as it opened. Merkle was in his mid-thirties with a clean-shaven head. He was not overly muscled but very solid looking. According to his driver's license, he was six feet tall or about two inches shorter than Jack.

"Good afternoon, Mr. Merkle," Beth said. "We're from the Atlanta Police. May we come in and talk to you?"

"What about?"

"It would be better if we speak inside," Beth said.

"Is something wrong?"

"Let's talk about it indoors."

Merkle looked from one to the other and then shrugged and stepped aside for them to enter.

Beth stayed where she was. "After you."

Merkle turned and walked back to his living room. Jack and Beth followed and took seats across from him on the couch. He sat facing them in an armchair.

"Either of you want a drink?"

"No," Beth said. "Thank you."

Jack also declined.

"So what can I do for you?" Merkle asked.

"We're investigating a series of murders and kidnappings. You may have heard about them on the news," Beth said.

"No kidding?"

"We're quite serious."

"Actually, I haven't. TV's been on the blink. What's this got to do with me?"

"Probably nothing," Beth said. "We've had reports of a white van seen in the vicinity of the crimes and we're trying to tie up some loose ends."

"I own a white van," Merkle said. "It's out in the garage. You wanna take a look at it?"

"We do," Beth said.

"There must be a million white vans around."

"Not quite that many," Beth said. "It turns out all the victims were also members of Parkwood, where you work."

Surprise showed on Merkle's face. "Oh man. Maybe I know them."

Beth read him the names. Merkle listened and shook his head thoughtfully.

"Donna Camp and Jerome Haffner sound familiar," he said. "I'm pretty sure they were in my intro fitness class. The other two don't ring a bell."

"Are you certain?" Beth asked. She glanced at Jack, whose attention seemed to be focused on a glass and drinking straw on the kitchen counter. Next to the glass were a tin can and a cigarette lighter.

"Pretty sure," Merkle said, leaning forward and resting his elbows on his knees. "I've got a good memory for my clients, you know?"

"That's helpful," Beth said. "Can you tell me where you were yesterday afternoon around five thirty?"

"At the club training."

"According to the manager, you checked out at four o'clock."

"Jesus Christ, lady. You brought my name up to the manager? I need this job."

"Your name wasn't mentioned. The club gave us copies of the time cards for everyone who works there."

The explanation was not quite true, but it seemed to satisfy Merkle. He sat back in his chair. "I stayed to train on my own. I do that four times a week."

"Do you smoke, Mr. Merkle?" Jack asked, speaking for the first time.

"What? No."

Merkle followed his eyes to the kitchen counter and saw what Jack was looking at.

"My mountain bike has a flat. I was gonna put a patch on the tube. Once it's in place, you seal it by burning off the cement around the edges."

"Sure," Jack said.

"Okay, so, if there's nothing else, I need to get back out and finish my lawn. Follow me and I'll take you out to the van."

"We'll get to that," Beth said. "Would it be okay with you if we take a quick look around?"

"Why?"

"It's just routine," Beth said. "We're trying to eliminate as many suspects as possible."

Whenever a cop says it's routine, it isn't. Merkle, who'd been to jail, probably knew that, too. His demeanor had changed. He was nowhere as friendly as when they walked in. He was also having trouble maintaining eye contact, which she interpreted as a tell. Jack, she was certain, noticed it as well.

"You're saying I'm a suspect?"

"Not at all," Beth said. "We're just trying to cover all the bases."

"I guess it's all right."

They searched the kitchen, then the bathrooms, and finally the two bedrooms. Beth nudged Jack with her elbow and motioned to a brown wig on a manikin's head sitting atop Merkle's dresser. Jack nodded. It took a real effort to keep her excitement from showing. Eventually, they made their way to the garage. Both walked around the van and then stooped down to examine the front tires.

"See the wear pattern?" she whispered.

"Mm-hm."

Merkle was still in the chair waiting for them when they returned.

"Everything good?" he asked.

"It looks that way," Beth said. "Would you mind coming with us to the precinct? We'd like to run a couple of tests. It shouldn't take more than a half hour."

Merkle stood up. "How come?"

"Like I said, it's just routine."

"Why don't you bullshit someone else, lady? I've been around, you know. I'm not answering any more of your questions. In fact, I'm gonna call my lawyer. I'd like you both to leave."

"We can do that," Beth said. "It's your right to have a lawyer present."

"That's great. Have a nice day."

"We can also take you in for questioning, which is our right. But we're trying to do this the easy way and not embarrass you in front of your neighbors. There's been a huge amount of publicity over this case."

The color in Merkle's face rose and he took a step toward Beth. "You threatening me?"

Beth held her ground. "It's not a threat, Mr. Merkle. We're asking you to cooperate."

"And I'm asking you to leave. This is a bunch of crap. You're not trying to help me. Cops always say that. I've never been to Jordan, and I had nothing to do with those people."

There was a pause before Beth said, "I never mentioned Jordan, sir."

Merkle realized he had just made a mistake. He looked at Jack and then at Beth. "For the last time, I've got nothing more to say. I want you both out of my fucking house now!"

With that he reached for Beth's arm.

Suddenly, Jack Kale was there, stepping between them. He caught Merkle's hand before it could make contact. The speed with which he moved surprised Beth and apparently Merkle.

One minute Merkle was standing, the next he seemed to do a cart-wheel through the air and landed heavily on his back. He started to scramble to his feet.

"Freeze!" Beth said.

Her gun was pointed at his chest. Merkle did as he was told.

"I haven't done anything. You got no right to come into my home and harass me like this."

"You invited us in, remember?" Beth said. "Assaulting a police officer is a serious offense, George."

"Assault? I never touched you! He's the one who assaulted me. I'm pressing charges." He looked at Jack. "You almost broke my wrist, man."

"We're not interested in arresting you," Jack said. "And we're not interested in the crack you were smoking, though your probation officer might be. Like Detective Sturgis said, we just came to talk with you."

Merkle mulled this over. He then asked Beth, "Is that true?"

"It is," Beth said, putting her gun away. "I'll need to check you for weapons."

Merkle said, "I don't have any, and I wasn't gonna hurt you, you know. I just get mad, is all."

Chapter 40

They went directly to the medical examiner's office, where a DNA sample was taken. Fingerprints weren't necessary since Merkle was already in the system. Before they left, Beth had him sign a consent form allowing a technician from the crime lab to come out and examine his van. Paula Desoto was dispatched.

Merkle decided not to call his attorney after all. Following further questioning, he explained he was working at the time Jerome Haffner and Betsy Ann Tinsley were killed and had flown to Florida that night. Beth sent a text message to Dwayne Stafford asking him to confirm it and then went back to her desk with Jack to await the lab's test results. After talking with the Parkwood's corporate office, the manager agreed to send the time cards for that day as well. They confirmed Merkle was out of work the days he indicated.

"He still had time to drive to Jordan before going to the airport."

"That wouldn't match with the neighbors' statements about seeing a black van the day after," Jack said.

"I'm still not convinced," Beth said. "He's tall. He has the right eye color, assuming Donna Camp was correct. He owns a wig. Everything fits."

"It's possible," Jack conceded. "But you may be overlooking—"

"You don't believe he's the one, right? I can tell that."

"I'm keeping an open mind."

"Me, too," Beth said. "Can I ask you a question? At Merkle's house, what was that thing you did?"

"What thing? Oh, you mean with his wrist? It's called aikido."

"I've never seen it before."

"It's a matter of using leverage and pressure against your opponent."

163

"You know martial arts?"

"Not really," Jack said. "I read a lot."

Beth blinked. "You're saying you got that out of a book?"

"Well, I practiced the move a few times when I was with the FBI, but basically, yeah. It's pretty neat. I can show you if you like."

Bemused, Beth shook her head and was about to ask another question when her cell phone buzzed.

"This is Detective Sturgis."

A conversation followed in which Beth did most of the listening. If she responded at all, it was with one-word answers. She finally thanked the caller and disconnected.

"Bad news?" Jack asked.

"That was Paula Desoto, Ben's assistant. The tires on Merkle's van don't match the prints we found at Lake Lanier. Neither do the hairs we recovered from Donna Camp."

"What about color and coarseness?"

"Different from his toupee."

"No help there," Jack said.

"It appears that way," Beth said.

Just when she thought it couldn't get any worse, Dwayne Stafford entered the room and walked up to her desk.

"His alibi's solid," Stafford said. "Delta Airlines has him listed as a passenger on the 9:25 PM flight to Ft. Lauderdale the day Haffner and Tinsley were killed. He also used his credit card to buy a shirt at a place called Golf Galaxy in Pembroke Pines the next day. The airport has him checking in and out of long-term parking. Sorry."

"Shit," Beth said. "We'll have to cut him loose."

"I'll take care of it," Stafford said. "Oh, and Lieutenant Fancher wants to see you in her office before you leave."

"And the hits just keep on coming," Beth mumbled.

Chapter 41

Jack returned to his office and occupied himself by searching VICAP, the FBI's computer database, for crimes with similar patterns while Beth was tied up with the lieutenant. He stayed at it for nearly an hour and came up with nothing.

The result didn't surprise him. Getting a hit would have. Sometimes knowing which road not to take was as valuable as picking the right one. Certainly the killer had initially followed in Howard Pell's footsteps. Pell unfortunately wasn't unique. Even he had a model, which Jack had learned during the original Scarecrow investigation.

Jack was working through the bones of his theory when he saw Beth exit Lieutenant Fancher's office. The tension in her face was apparent.

"Everything all right?" Jack asked.

Beth shrugged. "Fancher's getting pressure from up on seven. She's under the gun, which means I am, too. She asked if I felt up to the challenge."

"She actually said that?"

"Not in so many words, but the message was clear enough."

"You're doing a fine job," Jack said.

"I screwed up with Merkle," Beth said. "That doesn't sit well with the bosses. If the press finds out, it'll only make matters worse."

"Pulling him in for testing was the right call."

"You didn't think he did it."

"Well, I'm skeptical by nature."

"You think I jumped the gun?" Beth said.

Jack let several seconds pass before he responded. "You were in my class the day I said that you have very little chance of getting at the truth if you know in advance what the truth ought to be."

"I remember," Beth said. "You think that's what I was doing?"

"Somewhat."

"Tell me why."

"Because Merkle's right handed. When we interviewed Donna Camp, she told us the killer used his left hand to apply mortar to the wall he was building. He also hit her using his left."

Beth's jaw dropped slightly. "You knew and you let me proceed. That's pretty low even for the FBI, Kale."

"I'm APD now. How do you feel about Chinese?"

"The people or the food?"

Jack smiled. "The food."

"Love it. Lemon chicken's my favorite."

"How about Albert Lemon?"

Beth blinked. "What are you talking about?"

"Make yourself comfortable, Detective. I'll order in and explain over a working dinner."

When the food arrived, they went to the conference room and spread out the containers. Beth located some plates in the kitchen. She got her lemon chicken. Jack had ordered shrimp and lobster sauce, which Beth felt free to sample while they talked.

"When I saw the bodies being taken out of Underground Atlanta," Jack said, "I began to realize something was going on as far as the killer is concerned. We're not dealing with a pure copycat as I've said. It may have started that way, but the killer isn't following Pell's pattern any longer. Close, but definitely not the same."

"No missing finger this time," Beth pointed out.

"Exactly."

"And wrapping Donna Camp up. That didn't happen with any of Pell's other victims. Maybe this one is trying to put his own stamp on things."

"I think that's precisely what he's doing. He's also taking pieces from another serial killer named Albert Lemon, who lived here during the early part of the last century. Lemon was an archaeologist who went haywire. From the articles I read about him years ago, his specialty was early Middle Eastern cultures like the Babylonians and Assyrians."

Jack went on to give her the details he'd been able to pull out of the old newspaper stories regarding Lemon's killing spree. By all accounts, it was even more prolific than Howard Pell's reign of terror.

"So we're looking for what? A museum director?" Beth asked.

166

"Not necessarily, but perhaps someone who may have an interest in Egyptology and mummies."

Beth shook her head and took another shrimp off Jack's plate. "It's great you remember this stuff."

"Some I remember, some I'm learning, just like you."

"I'm not sure the next victim can afford to wait until I'm up to speed, Jack. I doubt the bosses will wait either. I was telling my dad that earlier."

Jack nodded. "Dan Pappas mentioned he's a cop in Charlotte."

"Sure is."

"Does he like the job?"

"I guess so," Beth said. "He's been at it long enough. He's due to retire next year."

"And how does he feel about you following in his footsteps?"

She was tempted to tell him that was only part of her reasons, but decided to keep the conversation uncomplicated. "He wasn't crazy about the idea at first but didn't discourage me either. We talk on the phone a lot about the job and he gives me advice. I think he thinks it might be a phase I'm going through."

"After five years?"

"Six in August."

"Is it a phase?"

"I don't think so. I finally feel like I'm making a difference, particularly now that I'm in Homicide. After college, I traveled for a while and worked for a magazine in New York, but there's never been anything like this."

"Making a difference how?" Jack asked.

She paused to refill his glass and then topped off her own.

"I don't know," she finally said. "Taking evil out of the world. Does that sound stupid?"

"Not at all," Jack said quietly.

Beth's expression grew serious, and she was quiet for a long moment. He was tempted to make some offhand remark to lighten the mood but stopped, sensing she had more to say.

"Everyone assumes I became a cop because my dad is one. Maybe that's part of it. The fact is, I had a sister who committed suicide when she was thirteen. We were really close. A bunch of kids started making fun of her at school and bullying her. None of us knew how bad it was until, well . . ."

Jack nodded slowly, encouraging her to continue.

"When I say evil, I don't necessarily mean fighting dragons. Sometimes it comes on two legs. Does that make sense?"

"Yes."

"There's a kind of viciousness you see in bullies and predators who focus on people who can't defend themselves. It lurks in the shadows and runs away when the lights come on. That's what I can't stand."

He wanted to tell her it was an impossible task. There were times when he was still with the Bureau it felt like he was using a glass to bail water out of a sinking ship.

Several seconds passed. Jack took a sip of the Blue Moon Ale he had ordered with dinner.

"My dad likes beer," she said, changing the topic.

"Oh, good," Jack said. "It usually comes with an orange slice."

"Really? How did you feel about it when you were with the FBI?"

"I don't think they had Blue Moon Ale back then."

"I meant about taking evil out of the world."

Jack nearly laughed at her change of direction. "It's a laudable goal."

"Can I ask why you left?"

"The decision wasn't entirely mine," Jack said.

He knew this was coming because he'd dealt with the question before, particularly after his marriage broke up. He and Morris Shottner had discussed the subject at length. The doctor's ongoing advice was not to seal himself off from others because it resulted in stagnation. His previous efforts at dating had failed, mostly due to him. Better to get it out of the way now.

"I wasn't trying to pry," Beth said. "Just curious."

"You're a detective. You ask questions. That doesn't offend me."

"You don't have to answer."

"No," Jack said. "I think you're entitled to an explanation. How much do you know about what happened to Howard Pell?"

She shrugged, then said, "After I met you, I asked around some, but no one wanted to talk about it. The file gives a bare-bones account of his capture. There were articles, of course. But they were all different from what Pell told me."

Jack's eyes held hers for a moment, then he smiled. "What did Pell tell you?"

"That you framed him for the murder of your partner. And that you tried to disembowel him."

Jack took a sip of his beer and said, "I didn't just try, Beth. I did. I tracked him to Cloudland Canyon and made the arrest. Unfortunately, I let my guard down. There was a fight. We went over the edge together.

"The canyon isn't a straight drop—a long way down, but fortunately not straight. I managed to lose my gun in the process. Pell still had his knife. He ran; I followed. There's a stream at the bottom of the gorge. He came at me while I was trying to cross it. We fought again."

Jack's eyes grew distant; he stared at some point over her shoulder as the memories came flooding back. At times, they crept silently into his dreams at night, images he'd never been able to erase.

Seeing the expression that clouded his features, Beth wanted to reach out and take his hand but stopped herself.

"There haven't been many times in my life where I can say I totally lost it. You've heard the expression about a person being so mad they saw red?"

Beth nodded.

"Well, it's true. We were struggling over the knife there in the water. All the time he kept talking. I finally snapped when he got to what he'd done to Connie."

"Your partner."

Jack nodded.

"Right. A red haze started in my chest and rose to my face, filling my vision. I can't remember every little detail, but I do remember thinking I was looking at something vile and base. Something that shouldn't be allowed to live."

"Jack—"

"I cut his stomach open and pulled his intestines out and dropped them on his chest."

Several seconds passed in silence.

"Did you want to kill him?"

"At first, but then I came to my senses and called for help."

"That's what matters. Don't you see?"

"Not really," Jack said.

"Listen to me—"

"What do you see when you look in the mirror?" Jack asked quietly.

"I don't understand."

"There's an old expression that one should be careful when fighting monsters lest you become one yourself. I don't know where it comes from. Nietzsche, maybe."

"Oh, Jack, you can't believe that."

"You think so?"

"I know so. You're no monster."

Jack smiled without humor.

"I know so," Beth repeated.

"The Bureau was sued over what happened. The DPR, that's our internal affairs, got involved. They met with the brass in some back room, and it was decided it would be best for everyone if I left, so I did." He shrugged. "You wanted to know."

"Thank you for telling me," Beth said. "I know that was difficult."

Jack looked down at his watch. "Gee, look how late it is. I'd better be getting home. Glad we had a chance to talk."

With that he stood and began putting on his jacket. Beth came around the table to him.

"Stop."

Jack looked at her.

"I'm not saying what happened was right. But you were in the most extraordinary circumstances imaginable. A fiend had just killed your partner and was trying to kill you. I can't even get my head around what that must have been like. One act doesn't define a person."

Jack nodded and said nothing.

"Do you understand me?" Beth prompted.

"What do you remember about John Wilkes Booth?"

"That's not a fair comparison."

Jack smiled. "I enjoyed the dinner, Beth. Drive safe."

Beth watched him walk out the door and down the hallway. He looked so sad. So hurt. She stood there for a moment, shook her head, and shut off the lights.

Chapter 42

The next morning, Dan Pappas was at his desk making notes on a yellow legal pad. He informed Jack that the judge had signed a subpoena for Jerome Haffner's client records.

"Great," Jack said. "Maybe it'll turn up a lead."

"I hope so. We've got bubkes so far. Hey, we're heading back to Mayfield later to interview Pell again. You interested in coming?"

"I'll pass."

"We wasting our time?"

"Maybe," Jack said. "Maybe not. Beth thinks he has something to say. I don't need to see him again."

"Understood."

"Any word from Furman on the Underground Atlanta victims?" Jack asked.

"Nope."

Jack was silent for a moment, then said, "Something's different about this killer. I told Beth he broke his pattern with Donna Camp. That's not impossible, but it's unusual. The first two victims were mutilated by having their fingers amputated. He didn't do that with her. There was also a sexual component with Pell that's missing from the other cases where the women are concerned."

"Is that significant?" Pappas said.

"I think it may be," Jack said.

"I don't get why the guy's leaving clues," Pappas said.

"Possibly he wants to be caught," Jack said. "Some part of the killer's mind may realize there's a demon lurking inside and that thought horrifies him."

171

"Seriously? A demon?"

"It's just an expression. I have a colleague at Columbia University who advanced that theory several years ago."

"Could he have left clues and we missed 'em?" Pappas said.

"Unlikely. Beth and I went over the scene thoroughly. So did Furman and his tech."

"Maybe the guy's fucking with us," Pappas said.

"Of that I have no doubt," Jack said. "You ever work a crossword puzzle?"

"Sure."

"Sooner or later, a picture starts to form. So you search around and find the piece you're looking for, but when you try it, it doesn't fit. I mean it looks perfect, but it won't go. Ever since the beginning of this case, that's the feeling I've been getting."

"Which means what?"

"Everything's too orchestrated," Jack said. "We're being played."

They were still discussing the possibilities when Jack's computer sounded. He bent to check his e-mail, and the sender's address stopped him cold. It was Betsy Ann Tinsley. He turned the monitor around so Pappas could see it.

The detective frowned and sat back in his chair.

"Looks like someone's trying to send you a video."

Jack debated whether to open it for several seconds. If whatever was coming through contained a virus, it could damage his hard drive.

"Do we have a tech around?" Jack asked.

"Several," Pappas said.

"I need to isolate this file before we look at it," Jack said.

Pappas nodded, picked up his phone, and made a call.

*

The technician turned out to be a twenty-five-year-old young man named Nathan Cohen who was attempting to grow a goatee. He entered Jack's office dressed in black jeans, sneakers, and a T-shirt with a picture of two people fencing on it. His hair was sandy brown and in a state of disarray as though he'd just gotten out of bed.

"You were right not to open this," he said. "If there's a virus embedded, it could crash whatever network you open it on."

"Recommendations?"

"Transfer the file to a stand-alone computer," Cohen said.

Jack's e-mail index was already open. The mysterious file had come in at 10:16 AM and was the most recent on his list. The one directly under it said, "Hugs and kisses from New York."

Cohen looked up at Jack.

"From my daughter," Jack said. "She's there on a class trip."

"Cool."

Cohen removed a small flash drive from his pocket, plugged it into a USB port at the front of Jack's computer, and then transferred the file to his own laptop.

The technician explained, "This isn't connected to anything. I backed it up this morning, so if something nasty is hiding here and it trashes my drive, I'll wipe it clean and reinstall the programs and data later on. First thing we do is run a virus and malware scan."

While he was busy doing that, Jack became aware of a presence at his side. He turned to see Beth standing there. She had changed into a chocolate-brown pantsuit with a yellow blouse and looked wonderful. The barest hint of a smile touched the corners of her mouth.

"Good morning, Lieutenant," she said with mock gravity.

"Uh, good morning, Beth," Jack said.

"Dan."

"Morning, Beth," Pappas answered. "Have you met Nate from IT?"

"I don't believe so," Beth said, shaking his hand. "What are we doing?"

Cohen told her, "The lieutenant just received a video file from one of the dead victims, which is totally creepy. We were just about to open it."

"Go ahead. I'd like to see this."

Jack nodded to the young technician, who double-clicked on the file. A moment later, the screen filled with the image of a woman who was definitely not Betsy Ann Tinsley. She was tied hand and foot and obviously terrified. One of her eyes was purple and swollen shut. Her mouth was taped.

The camera stayed on her for a time and then panned across her body to a small figure huddled in the corner.

Beth inhaled sharply.

"Shit," Pappas said. "He's got a kid."

The camera continued moving until it came to rest on a toy sailboat lying on its side. Wherever they were, it was dark, which came as no surprise to Jack. Off to one side was a faint light source. It looked artificial and was out of the camera's field of view.

Eventually, the lens focused on a face in a ski mask. An unblinking pair of cold, gray eyes looked back at them.

"Here you are, Clever Jack," the man said in a hoarse whisper. "Let's see what you can do with this."

The video ended. No one spoke.

"Where the hell are they?" Pappas said eventually. "I couldn't see anything in that room."

"Someplace underground." He turned to Cohen and asked, "Is there some way you can bring up more detail?"

"I can raise the monitor's resolution, but if I do the picture will get smaller. Ben Furman has a program that fills in and sharpens the individual pixels. I've seen it work."

Jack said, "Take this file over to him. There's a yellow area above the killer's shoulder I'd like to focus on. The sailboat, too. It had some kind of writing on the side that might tell us where it was sold."

"We need to check missing persons. If that was a mother and child, someone must have noticed they're gone."

"I'll jump on it," Pappas said.

"No," Beth said. "Let Stafford and Mundas do it. I want you with me at Mayfield when I meet Pell."

"You sure?" Pappas asked.

"Positive," Beth said. She then asked Jack, "Did you hear what he called you?"

"Clever Jack?"

"Those are the same words Pell used when we met."

*

After they left, Jack spent some time thinking about what Beth had said. It was another indication they were being manipulated. Howard Pell was too smart to make a mistake like that. The killer might not possess Pell's intellect, but he doubted the comment was accidental. Certainly there was a connection between the two, though what that was he had no idea at the moment. He turned his attention back to the computer and resumed reading the old newspaper accounts.

*

Beth was silent as she and Pappas drove up I-75. Despite the sobering video, her thoughts kept returning to her conversation with Jack the other night. She was certain he had shared with her something he rarely talked about. For all his quiet manner and brilliance, he was clearly capable of violence if provoked sufficiently. Maybe everyone was. That realization scared her a little.

After thinking about this for a while, she decided to send him a text message.

"Interested in another working dinner? Just arrived at Mayfield. We can compare notes."

Thirty seconds later, Jack's response arrived. "Sure. What should I bring?"

"Yourself. My place. I'll cook. Six o'clock?"

"Deal. See you later."

Dr. Charles Raymond was waiting for them in the lobby. He seemed disappointed that Beth had brought Dan Pappas along. After introducing them, Beth told him she wanted to review the institution's security procedures.

"For heaven's sake, why?" Raymond said. "No one's escaped from here in forty years. It's a complete waste of time."

Pappas gave the doctor his best cop stare.

"Oh, very well," Raymond said.

While he and Pappas were staring at each other, Beth decided Raymond looked more like Henry the Eighth than Sigmund Freud. He just needed a large turkey leg in one hand to complete the picture.

She said, "I understand how busy you are, Charles. Perhaps Dr. Cairo could take us around."

"He won't be in until tomorrow," Raymond said. "It's his day off."

"Someone else then?"

Raymond let out a long breath. "There is no one else. We're short-handed at the moment."

"What about that nurse?" Beth said. "Curry?"

"Unfortunately, Ron's no longer with us."

"Oh?"

"He's part of a medical group the state has a contract with. They transferred him to Ellenwood Regional in Savannah. We'll get a replacement, but it probably won't be for a week or two. I suppose you'll have to make do with me. Come along," Raymond said and started down the hallway.

Pappas looked at Beth and shrugged. Before she could comment, Raymond turned and clapped his hands twice, "Chop-chop, people. Time is money."

"How original," Beth muttered and started after him.

They went through a pair of double doors at the far side of the lobby. Beyond it was a room enclosed by a barred door. Raymond spoke into the walkie-talkie he was carrying.

"Warren, this is Dr. Raymond at the east portal with two detectives. Would you be good enough to let us in?"

"Sure thing, Doc. I see you," came the reply.

A moment later, the bars slid to one side. After stepping through, they found themselves in a large room occupied by twelve men. Some were reading, three were playing cards, others were writing, and some simply sat on plastic chairs staring off into space. A few looked up at their entrance. The rest went about their business.

Raymond informed them, "This is our day room. We have a track outside where the residents can walk. If they're not inclined to do so, they spend time in here. None of these people are dangerous."

"Good to know," Pappas said, scanning the room. "Is Pell in here?"

"Hardly," Raymond said. "This is a low-security area. The women have a similar arrangement on the opposite side of the building. Medium- and high-security patients are located on the upper floors."

"How many people do you have?" Pappas asked.

"At the moment, fifty-six, but the figure varies. Some are here for evaluation. Some are awaiting trial. Others are permanent. Follow me, please."

Raymond moved to a door near the corner of the room and used a key card to open it. He pointed out their medical clinic and pharmacy, where patients lined up each day to receive medications. Across from the pharmacy was an elevator with a security camera above it.

"Warren, would you send the elevator, please?"

"On the way."

"This elevator," Raymond explained, "is one of two methods used to gain access to the upper floors. The other is a staircase used only for emergencies, such as a fire. Access is controlled by key cards issued to each staff member. They're never allowed out of their possession. In the four years I've been here, the staircase hasn't been used."

Pappas started to ask another question but Raymond anticipated it and continued.

"There are eight residents in the men's wing and three on the women's side."

The inside of the elevator was entirely metal and smelled of antiseptic. They emerged into a dismal area of gray-painted cement walls and floors. Directly in front of them was a glass-enclosed control room with three guards and a bank of video monitors. One of the guards, presumably Warren, waved his acknowledgment. Dr. Raymond waved back. Every so often, the screens changed their view. One showed the elevator they'd just stepped out of.

Dr. Raymond said, "Patients on this floor stay in their rooms twenty-three hours a day. One hour is allotted for exercise. They have a special yard, completely enclosed and separate from the rest of the population. Cells are checked every four hours to ensure everyone is where they're supposed to be and no one has harmed themselves."

Beth said, "Howard Pell isn't on this floor."

"Absolutely not. He's housed on three, which is for maximum-security patients. At the moment, there are only two in residence."

"In residence? Sounds like what they say about the Queen of England," Pappas said.

Raymond glanced at him and continued, "Third-floor prisoners are considered the most dangerous. They're locked down twenty-four-seven, except for a one-hour exercise period three times a week. They don't eat with the general population or interact with them in any way. In the past, we allowed the groups to mix, but that didn't work out."

"What happened?" Beth asked.

"A patient thought he would make a name for himself by killing Howard Pell. I assume being detectives, you know what a shiv is?"

Beth and Pappas both nodded.

"The whole thing happened so quickly," Raymond said. "When the guard turned his back, the inmate came at Pell on the exercise yard. There was a fight."

"And?" Pappas said.

"By the time the guards pulled him off, Pell had nearly bitten through the man's throat."

Beth clenched her teeth. "Is the third floor like this?" she asked.

"It consists of eight cells," Raymond said. "Four on either side of the hall. We've never had more than three people up there as far back as I can remember. Access is also by elevator. Two guards are required to verify the visitor's identity and clearance level. Once that happens, they both simultaneously press a button to send it. There's really not much to see."

"Let's take a look anyway," Pappas said. "It was a long ride out here. We'll tackle Pell afterward."

"Exactly what's wrong with him?" Beth asked.

Raymond shook his head. "There's no name for it, at least none that I know of. Neither sociopath nor explosive rage control come close. Dr. Cairo's diagnostic notes describe him as evil. That's not an exaggeration."

The rest of the tour went quickly. Raymond was right: there wasn't much to see. Save for two, the upper-floor cells were all empty. Pell had already been taken to the interview room.

"Normally, we wouldn't allow another visit. He was quite difficult after you left, Beth," Raymond explained. "But since you insist, I've made an exception. To be quite honest, I'm not crazy about it."

"I understand," Beth said. "Please show me his room."

The cell was yellow cinder block, about 175 square feet. A single window with bars looked into the woods behind Mayfield. The only furniture consisted of a desk and a chair opposite a narrow cot. The mattress was nothing more than a vinyl pad. Pell's clothes—two pair of orange jump suits and several white T-shirts—were hanging from a series of metal hooks above a storage locker.

Beth's eye came to rest on three different chess sets, two on the table and one on the floor. From the position of the pieces, they appeared to be games in progress. Curious, she asked Raymond about it.

"Oh, people write him all the time. He keeps several games going at once. Dr. Pell is quite the chess player."

"Talented," Pappas said.

"Very," Raymond said. "It's a shame he didn't put his talent to better use. Have you seen enough?"

"Looks pretty secure to me," Pappas said. "The elevator's the only way on or off the floor, right?"

"Right. Other than the fire exit, as I've mentioned."

"Has Pell had any visitors since I was out?" Beth asked.

"Two reporters requested interviews," Raymond said. "He turned them down."

"That's it?"

"Yes," Raymond said.

"What about over the last year?"

"If you recall, I gave those names to you, Beth."

"Any chance someone slipped through the cracks?" she asked.

A note of exasperation crept into Raymond's voice. "None. The people who work here are quite efficient. Now, if you don't mind, I have other things to do today."

Chapter 43

Howard Pell was waiting for them in the interview room along with a security guard. After placing their weapons in a locker, they went in. A thin smile appeared on Pell's face when he saw Beth. His brown eyes flicked toward her companion.

"Detective Pappas, isn't it?" he said.

"Good memory, Doc. It's been a few years," Pappas said.

Pell turned to Beth. "And you've changed your perfume."

"Correct, Doctor," Beth said. "Your powers of observation are still intact."

"A lover's gift? From Clever Jack, perhaps?"

"Hardly," Beth said. "Thank you for seeing us."

Pell inclined his head and said, "My pleasure. I seem to have no appointments today. I trust your case is proceeding well."

"You were right about the Historical Society and the satchel," Beth said. "Those clues helped rescue that woman."

"I'm so pleased."

"There were other bodies recovered, Dr. Pell," Beth said.

"Really?"

Beth searched his face for a tell and detected nothing other than idle curiosity. This was one of the reasons she'd asked Pappas to come with her. He might notice something she didn't.

"Five bodies," she said.

"A private graveyard," Pell said. "It sounds macabre."

"Three of them were very old. About eighty years or so. But the other two were more recent."

"How recent?"

"Nine years," Beth said. "About the time you embarked on your, ah . . ."

"Hobby?"

Beth ignored the comment. "Do you know anything about them?"

"Such as?"

"Who those people are. How they got there. What killed them."

Pell leaned back in his seat and feigned surprise. "You think I'm responsible?"

"Are you?"

Pell didn't seem to like the directness of her question. He stared at her through lowered brows. She held his gaze. For the first time, she caught a glimpse of the malevolence lurking behind his mask.

"Did your scientists say what those poor people died of?" Pell finally asked.

"They're still testing," Beth said.

"You sayin' it wasn't you?" Pappas said.

"You know, Dan, there are wonderful medicines now for acne. You might also consider dermabrasion to smooth the skin," Pell said.

"First chance I get," Pappas said. "So you don't know nuthin' about the other bodies?"

"Perhaps if you told me a little about them, I could make some educated guesses."

"The most recent are two women," Pappas said. "Both in their late twenties. Both around five foot six with auburn hair. Both walled up alive. Both had fingers missing."

"How horrible," Pell said. "That's really not much to go on. What interests me are the older bodies."

"Why?" Pappas asked.

"It's something of a stretch to think two killers happened to bury their victims in the same place by coincidence."

"That was our thought," Beth said.

"Tell me, Elizabeth, were you the one who figured out the hiding place?"

"It was mostly Jack Kale," she said.

"Of course." Pell's smile never touched his eyes. "Perhaps you should start your investigation closer to home."

"What do you mean?" she asked.

"I just mentioned coincidence. Do you really think it's a coincidence Mr. Kale solved my case and pieced together all those clues that led to the new victims? Two at the farm, the woman at Lake Lanier, and now the lady at Underground Atlanta. Yes, I saw that on TV. Incredible luck, wouldn't you say?"

"Jack Kale is a very intelligent man," Beth said. "You said that yourself."

"I said he was clever, Elizabeth. Consider this: he may be the one you're looking for."

Beth laughed to herself at the statement. "Is that so?"

"A killer, pure and simple. Not much different from me, really."

"Ridiculous," Beth said.

"Is it? Do you remember how I told you he framed me for the murder of his partner?"

"I do."

"Ask yourselves this question: if I didn't do it, who did?"

"Maybe the Easter Bunny," Pappas said. "We're spinning our wheels with this looney."

Pell looked at him and smiled. "You came to see me, Dan. I'm afraid the truth can be unpleasant."

Beth told Pell, "The reason Detective Pappas doesn't believe you— and frankly, neither do I—is that the killer sent us a video. He's taken another woman and a child—a *child*, Doctor. You helped us before. We were hoping you'd help us again."

"Believe me, I'm trying to," Pell said.

"I'm sure you are," Beth said. "Interestingly, the man sent us a video recording of the people he kidnapped. Like you, he referred to Jack Kale as Clever Jack. Why do you suppose he did that?"

"I haven't the faintest idea. Coincidence, I suppose."

"Wasn't that something you did?" Beth said. "Send letters and recordings to Jack Kale?"

"Possibly. It's been quite a while and memory fails. I was a different person then."

"Of course. You got that from Albert Lemon, didn't you?"

Something shifted behind Howard Pell's eyes when she mentioned Lemon. The change wasn't much. It came and went so fast, Beth wasn't certain she'd seen it at all.

For the next half hour, Pell reverted back to his cat-and-mouse game, suggesting directly and indirectly that Jack was a murderer. In the end, they learned nothing that would help them find the missing woman and her little boy.

*

As soon as they were alone, Pappas asked, "What was that stuff about Albert Lemon?"

"Jack and I worked late last night. He told me what Pell did wasn't original. There was a serial killer in Atlanta around the turn of the century by that name. According to Jack, Pell was fascinated by him and apparently modeled what he was doing after Lemon. But he took it one step further and put his own spin on the way he killed his victims. He thinks the killer may be trying to pick up where Pell and Lemon left off."

"That's great," Pappas said. "It would be a good idea to let me in on that information before you decide to spring it. That's what partners do."

Beth realized she had made a mistake. Pappas was completely right. "I'm sorry, Dan. My bad. It won't happen again."

"No problem, kid. We're all about communication."

"It's really amazing how his mind works."

"Pell?"

"Jack."

"Yeah, if you figure it out, let me know."

*

On the return to Atlanta, they had to stop for gas. Pappas pulled into a service station one exit north of Jordan. Wanting to stretch after sitting so long, Beth volunteered to do the pumping. When she got back in the car, she caught Pappas studying his face in the rearview mirror. He noticed her looking and quickly put it back in position, started the engine, and pulled onto the highway.

"What were you doing?" Beth asked.

"Nuthin'."

A mile rolled by before he asked, "You think there's anything to that derma stuff Pell was talkin' about?"

"Daniel Pappas, if you listen to one word that idiot said, I'll shoot you myself."

Pappas shrugged and kept driving. Then he said, "Didn't bother me none. I was just curious, is all."

"You look just fine," Beth said. "You have a nice, strong face."

"When my kids were young, they'd touch the scars and ask, 'Daddy, do they hurt?'"

"Pell was just trying to get in your head. He took a cheap shot."

"I know. You buy any of that crap he was shoveling?" Pappas asked, changing the subject.

"What's it supposed to do? Make the new murders go away? He hates Jack for catching him. It's an attempt to undermine the investigation."

"That's when you sprung your Albert Lemon question," Pappas said.

"He danced around it. He also tried to pass off the killer's comment on the video as coincidence."

"You buy that?"

"Not for a minute. Did you see his face? He was royally pissed."

"Yeah, I caught it," Pappas said. "He tried to cover, but—"

"He's full of shit," Beth said. "They're communicating somehow, and I think Pell is calling the shots."

For the next twenty minutes, they speculated how the killers were accomplishing that and came up empty. Mayfield's procedures were airtight.

Pappas asked, "What about his phone calls? Has anyone checked them yet?"

"Supposedly their security people did that. I'll speak with Dr. Raymond in the morning and ask for copies. Maybe Pell is talking to someone in code."

They were still discussing the possibilities when Pappas pulled up to Beth's house and let her off at the curb. She got out, told him to get some rest, and shut the door.

Pappas didn't drive off immediately. Beth heard the sound of the passenger window roll down and turned back.

"You know when I said what Pell said didn't bother me?"

Beth nodded. Several seconds passed.

"It did," Pappas said.

Before she could reply, the detective put the car in gear and pulled away from the curb.

Chapter 44

Jack decided to stop for a cappuccino at a local coffee bar on his way to the library. He'd taken his Internet research as far as he could and was now looking for an old and very specific book.

He found a self-pay lot with space available near the Equitable Building and dropped his car off. The lot had a box with numbered slots that corresponded to the space numbers painted on the asphalt. He spent a full minute folding a five-dollar bill into the approximate size of an electron and jammed it in the appropriate slot using a small tool hanging from the box on a chain.

At that hour of the morning, the streets weren't crowded. For no reason he could see, the traffic on Broad and Luckie Street was at a standstill. He threaded his way through the cars, past a woman driver who had decided to spend her time more profitably by touching up her eyeliner. She looked up at him as he crossed in front of her car. Jack gave her a thumbs up. She smiled, flicked her hand at him in a go-away gesture, and went back to her makeup.

Before leaving the office, Ben Furman called to let him know his photo enhancement program was running and the results looked promising. The yellow area over the killer's shoulder was, as Jack thought, a pipe of some sort. The question now was *where* was it?

Dwayne Stafford, one-half of Frick and Frack, checked with missing persons and reported that a call had come in late the previous night about a mother and missing child. Stafford and his partner interviewed the distraught father, who told them that Pamela Dorsey had taken their young son, Aaron, to Piedmont Park to play with his new sailboat. If the killer snatched them from there in broad daylight, it meant he was getting bolder. It might also mean he was getting careless or that he was feeling confident that he wouldn't be caught.

The pattern they thought existed with the other victims was now pretty much out the window. The Dorseys weren't members of the Park-wood Health Club, which put them back to square one.

There was a pattern. Of that, Jack was certain. He just hadn't found it yet. Pamela and Aaron's lives depended on his doing so quickly. It didn't help that the newspapers were contributing to the rising tide of alarm in Atlanta. The *Constitution*'s headline read, "Is It Happening Again?" Beneath it was a photo of a body bag being carried out of Underground Atlanta by the medical examiner's assistants.

For the last two days and most of the morning, Jack had been formulating a theory about how the killer was thinking, about what he would do next. Albert Lemon was central to that. But, there were still large gaps he needed to fill in before he shared it with the others. He took a breath and continued walking.

*

Throughout the day and late into the afternoon, Jack searched through the stacks without success. In the back of his mind, he recalled seeing a reference an author had made to Howard Pell and the patterns serial killers tended to follow. Unfortunately, that had been years ago, and he couldn't remember whether it was in a book, a magazine, or perhaps a newspaper article. It was nearly six o'clock when he quit. He called Beth to say he might be a few minutes late for dinner. The phone rang four times before going to her answering machine.

"You've reached Beth and Peeka's house. I'm not in right now. Please leave a message."

It took a second for him to remember Peeka was short for her cat, Peekachu.

"Hi, this is Jack. I was doing some research and let the time get away from me. I may be a couple minutes late. I need to stop at my house and take care of Marta. See you later."

He disconnected and immediately second-guessed himself for not leaving something a little friendlier.

*

The Soul Eater stood in Beth's kitchen and listened to the message. Beth and Clever Jack together. What could be more perfect? When it was through, he played it again.

Getting past her burglar alarm was easier than he thought. Facebook and her cat did her in. The private information people were inclined to put out to the public never ceased to amaze him—everything from their birthdays to the places they were born and the names of pets and family members. It was beyond stupid. He conjectured that social media was the rough high-tech equivalent of carving your initials on a tree. Once, when he visited Stone Mountain, he was astonished to see how many people had gone to the trouble of using a hammer and chisel to tell the world they were there. The names and initials went back to the mid-1800s. Basically, it came down to this: no one wanted to disappear. It took only two tries to find the password to Beth's burglar alarm using her cat's name.

The Soul Eater wandered through the house looking at this and that. Interesting woman. Her taste in books was eclectic, running the gamut from historical fiction and memoir to romance novels. In her bedroom, he examined her dresser drawers. Her lingerie was in the top drawer.

The second and third drawers contained sweaters and slacks, all neatly folded. As he was browsing, a large, gray cat with green eyes came into the room and sat watching him. He didn't like cats, and he didn't like being watched.

"Scat."

The cat's tail flicked, but it stayed where it was. The Soul Eater gave it a sour look and continued to browse. In the bottom drawer were several nightgowns and teddies, which he thought were more for show than function.

Atop the dresser was a photo of Beth and another woman he took to be her sister. Their facial features indicated as much. Both were extremely photogenic. He could change that. Her closet held no surprises, save for a box of photographs. He went through them one by one. Past lovers? Odd that she'd kept them. He'd have to ask why when they met.

The work on his basement was nearly complete, which was good. The sarcophagi had taken up more space than he thought. They were beautiful and elegant and the occupants looked serene lying there. No more cares. No more worries. All safe and secure with him to watch over and protect them forever. Elizabeth would make a shining addition.

The annoying cat approached the closet door and continued to watch him. He could feel the pressure building in his chest. The cat was beginning to get on his nerves. Very slowly, so as not to spook it, his hand crept to the scalpel in his pocket. But the moment he took a step toward it, it darted away. Fine. Back to business.

The good detective's bed had antique head- and footboards and a queen-size mattress. He lay down and held the pillow to his face, breathing in the scent of her shampoo. On the nightstand alongside the bed was an anniversary clock, its pendulum turning first one way and then the other. The time was 6:05 PM. Not much longer to wait. Not much longer until the pressure was released.

The bedroom was cool and lit by ambient light from a window. Above him, a fan with blades shaped like palm leaves moved air around in a desultory fashion. In a small garden just outside the window was a fountain with a lion's head that poured water into a bowl from the lion's mouth. The stupid cat apparently found a way outside and jumped onto a table, then stretched out in a square of sunlight. That didn't matter either. He'd deal with it, too, in due course.

Chapter 45

Despite his fondness for beer and Scotch, Jack knew almost nothing about wine. They all tasted the same to him. Even though Beth said not to bring anything, he thought a bottle wouldn't be out of place. She hadn't mentioned what she was making, so choosing the right one now presented a problem. He knew red went with meat and white went with fish, but that was about it. The salesman wasn't much help either.

"How much do you want to spend?"

"I don't know," Jack said. "It's an informal dinner with a colleague."

"Hmm. Fifteen dollars should get you a nice selection," the salesman said. "Do you prefer something fruity?"

"Aren't they all fruity? They come from grapes," Jack said.

A quick explanation followed on the merits of fruity versus dry wines and light versus full-bodied wines, which went in one ear and out the other. The salesman remained tolerant. This was followed by the inevitable question about whether he wanted a white or red. Jack admitted he had no idea what Beth was serving. Even the salesman was stumped now. To solve the problem, he suggested a rose, which apparently fell somewhere in the middle. Jack decided to purchase one bottle of each. The salesman wished him good luck.

*

Beth lived in a subdivision of detached townhomes called Garland Square. All thirty-two of them were situated around a small, well-landscaped park with a gazebo at the center. The gazebo's roof was green and its sides were white. According to directions sent while Jack was in the library, her home was at the end of the first street. She told him to park in the driveway.

The house was three stories high. Each of the windows had plantation shutters rather than shades. As Jack approached the front door carrying his bottles of wine, he noticed the purple and orange pansies growing along her walkway. They added a nice welcoming touch. On either side of the door, a low English Ivy hedge and azaleas lined the foundation wall.

He knocked.

After several seconds, there was no response. He knocked again and waited some more with the same result. This time he tried the doorbell. Still nothing. He listened for any sounds coming from the inside and heard none. Perhaps she was also running late. But if that were the case, she would surely have called to let him know. There were no messages on his cell phone.

Uncertain what to do, Jack called Beth's cell and then her house phone. He could hear it ringing inside.

"You've reached Beth and Peeka's house. I'm not home right now. Please leave a message."

"This is Jack. I'm outside your door. It's six fifteen. Call me back if you're stuck someplace."

Jack stepped away from the door and looked in the window. Toward the rear of the house, he could see a light on. Beyond that, there was no indication anyone was home.

There wasn't much option other than to wait.

Jack returned to his car and placed the wine on the driver's seat then leaned against the fender. Except for a single white cloud, the sky was blue and clear. While he was waiting and trying not to look suspicious, a neighbor walking her dog passed by and smiled at him. He gave her a small wave in return. The woman continued down the street.

Random thoughts came and went in his head. She and Pappas had gone to see Howard Pell, and that made him uncomfortable. He tried never to dwell on Howard Pell. Without warning, an image of his ex-partner surfaced in his mind as she lay dying in her bedroom, the victim of Pell's insane surgery. To this day, it remained the single most horrific sight he'd ever encountered. In the years that followed Connie's death, he'd often lay awake into the early hours of the morning staring at the light seeping through his curtains. That was preferable to the nightmares and the events he pushed into the recesses of his mind.

Before he was conscious of the fact, Jack's breathing began to increase. His heart was now thumping heavily in his chest. Instinctively, he reached for his pills only to find that he'd left the bottle at home.

Next, he went through the mental exercises Morris Shottner had shown him in an effort to calm down. After a minute or two, they began to work. He took a deep breath and looked up. The cloud was still there, just over the edge of Beth's rooftop, only it had moved higher and there was a tinge of gray at the bottom.

Fearful that she would come home and find him in the throes of a panic attack, he decided to distract himself. Pushing off the car's fender, Jack walked to a narrow path that separated Beth's home from the one on the right. Her backyard was visible from where he stood. Like the house, it also looked deserted. He was nearly to it when he heard a man curse. That was followed by the sound of something heavy hitting the ground. Metal scraped against metal. Jack immediately drew his weapon and broke into a run, rounding the corner at full speed.

"Freeze!"

A startled man in jeans took one look at him and the sight of his revolver and yelled, "Jesus!" Throwing his hands up defensively, he stepped backward and tripped over a toolkit lying on the ground. He landed heavily on his rear.

"Jack!" Beth yelled. "It's my air conditioning man."

"What?"

"It's Rudy Volkmann, my air conditioning man," she said, stepping between them. "It's okay. I called him."

Jack finally let his breath out, holstered his weapon, and shut his eyes. He now remembered the Cool-Tech van parked in the visitor spaces as he drove in.

"I'm sorry," he said, offering a hand to Rudy.

Rudy pushed his hand away and said, "Are you crazy?" He got to his feet and turned to Beth. "What kind of people do you hang out with?"

"This is Lieutenant Kale," she said contritely. "Jack, Rudy Volkmann. Rudy's the owner of Cool-Tech."

He apologized again. This time the technician shook hands, though not with much enthusiasm.

"Everything should be good, Ms. Sturgis," he said, keeping his eye on Jack. "The system's completely charged."

"Thank you for coming out so quickly," Beth said in a small voice.

"No worries. I was in the neighborhood."

Rudy snapped his toolkit shut and shook hands with Beth. He nodded to Jack and headed back to his van, shaking his head.

When they were alone, Beth moved closer and kissed Jack lightly on the lips.

"You came to my rescue," she said.

"I feel like the village idiot. For my next trick, maybe I can break down your neighbor's door and let their pets run loose."

Beth's efforts at remaining somber were in danger of collapse. She was trying desperately not to laugh and not succeeding.

"You looked so serious. Ferocious, actually," she said, struggling to get the words out.

"Thank you," Jack said, blandly.

"I'm sorry Rudy didn't stay longer. He's really nice."

"Probably had to go home and change his pants," Jack muttered, which caused Beth to lose it completely.

When she regained her composure, she took him by the hand and led him inside. The gesture was wholly unconscious, but it surprised him in a good way. As they walked, the sound of her laughter remained on his mind. Pure unrestrained glee. What would it be like to make a woman like this laugh all the time? Could he allow himself to be with another person? These thoughts made him uncomfortable. Would catching the killer earn him a chance at redemption? He had no answers.

Beth informed him they were having veal scaloppini and pasta, which sounded great. Italian food was his favorite and he was famished. In view of the late start, she asked if he would lend a hand and cut up some tomato and mozzarella slices for their appetizer. Jack came into the kitchen and set about the task. When he was through, he drizzled a little olive oil and balsamic vinegar over them. Beth paused to inspect his work, nodded her approval, and returned to the veal preparations.

"I bought some wine," Jack said. "With all the excitement earlier, I nearly forgot about it."

"That was thoughtful."

"Be right back."

When he returned carrying three bottles, she looked at him quizzically.

Jack told her, "I wasn't sure what you were making tonight, so I bought one of each to be safe."

*

Beth came into the room carrying their dishes. She'd changed into a light-blue cotton dress that buttoned up the front and came nearly to her knees. They were joined by Peeka, who sat under the table and occasionally rubbed against their ankles to let them know he was there. Basically, an advanced form of begging.

"Do you feed him from the table?" Jack asked.

"Never," Beth said, pinching off a tiny piece of veal with her fingers and handing it to the cat. Jack stuck his lower lip out and followed suit with a piece of his own. Peeka grabbed it and dashed off to another part of the house with his treasure.

"Well," Beth said, "I have to say I'm surprised."

"Oh?"

"Peeka likes you. He's usually not fond of my dates."

For some reason, the idea of her dating rankled him.

"Do you date much?" he asked.

"A little," Beth said. "You?"

"Not really," Jack said. "At least not for a long time."

Beth took a sip of her wine and processed this without comment.

Jack added, "After the divorce, I tried a few times. It . . . they didn't work out. It was mostly me."

"Haven't you been lonely?"

"Some."

Beth was becoming attuned to his one-word responses. They were generally accompanied by a wooden expression because the topic made him uncomfortable. It was frustrating because he'd begin to open up, approach the ledge but then pull back, like sticking your toe in a pool before diving in. His reaction only served to make her more curious. But if she pushed, he'd only retreat further.

"So, did you find what you were looking for in the library?"

Once again on familiar ground, Jack said, "Not really. But I did locate a few more references to Albert Lemon and his crime spree. One article mentioned the author had used Lemon's diary. That would be a gold mine if I could get my hands on it."

Beth agreed. She then informed him of Pell's reaction when she brought up Lemon's name.

"Did he say anything that might help locate the victims?"

"He claimed not to know anything about Lemon or the other bodies. Nothing. Just a bunch of lies."

"Actually, that's helpful," Jack said. "Because I know he's lying."

"What good does knowing he's lying do us?"

"Ask yourself this: Why do people lie?"

"To cover something up," Beth said.

"Or because they believe the lie will benefit them."

"Because the consequences of telling the truth will be unpleasant," Beth said.

Jack smiled. The girl had a quick mind.

Beth sat back in her chair and looked at him. "Do you ever get tired of being a teacher?"

Jack smiled and took a sip of his wine. "That depends on the student, Miss Elizabeth."

*

The Soul Eater was frustrated. Everything had been working out so beautifully. Beth Sturgis was just pulling into her garage. Clever Jack was on his way. Even the miserable cat had come back inside. Then the air conditioner man showed up. Of all the rotten luck.

There'd be other chances. He was a patient man, and there were always other chances. The basement still had a way to go, and the delivery from the antiquities dealer wouldn't arrive for two more days.

He sat in his den studying the book again, marveling how history had a way of repeating itself. What was that expression? Those who don't learn from history are doomed to repeat it?

Clever Jack was doomed. So were Pamela and little Aaron. He did feel rather badly about the boy. Well, life wasn't fair, was it? Time was running out for all of them.

Chapter 46

Beth's eyes felt dry. She and Jack had wound up staying up late, talking about what seemed like everything under the sun. She loved the sound of his voice and wanted to know more about him as a person, which was why she suggested meeting at her house, where it would be natural to touch on things other than the case. And it seemed to be working—almost.

At one point, he asked what she liked to do when she wasn't being a cop. She told him she was taking ballroom dancing lessons at a little place in Sandy Springs. That seemed to surprise him almost as much as he surprised her when he said he wouldn't mind learning to dance. The talk continued with Jack growing more comfortable by increments when they touched on personal subjects. But no matter what the progress, he always shied away when it got too personal. Beth finally gave up and went back to talking about business.

One thing she and Pappas had agreed on was that there was no way Pell could have gotten past the cameras, key cards, and personnel on duty. Which meant her theory that he was working with someone on the outside had hit a wall. Over the past thirty-six months, he'd only had two visitors: his mother and some college student writing a paper about him. His mother had passed away the following year and the college student had graduated from the University of Georgia and was now doing a fellowship at a New York hospital.

Jack was inclined to agree: Pell was somehow working with the killer. The missing finger signature withheld from the public virtually confirmed it. He explained this was a trait psychologists had observed among serial killers. For reasons known only to Pell, after killing his victims, the serial killer had cut off one of their fingers as a souvenir. That made their connection certain. Add to that the "Clever Jack" comment and it only reinforced the theory.

Beth was in the process of making out her notes regarding her meeting with Howard Pell when Lieutenant Fancher signaled for her to come into the office.

"How's it going?" Penny Fancher asked after Beth was seated.

"Not great," Beth said. "We've been getting the typical mix of calls from the public wanting to help. Two gave us conflicting descriptions of suspicious men they saw at Underground Atlanta and a bounty hunter called several times to ask if a reward's been posted yet."

"Wonderful. What about the others?" Fancher asked.

"You don't want to know, boss."

"That bad?"

Beth rolled her eyes. "Two angry ex-wives sure it was their former husbands. We checked anyway. Both have solid alibis."

"Maybe I'll call in about my ex," Fancher said. "We're taking a beating in the press."

"I know," Beth said.

"Chief Ritson wants to meet in the conference room later this morning to discuss our progress. He'll probably assign two more detectives to the task force."

"That's fine," Beth said noncommittally.

"He's also thinking of calling in the FBI."

This was the last thing Beth wanted to hear.

"If he does, we'll lose the case, Lieutenant. You know how they operate. Besides, we already have Jack Kale."

"Losing the case may be the point, Detective," Fancher said.

"That's not fair. We've only had it two weeks. If it wasn't for Jack Kale, Donna Camp would be dead."

"Let's see how things shake out in the meeting," Fancher said. "Right now, the chief wants to get a feel for where we are."

"Fine," Beth said.

"By the way, where is Jack? I left a message on his phone, but I didn't see him come in."

"He mentioned something about going over to Atlanta Gas Light to talk to an engineer," Beth said.

"Why?" Fancher said.

Beth raised her shoulders.

"See if you can get hold of him," Fancher said. "Burt Wiggins said they're shooting for nine thirty."

"Will do."

She was in the process of texting Jack when he walked in the door. She was immediately conscious of his aftershave, which she'd come to associate with his presence over the last few days.

"Morning," Jack said.

"Good morning. I was just texting you."

"How come?"

"Chief Ritson wants a nine thirty status meeting. According to Penny Fancher, he's toying with the idea of calling in the FBI."

To her surprise and annoyance, Jack wasn't upset.

"They have lots of resources," he said. "It might not be a bad idea."

"We don't need them," Beth said. "This is our case and we'll solve it."

Jack smiled without humor. "I wish I was that certain."

"What were you doing at Atlanta Gas Light?" Beth asked.

"Ben identified the yellow area in the video as a pipe. I was trying to pin down who it belongs to."

"Any luck?"

"Nothing. Someone from Georgia Power's coming by later."

"What about telephone and cable?" Beth said.

"Ben Furman has calls into them. The problem is we have so little to work with. We were hoping to get lucky. I've looked at that damn video twenty times and can't shake the feeling I'm missing something."

"It'll probably come to you when you least expect it," Beth said.

"It had better be soon," Jack said.

*

Pam Dorsey couldn't feel her fingers any longer. Her hands were still tied behind her back. The plastic restraints had cut off the blood supply. Her son was bound as she was. The poor thing was plainly terrified. At first he'd struggled wildly trying to get free and help her. She loved him for that. But gradually, his struggles had grown weaker and weaker. He lay on his side now, staring numbly into the darkness. She tried to catch his eye to reassure him. Too bad there was no one to reassure her. She had no idea where they were or where the madman had taken them. She only knew they were in trouble. Big trouble.

The only thing she was certain about was the person who kidnapped them was the same man who tried to wall up that woman at Underground Atlanta. Pam had watched the newscast with a neighbor as she prepared dinner only two nights earlier. How could she have been so stupid going to the park at dusk? She should have said no. But Aaron wanted to play with his boat so much. She looked at her son lying a few feet away, wanting to hold him, comfort him, and tell him everything would be all right.

Mostly she wanted to convince herself that she hadn't sacrificed his life over a toy sailboat.

Chapter 47

They had to bring more chairs into the conference room to accommodate everybody. The mood was somber. No one was talking. No one was on their phone. A few people were busy scribbling notes. On the wall were photographs of the three murdered people. Next to them was a chart Beth had constructed setting out what they knew of the killer along with the location for each of their deaths. Jack watched the second hand on a wall clock move and waited along with everyone else.

Two detectives who generally worked white-collar crimes were also present. Beth had met both men but didn't know them well. Dave Childers, the older of the pair, had a salt-and-pepper moustache and was in his late fifties. He was wearing a gray sport jacket and black pants. His partner, Jimmy Lee Spruell, was the one who had the run-in with Jack at the last meeting. He was approximately thirty years old, about six foot two, and had a reputation around the department as being a hot head. The few times she had any contact with him he had come off as arrogant. Considering the earlier friction between Spruell and Jack, she wished the lieutenant had asked another pair of detectives to join them. But from what Dan Pappas had told her, Jack seemed to have handled the situation well enough. Hopefully, they would put aside any personal issues and concentrate on the task at hand.

Stafford and Mundas were also there, as was Dan Pappas. Despite the early hour, he already looked rumpled. Deputy Chief Ritson and his aide, Burt Wiggins, entered the room at 9:31 AM. The chief began without preamble.

"We've got a mess here, people. I assume most of you have seen the newspapers and television reports by now."

He looked slowly around the room at the assembled faces indicating there was more to his point than he had articulated, then pulled a *USA Today* from under his arm and opened it for everyone to see. The headline read, "Atlanta Police Baffled."

"This doesn't make our department look good," Ritson said. "Are we baffled?"

The question hung in the air. As the case lead, Beth knew she ought to respond. Dan Pappas surprised her by saying, "We don't have all the answers, but we're making progress." He pointed to the wall with the photographs and continued, "We know the bastard's white, he's tall, left-handed, and has light-blue or gray eyes. We also have his DNA, courtesy of that gal who tried to coldcock him at Underground Atlanta. There were enough skin cells on her shoe for a match."

"We knew these things two days ago. Tell me something new." He turned to Beth, as she expected he would, with his next question. "What happened to that subject you picked up?"

"Merkle? We had to cut him loose, Chief. He looked good, but his alibi checked out."

"Did you happen to catch WGST this morning? 'Atlanta Police Stumble Again,' I think the topic was."

"No, I didn't," Beth said. "We're doing our job and we're doing it the right way. When a subject looks solid, we pull him in for questioning. It's important to eliminate the good ones from the bad."

"She's right, Chief," Pappas said.

"So what are we dealing with?" Ritson asked.

Beth hesitated, waiting for Jack to respond and tell them about Lemon, but for some reason, he remained silent. It looked as if something was distracting him. After several seconds, the silence began to feel strained.

She said, "We're not sure, and that's the truth. No question the killer's a copycat, but there's a big wrinkle involved."

"Such as?"

"In each of Howard Pell's kills, he cut off a victim's finger. Initially, the killer did the same. As you know, that information was never released to the public."

"You're telling me we have a leak?" Ritson said.

"Have or had," Beth said. "If the killer's trying to pick up where Pell left off, he had to obtain that information someplace. He could've gotten it from Pell. But no one's visited Pell in quite a while. So if he didn't communicate the details, someone else did."

"What if he used the mail?" Childers asked. "They don't monitor outgoing stuff from what I hear, only the incoming."

"Dan's going through Pell's contact list. Prison regulations require the people who correspond with inmates be approved by the warden, or in this case, Dr. Charles Raymond, Mayfield's resident psychiatrist. Dan?"

"Pell has about thirty-five names on his list," Pappas said. "One or two are relatives. A couple may be reporters or fans."

"Fans?" Ritson said, surprised.

"I know it's crazy," Pappas said. "But some people think the guy's a rock star. One lady actually wants to marry him."

"Be a helluva honeymoon," Spruell commented.

"What about the other bodies we found at Underground Atlanta?" Ritson asked.

"They're likely the work of Albert Lemon," Jack said, speaking for the first time.

Heads in the room turned toward him.

"I did some research yesterday. Albert Lemon lived around the turn of the last century and was, by all accounts, the first serial killer Atlanta ever encountered. There are newspaper reports chronicling his exploits. There's also a book about him that came out in 1972."

"How can you be certain it's Lemon?" Ritson asked.

"I'm not," Jack said. "But everything fits. Pell basically picked up where Lemon left off."

"Why?" Ritson asked.

"Pell was a student of history. After his arrest, we went through his house. There were books and articles everywhere about killers from the past."

"With references to Lemon?" Childers asked.

"Not that we found. But there's every chance Pell knew about him and was familiar with the details of his crimes. Pell dressed his first victims up as scarecrows, just as Lemon did."

"And cut off their fingers, too?" Childers asked.

"That was something Pell added as his own signature. I suspect to branch out on his own."

"And the other victims?" the chief inquired.

"Lake Lanier and Buford Dam didn't exist when Lemon was around. He murdered the third woman by drowning her in the Chattahoochee River, quite similar to what the killer tried to do with Sandra Goldner."

"Go on," Ritson said, folding his arms across his chest.

"One of Lemon's victims was buried alive in an old part of the city, a prominent banker named Joseph Elkins. His body was recovered when the building was torn down in 1906. A newspaper account I read talked about a man and woman who also went missing back then. The speculation was that they had fallen prey to Albert Lemon. From the style of their clothes, I suspect they're two of the people we found in Underground Atlanta."

Childers said, "So Pell found Lemon's hiding place and continued stashing the bodies there."

"The missing fingers on the three newer bodies make it seem that way."

"That is weird, man," Spruell added.

"It also means Detective Sturgis is right about a connection between Pell and the killer. The attempt at partial mummification is a new wrinkle. It means the killer is trying to branch out on his own. That may sound odd to the rest of us, but serials tend to view the world through a filter. In other words, his actions are logical to him."

"You said 'attempt,'" Childers said. "That woman was pretty well wrapped up. How much more do you need to make a mummy?"

"If he had followed the ancient practices, he would have removed her organs and placed them in Canopic jars. Entombing Donna Camp in Underground Atlanta is too much to write off as chance."

Beth and Pappas exchanged glances. That was basically the same comment Pell made regarding Jack.

"What the hell are we dealing with?" Ritson asked.

Jack was silent for a moment as he composed his thoughts.

"Despite what television and movies would like you to believe, we don't have a large population of killers to study. Some comparisons are possible. Generally speaking, serial killers fall into two groups: sociopaths and psychopaths. The latter being the easiest to identify and catch."

"Why?" Penny Fancher asked.

"Because they stand out and are easy to spot due to their behavior. As a rule, they're white males between the ages of twenty-one and forty-two, badly adjusted, with little education, and often unemployed."

A number of detectives in the room began taking notes. Jack paused to give them time.

"Sociopaths, on the other hand, are a cop's nightmare. What's the first thing we look for in a murder?"

"Motive," Beth said.

Jack nodded. "With sociopaths, there isn't always one, or at least their motives aren't apparent. They're generally well educated, follow what the police are doing carefully, and are adept at blending into a crowd and disappearing. Most of them are highly intelligent. This type often gets a kick out of seeing the police struggling to solve the case."

Beth said, "The killer had an observation point set up at Lake Lanier."

"But he didn't do that at the farm or at Underground Atlanta, as far as we know, which is one of the inconsistencies that's been bothering me," Jack said. "Possibly the lack of cover didn't allow for it."

"What about the clues he's been leaving?" Pappas said.

"According to Beth, he's calling me out or trying to send me a message," Jack said.

"I still think that," Beth said. "I think he's saying that if you don't figure out what he's up to, the victims' deaths are your fault."

"I agree," Jack said. "To an extent. But there was no way for him to know I'd be called in where the first three people were concerned."

"Unless he started keeping tabs on Beth or you," Penny Fancher said.

Her comment brought silence to the room.

"Interesting," Jack said. "Watching me, certainly. The scarecrow motif might have been enough to ensure that I'd be brought back. At best, it was a calculated gamble on his part. I hadn't considered that he might be watching Beth, too."

"What about territory?" Childers asked, looking at the map.

"Another good point," Jack said. "There tend to be three types. The ones who lure you to their place, be it a home or someplace else they're using—"

"That doesn't work here," Penny Fancher said.

"No, it doesn't," Jack agreed. "The second type stakes out an area to prey on, like the Boston Strangler or David Berkowitz in New York. By far, they're the most common."

Jack continued, "The last type seems to roam around when they go on their killing spree."

"Which is what we're dealing with," Pappas said. "The asshole started in Jordan and he's worked his way to Atlanta."

"Is there a chance he'll move on?" Beth asked.

"Maybe he's like a shark," Spruell said. "You know, he's found a good feeding ground."

"Possible," Jack said. "The killer certainly seems more directed, particularly where I'm concerned. Everything he's done has a purposeful feel to it, which is highly unusual in a serial killer."

"This is all well and good," Chief Ritson said. "Are we anywhere close to catching him?"

"I can't say we are," Jack said. "Obviously, we're still trying to pin down the location of his latest victims. It's been slow because he hasn't left us much to go on."

Ritson nodded.

"If you're thinking of bringing in the FBI, I won't argue against it," Jack said.

Ritson considered this for a long moment. "No," the Chief said. "This is our case and we've got a good team. Let's find this bastard and put him out of business."

Chapter 48

Noah Ritson caught Jack's attention after the meeting ended and motioned with his head for him to follow. He nodded at Beth, "You, too, detective."

Ritson's office was large and contained photographs of him and Atlanta's last five mayors, two governors, and a senator or two whose names Jack couldn't remember. On a credenza to the left of his desk was a baseball bat autographed by most of the Atlanta Braves. Next to that was a football signed by the Falcons.

The deputy chief pointed them to two chairs and took a seat behind his desk.

He began, "Downstairs you asked me about bringing in the FBI. What about in a limited capacity as consultants?"

"In addition to me or as a replacement?" Jack asked.

"In addition."

"I wouldn't have a problem with that," Jack said. Sensing the tension in Beth, he added, "Detective Sturgis disagrees, and she has a point where Pam and Aaron Dorsey are concerned. Until we know otherwise, we're dealing with a kidnapping, and that's FBI territory. We could easily lose the case. But I think that's a secondary consideration."

Ritson looked at Beth. "Your thoughts?"

"Finding Aaron and Pam Dorsey is our first concern," she said. "That overrides everything else."

Ritson nodded thoughtfully. "I'm glad you see it that way. You've both done excellent work. Unfortunately, the public and media have short memories. It all comes down to 'What have you done for me lately?'"

"I still think we can crack this," Beth responded.

"Professor?" Ritson said.

Jack took a deep breath then said. "If we're going to catch him, the odds are increasing in our favor. Traditionally, serials go through several phases. The first is the buildup stage. After that, they're often consumed by guilt or even horror at what they've done, on a subconscious level if nothing else. The second stage, which is typically more thought out and better planned, follows. Eventually, they reach the last stage."

"Which is?" Ritson said.

"The time between the killings becomes shorter and shorter. The killer feels driven and compelled to act. Planning is more haphazard. Hopefully mistakes are made. I think we're seeing that now with the abduction from Piedmont Park. It wasn't exactly in broad daylight, but he's taking chances. The video he sent is a prime example. There's more information on it than he planned to let out."

Ritson was quiet for a while. Seconds ticked by. From somewhere down in the street, the sound of a siren drifted up to them. "This is Monday," he finally said. "Let's keep working on those leads. Maybe we'll get lucky and a few more will fall into our lap. I've authorized overtime and will give you more personnel if you need them. If we don't turn up anything by the end of this week, we may have to revisit the situation."

"We'll catch him, Chief," Beth said.

"You sound confident."

"I am."

"That settles it then," Ritson said, standing up. "I'll leave you to your work."

Beth and Jack stood as well. Jack held the door open for her. Ritson waited until she walked through and then said, "Oh, Kale, give me another minute, would you?"

Beth's eyes flicked to Jack momentarily. She kept going.

"Close the door."

Once they were alone, the deputy chief informed him, "There are a couple of things I want to clear up. We haven't had a chance to talk."

Jack's mind immediately turned to the incident outside Wellington's. Noah Ritson was known for having his finger on the department's pulse and everything that went on inside it. He assumed Pappas, the cops, or possibly someone at the Detention Center had let word leak.

"What's on your mind, Chief?"

"Have you ever wondered why I asked you to consult with us?"

"I think we both know the answer," Jack said. "If I don't help clear the case, the department can hide behind my failure. If we're successful, so much the better for everyone concerned, particularly the victims."

"You're a cynical fellow, Dr. Kale. Has anyone ever told you that?"

Jack didn't respond.

"I assume you know who Janet Newton is," Ritson said.

"My former boss—Deputy Director Newton, now," Jack said.

"When I first heard that Detective Sturgis asked for your help, I made a few calls. Janet Newton's a friend of mine. We spoke. Afterward, I talked to SAC Bennet Harbaugh. They both share the same opinion of you—brilliant but wasting your talents teaching at Georgia Tech."

Jack had nothing to comment, so he kept quiet.

"Interestingly, I learned both invited you to rejoin the Bureau after you completed a detox program, if I'm using the term right. You never took them up on it. I'd like to know why."

"I've moved on since then," Jack said. "Besides, Internal Affairs wouldn't be thrilled to have me back."

Ritson held his eye for a long moment, then said, "I hear things now and then about people in this department. Most of it is none of my business, but every once in a while, something falls into my lap that bears looking into."

Here it comes, Jack thought.

"A couple of nights ago, one of our mobile units noted a silver BMW parked after hours at a bar in a seedy part of town. They ran the plate and it came back belonging to you."

"That's true."

"Normally, that wouldn't bother me," Ritson said. "A man's entitled to take a drink when he's off duty. But when you couple that with a passing motorist calling nine-one-one about nearly hitting a man staggering across Peachtree Road at three thirty in the morning, it raises some concerns. Was that you, Professor?"

"It was," Jack said.

Ritson nodded, glanced out the window for a moment, and then turned back around. "My job is to protect the people of this city. I've been doing it for a long time. Sometimes that means putting our people in harm's way. It doesn't mean turning my back on a problem staring me in the face. You don't strike me as an alcoholic. Why the detox?"

"Possible addiction to prescription medication. I suffer from panic attacks."

The chief processed that for a moment. "I appreciate your honesty. What I really need to know is, can you do your job?"

"I can."

"And not compromise the people working with you?"

"I can control it," Jack said.

Ritson smiled at the comment.

Jack had had this conversation in the past . . . with Pappas, his wife, his father, his boss, even the DPR, FBI's internal affairs unit. He was tired of explaining himself. Tired of being afraid. Tired of hiding the truth. He waited because there was no other choice. The possibility of being shut out of the case suddenly loomed very large. He didn't know if he had convinced Ritson or not. He simply wanted to see it to an end.

Jack informed him, "I know that's what every addict says. With the help of a psychologist, I've been trying to wean myself off the medication. I give you my word, the first minute I feel I can't hack it, I'll take myself out of the equation."

"I think," Ritson said, "the help you've given us has been substantial, possibly brilliant. According to Lieutenant Fancher, Detective Sturgis shares this opinion. Your efforts certainly saved that woman's life at Underground Atlanta. Two minutes sooner and we might have done the same for Sandra Goldner. Not your fault, though.

"The one thing I won't allow is for this department to be hurt, and by hurt I mean embarrassed. Continue with the investigation. Your colleagues like and trust you. That means something. If there's a repeat of this behavior, you won't have to worry about pulling yourself off the case. I'll do it myself. Are we clear on that?"

"We are," Jack said.

"You didn't ask to be here. Maybe you were happy doing what you were doing. This is a chance for you to get back in if you want it. I know about your partner and what you must have gone through losing her like that. Unfortunately, it's a dangerous business. Every time we go out there, we're at risk. You understand what I'm saying?"

"I think so," Jack said, fighting to keep his expression and breathing neutral. Connie Belasco's face stared at him from inside a cloud drifting past the chief's window.

Ritson went on. "Whatever led to that binge a few nights ago, put a cap on it and let's catch this sonofabitch."

*

Cold fingers touching her face caused Pam Dorsey to jump. She opened her eyes and was stunned to see her eight-year-old son leaning over her.

Somehow, he had managed to free himself from the plastic restraints. He was trying to peel the duct tape off her mouth. Once that was done, he went to work on the ties securing her hands. But there was nothing to cut them with.

"I can't get them off, Mama," he whispered.

Pam struggled into a sitting position. "It's okay, Aaron. Let me think for a moment."

Across from her, atop a box on the wall, a digital timer the police-man had left was counting down to zero. The display now read *178*. Something bad was going to happen. She couldn't understand why he had taken their shoes and socks and left them lying in four inches of water, but she was certain the two were related. She looked around again.

What was this terrible place?

A tunnel of some sort, but like none she'd ever seen before. Over-head, a single bulb revealed a series of colored pipes that disappeared into a dark opening at the other side of the room. Ten feet to the right of the box on the wall was a flat, gray door that was probably an access panel like the one in her garage that led to their crawl space. It was more than three feet high. Other than the tunnel, it seemed to be the only way in or out. There was no way to be certain if the policeman had used it because she'd been unconscious at the time.

"Where are we?" Aaron whispered.

"I don't know," she said.

"It smells weird in here."

"I know."

"Can we get out?"

"We're gonna try," Pam said. "See if you can open that door."

Aaron crawled through the water and tried only to find it was locked. He wedged his little fingers in the opening at the frame and pulled as hard as he could. After several seconds, he gave up and turned to his mother, shaking his head.

There has to be another way, Pam thought.

She considered the tunnel again. No choice. The pipes took up most of the space, but if they walked single file, there was enough room. Even pipes have to come out someplace.

Aaron was back at her side looking at his mother hopefully.

"C'mon," Pam said, keeping her voice down. "We're leaving."

Despite her hands still being secured by the plastic restraint, Pam Dorsey struggled to her feet, and together, mother and son started down the tunnel. They'd gotten no more than ten feet before Aaron said, "Wait."

He scrambled back into the room and returned carrying his sailboat.

Chapter 49

Jack returned to his desk to find Beth and another man waiting for him. She introduced Steve Jamison, a supervisor with Georgia Power.

"We've just been going over the video the killer sent," Beth said. "Steve has a couple of ideas."

"Wonderful," Jack replied. "We can use the help."

"The picture quality's not great," Jamison said, motioning to Beth's computer. "But I think there's a chance that yellow area over the woman's head might be one of our conduits."

"I thought electricity's delivered through overhead wires," Jack said.

"In the suburbs it is. Inside the city, the grid runs through a series of underground tunnels."

Jack's attention sharpened. "Georgia Power has their own tunnel system?"

"Not really. Some we put in. Some are shared with other utility companies. Gas, electric, and telephone run side by side. Cable's been leasing space from us for a number of years. Those green dots in the picture could be their wires. And I'm thinking the gray are gas lines."

"You can tell from the dots?" Beth asked.

"It's more the arrangement and combination of colors and the fact that they stretch across the screen. That's just what they remind me of."

"I wasn't aware utility lines ran together," Jack said.

"Better than tearing up the city every time you need to bring new services in," Jamison said.

"Are they always together?" Jack asked.

"Whenever it's feasible. But sometimes it's necessary to create new infrastructure if none exists."

"Meaning the tunnels where the pipes or whatever run," Beth said.
"Exactly."

Jack said, "I take it there are access points every so often for maintenance issues."

"Of course."

"Is the conduit Georgia Power uses always yellow in color?" Jack
said.

"Honestly, the older stuff could be anything," Jamison said. "We've
been using yellow exclusively since 1983, particularly with any replacement work."

Jack inquired further, "Did you notice both the woman and boy
aren't wearing shoes or socks?"

"As a matter of fact, I did," Jamison said. "That doesn't make sense."

"There appears to be water on the ground where they're lying," Beth
said.

Jamison's brows came together and he looked at the screen again.
"Where? I don't see that."

Beth backed up the disc and replayed it. She pointed at the screen.
"The camera pans across them quickly. But if you look close, you can see
a water mark on the woman's clothes. It's the same with her son."

Jamison studied the picture again and muttered, "Damn" under his
breath. "That's not good. If a water main's leaking down there and it
comes into contact with one of our transmission lines, whoever's in the
vicinity's going to get fried."

"Wouldn't the water company know if there's a leak?" Beth asked.

"If it's large enough. But a small one, who knows?"

"Is there a master map that shows where all the utility lines are
throughout the city?" Jack asked.

"Sure. The Planning Commission maintains one. When a contractor applies for a permit, they check to see where everything is located
and then notify the companies. We have crews that go out and flag the
areas to prevent accidents."

"What about the water lines?" Jack asked. "Are there tunnels where
they meet the other utilities?"

"There are probably a few left," Jamison said. "When we run across
a situation like that, we have to reroute."

Beth and Jack exchanged glances.

"I need to know where they are," Beth said. "There's a good chance
that's where he's holding that woman and her son."

Chapter 50

Isaac Worley, the city engineer, was waiting for them in his office at City Hall. Next to his desk was a drafting table. On it was a large book showing Atlanta's layout street by street. Worley responded to Jamison's request for a meeting immediately.

He informed them, "There are probably a dozen or so places where the lines run together. Atlanta's ordinances were amended in 1960 to require separate routing of water and electrical services."

"Because of the danger of electrocution," Beth said.

"Actually, it's a little worse than that," Worley said. "Did you ever hear of the old Crawford Hotel on Ponce de Leon Avenue?"

"Before my time," Jack said.

"Mine, too," Beth said.

"I was just a kid then, but I remember the fire clearly. It took about every emergency vehicle in Atlanta two days to put it out. People were jumping out of windows to escape the flames."

"It sounds horrible," Beth said.

"It was," Worley said.

"The fire was electrical?" Beth asked.

"A burst pipe shorted out an underground junction box and caused an arc flash."

"A what?"

"An arc flash. That's where the electrical current running in the line jumps. Once that happens, look out. The result can be catastrophic, like a runaway train. A flash can travel along pipes or anything conductive. It's even been known to jump across rooms."

Jack's face had assumed that intense look Beth was becoming familiar with when he was concentrating. He moved to the map book on

213

Worley's drafting table and said, "Show me where the electricity and water lines meet."

"I can't."

"Why?"

Worley explained. "I mean, there's no index that points them out. Most everything was rerouted after the 1960 ordinance, but there are still some spots we come across every now and then. Usually it's the case of a side line running off one of the mains. When that happens, we start digging and move the utilities."

"But this map shows where everything is, doesn't it?" Jack said.

"Sure, but you'd have to go through it page by page."

Jack considered the book again. It was probably two feet wide and eighteen inches high. He shook his head in dismay when he saw how many pages there were.

Worley added, "That's just volume one. We have three more books in the map room. I was working on that one when Steve called."

"Jeez," Jack said.

"It's a big city, Detective," Worley said.

Within an hour, Beth had assembled three teams of investigators at City Hall. Stafford and Mundas made up one team. Dave Childers and Jimmy Lee Spruell made up the other, while she and Jack composed the third. Dan Pappas put out a call to Corey Harrison, the patrolman who helped them at Underground Atlanta, and headed for the Fulton County Planning Commission where yet another set of maps were maintained. Technically a separate political entity, Fulton County's jurisdiction took up where Atlanta's left off. The recent census put the county population at more than two million people.

The detectives began going through the street maps one by one. Sometimes the lines were clearly marked and sometimes they found notations referring them to a supplemental map book. The process was painstaking and frustrating.

It was close to seven by the time they finished. Stafford and Mundas found six streets where the electric and water lines shared a common route. Beth and Jack found six, and Childers and Spruell located four. Pappas and Harrison were more fortunate. Having identified one quickly, they eliminated it as a possibility because the only point of access was through the basement of a fire engine company. The plan was to descend into the tunnels and begin searching for Pam and Aaron Dorsey.

Beth called everyone together to let Steve Jamison address them on the safety precautions.

"It's important to understand what you're dealing with," Jamison said. "The average transmission line carries over two hundred thousand volts. A hair dryer with a hundred and ten volts can kill you. Heavy-duty protection gear should be waiting for you downstairs. It's important that you wear it at all times."

"We all carry latex gloves for crime scene work," Childers said. "Won't they do?"

"I wouldn't want to bet my life on them," Jamison said. "The heavy-duty stuff is the way to go, but even with it, there are no guarantees."

"Well, that's encouraging," Childers said.

"Dealing with that much current is like holding a rattlesnake. First rule of thumb, you don't go near the juice if you don't have to. In other words, *avoid all contact.* It's dangerous and can jump without warning. If you can't avoid contact, you'll have to make the call. Should you locate the woman and her son, get in touch with me immediately and I'll kill power to the area."

Looks were exchanged around the room as the reality of what they were dealing with began to sink in. No one offered a comment.

Jamison continued, "The next rule of thumb is to stay as dry as possible. From the photographs I've seen, it looks like there's water down there. Dry human skin isn't a great conductor. Wet skin is another matter."

"Oh mama," Dwayne Stafford muttered.

Jamison glanced at him, then said, "Third rule of thumb, you can't outrun the juice so don't try. Even the most fleeting contact is enough to complete a circuit. And if part of that circuit is you, well, the results could be unpleasant."

"Unpleasant," Stafford echoed.

"I've seen an arc flash melt steel. Do not, I repeat, *do not* challenge it by thinking you can pull your hand back quickly enough. You can't," Jamison said.

"If you're trying to scare us, you're doing a good job," Spruell said.

Jamison looked down at the floor for a moment and took a deep breath before he responded.

"I had a friend named Lou Boedner who worked as a maintenance supervisor for Florida Power and Light in West Palm Beach. About five years ago, three different hurricanes hit the area, all within a couple of weeks of each other. The place was a total mess. Trees and lines were down everywhere. Utility companies from all over the Southeast rushed crews down there to help restore power.

"Lou and another man had just climbed out of a cherry picker. They were replacing a blown switchbox. Two blocks away, a tree came down and landed in the middle of a substation. Even though the power was off at their unit, the arc flash from the substation jumped to Lou's line and traveled two blocks. I was ten feet away when he burst into flames. So yeah, I'm trying to scare you. It might just save your life."

Beth had heard the expression about the air being sucked out of a room. If this wasn't a good example of it, she doubted she'd ever see one.

Ever since the meeting began, she knew where things were heading—back underground and into the dark. A drop of perspiration slid down the side of her forehead. Hopefully the next time they would land a killer partial to heights. She didn't mind heights.

Jamison was finished talking. The rest of the detectives were waiting for her. It took a second to find her voice.

"Assuming the protective gear is here, we'll divide into four teams and begin checking the intersections one by one. You all understand what we're walking into. We need to find that woman and her son and get them the hell out of there."

Chapter 51

Pam Dorsey was now certain they were not in a basement as she first thought. It was far too large for that. They were someplace underground. But where? The pipes seemed to go on forever. One section looked exactly like another. Like moths to a flame, she and Aaron were drawn to them only to be disappointed.

Due to their lack of shoes and Pam's inability to use her hands for balance, progress was slow. Mold and algae covered the floor. To make matters worse, the trickle of water that followed them after escaping from the room had turned into a stream. It was now up to their ankles. Thoughts of drowning began to gnaw at her and increased with each passing minute. She made an effort not to let it show. Aaron trudged along behind, clutching his sailboat.

If she didn't make it out, her son would. She kept repeating that mantra over and over in her mind, praying the words would push away the fear. She'd never considered herself a brave person. Quite the opposite. Timid by nature, she avoided conflict wherever possible. Even something as simple as learning to ski this past winter had terrified her. Roger's idea of a fun family vacation. Hers was sitting in front of the fireplace at their hotel sipping hot chocolate.

Pam spared a glance at her son and smiled. He was as stubborn as his father, lugging that silly sailboat with him. She shook her head. Children trust their parents to keep them safe. She had no idea how she would accomplish that, but try she would. Aaron chose that moment to look at her. She smiled. He smiled in return. And in that look, she found the strength to keep her legs moving to the next light.

*

Clad in knee-high rubber boots and wearing gloves that came halfway up their arms, Beth and Jack removed the access panel, ducked down low, and entered the relay junction room. It was approximately ten feet square and quite empty, save for the electrical conduit and different colored pipes overhead. Jack swept his Maglite across the floor. Dusty. Bone dry. On the wall in front of them was a black metal box with the words, "DANGER—HIGH VOLTAGE" stenciled in yellow letters. An ominous hum was coming from inside the box, reminding them there was something alive in there. Something extremely dangerous. Apart from their Maglites, the only other source of light came from a single overhead bulb surrounded by a metal safety cage. It was obvious no one had been there in quite a while. According to the map, the pipes would lead them into the tunnel system.

Beth had issued hand communicators to all the detectives. Steve Jamison thought reception would be hit and miss at best. All twenty-two locations where electrical conduit met the city's water pipes had been circled on their maps. The plan was to eliminate them one by one.

Dan Pappas, whose location in the suburbs had been scratched off early on, was now in the mobile command van that would function as a central relay to communicate with the other detectives and the utility companies in the event services had to be cut. Ironically, the place they chose to enter the grid, as it was called, was directly below City Hall, barely a block from where Donna Camp had been rescued.

Steve Jamison elected to stay with Pappas and answer any technical questions that might come up. Roger Dorsey, after being advised of the situation, had left work and arrived a half hour earlier. It looked like the man hadn't slept in two days.

Jack's voice came over the van's speakerphone.

"This is Kale. Detective Sturgis and I are in. Area One is negative. We're heading into the tunnels now."

"Acknowledged," Pappas said. "Be careful." He then turned to Jamison and asked, "How long 'til they reach the next junction?"

"Maybe fifteen minutes for Kale and Sturgis. Thirty minutes for Childers and Spruell. Stafford and his partner should be at theirs in about twenty."

The detective sat back in his chair and began tapping a pencil against the desk. He didn't mind Jack taking his place. The truth was he hated tunnels and confined spaces as much as Beth did. She was too competitive to admit it. So was he. He'd seen what she'd gone through at the barn as she tried to hold it together. Considering where they were, that didn't bode well. Still, Jack was a bright guy, and a psychologist to boot. If a problem did crop up, he was more likely to recognize it than anyone else.

But that left him sitting in a van, tapping a pencil, while they walked into who knew what.

Chapter 52

The water appeared to be increasing. The flow, coming from some-where behind them, was now up to her calves. What progress they made was laborious and exhausting. Thankfully, her son seemed to be managing well, still clutching his sailboat in one hand and her arm in the other. They stumbled along, hoping to find a door that would lead to their freedom.

After two hours in the semidarkness, Pam's sense of direction became hopelessly muddled. For all she knew, they were retracing their steps. The single access panel they found shortly after starting out gave them momentary hope, but it was also locked. So on they went, down one corridor after another with the water trailing behind them. The tunnel had finally widened, allowing them to walk side by side.

The brave little man next to her remained stoic, but she could see his strength was waning. Every so often, Pam stopped to give him a rest. Aaron's eyes had assumed a vacant, hollow look. A hundred-yard stare, her husband called it.

My little boy.

The thought of getting him to safety became all consuming. No matter the cost, she would see it done. Even if that meant her own life in the process. The next door couldn't be that far. Despite the bravado, doubts began to take over. She was a weak, overweight housewife, frightened of everything for as long as she could remember. Well, not anymore. She snuck a glance at Aaron again.

My baby.

Her son would live. She swore a silent oath on that.

*

Nearly a mile away, Beth and Jack continued along the tunnel to the next point on their map. The farther they went, the worse the reception was becoming on their hand communicators. After an hour of walking and feeling their way along portions of the tunnel where maintenance lights had burned out, Beth suddenly stepped in water that covered the tops of her boots. Despite the heavy rubber, she could feel its chill.

Electricity and water don't mix.

Right. I'll remember that when I light up like a Christmas tree, Beth thought.

Somewhere, air was moving. As the breeze passed over Beth's skin, she realized she'd broken out in a cold sweat. Annoyingly, Jack seemed fine. His face was grim, but his eyes were very much alive, taking in the details of their surroundings. He finally realized she was looking at him and smiled at her.

After several minutes, he came to a halt and studied the map. They were at a junction of some sort where the tunnel split in opposite directions.

"You know where we are?" Beth asked.

"In a tunnel," Jack muttered, without looking up.

"You're just irritated because you have to look at a map. Admit it."

He seemed to find that funny. "It's that way," he said, pointing.

"Good. Do we still have a signal?"

Jack took the hand communicator from his belt and checked it. "Two bars."

"Better let Dan know where we are," Beth said.

Jack keyed the unit and said, "This is Team One. We just encountered water. It seems to be coming from up ahead of us in the direction of our next stop. Can you check with the utility company and see if they're reporting any leaks?"

"Will do," Pappas said. "Hang on."

Jack waited while a conversation took place in the background. He couldn't make out any of the words. Pappas returned to the call.

"Sorry. That was Childers checking in. They cleared the first four doors. No sign of the woman or the kid. Anything on your end?"

"Nothing," Jack said.

"I'll make the call and get back to you."

221

"What about Stafford and Mundas?"

"Same. You sure about this search?" Pappas said.

"Best guess," Jack said. "It's the only game in town."

"Yeah. Good luck," Pappas said and disconnected.

"How long 'til the next door?" Beth asked.

"Thirty, maybe forty minutes," Jack said. "Basically, we're following Spring Street now. According to the map, the tunnel intersects with a feeder line up ahead at Tenth Street."

"What's with all this water?" Beth said. "This can't be right."

"No," Jack said. "It can't."

On they walked. Thankfully, the water level remained constant, perhaps even receding in some areas as it drained into the side tunnels.

Dan Pappas called back five minutes later.

"The water company says they have no indication of any leaks, but that's not unusual. Until there's a major drop in pressure along a specific line, they have no way of knowing."

"Wonderful," Beth said. "We could drown down here and they won't have a clue until someone's faucet runs dry."

The detective added, "Team Two's coming in. That's Childers and Spruell, in case you were wondering. All four of their locations are clear. Stafford and Mundas have two more to check. You want them to hook up with you when they're done?"

"No," Beth said.

"What about the water company? They're asking if you want them to send a repair crew down and start tracing the problem."

"Negative," Beth said. "Let's keep the civilian risk to a minimum until we locate that woman and her child."

Gutsy gal, Pappas thought to himself, then remembered Jack's comment about it being politically incorrect to call women "gals." His daughters were always getting on him for being a dinosaur. He figured it was okay as long as you didn't mean anything bad by it. Steve Jamison interrupted his thoughts with a question, which he relayed to Beth.

"Jamison wants to know how much water you're in right now."

"It's backed off some, but it's over the soles of my boots," Beth said.

"And where exactly are you?"

"According to Jack, somewhere under Spring Street approaching the Tenth Street cutoff."

Jamison came on the phone.

"The map doesn't show it, but that line runs straight down and crosses I-75/85. Eventually, you'll come to the fifth relay station at Northside Drive."

"Isn't that near the reservoir?" Jack asked.

"Close. The reservoir's on Howell Mill Road, one street up," Jamison said.

"Maybe it's leaking," Pappas said.

"I don't think so," Jamison said. "Those holding tanks are pretty solid. Still, you can't underestimate the danger. I've seen an arc flash travel over two hundred yards."

I wish he'd stop saying that, Beth thought.

"I'll call Water just in case and have them check the levels. Let us know immediately if you see any increase."

"Oh, you'll hear from us," Jack said.

"Once you reach Northside Drive, the electric and water lines split in different directions. Our conduit routes toward your school."

"That's fine," Jack said.

"Your sixth stop will be at Moore's Mill Road, where they meet again."

"Acknowledged. We'll let you know what we find."

With the water slowing their progress, it took nearly an hour to make their way to the Tenth Street intersection. There, they found a ladder that descended into a hole. Water spilled over the edge like a miniature waterfall. On the wall next to the ladder, someone had spray-painted, "Welcome to Disney World."

"Oh, this just gets better and better," Beth said, zipping her rubber jacket closed. "These damned pants have a leak."

Jack seemed to bite back a smile and said, "I'll go down first. Give me as much light as possible. If it's safe at the bottom, I'll call up to you."

"Wait, what? Why wouldn't it be safe?"

"Let's see how much water's down there."

Twenty seconds later, he yelled up, "We're good."

Beth started down, muttering to herself about tunnels and water and suits. Two rungs from the bottom her foot slipped. Jack grabbed for her waist to stop her from falling, then eased her down the rest of the way. When she turned to thank him, their bodies were close and their faces inches apart.

Great, I finally get him to touch me and I'm dressed like a lobster fisherman.

"Thank you," she said.

Jack held her a moment longer than strictly necessary then asked, "Ready?"

"Ready."

He nodded and turned back to the tunnel, not seeing the swipe she took at the back of his head.

Chapter 53

Pam and Aaron Dorsey were cold, wet, and completely lost. Every tunnel they turned down looked exactly like the one they'd just come from. Getting out seemed hopeless. Pam knew they had to keep moving. The timer was still ticking. Whatever that lunatic was up to, it was going to happen soon. She willed her feet forward.

Keep following the pipes. Sooner or later, they'll lead the way to another door.

Her son was nearing the end of his strength. When they paused to catch their breath, he leaned against her, resting his head on her hip. It wasn't fair. His life was just beginning, and no madman was going to rob him of it.

"Look, Mom," Aaron said.

Pam followed where he was pointing.

Above their heads, a line of mice and rats were scurrying along the highest of the pipes.

Pam fought down a wave of revulsion and said, "Guess they know something we don't."

"Where are they going?"

"They're getting out of here. And so are we."

They had only taken a few steps before Aaron froze. He tugged on his mother's arm.

"Honey, I've seen the rats. They won't hurt us. We have to keep walking."

"No, look!" Aaron whispered.

Pam turned and gazed into the darkness behind them. A light was moving against the wall. A moment later, the shadow of a man appeared. Panic seized her. The policeman was coming for them. Desperately, she tore at the restraints binding her wrists. There was just a little play. If she could just get her hands free, she could fight him. Claw his eyes. Hurt him. Give Aaron a chance to escape.

"What do we do?" he whispered.

"Stay very still," Pam said. "He's going down a different tunnel."

"He's getting closer."

Pam Dorsey made her decision. She could now make out a shape behind the light. An ominous malignant shadow.

"Run," she hissed. "Keep following the pipes."

Aaron stayed where he was.

"Do as I say."

"No, ma'am."

Pam's heart nearly broke. She loved him for his loyalty. His courage. She loved him more than her life.

Yes, she'd never been brave. That was about to change. Her arms and face were bathed in perspiration as she pulled against the restraints with every ounce of strength she possessed. The pain was unbearable, so much so she started to become faint. Pam clenched her teeth. Pulled harder. Finally, her hand came free. The skin had been rubbed raw and was covered in blood, but she was free.

Pam Dorsey stepped in front of her son and turned to face the monster.

*

Immediately behind the first light came a second one. Both beams were sweeping back and forth, searching. Two shadow shapes moved past the tunnel they were in. For the first time in hours, hope blossomed in Pam's heart. They were coming to rescue them.

"Here!" Pam shouted. "We're here!"

The lights paused. Swung back.

"Mrs. Dorsey? It's the Atlanta Police," a woman called out. "We're here to help you."

The sound of feet sloshing through water followed as the lights turned around in the direction of her voice.

"Stay where you are, Pam," the woman yelled. "We're coming."

The shapes behind the lights took form. A man and a woman. Both were tall and wearing rubber boots and jackets.

"Thank God," Pam said, nearly collapsing with relief.

"Are you all right?" the woman asked.

Pam's voice deserted her. She nodded.

"I'm Beth Sturgis. This is Lieutenant Kale. I'm so glad we found you."

Aaron said, "If you're the police, let me see your badges."

Beth's eyebrows rose, but she pushed the yellow coat aside to reveal the badge pinned to her belt. Jack had to dig around in his pockets to find his. She noticed he had started carrying his gun, which was a good thing given what they were dealing with. The badge seemed to satisfy the young man.

"My mom's hands are hurt," he said.

Beth trained her light on Pam Dorsey's hands and winced when she saw they were covered in blood. Using a pocket knife, she forgot about fashion and cut off a piece of her blouse, creating two makeshift bandages, and tied them around Pam's wrists.

"Why did you ask to see our badges?" Jack asked.

"Because the man who took us said he was a policeman," Aaron said. "He put a cloth over my mouth."

"That man lied to you, son," Jack said. "He was no policeman. Are you all right?"

"I guess," Aaron said.

Jack dropped down to the boy's level and said, "Hey, that's a neat-looking sailboat you've got there."

"It's my birthday present."

"Awesome. What do say we get you out of here and you can show me how it works?"

"We've been trying to get out," Aaron said. "We're lost."

"No worries," Jack said. "I've got a secret map that'll show us the way." He took the map out of his pocket.

"Bull," Aaron said.

"Aaron!" his mother said.

Jack held his right hand up in an oath gesture. "Honest. Want to help me read it?"

"Okay," Aaron said, though he still didn't sound convinced.

"We need to hurry," Pam Dorsey said. "That man had us in a little room. There was a box on the wall with a timer. I think he's going to blow it up."

Beth reached for her hand communicator to relay the information. There was no way to tell which transformer box it was. Jamison would have to cut power to all of them. His words about arc flashes and molten metal surfaced in her mind. As quickly as her hopes soared, they came spiraling back to the tunnel. There was no signal.

"We're too far underground," Jack said, seeing her expression. "The next maintenance door isn't far. Let's move."

Beth looked at the water. It had risen another inch.

"Do you know where this is coming from?" she asked Pam Dorsey.

"No. We were lying in it when we woke up."

"Was a pipe leaking?" Beth asked.

"Not where he had us. I thought maybe one had broken farther up the tunnel."

Apparently, the killer knew better than to mix electricity with water, at least when he wasn't around. All at once, his plan became clear. Blow the transformer box and electrocute everyone in the tunnel. Great way to make sure no one was following you.

Aaron said, "He put a camera on one of the pipes before he left. I saw him do it."

The news didn't surprise Beth. Apparently, Jack was right about him wanting to watch his victims die. If there was enough time, they might be able to find it and trace the signal. Maybe find a fingerprint or a serial number that would lead to him. What she really wanted was to put the bastard down. Something else Jack said when he was talking about Howard Pell now made sense: "I perceived I was looking at an aberration that shouldn't be allowed to exist in this world."

You don't rehabilitate cancer. You cut it out.

Chapter 54

On the other side of the highway, the tunnel began to rise. Oddly, they encountered another flow of water coming at them from the opposite direction.

Not good, Beth thought. *That means a second leak.*

From the expression on Jack's face, he'd reached the same conclusion. Young Aaron, who had been so brave and stoic throughout the ordeal, was at the point of exhaustion. He was fighting hard not to show it but losing the battle.

When Jack picked him up, the boy didn't resist.

"Let me give you a hand there, buddy."

Aaron closed his eyes and put his head on Jack's shoulder. After a minute, he went to sleep, still clutching his sailboat. Pam Dorsey gently pried it from his fingers.

The second stream of water was far stronger than the first and rising quickly. Despite the rubber boots, Beth could feel her legs going numb. They should have reached the maintenance door by now.

Somewhere, a digital timer was counting down.

We need to move quicker.

"There's the ladder," Jack said, drawing her back to the moment.

Beth checked her communicator again. The signal indicator read one bar. It might be enough for a call. Steve Jamison answered immediately. His words were filled with static.

"Thank God," he said. "Where are you?"

"Almost at point five on the map," Beth said. "We have Aaron and his mother. Repeat. We have—"

"You need to get out of there now. I just hung up with the water company. Pressure all over the city started dropping about eleven minutes ago. We think your man tampered with a number of lines."

Beth said, "You may be right. When we got down there, the water was coming from behind us. Now it's in front."

"Shit," Jamison said. "That could mean the reservoir. The water company's repair crew is standing by."

"Tell them to hold off," Beth said. "We have a bigger problem."

She quickly told Jamison about the timer Pam Dorsey had seen.

"It'll only take us a few minutes to shut down power. I'm making the call now."

"Good. We're starting up the ladder—"

Beth's words caught in her throat as a tremor shook the ground under her feet. The muted sound of a distant explosion followed.

"Are you there?" Jamison asked.

"Something just happened," Beth said. "An explosion—"

"Out! Out now!" Jamison yelled. "If he blew the relay and those lines come in contact with the water—"

"On our way," Beth said.

Jack told Pam Dorsey, "Up you go."

Aaron finally lifted his head and looked around confused.

"Can you climb, son?"

"Uh-huh."

"It's just like the jungle gym at school. Follow your mom. I'll take the sailboat and be right behind you."

Jack removed his protective jacket and wrapped it around the boy, then hoisted him onto the ladder and told him to keep his hands inside the sleeves. Beth gave her jacket to Pam Dorsey, who began to climb with surprising ease.

"You're next," Jack said to Beth.

Before she could reply, a rumbling noise from deeper in the tunnel snapped both their heads around. One after another, the safety lights two hundred yards in began to go out as a torrent of water came rushing at them.

Jack put the sailboat down, grabbed Beth, and swung her up onto the ladder. The water was on them before she had gone three rungs. So great was its force that it nearly tore Jack's grip loose.

"Jack!"

A head emerged followed by a hand and then the masts of a toy ship. Incredibly, he'd managed to retrieve the stupid sailboat.

"Go!" he yelled up at her.

In what seemed like the blink of an eye, the water started to fill their escape route. It was up to Jack's neck.

Beth began to climb. She trained her light upward and could see the top of the ladder and an opening where it terminated. The water continued to rise. Try as she might, she couldn't shake the memory of Sandra Goldner dying beneath Buford Dam.

Don't try to outrun the juice. You can't do it.

Hand over hand Beth climbed, steadily gaining on the access room. Fifty feet. Forty feet.

Dry skin isn't a great conductor. But wet skin is another matter.

The opening was only about twenty feet away. Aaron disappeared into it. Pam Dorsey scrambled in after him, then reached back to help Beth the last few feet. Below her, she saw Jack come to a halt. The expression on his face seemed confused. He blinked several times and looked around him, clinging to the ladder, shaking his head as if he was trying to clear it.

"Are you all right?" Beth called back.

Jack hung there, not moving. For a moment he appeared not to have heard her. She was about to start back down when he recovered and started to climb again.

"Everyone keep your hands and feet away from the ladder," Beth said as Jack tumbled through the opening. He still appeared disoriented. There was no time to ask what was wrong. The water was still rising.

Beth swept her Maglite beam over the walls and quickly spotted the access panel. The area they were in could hardly be called a room. Fortunately, the utility pipes and electrical conduit were far below them in the tunnel. She tried the door. Like the others, it was locked from the outside. Beth drew her gun.

"Cover your ears," she instructed. The muzzle flash lit up the room for an instant, and the resulting bang echoed in the narrow confine. The door stayed locked.

Using both arms, Beth took aim again and was about to pull the trigger when someone on the opposite side of the door shouted.

"Hold your fire!" It was Childers's voice. "We're right outside the door."

"Jesus. Did I hit anyone?"

"No, but the maintenance guy just had a heart attack. Hang on. We'll have you out in a minute."

As soon as the door opened, Jack instructed Aaron to go first and help his mother through. He told Childers, "This lady needs medical attention."

Beth started to call Steve Jamison about the power when the situation changed for the worse. A buzzing sound filled the room. A second later, both the ladder and the metal door frame around it turned blue.

The buzz morphed into a crackling sound as a jagged bolt of electricity appeared out of nowhere snaking its way across the metal frame. Moving. Changing shape. Like something out of a Star Trek movie.

Childers reacted quickly. He pulled off his rubber jacket and tossed it to Beth.

"Put that on," he yelled.

Jack appeared to have recovered from the fugue he was in. His eyes were glued to the electricity shifting in front of them, seemingly with a life of its own. Beth slowly put her arms in the jacket. The arc flash or whatever it was changed shaped again, extending completely across the frame, moving first upward, then down again.

In the hallway outside, Childers was shouting over his com unit for Jamison to kill the power.

Slowly, cautiously, Jack and Beth began to inch toward the access panel, never taking their eyes off the metal frame. Time seemed to stretch. Then finally, without warning, the blue snake winked out of existence, leaving an acrid smell in the room. Beth let out the breath she was holding and slid down the wall to a sitting position. She drew her knees up to her chest. Hugged them. Jack dropped down next to her. They looked at each other for several seconds before she rested her head on his shoulder. After several seconds, she looked up at him. When she replayed that moment in her mind, and she would do so many times, she knew the decision had been reached. Jack brought his mouth down on hers and kissed her. She responded by wrapping one arm behind his neck, the other going to the side of his face. The kiss continued.

"Jeez, get a room, you guys," Childers said from the doorway.

The world stopped spinning as they separated. A smile spread across Beth's face and crossed over to Jack. They both began laughing.

"We have a room," Jack said.

Chapter 55

Once they were outside and dried off, Childers informed them Pam and Aaron had been taken to Piedmont Hospital for treatment. The stocky detective looked at them and shook his head.

"Good work. You need a lift to the station?"

"I brought my car," Jack said.

"Pappas drove me," Beth said.

Childers further informed Beth that Noah Ritson wanted her to handle a press conference the following morning. She thought that was odd, since Jack had been the one talking to the media, but didn't comment. The detective said good-bye. They were alone on the street.

Jack was about to do the same when he noticed a toy sailboat leaning against the building.

"Uh oh, that won't do," he said, picking it up. "C'mon."

There were already two news trucks at the hospital. Reporters started shooting questions at them as they approached the entrance.

Jack slowed. "Detective Sturgis, the team's investigative leader, will hold a conference tomorrow. Both kidnap victims were recovered and appear to be in good health. There were some injuries to Mrs. Dorsey's hands, which the doctors are looking at now."

Aaron was in the waiting room with his father. He jumped up as soon as he saw Jack and Beth get off the elevator and ran to them.

"I think this belongs to you," Jack said, handing him the sailboat.

"Thank you. The doctor's fixing my mom's hands. They were hurt real bad."

"We know," Beth said, dropping down to his level. "Your mom's really brave and so are you. She'll be just fine."

They spent a few minutes talking to the husband before excusing themselves. When they were at the elevator, the sound of running footsteps caused Jack and Beth to turn. Aaron Dorsey came charging up and threw his arms around Beth's thighs, then did the same for Jack.

*

"I look like a drowned rat," Beth said, seeing her reflection in the side window of Jack's car.

"You look fine," he said. "Get in. I'll take you home."

"What about Dan?"

"He has a home."

"Jack."

"I texted him a few minutes ago. He said he'll see you tomorrow."

Jack was quiet on the ride to Beth's house. He appeared to be preoccupied, which wasn't unusual for him as Beth was coming to learn. She attributed this to him thinking about the case and didn't try to force the conversation. She was thinking about their kiss, the way he smiled at her in the elevator and put his arm around her shoulders as they walked back to his car. Something had changed, something fundamental. She wanted to know what was going through his head. But he wasn't talking. He'd come out of it when he came out of it. Maybe he was thinking about the kiss, too.

At home, she fixed him a Scotch with a little ice and told him to make himself comfortable in the den while she showered and changed clothes. Peeka the cat jumped up on the couch and sat beside him.

*

Ten minutes later, they were still sitting there when he heard the water come on. What happened in the tunnel had rocked him. Not a panic attack exactly. More a recognition about what was causing them. It was the trigger he and Moe Shottner had been searching for. He'd been so unprepared for it he nearly lost his grip on the ladder and was certain Beth had noticed. She would have questions. Any partner might. But what to tell her. Jack took a sip of the Scotch. It produced a mixture of sensations. Clean and smooth in his mouth. Warming as it went down.

He was still immersed in his thoughts when he heard a noise to his right and turned to see what it was. Beth was standing in the doorway with a towel around her that came barely to the top of her thighs. Jack's drink nearly went down the wrong way.

"Care to join me?" Beth asked.

234

Jack slowly put the glass down on the coffee table and got up. They stood staring at each other for several seconds before Beth smiled and held out her hand.

As they lay in the bed afterward, Jack decided, all in all, it may have been the best shower of his life. Maybe the best shower in history. He'd nearly drowned trying to be creative.

Beth had fallen asleep on his chest. Her mass of brunette hair was a tumble around the pillow. When he leaned down and kissed her on the forehead, she smiled, made a little contented noise, and snuggled closer, molding herself against his side.

Through the window, he could see the lights had come on in her garden. Water poured from the lion's mouth of her fountain into a catch basin below it, creating a series of shadows. A mild rain had begun falling. Drops slid down the windows and off the plant leaves. If there was anything better than lying there together like that, he didn't know it. He felt at peace.

*

At eight o'clock that night, they finally stirred. They went down to the kitchen to fix a bite to eat. Beth made omelets, which they ate at her breakfast table.

Beth said, "The last time we were here, we were talking about relationships and I asked you if you've been lonely."

"You did."

"And you said, 'Some.'"

"I did."

"So there's really no one special in your life right now?"

"I'm having dinner with her," Jack said.

The compliment produced a smile, but then her face became serious. "We might as well get this out of the way right now. I really care for you, Jack, but I'm not good at sharing."

Jack blinked. "Well . . . neither am I."

"Good," Beth said, with an emphatic nod.

"Good."

There was a pause. They sat facing each other.

"Did we just decide something?"

"Maybe."

"*Maybe?*"

"I need to tell you something before you make your decision," Jack said. "I have a problem with panic attacks, and I may take my pills more than I should."

235

"Okay," Beth said. "We can deal with that."

"And there are times that I drink too much."

Beth stood, walked around the table, and picked up Jack's wine glass. Along with hers, the contents were emptied down the kitchen sink. Jack frowned.

He was still sitting there when she returned and sat down.

"So," Beth said, "did we just decide something?"

A smile slowly spread across Jack's face. "Yes, ma'am. I believe we did."

Chapter 56

Because Dan Pappas was coming by to pick her up, they decided it would be best for Jack to leave early. Technically, he outranked her, and, consultant or not, their relationship, if it became known, was a violation of department rules. Not a major one, but sufficient to raise eyebrows and possibly sidetrack her career. Beth told him she would speak with Dave Childers and ask him to keep their kiss quiet. She felt he was a decent man who would go along with it. Beyond that, they decided discretion was the wisest route.

Jack thought about Beth as he showered. It had been a long time since he had anyone to share the foxhole with, as his father used to say. Was she impetuous? Definitely. Headstrong? Certainly. She was also funny and intelligent. She might be able to handle panic attacks. But could she deal with what he'd become?

While he was getting dressed, he turned on the television. According to the news reports, the killer had blown not only a water main but one of the city's reservoir holding tanks. He switched channels to find Noah Ritson being interviewed about the rescue of Pam and Aaron Dorsey. Beth was standing beside him.

The deputy chief was measured in the information he was doling out. An old hand at the job, Ritson knew better than to disclose any strategies that might compromise the case. At the bottom of the screen was a banner that read, "Terror Attack?" Sad.

As team leader, much of the credit went to Beth, which was fine. She deserved it. Ritson had apparently decided it was time to bring her into the spotlight. Also fine.

When it was Beth's turn, she fielded the questions smoothly as if press conferences were a daily occurrence for her.

At one point, a reporter called out, "Are you close to making an arrest, Detective?"

"We are. It won't be long, I assure you."

Jack blinked. It was a pretty aggressive statement to make. He wished he were that confident. He glanced at Marta, who was lying on the floor watching him. Her ears perked up. You never knew when someone might toss you a treat.

"She's good, isn't she?"

Marta's tail rocked back and forth twice, which he took for a yes.

"I need to see Morris Shottner. I won't be home late. Promise."

The deputy chief stood, indicating the press conference was at an end. Beth followed suit. Marta, finally concluding that no treat was forthcoming, also stood and walked over to the window. She turned around twice and lay down in a square of sunlight closing her eyes.

On his way to Morris Shottner's office, Jack continued to reflect on what had happened in the tunnel. He'd been able to think of little else. Intellectually, he understood what traumatic amnesia and repression were—defense mechanisms the mind develops to deal with emotional trauma—but understanding them wasn't enough.

His recognition of what was causing the attacks happened so suddenly and with such frightening clarity, he was literally speechless. Scenes buried deep within his subconscious came hurtling into the present, leaving him appalled. Stunned.

*

Morris Shottner was using a finger to tamp down the tobacco in a white Meerschaum pipe with a translucent orange-colored stem. He went about the task methodically as he waited for Jack to continue.

"When I lost my grip on the ladder, saving that boy's boat suddenly became the most important thing in the world to me. That's when I knew."

Shottner nodded but said nothing.

"The dream I've been having since Connie died always involves a boat, Moe."

"And you know what that means now?" Shottner asked.

"I think so. There was a painting over her couch of an old sailing ship moored at Maiden Lane in New York. Turn of the century stuff. It's the same one in my dream."

"You're sure of this?"

"Absolutely. Everything was there, right down to the cobblestone street and the gaslights."

Shottner nodded. He didn't appear surprised.

"It fits," Jack said.

"So you remember everything," Shottner said.

He had always known what happened with Connie, but the trauma was so great that his mind had automatically applied its own bandage and shunted the event into the furthest corner of his consciousness. Now in one single instant of awareness, he realized not only what he had done and how he'd been avoiding dealing with it but what he believed was the trigger to his panic attacks.

"Have you shared this with anyone?"

"You mean Beth?"

"Yes."

Jack shook his head slowly. "I needed to speak with you first. There'll be consequences."

Shottner finished loading his pipe and placed it in a rack on the side of his desk. The tobacco consisted of black, brown, and gold shreds. Its pleasant smell filled the room.

"I'm not sure what to tell you about the consequences," Shottner said. "People, your relationships, and your mental health are another matter. I suppose the easiest way to say it is there are times we have to give up the dead and accept the living."

"Nice platitude," Jack said.

"Most platitudes are based on the truth. Or if not the truth, then on common sense. The legal part is problematic, I agree. But I can say, any relationship that rests on a lie has a poor foundation and very little chance for success."

Jack made a face. "Sounds like something off a Hallmark card."

"Actually, Hallmark got it from Carl Jung," Shottner said.

"Trite."

"Doesn't mean it's not true."

Jack went quiet and looked out the window at the old oak tree where he had seen the squirrels. There was no sign of them. He wondered what they were up to.

"You think I should tell her?"

"What are your feelings on the subject?"

"Truthfully, scared," Jack said.

"Not surprising," Shottner said.

"That doesn't help, Moe. I feel like I'm standing on the edge of a black hole."

"Which do you suppose is greater?" Shottner asked, "Living with the fear of her finding out on her own or her reaction when you tell her?"

"I don't know. She sees things pretty much in black and white. There's not much middle ground where Beth's concerned."

"You don't have to decide. Just mull it over."

Jack nodded.

"I suspect the answer will become clear in due course. Once the clouds lift, things have a tendency to start falling into place."

"Meaning there may be more than one cause for the attacks?"

"Possibly."

Jack stared at him. "You don't think they'll go away now?"

"I sincerely hope they will," Shottner said. "I'd like to talk about your reaction to what happened the night Connie Belasco was killed."

"Let's do it another time," Jack said.

"All right," the doctor said and shifted topics. "Are you making any progress with your case?"

"Apart from rescuing those people," Jack said, "not a great deal. We've been a step behind since day one."

"Saving lives counts for something."

"We've been lucky."

"Is that what you think it is? Luck?"

"To some extent."

"I'm curious. Why do you suppose the killer contacted you?" Shottner asked.

"It's part of the game he's playing," Jack said.

"As in a challenge. *You can't catch me.* That sort of thing?"

"Right."

"Immature, but it makes sense," Shottner said. "Are you expecting him to strike again?"

"Unfortunately, yes. He's begun taking more risks, particularly after we stopped him at Underground Atlanta."

"How are the woman and boy you rescued?"

"Resting," Jack said. "Her husband's taking time off from work to be with them."

"Good to hear," Shottner said. "Any more panic attacks to report since the last time you were here?"

"No."

Shottner nodded as if this was something he had already concluded.

"Let me jump back a moment," the doctor said. "This game the killer is playing, would you say it's more like chess than hide and seek?"

"Definitely," Jack said.

"Is it just between you and him, or will anyone do?"

Jack sat up straighter in the chair.

"No," he said slowly. "It's definitely directed at me. The victims are pawns. Incidental, when you think about it. Knowing I was involved, he needed to draw me into that tunnel. That's why he sent the video to me. Why he put my name on the satchel."

"You sound sure."

"If he wanted to kill Pam Dorsey and her son, he could have done so right away. Instead, he rigged a bomb with a delay timer and waited for me to show up."

"Out of curiosity, did he try to mummify these people as he did that woman in Underground Atlanta?"

Jack didn't answer immediately. Instead, his eyes grew unfocused, staring off into the distance. It was something Morris Shottner had seen him do before. The doctor waited.

"There was no mummification this time," Jack said slowly, speaking almost to himself. "No mummification." He finally looked at Shottner. "Which means he's changing again. The tunnels are like the passages and false doorways and traps in the pyramids. The pharaohs' builders set them up to kill thieves and anyone who entered the burial chamber. He started off following Howard Pell, but now he's imitating Albert Lemon.

"When the police were digging through the rubble of Lemon's home after the fire, they discovered he had dug out and expanded his basement to resemble a maze, complete with pitfalls, a spring shotgun, and doors that opened into a wall or a hole. They discovered four more bodies buried there."

"So the tunnels were your killer's trap?"

"A very deadly one."

"And he didn't care if other people were killed?"

"Their deaths wouldn't matter to him. I'm the only one with a connection to Howard Pell."

"Something to think about," Shottner said. "When will you see Beth again?"

"Tonight, I imagine. We didn't make any specific plans. It might be a good time to talk with her."

"It might," Shottner said.

*

The Soul Eater sat in his den watching Deputy Chief Ritson's press conference. Not only did Clever Jack and the others survive, but that miserable woman and her child gave the police a description of him. His face was now all over the news. Not that it mattered. They only saw what he wanted them to see.

On the desk next to him was a prosthetic nose he used along with the jaw and cheek additions that altered his face and made him unrecognizable. Alongside them were three contact lens cases. Due to the miracle of modern science, it was easy enough to change eye color using contact lenses. Let them show their stupid sketch.

They were getting closer, just as Howard said they would. His prediction of Jack Kale being a worthy opponent was correct. Everything Howard said was coming to pass. The man was brilliant.

The woman detective couldn't be underestimated either. She'd shown a great deal of resilience. Worthy or not, they were no match for him. So they figured out the clues more quickly than he gave them credit for. Luck is always difficult to factor in. Perhaps he should start calling Kale "Lucky Jack" in the future.

The Soul Eater smiled. He turned to the next chapter in the book he was reading.

A few more days one way or the other wouldn't make a difference.

Chapter 57

Instead of feeling pleasure at the praise she was receiving for her part in saving Pam and Aaron Dorsey, Beth left the press conference distracted and fighting a headache. Her night with Jack had been wonderful. The physical part aside, she thought they had connected on an emotional level. In fact, she was positive of it, which was why his failure to explain what happened in the tunnel was so perplexing. On the ride back from the hospital and later at her home, she waited for him to talk about it. Something had clearly happened. If she didn't know better, she would have described his initial reaction on the ladder as someone who was in shock. She'd seen those symptoms before in others. So she didn't press and waited for him to speak on his own. He didn't. It was frustrating because there wasn't much she could do except wait and see what the new day would bring.

By lunchtime, Jack still hadn't called or made an appearance. Beth began to wonder if he was having second thoughts. She certainly wasn't. But there was no time to dwell on it because a number of other matters were competing for her attention. The inklings of an idea had begun to form in her mind about how to catch the killer. It was something she and Pappas had initially missed when they viewed Mayfield's security tapes.

As quickly as the possibility of a solution dawned on her, doubts began to form. What if she was wrong? She'd already made a mistake putting all her chips in one basket with Gary Merkle. That couldn't happen again. She thought about calling Jack and Pappas, then shelved the idea. Wouldn't it be interesting to see Jack's face if she solved the case before he did?

Beth made her decision and placed a call to Charles Raymond's office.

*

When she arrived at Mayfield, she was relieved to find Dr. Raymond had been called out of the office. Just as well. He'd left the personnel files she requested with his secretary and word that she could view the security tapes on Pell's cell again.

Tony Gillam, the officer in charge, set her up on a video monitor and showed her how to operate the equipment, then left her alone. Five hours later, Beth had what she wanted, or thought she did. The techs would be able to tell for sure after they analyzed the film. She shut the monitor, thanked Officer Gillam, and headed for the parking lot at the rear of the building where she had parked.

It was late afternoon and surprisingly warm, almost as if someone had flipped a switch to get spring under way. On cue, the azaleas and dogwoods had come into bloom, something about Atlanta that never ceased to impress her no matter how many times she'd seen it.

Behind the main building was Mayfield's exercise track, where non-violent inmates could walk or run. Except for a solitary figure approaching her around the turn, the track was deserted.

"Why, if it isn't Ms. Sturgis. What a nice surprise."

"Dr. Cairo, how are you?"

"Very well. And you?"

"I'm fine."

"What brings you here today? Your case?"

"I'm afraid so. I wanted to review your personnel files again. Dr. Raymond was kind enough to make copies for me."

Beth showed him the file she was carrying.

"Excellent. Care to stretch your legs? I'm on my last lap."

Beth fell into place beside him. The track was hard packed dirt and wound through a fair number of trees, bucolic except for a chain link fence topped with coils of razor wire. As they walked, the azaleas' scent carried on a mild breeze drifted past them.

"So, how is your investigation coming?" the doctor asked.

"Slowly. But I may be onto something," Beth said.

"Oh?"

"How well did you know Ron Curry?"

Cairo looked surprised. "Curry? Barely at all. He was a contract nurse here for a while."

"Did you ever notice him acting oddly?"

Cairo frowned. "Not that I could see. But to be honest, everyone out here is a bit odd."

Beth smiled.

"Is there a problem with him?"

"It may just be a clerical error. I'm still checking."

"He seemed pleasant enough and competent. To tell the truth, I didn't have much contact with the man."

"I understand," Beth said. "What about Dr. Raymond?"

"Charles?"

"Did he ever mention observing anything out of the ordinary?"

"Well, I can't speak for Charles. If he did, he never said anything to me. Mostly I just do my therapy and head home."

"No friends here?" Beth asked.

"Not really. Charles can be a bit much to take on a regular basis."

Beth nearly laughed. "I thought he was a pompous ass."

"That might be one way to describe him," Cairo said.

"When we spoke, he mentioned you've had a number of sessions with Pell."

The doctor frowned at her statement. "I've handled virtually all of Howard's therapy since he arrived here. He's a fascinating individual."

"A colleague of mine says he has no conscience."

Cairo glanced at her as they rounded the far end of the track and took a moment to compose his response.

"I don't think I'd argue with that. Somewhere along the line, How-ard took a wrong turn. I've worked with him for years now and have come to believe I'll never understand the engine that drives him."

"He's an unusual man," Beth said.

Cairo kicked a branch out of the way as they walked, then said, "May I ask what it is about Mr. Curry you're looking into?"

"I can't say at this point."

Cairo smiled without humor. "Just curious. The recent murders in Jordan have put everyone a bit on edge. Do you feel you're close to an arrest?"

"Honestly, yes," Beth said.

"I can assure you a great many people will be happy to hear that. What happened is just horrible. Did you learn anything useful from your talks with Howard?"

"He thinks Jack Kale framed him for murder and killed the people we found at Underground Atlanta."

"Ah, Jack Kale," Cairo said. "He's a name I recognize from my therapy sessions. Howard's quite fixated on him. I take it Mr. Kale is not considered a viable suspect?"

"Hardly. The earliest bodies we found are about eighty to eighty-five years old, Doctor. They're likely the work of a serial killer named Albert Lemon who operated in Atlanta during the early to mid-1900s."

"There's another name I recognize. Lemon is a favorite of Howard's. Perhaps I should let you do the therapy."

"I'm afraid I wouldn't be much good at it," Beth said. "I don't need to understand criminals, just put them away."

"And is that why you went into police work?"

The question was unexpected. She thought for a moment, then said, "I suppose so. That and the belief I could do some good. Does that sound silly?"

"Not at all. It's quite admirable," Cairo said.

"I do have a question," Beth said. "Can someone like Pell be cured?"

This time it was the doctor's turn to pause.

"We're making advances all the time, not only in the psychotropic medications we prescribe, but in our therapeutic techniques. While I'm reluctant to say no," he stopped to look up at a window on the third floor where a solitary figure was watching them, "I wouldn't hold my breath."

Beth followed his glance. The chill that seized her stomach stayed with her until she was well onto the highway.

Chapter 58

Jack returned to the North Precinct to find the mood upbeat. A kind of charged anticipation hung in the air, the kind every cop feels when a case is about to break. The reason was one Walid Zirmann.

Working overtime, Stafford and Mundas continued to canvas the neighborhood where the Dorseys had been kidnapped hoping to find a witness to their abduction. They found Mr. Zirmann, or rather he found them.

Zirmann was the owner of a convenience store on Dresden Road and lived in the area. He saw the detectives' car and approached them to complain about a cop who thought he was above the law. Zirmann explained he was on his way to work when he saw a policeman get out of a black van on the day Pam and Aaron were taken. Ordinarily, he wouldn't have paid much attention to it, but the cop had parked his vehicle on the wrong side of the street. Thursdays were reserved for street cleaning and trash pickup in the neighborhood. If he had to obey alternate side of the street parking, why didn't the police? Public-spirited Walid had gone so far as to take a picture of the van with his cell phone and was thinking of posting it on Facebook.

Unfortunately, Walid's camera had captured only a portion of the license plate. Stafford, Mundas, and Pappas were trying to run down various combinations of the license with the DMV.

"Where's Beth?" Jack asked.

"Piedmont Park. They have a security camera on the old stables. She's checking the disc to see if it might have caught the killer." He pointed to a small Middle Eastern–looking man sitting in a chair at Mundas's desk. "Walid over there saw the guy who was driving the van and says it was a cop."

Jack looked at Walid, who stood and smiled back at him. He motioned for him to sit. Walid looked very pleased with the attention he was getting.

"I think I'll run up there and see if I can help her," Jack said, seizing on the opportunity to speak to Beth alone.

"Good idea," Pappas said and went back to his computer screen.

En route to Piedmont Park, Jack's walkie-talkie beeped to show a BOLO for the black van had gone out. On arrival, the manager told him he had just missed Beth.

"Did she say where she was going?"

"Something about grabbing a bite to eat at the Flying Biscuit."

"She find anything useful on the camera?"

"I guess. She left here in a kind of a hurry."

Jack thanked him and started walking. He dialed Beth's phone but the call went to voice mail. The restaurant she was heading for was on Tenth Street, only a short distance from the park entrance.

After a few minutes, he spotted the familiar figure of Beth Sturgis in a black pantsuit about five blocks ahead. Crawling along behind her was a black van, the same make and model the cops were now looking for. Was it possible? Her appearance at the press conference that morning had placed Beth squarely in the public eye.

Jack picked up his pace. He couldn't be certain but it looked as though the van was shadowing her. He'd told the chief as the pressure on the killer increased, the time between his kills would shorten. Beth's statement about being close to an arrest could have been the straw that broke the camel's back. If this was the killer's territory, they were right in the middle of it.

Jack pulled his walkie-talkie out and called the central switchboard.

"Connect me with Glen Sheeley."

Sheeley answered within thirty seconds.

"This is Kale. I'm on foot, heading south on Piedmont Road at Fifteenth Street. Detective Sturgis is up ahead of me and about to turn onto Tenth Street. There's a black van following her that may be the UNSUB. I think he's going to make a move on her."

"On our way."

"Silent approach," Jack said, breaking into a jog and drawing his weapon.

"Roger that."

Beth was nearly at the corner with the van still maintaining its distance. He could just make out the silhouette of a man behind the steering wheel.

Ahead on Tenth Street, he saw a police cruiser's light bar come on as it swung about in a U-turn. There was no reaction from the van. It continued around the corner after Beth as Jack accelerated into a full run.

He didn't need to shout for people to get out of his way. Seeing a man with a gun charging up the street cleared the path. Running for all he was worth, Jack rounded the corner and was startled to see what looked like every cop in Atlanta on the scene.

The van was completely surrounded with at least twenty guns trained on it. An astonished Beth Sturgis stood on the sidewalk watching her brethren flood the street. Jack showed his shield and approached the van keeping his gun trained on the driver, who had his hands up and was shouting something through the glass. Two more uniforms, each holding shotguns, were cautiously approaching from opposite sides. Officers crouched behind patrol cars, revolvers drawn and aimed at the driver.

When Jack opened the door and hauled the man out, he finally heard what he was screaming.

"Hal Loehman! I'm Hal Loehman, with the *National Star*! I'm a reporter!"

No one was taking any chances. Loehman was placed on the ground and handcuffed. Glen Sheeley's unmarked cruiser came flying down Tenth Street and screeched to a halt as a SWAT officer hauled the man to his feet.

"My ID's in my wallet!" Loehman yelled. "Jesus Christ, I'm a reporter."

The cop handed Sheeley the wallet and waited. Beth stuck the file she'd been reading under her arm and joined them.

"Jack, what—?"

"He's a reporter," Sheeley said.

"I saw him following her," Jack said.

"It's true," Loehman said. "At the press conference, she said an arrest was imminent. I was trying to get the story."

Jack let out the breath he'd been holding as a flush built in his face. Loehman was considerably shorter and wider than the descriptions the victims had given. He was also mostly bald and had to weigh at least 275 pounds.

"Jack?" Sheeley asked.

"Let him go."

As soon as he heard that, Loehman recovered some of his bravado. "You're lucky I don't sue for false arrest. I won't 'cause I like to get along with the cops."

The officer holding his arms turned him around and released the cuffs.

Loehman said, "Haven't you people heard of freedom of the press down here?"

The cop gave him his best deadpan stare and said, "You'll want to move your car, sir. You're blocking traffic."

Sheeley gave the order to disperse and motioned Jack over to the side. Beth joined them.

"Well, you got our blood pumping there, pal," he said.

"I apologize."

"No apology necessary. You did the right thing. Unfortunately, this went out over the air. Don't be surprised if the chief gives you a call."

Jack nodded. "Sorry again."

Sheeley put a hand on his shoulder. "Not to worry. We don't win 'em all. Next time's the charm."

Before Jack could reply, his cell phone went off. He turned the screen around and showed it to Sheeley, who shook his head. It was Noah Ritson's secretary calling to advise him the chief wanted a few minutes when he had a moment. Jack told her he'd be there in the morning.

The SWAT commander gave them a sympathetic look, got back in his cruiser, and left.

Chapter 59

Once again they found themselves alone on a street. It was obvious Jack was embarrassed by the incident. Beth knew he'd made the right decision, and she was prepared to tell the chief that. If an officer believed another's life was in danger, they were obliged to protect it. She would have done the same had the circumstances been reversed.

The silence between them grew heavy. It had been over a day and they hadn't spoken since the morning he left her house. She wanted to know what he was thinking. Feeling. She wanted to say something to make him feel better. Jack's mouth was drawn in a tight line.

"What you did wasn't wrong. The chief will understand."

"I know that," Jack said. "I thought you were in danger. I'd make the same call again in a heartbeat."

"Then I don't understand. What's bothering you?"

"We need to talk."

Oh boy. He's going to tell me we made a mistake. Shit.

"All right," Beth said, clasping her hands in front of her.

Jack opened his mouth, then closed it again and glanced up and down the street.

"Would you like to talk someplace else?" Beth prompted quietly.

Several seconds ticked by.

"My place," Jack said, taking her by the elbow.

Chapter 60

Beth went directly to the living room and sat down. She sat with her knees together. Hands folded in her lap. Jack took a seat at the opposite end of the sofa, one cushion between them. He unclipped the holster and gun from his belt and put them on the coffee table.

"I've been trying to figure out how to say this for a while now."

"Go ahead," Beth said quietly.

Jack took a deep breath and began. "Something happened in the tunnel. Something I wasn't prepared for. Do you remember I mentioned my panic attacks?"

"Yes."

"I've been trying to get a handle on them for some time now. In my case, bits and pieces have been coming back for a while, mostly in my dreams. But until I was on the ladder holding that boy's sailboat, they were nothing but shadows—smoke."

Beth nodded and let him continue.

"I've mentioned Connie Belasco to you."

"Your partner," Beth said.

"She was a year or two younger than you are now," Jack said. "We worked the Scarecrow case. For the longest time, it felt like we were walking through mud. Then things started coming together. Some of the stuff our expert advisor was saying didn't add up."

"Howard Pell," Beth said.

"Exactly."

Jack leaned forward and aligned the holster so that its long edge was parallel to the side of the coffee table. He looked at Beth and went on. "Little by little, Connie and I began to suspect Pell was leading us around by the nose. It didn't make sense. She wanted to confront him. I was in favor of giving him enough rope to hang himself. She was always a little impetuous. Somewhat like you, actually."

Beth had no comment to that. She nodded for him to continue.

"Something Connie said must have spooked him. Pell followed her home and used a Taser to knock her out. Then he started cutting."

Jack squeezed his eyes shut and shook his head as if that could clear away the images he was seeing. Marta got up from where she was lying, walked to the sofa, and rested her head on his lap. He scratched her absently behind the ears. For a moment his eyes settled on the gun before he continued.

"I tried calling her several times that night. Connie was always good about answering her phone. At first I didn't think much of it. But then I became worried. The more I thought about her not answering, the worse it got. I finally decided to stop by her place and check that she was all right."

A sheen of sweat had broken out on Jack's forehead. His breathing was heavy. If he was aware of this, he didn't show it. Beth watched him carefully. At one point, she thought he might actually become sick right there in the living room. She knew what was coming and forced herself to sit quietly and listen.

Jack gathered himself and continued.

"All the lights were off when I arrived. Her car was in the driveway. At first, I thought she might be out on a date. Maybe that she had fallen asleep. That's when I noticed the front door was ajar.

"I called her name several times. No answer. Then I heard it. A sound unlike any I'd ever heard before. Almost like an animal was in pain. I went in. Flicked on the lights."

Jack took in a gulp of air. Then another. Beth didn't know whether to get him a glass of water or sit still. He solved the problem by resuming his story.

"I found her in the spare bedroom. Pell had cut off her arms and legs. Tourniquets were applied to the stumps. He'd done other things to her face I won't tell you about. At first, I wasn't sure what I was looking at. Then I realized it was my partner. The pain she was in was horrendous. Beyond what any human being could bear.

"I consider myself a reasonably calm man. But the truth is I panicked. Nothing in my experience prepared me for what I was seeing. I'd been in combat. Seen injuries in Afghanistan. Terrible, terrible wounds. Seen men shot. Bodies blown apart. The worst sights imaginable. They paled in comparison.

"I finally got myself together and was reaching for the phone to call an ambulance when I realized Connie was trying to say something."

Jack's voice trailed away.

It took a moment before Beth asked, "What?"

"She was asking me to kill her."

Chapter 61

Beth's eyes went wide. All at once she knew what had happened. "*You* killed her," she said. Her words were barely audible.

Jack stared at her for a long moment, then said, "That's right."

No explanation. No excuse. Just "That's right."

"Dear God," Beth said.

"Pell told you the truth . . . about that, at least."

Her mind went into a tailspin. Without realizing it, she stood as the tentacles of what happened that night reached into the room. It took several seconds to bring her emotions under control. Jack was still sitting on the couch watching her. His face had the strangest look. One she'd never seen before. His hand was within inches of his gun. A trickle of fear ran up her spine.

How well did she know this man? Her own gun was across the room in her purse.

Jack said, "Do you remember what I told you about fighting monsters?"

"Be careful you don't become one yourself," Beth whispered.

Jack's fingers closed around the handle of his weapon. There was no way for her to stop him.

"Here," he said, picking it up.

"What?"

"Take it. I'm surrendering myself to you."

"What?" she repeated.

"I'm turning myself in."

She stared at Jack, at a complete loss for words. It wasn't a joke. He appeared completely serious. After a moment she pushed his hand away and sat back down.

"Could she have lived?"

Unable to maintain eye contact, Jack stared out the window for several seconds. He finally lifted his shoulders. "There was a very small chance. Pell had applied tourniquets like I said, but they were ineffective. The bleeding wouldn't stop. I've never seen so much blood."

A vision of what it must have been like rose in Beth's mind with appalling clarity. She shuddered. Then another thought occurred to her.

"Did that have something to do with your marriage breaking up?"

"After what I had done to Pell, it wasn't safe to have them around any longer," Jack said. "Just couldn't take the chance I might snap again. There's a doctor I see who's been helping me. I'd become so good at avoiding dealing with the problem, the process became automatic for me. Then in one instant, everything became clear. At least I think it was everything."

Beth shook her head trying to make sense of it all. This was insane.

Jack added, "Believe it or not, you've both helped me."

"I don't understand."

"My doctor and you."

"Me?"

"Yes."

Beth looked at the man sitting across from her. There was no way to tell what he was really thinking. His voice in recounting the story had little inflection. Almost mechanical, as if he was reading a report someone else had written.

Shit, Beth thought. *What the hell do I do now?* To have kept this bottled up all these years. It was a mess. The biggest mess she'd ever come across. Dating an accountant suddenly seemed to have its advantages. A nice, safe accountant. *I'll talk it over with Dan Pappas. No. Bad idea. Wrong to involve him.* She recalled reading a quote years ago that said, "Three people could keep a secret if two of them were dead."

Other pieces began to fall into place. Things she'd heard about Jack suddenly began to make sense. His becoming a recluse after the Pell trial. His avoidance of publicity. The separation from the FBI for "medical reasons." How much did they actually know? She needed time to think. Needed to get away and process the implications.

"I have to go," Beth said.

Jack sat there silent.

She didn't kiss him good-bye. He didn't see her to the door. He leaned back on the couch and closed his eyes.

Chapter 62

The last thing Beth wanted was to be alone with her thoughts. Too many scenarios were competing for her attention. It was clear: her duty as a police officer was to report the crime. Concealing it would only compound the problem. Considering her involvement with him, any pretense at objectivity was out the window. The situation was making her ill. Was it something that could be handled discretely? Certainly the consequences surrounding a disclosure would be dire. No question about that. She knew the department was good at protecting their own, but Jack was an outsider. They'd throw him to the dogs in a heartbeat. This was a disaster in the making.

At a little past midnight, Beth found herself back at the North Precinct. The night shift was never very crowded, something she was grateful for at that moment. If anyone thought her appearance was unusual, they didn't mention it.

The file room was located in the basement. Beth hated the place. It smelled musty and generally gave her the creeps. Its lone saving grace was a civilian clerk the department employed to handle requests. At least she wouldn't be alone.

Evening Watch Supervisor Belinda Washington put down the crossword puzzle she was working on as Beth approached her desk. She eyed her without enthusiasm and didn't get up.

"Good evening," Beth said.

"Evenin'," Belinda replied.

"I need to see a file."

"That's generally why y'all come down here."

"It's about seven years old."

"You kiddin' me?"

"I'm not."

"Most files that old are downtown at the archives."

"Maybe we'll get lucky," Beth said.

"We? Ain't no we about it, honey. I'll be the only one gettin' dusty huntin' it."

"I'd really appreciate your help," Beth said.

"Uh-huh."

"Please," Beth added, remembering her father's advice to be nice to the clerks. They run the world.

Belinda sighed and asked for the file name.

"Constance Belasco. Her homicide occurred at the Prado."

"You need to fill out a request form," Belinda said, pointing to a stack of five-by-seven cards on the counter. "If you want somethin' outta property, use the green one on the right and take it to the second floor."

"Thank you," Beth said. "The file will be just fine."

Belinda finally concluded that Beth wasn't going away. She tossed her pencil onto the crossword puzzle. She heaved herself out of the chair, frowned at the form Beth had completed, and then took it without comment and wandered off down the hallway at slightly better than a glacial pace.

After waiting for ten minutes, Beth was about to climb over the counter and go looking for her when Belinda reappeared carrying a brown folder. Beth thanked her again and wished her a good night. Belinda waved and went back to her crossword puzzle.

At her desk, Beth turned to the initial investigative report, put together by a senior detective named Patrick Canfield. As she started to read, there were no surprises. The narrative tracked closely with Jack's version. Next up was the medical examiner's report, which recounted the obvious facts of Connie Belasco's injuries. Her blood loss. The extensive damage to her face. Her limbs. It was a chilling account.

She'd read a number of medical reports and was surprised at the number of adjectives used to describe Belasco's injuries. Clearly, the doctor writing it was deeply affected by what he had seen. Repulsed might have been a better word. Phrases like "amateurish hacking" and "callous use of tourniquets at improper tension levels" jumped out at her. Her eye eventually came to rest on "horrific facial injuries resulting from the gross removal of all three epidural layers."

Though prepared for it, Beth's stomach did a flip.

The report went on to say, "After torturing the victim, the assailant put a 9 mm bullet in her head at close range, an act largely unnecessary since the outcome of Detective Belasco's death was by then a foregone conclusion."

She let her breath out slowly. What Jack did was wrong, but given the circumstances, it might have been considered a mercy. Beth turned the last page of the narrative and sat there for a moment deciding whether to go on. She wasn't sure if she'd be able to handle the crime scene photos. No choice. She took a deep breath and turned them over. After the third one, she stopped, went to the ladies' room, and threw up.

The decision about what to do came as she was walking back to her desk. Her mind was quiet. There would be no report to the bosses. Jack would not turn himself in. Howard Pell had claimed enough victims. Ruining Jack's life would only add to that total. The past needed to stay buried. In the morning, she'd let him know. At the moment, she was exhausted. No, it couldn't wait.

They still had a job to do. Time to go on.

Beth picked up the phone.

Chapter 63

Jack's phone rang four times and went to voice mail. Beth left a message then tried his cell phone with the same results. She was careful not to say anything damaging.

When she disconnected, it felt like a weight had been lifted off her shoulders. Other than in the obvious way, she wasn't sure how repression worked, but if it helped Jack deal with the trauma, it couldn't be a bad thing. If he'd discovered what set his panic attacks off, they'd deal with that, too. Beth placed the file in her desk and locked it. On the way out, she ran into Mickey Barnes, a detective she knew.

"Late night, Sturgis?"

"Just some cleanup work."

"I heard about your big adventure today," he said. Barnes glanced at the wall clock, saw it was nearly one o'clock in the morning, and then added, "Guess it was yesterday. Tell Kale not to sweat it. There'll be a few jokes, but that's how cops are." He looked up at the ceiling. "The DC, I don't know. I'm not sure the guy has a sense of humor. Bottom line—solid call."

"Thanks, Mickey. I'll tell him."

"Heading home?"

"Yep. I'm beat."

"New day tomorrow. We never close."

Beth smiled and patted him on the arm. "Can't wait."

*

The streets were silent. Inert. Waiting for the sun. As she drove, the faces of Betsy Ann Tinsley, Sarah Goldner, and Jerome Haffner came to her.

Beth spoke their names aloud. It was a tradition with the RHD detectives. No one disappears without someone to speak for them.

After studying the employee list and the videos Dr. Raymond had left for her, she thought she could prove Pell's involvement now. Nailing him as an accessory to felony murder would be the icing on the cake. Of course, he would fall back on his insanity defense. That was for the courts to decide. She'd do everything in her power to disprove it. The bastard deserved a one-way ticket to the needle. When that happened, the world would celebrate one less monster.

New thoughts pushed out the old ones. Thoughts of what her future could be like with Professor Jackson Kale. Jumping the gun? Maybe. Was her house large enough for two? What if there were more? Jack's home was bigger, and children deserved a yard to play in. Did he even want more children? They'd known each other, what? Two weeks? Didn't matter. When you know, you know. They'd tackle those subjects one at a time. Life was looking up. Beth smiled.

She was still reviewing the possibilities as she rolled up to her garage. She pressed the remote-entry fob, pulled in, and shut off the engine. Beth entered through the hallway door and looked around. Peeka wasn't there to greet her. Normally, he'd come charging around the corner, then rub up against her legs. Easy way to score a treat. Beth called his name and listened. No meows. No sound of little claws racing across the den. For no reason she could point to, she grew concerned.

That stupid file probably spooked me.

The house had a different feel to it. She walked into the kitchen and then the dining room. Everything seemed normal. But no cat. Something was wrong.

Beth slowly removed the gun from her handbag and went into the living room. At first her eyes refused to accept what she was seeing. She gasped.

Peeka was lying in the middle of the rug in a small pool of blood. His head had been caved in.

She sensed rather than heard the movement behind her. Swinging around, Beth brought her weapon to bear. The killer's first blow struck her arm, knocking her gun to the ground. She screamed and instinctively threw up her other arm to protect herself. The second blow shattered her collarbone. The third grazed the side of her head. The blow was deflected but was hard enough to send her crashing backward. Beth lost her balance and fell hard. Waves of pain shot through her body.

Survival instincts took over as she scrambled away, trying to put some distance between them.

A pair of unblinking, gray eyes behind a ski mask regarded her. Desperate, Beth searched for a weapon. It was no use. Her arms weren't working properly. If she could only get to her feet, she might be able to fight him or reach the panic button on her burglar alarm. The furniture was beginning to swim. Beth struggled to her knees and collapsed. As she fell, some part of her brain registered the light on her fountain was out.

I'll get a new bulb tomorrow.

The killer advanced on her, holding a crowbar in his left hand, gently slapping it against his right.

Maybe another fountain to balance the garden.

*

A tick had started under the Soul Eater's left eye. It took an effort to compose himself. He stood there until his breathing returned to normal. He felt buoyant. What he had planned so meticulously was finally coming together.

Clever Jack was next on the agenda.

Chapter 64

Jack heard Beth's voice mail and called her back immediately. It was a noncommittal message, and he desperately wanted to speak with her. It had been two days now, and she hadn't returned his call. The fact that she hadn't spoke volumes. He didn't blame her. Some things were simply too hard to accept. Gradually, the realization that she wasn't going to call took hold. Dejected and depressed, he withdrew into himself. He sat on his patio looking out at the live oaks. The others could take it from there. A bottle of Jack Daniels and a half-filled glass were on the table next to him. The day was overcast with the promise of rain yet to be delivered. In the west, the clouds were alive with flashes of electricity. He picked up the glass, raised it to his lips, hesitated, and put it back down again. It was the third time in the last hour he had done so. Marta lay close by in the grass watching him, a yellow tennis ball next to her. Every so often she'd nudge it in his direction. Canine psychology.

Leaning back in his chair, he shut his eyes and speculated whether what he had done made him a sociopath. Probably. The definition was broad enough. Regardless of the label, one thing was certain: he was unfit to be around other human beings. The previous evening, Morris Shottner had called. They talked for an hour about the old nature/nurture question. He leaned toward nurture. The former might give you a push, but nothing was written in stone. Eventually, he opened his eyes and stared at the amber liquid in his glass. Droplets of water had formed along the outside. Once again, he pushed it away. The gesture was symbolic and ultimately meaningless.

Marta abruptly sat upright, her ears erect. A moment later, the doorbell rang. Whatever hopes he had that it was Beth were quickly dispelled when he saw Dan Pappas's car in his driveway. Sometime later, he would recall their meeting as akin to a tremolo running through the floor, the kind you might feel on the deck of a ship a moment before it hits an iceberg. In all likelihood, Beth had told him about their conversation and didn't want to be there when he was arrested. The moment he opened the door and saw the expression on Pappas's face, a cold vapor wrapped itself around his heart.

"What is it?" Jack said. He expected the detective to ask why he'd been away from the investigation for two days, but he didn't.

Pappas took a breath and said, "About an hour ago, dispatch took a call from one of Beth's neighbors. She was out for a walk and looked in Beth's living room. The cat's lying there in a pool of blood. Someone bashed its head in."

"Jesus," Jack said. "What about Beth?"

"I've tried calling her cell and landline and can't raise her. Two uniforms responded and went through the house. According to them, there's blood all over the place. I'm on my way. So's Ben Furman. Thought you'd want to come, too."

Jack felt like he'd been hit in the stomach. He leaned against the doorjamb to steady himself, his face ashen. He tried Beth's cell phone again. It went straight to voice mail.

*

They were in Pappas's car. Since he hadn't arrested him or mentioned the conversation, he assumed the detective was still in the dark. Maybe she needed some time alone to process what they talked about. But even if that were true, it didn't explain the blood and her dead cat.

"We're supposed to be available twenty-four-seven," Pappas said. "Except for one guy, no one's seen her since that, uh . . . confusion over on Tenth Street. She's not on the board this weekend and isn't due in 'til Monday. Mickey Barnes was the last man she talked to."

"And he is?"

"A detective who works out of the North Precinct. Apparently, she stopped by records late Friday night and pulled the file on your partner. Any idea why?"

"Not really. I guess she was curious," Jack lied.

Pappas let several seconds pass before he spoke. "Between you and me, maybe it was a little premature, but hey, what was the alternative?"

Jack started to reply, but the detective held up his hand stopping him.

"Look, this ain't the time or place to discuss it. Shit happens. Sometimes things go south. Right now we focus on finding Beth. I gotta tell you, there's a knot in my stomach the size of a grapefruit."

"You're not alone," Jack said. "Maybe there's a simple explanation."

"That what you think?"

"No," Jack said.

Pappas slowed at an intersection, then ran the red light, drawing an angry beep from a motorist he had just cut off. They each raised their middle finger to the other. He informed Jack, "Childers and Spruell are meeting us at the house. I know Spruell smarted off to you the other day, but I think he'll be all right. Sometimes Jimmy's mouth gets going before his brain's in gear. They're both solid cops, particularly Dave Childers. Spruell comes from old Atlanta money and can be a little flaky at times, as you probably know. He's okay. It's just that his mouth gets going before his brain's in gear every now and then."

Jack nodded but said nothing.

"According to the lieutenant, they drew the case, which means they'll treat it like Beth's missing in action, but if the blood turns out to be hers, they'll obviously upgrade to probable homicide."

Jack felt the bile rise in his throat. Everything was coming at him faster than he could process. His head was spinning. Dan Pappas's voice sounded like it was in a tunnel. He was talking, but the words weren't registering.

"I'm sorry," Jack said. "What did you say?"

"I was saying that, for obvious reasons, after today, neither of us can go near the case, at least as it relates to Beth. I'm her partner and technically you're a task force supervisor. You get my meaning?"

"So what do we do? Try to find the killer and pretend Beth wasn't kidnapped or murdered?"

"We have a conflict of interest, and there's a department rule on it. Kinda hard to be objective under the circumstances or keep from blowing the bastard away if he hurt her. Much as I hate to admit it, it makes sense."

"So what am I doing here? What are you doing here?"

"You get first crack at the scene. Childers and Spruell will be fine as long as you agree to share. We both know you see things."

"Right," Jack said.

"There's bound to be overlap between the killer and Beth. We just have to tread lightly in some areas," Pappas said.

Jack said nothing.

Pappas continued, "Ben Furman's probably there already. He's holding off 'til you arrive."

"That's fine," Jack said. He wanted to talk more about the overlap but thought it best to let the matter rest. What he needed was time to clear his head and focus.

Pappas continued, "Look, if she's dead, he'da left the body, right? I mean, there's no sense in taking it."

"No sense," Jack said.

Pappas was probably correct, but he had a feeling from the detective's nervous speech that he was trying hard to convince himself she was okay. The alternative was just too horrible to contemplate.

"I'm thinking we'll probably receive more of those fucked up clues the killer likes to leave," Pappas said. "Then you can work your magic on them."

My magic, Jack thought morosely. His hands were shaking with worry, and it was difficult to keep a coherent train of thought going.

Three police cruisers, two unmarked vehicles, and the crime scene van were parked in Beth's driveway and in front of her house. Penny Fancher had arrived in her personal vehicle and was leaning against its front fender smoking a cigarette. In the time since he had left his house, the weather had undergone an audible change. The wind was up, bending the caladiums and flowers along Beth's walkway to the side. In the little park at the center of the subdivision, it was blowing leaves off the tree branches and scattering them through the air to the ground. They soared upward like green butterflies as if blown by a vacuum.

Penny Fancher shook Jack's hand. Childers and Spruell nodded to him.

Fancher informed him, "Furman's waiting for you inside." She handed him a pair of blue paper covers to put over his shoes.

Childers advised him, "The two uniforms who responded to the call are going door to door canvassing the neighborhood. So far no one's seen anything."

Jack told him, "There's a security camera by the gates as you drive in."

"I saw it. As soon as we find the property manager or whoever's in charge, I'll have the tape pulled. We'll go in once you're finished."

"That's fine," Jack said. He glanced at Spruell, who didn't seem to be paying attention to the conversation—basically ignoring him.

Childers added unnecessarily, "If Detective Sturgis is still alive, we're gonna get her back. You can count on it."

"I know you'll do your best," Jack said.

Childers looked at his partner to see if he had anything to add. It appeared he didn't.

"All right, good luck inside. Let us know what you come up with."

Jack found Ben Furman sitting at the dining room table in the same chair he had occupied when he and Beth dined together. Everything looked the same, but it wasn't. Furman's presence and that of the others was an incongruity. They didn't belong in her home. The thought was irrational and he knew it. They were there to help. Any cop would be. Jack motioned for Furman to follow him. Together they headed for the living room.

The description Pappas had relayed from the officers was inaccurate. There was blood, but it wasn't everywhere. In fact it was concentrated mostly in front of the couch and in the hallway leading to Beth's garage.

The blood around the cat's head was obvious. It was darker in color than the spatters on the floor and walls, indicating it had been there longer. Jack looked at Peeka and shook his head sadly. Killing a harmless animal was an act of unspeakable cruelty.

In the corner of the room lay Beth's service piece, a 9 mm Browning. He picked it up and sniffed the barrel. There was no smell of gunpowder. He then checked the clip. All the bullets were present, including one in the chamber. Jack handed it to Furman to bag.

A short distance away lay Beth's cell phone. The battery was still good. Jack showed it to Furman and dropped it into his pocket.

"I'll give it back in a minute. I want to look at the call register first."

Furman nodded.

With arms folded across his chest, Jack stood in the entrance absorbing the room's details. Out of the corner of his eye, he saw Ben Furman point to the outline of what looked to be a man's shoeprint. Jack gave him a thumbs up without taking his eyes off the room and continued to study it. In all his years with the FBI, he never devoted more attention to any task.

An unspoken faith exists among criminal investigators that a crime scene will give up its clues. When Jack was satisfied he had gotten all he could, he mentally divided the room into a grid and began to walk it. No question the attack had taken place here. None at all. Most of what he assumed was Beth's blood was at the corner of the couch. He noted that the additional spatters on both sides of the wall by the entrance were at different heights and angles and discounted them as more of the killer's staged clues. Ben Furman's expression indicated he'd reached the same conclusion.

Fifteen minutes passed before either man spoke again. Outside, the light in Beth's garden was tea colored as one or two rays of sun tried to break through the clouds. The result was short-lived, because the sky closed up again. If anything the wind was stronger than before. With painstaking effort, they went through the rooms one by one, learning nothing of value.

In Beth's bedroom, the sense of trespass he felt earlier reasserted itself. The drawers of her dresser were open, leaving her undergarments on display. Jack wanted to shut them but restrained himself. His job was to analyze and form a theory as to what happened. The longer he worked, the clearer his mind was becoming and the more his anger grew. He forced the thoughts away and concentrated on the task at hand.

The bed had been made using only a blanket. The comforter lay folded across a bench at the foot. On her blanket the outline of a body was visible, deeper and wider than an impression Beth might make. Seeing it gave him a sick feeling, not so much because of the invasive nature, but because it implied a sexual component. Truth or more game playing? A chill went up his spine.

Jack bent low and sniffed the pillows. A familiar coconut scent was faint but recognizable as Beth's. The scent on the opposite pillow was stronger and reminded him of the Club Man aftershave his father had used for years.

Ben Furman asked if she had a boyfriend.

"Possibly," Jack said.

Warning bells were going off in his head. Now was the time to speak up and tell Furman they were involved. He was already on shaky ground with the department, and it could be considered withholding evidence if their involvement came out later. A belated explanation definitely wouldn't look good. After a momentary debate with himself, he decided to say nothing.

Ben Furman used a sticky roller to go over the bed and pillows and picked up a few hairs that seemed promising. From their length and color, Beth's were a no brainer. The shorter ones belonged to either him or the killer.

"I don't see any sign of a struggle," Furman said. "Looks like the main event took place downstairs."

"Right," Jack said.

"I'll test the blood on the wall, but it's probably misdirection."

"Agreed," Jack said. "Let's take a look out back."

The backyard confirmed the living room's story with one wrinkle. There were two sets of men's shoeprints in the grass. Both were evenly spaced and far enough apart to indicate the killer and whoever was with him were carrying something—namely, Beth Sturgis. Furman marked the locations with little white flags on wires and then called his assistant and told her to hurry with the images. From the wind and dropping temperature, it was obvious a storm was coming. Nothing jumped out at them, so it appeared the security camera at the subdivision entrance was now their best hope to identify the vehicle that took her out.

Foremost in Jack's mind were not the clues but the lack of them. In the previous murders, the killer had deliberately left a trail to follow. The evidence buried in Jordan, the carpetbag at the Historical Society, even the video of Pam and Aaron Dorsey—all appeared in the first twenty-four hours. Jack removed Beth's cell phone and examined the call log. There were several incoming messages on Saturday and Sunday, but the last outgoing call, which was to him, had been placed in the early morning hours on Saturday, a little past midnight. This meant she'd been gone two days. This was another break in the pattern and one that concerned him more than any of the others.

Chapter 65

The storm that broke over Atlanta was short and violent followed by a purposeful rain. Jack could hear it beating against the roof and windows in Beth's dining room. Ben Furman and his assistant had to scramble to complete their electrostatic images. All the detectives were now assembled around the dining room table. Furman had returned to the lab to process what he found, leaving a technician to go through the house looking for fingerprints. If it was like most homes, 99 percent of them would be worthless. Jack finally made his decision and advised them they would probably find his there as well but didn't elaborate beyond saying he and Beth had had dinner together. Childers held his eyes for a moment, then nodded and informed him they'd reached the property manager who was en route and would furnish them the last two days of tape from the security camera once he arrived.

"I think what happened is pretty clear," Jack said. "An attack took place. One or more people gained access to the house, overpowered Beth, and abducted her."

"You only found one set of shoeprints in the living room," Spruell said.

"But there were two outside. The fact that we didn't locate the second set in here doesn't mean much, only that they weren't obvious. Let's start from the premise that the assault was the killer's work. Unfortunately, Ben Furman and I turned up very little that's helpful. Did either of you have any luck?"

Childers said no, as did his partner.

"So where does that leave us?" Penny Fancher asked.

"Waiting for the killer to make contact," Jack said, "and pursuing what leads we do have from the other cases."

"Which isn't much, from everything we've heard," Spruell said.

"No," Jack admitted.

"Has the chief talked with you about bringing in the FBI?" Childers asked.

"He did. And I told him I was fine with that."

Dave Childers turned to Penny Fancher and inquired, "Was Sturgis working on any other cases?"

"This was it."

"Any open on her books?"

"No."

"I understand she wasn't married. What about a boyfriend or ex-husband?"

Penny Fancher turned to Dan Pappas. "Dan?"

"Her ex is William Camden, the writer. As far as I know, he lives someplace in Connecticut, and they haven't spoken in years. She never mentioned being involved with anyone, but I'll check with Lenny Cass. Her dad's a cop in Charlotte. I imagine he'll be in her cell phone."

Childers glanced at the phone, which was now sitting in a plastic evidence bag on the table, and then said, "Jimmy and I can run down the brother and sister. You want to make the call to her father, you being her partner and all?"

"I'll do it," Jack said. He was about to continue when he realized he was being stared at by James Spruell. Whatever the reason, he was in no mood to deal with him. He swiveled his chair and returned the gaze until Spruell looked away. Peggy Fancher decided to end the meeting.

"All right, let's secure the house and get on with it." Penny Fancher turned to Dave Childers and informed him, "I want daily status reports. We'll meet in my office at eight AM on Tuesday to see where we are. Hopefully, we'll have heard from the killer by then."

Once again, Jack considered letting them know of his relationship with Beth but decided to hold off, at least for the time being. If he disclosed they were sleeping together, even if it had only been once, it could result in his being summarily removed from the case. That was unacceptable now. Beth's life was at stake.

On the ride home, Jack and Pappas were quiet. Neither had much to say. The enormity of what had happened was like a boulder teetering precariously above their heads and waiting to break loose from its foundation.

The rain continued, coming down in gray sheets that turned the streetlamp on Jack's corner into a haze. At eight o'clock that evening, Pappas touched base to tell him Childers and Spruell had looked at the security camera with two of the neighbors. They saw a late-model, brown Toyota Avalon pull into the neighborhood around 7:00 PM and leave a little after 1:40 AM. Neither thought the car belonged there.

"That jives with what the detective told me about seeing her at the precinct. According to Mickey, she left just after one."

"They were probably waiting for her when she got home," Jack said.

"What puzzles me," Pappas said, "is there was no sign of forced entry. Maybe she knew them and let 'em in."

"Or they got past her alarm," Jack said. "It doesn't sound like Beth to let someone in at that hour. Besides, we found her gun in the living room."

"She might have drawn it after they were in," Pappas said.

"I suppose so," Jack said.

"You speak with her folks yet?"

"I called earlier. The answering machine picked up. It's not the kind of message you want to leave. I was about to try again when you rang."

"You doin' okay?"

"Not really," Jack said.

"Listen, we got a guest bedroom if you feel like company."

Jack smiled. "Thanks, Dan. I'll be fine. I'd better make that call now."

"All right. You change your mind, we don't go to bed until eleven or so."

"Understood. Thanks again."

Jack was about to disconnect, but Pappas wasn't ready to hang up yet. He said, "Something else has been bothering me."

"What?"

"Why her?"

"What do you mean?"

"If the guy's got a hard-on for you, why go after her?"

"Pell went after my partner, remember?"

"Sure. You figure he's tryin' to get to you through her?"

"It would be consistent," Jack said.

"So why not go after you directly?" Pappas said.

"Beth might have been an easier target," Jack said.

"Why kill her cat, man? What'd he ever do to anybody?"

"I need to make the call, Dan," Jack said.

After they disconnected, Jack pinched the bridge of his nose, waited for a second, rehearsed what he would say, and then dialed the number. Beth's father answered. He related what they knew for certain and how they planned to proceed. Joe Sturgis listened quietly and waited until Jack was through before asking any questions. He seemed calm enough as one might expect of a cop with his experience. Jack wasn't surprised that he knew about the case and about the Scarecrow years earlier. Beth told him they talked frequently. The only surprise was that Joe Sturgis also knew about him.

In the end, Joe Sturgis thanked him for the call and said he and his wife were looking forward to meeting him in person.

"Thank you, sir. Me, too."

There was a pause on the line.

"You can call me Joe. I lost one daughter a long time ago. I don't want to lose another. Get her back, son."

Jack ended the call feeling worse than when it began.

When the rain finally let up, he decided to go for a walk to clear his head and allow himself time to process what happened. The streetlamps were on and the air was clean and fresh, though the wind was still blowing. A full moon rose, bathing the streets in cold light. As he moved through the neighborhood, the frenetic shadows of the tree limbs and their leaves made him think of children running from trunk to trunk in a nocturnal wood. It called to mind the games his daughter and her friends played when they were little.

The epiphany didn't hit until he turned for home. Something at Beth's house was out of place. The realization, when it came to him, was like descending a set of stairs in the dark and thinking there's one more at the bottom only to find you've reached the landing with a thud. It was so obvious that he was amazed it took so long to put two and two together. He called Dan Pappas immediately.

"Change your mind about a sleepover?" Pappas said.

"I'm going back to Beth's house," Jack said.

"What? Why?"

"Did Childers and Spruell take her computer?"

"I don't think so. No reason to."

"You look at it when you were there?"

"Briefly."

"Well, I did," Jack said. "I found a note to Dr. Raymond thanking him for compiling the Mayfield employee list."

"Okay," Pappas said.

"It was dated three days ago," Jack said.

Pappas took a moment to digest this. "How come she was asking for it again? Mundas and Stafford went through the employees at the beginning of the case. Everyone had an alibi. On top of that, they double-checked their DNA against what we got off Donna Camp. They were all cleared."

"You asked why the killer targeted her," Jack said. "What if she hit on something?"

More silence followed. Jack began walking faster.

"Okay," Pappas said. "I'm with you. That's a possibility."

"Remember the legal pad in her bedroom?" Jack said.

"Yeah, on her nightstand. It was divided in columns. *L, R, S*, something. But they were all blank. We figured she was doing some work at her house. What do they stand for?"

"No idea," Jack said. "But I think the names she wrote on the first page are Mayfield employees. Some were crossed out; some weren't. I want to check them against what Raymond sent."

"Sure, but if their DNA results were negative, it's a blind alley."

"We missed something," Jack said. "I don't know what, but we missed something."

The silence was even longer this time.

"I'll meet you there in an hour," Pappas said.

*

Pappas showed up wearing the same tan slacks and white shirt he'd worn earlier. He added a black windbreaker to the outfit and looked only slightly more rumpled. Jack left his car in one of the visitor spaces and was waiting for him by the front door.

"You been inside yet?" Pappas asked.

"No."

"I've been giving some thought to what you said. If she wanted the employee list, why didn't she make a copy from the one in our file?"

"I intend to find that out," Jack said.

The door was locked, but Pappas surprised him by producing a key. Jack's eyebrows rose when he saw it.

"When we were out earlier, I noticed she had an extra key sitting in one of her kitchen drawers," the detective explained. "I thought it might come in handy."

They ducked under the yellow crime scene tape and entered.

The computer was still there. Jack flicked it on, brought up her e-mail, and printed the note and list Charles Raymond had sent. Then they went up to Beth's bedroom and retrieved the white legal pad and compared the names she'd written down. There were thirty-four in total.

Jack now saw all the female names were crossed out, leaving twenty-one men.

Pappas flipped the page to the columns labeled *L*, *R*, *E*, and *S*.

Jack shook his head. "She ever mention this to you?"

"Nope. And I don't recall seeing any notes about it in the murder book."

"Maybe they're in her desk at the office and she didn't have a chance to update the file. You know how cops are about paperwork."

Jack and Pappas returned downstairs and spent a half hour going through Beth's e-mail, starting from the time she caught the case in Jordan. Nothing seemed even remotely relevant.

"I feel like a shit pawing through her personal stuff," Pappas said.

"Me, too," Jack said. "No choice though."

As a last resort, Jack opened her Internet browser and checked the search history hoping it would give them some insight into what the mysterious letters meant.

"You just know this crap?" Pappas commented.

"I read a lot," Jack said without looking away from the screen.

Pappas shook his head.

Their search ended in frustration. There was nothing in the computer to help them. Jack shut the machine down, and they went outside. Pappas relocked the door. The detective took Raymond's list and Beth's legal pad with him.

"I'll fill Dave Childers in and enter these in the book first thing in the morning. Will you be in?"

"I have a quick stop to make. I'll be there around ten thirty."

"All right. Get some rest. Maybe the letters'll make sense in the daylight."

"Maybe," Jack said, walking Pappas to his car.

He was about to get in when Jack continued, "Dan?"

"Yeah?"

"Beth and I are seeing each other."

Pappas stared at him for a beat, then said, "Seeing as in dating-type seeing?"

"Right."

Pappas responded by slowly banging his head against the car's roof.

"Are you nuts? Never mind, I already know the answer. You've gotta be out of your minds; the both of you. During an investigation?"

"We didn't plan it. It just happened."

"Nobody ever plans this shit. Jesus, Kale, you're giving me an ulcer. That's why you looked funny when Childers asked if she had a boyfriend. Why didn't you speak up then? He could nail you for withholding."

"I know. It's more important than ever for me to stay on the case. This could get me bounced off."

"You bet your sweet ass it could," Pappas said.

"I can call Childers tonight and talk with him," Jack said.

"Negative. Don't do anything 'til I think this through."

"I told you Dave is fine, but Jimmy Lee's got a stick up his ass. His father's some kind of deacon with the church. The whole freakin' family comes off holier than thou, and it's rubbed off on the kids. I went to school with his older brother, Teddy."

"Okay," Jack said. "Sorry."

A lengthy silence followed. Jack thought Pappas was going to ask for details. He didn't.

"All right," he said, "it ain't the end of the world. But it sure don't help right now."

Jack turned his palms up and didn't comment. Anything he had to say might only make matters worse.

Pappas looked up at the stars and shook his head. "The only thing that can complete this day would be to call my ex-wife and have her come over and kick me in the balls a few times."

Jack remained silent.

"All right, don't stress over it, kid. We'll work it out. Get some rest. You look like shit. I'll see you in the morning."

With that, the detective got in his car and drove off, leaving Jack standing there feeling like an idiot.

276

Chapter 66

Jack lay on his back in bed wracking his brain over what *L*, *R*, *E*, and *S* meant into the small hours of the morning. Why would Beth ask for the Mayfield employee list again?

"Talk to me. Tell me what you were thinking," he whispered to the dark.

Still agitated and having trouble thinking, he reached for the glass of Scotch on his nightstand and took a swallow. The amber liquid slid down his throat, warming him, restoring coherence to his thoughts, driving the gargoyles back into the unlit recesses of his mind. He took a breath, slowly let it out, and settled onto his pillow. Exhausted, sleep finally crept into the room.

The familiar dream about being on the old sailing ship returned. Leaning hard into the wind, the ship drew away from the harbor. Sails were full. Lines sang with tension. A wooden deck swayed under his feet. In the distance along the shore, he could see gas lamps flooding light onto cobblestone streets.

In the past, only he and Connie Belasco were present. From the quarterdeck on which he was standing, he looked toward midship expecting to see her staring out over a black handrail. Only this time it wasn't Connie. Beth Sturgis, wearing a white dress, looked back at him over her shoulder and said something. In the rising wind and with the splash of water against the sides of the ship, he couldn't make out her words. He started forward but couldn't seem to find the stairs leading down to the main deck. Beth was speaking again. Instinctively, he knew it was something important. Something he needed to hear.

Jack finally decided to jump to the main deck, a distance of five feet. But by the time he did, Beth had turned and was walking toward the bow. He called after her. She didn't turn nor offer any sign she heard him. She simply kept walking into the sun's glare. The light was so bright, it hurt his eyes. Putting up a hand to deflect it, he continued forward, shouting her name.

When he reached the bow, he found himself alone. Jack turned in a circle trying to locate her as a flood of trepidation washed over him. Leaning over the rail, he looked down at the foaming wake, then beyond it toward the land. Still no sign of Beth. His anxiety grew into panic as he ran through the ship calling her name.

He awoke with a cold film of sweat covering his face, his shirt damp and plastered to his body. His breath was coming in ragged gulps. He reached for his pills and took just one this time. A minute passed before his respiration returned to normal. What did the dream mean? He had no clue. *Some psychologist I am.* Jack rubbed his face with his hands and reached for his cell phone to see if any messages had come in. Nothing. He put on a bathrobe and went downstairs to check his e-mail. Same result. Instead of feeling calmer, he was more on edge than ever. This was the start of the third day and still no contact from the killer.

Probably part of the bastard's plan.

*

Contact came in a form he didn't anticipate. The moment Jack left the house to take Marta for her morning walk, he saw the bloody scarf draped over the handrail on his porch. He recognized it immediately as the one Beth had been wearing the last time they were together. That he managed to examine it dispassionately surprised him. It meant the game was still on and Beth was still alive. At least he prayed she was.

The killer had probably driven up to the house, got out, and placed the scarf on his porch. He was confident there'd be other clues, and that filled him with hope. The UNSUB was consistent in that regard at least. Jack used his cell phone to call Dan Pappas and told him what happened.

"Prick," Pappas said. "Where's the scarf now?"

"In the same place."

"Great. I'll let Childers know. He'll probably send Furman to pick it up."

"That's fine," Jack said. "I'll be at the precinct in a while."

"You need to be careful. Coming to your house is a ballsy move. There's a good chance he's been watching you. He might still be hanging around somewhere."

"I think I said something like that to you at the beginning of the case."

"It's still true. Listen, is there something personal going on between you and this guy I need to know about?"

The unspoken message was clear. Trust had taken a shot. *You held out on me before, pal. Don't leave me swinging in the wind.*

"That's everything, Dan. I'll see you later."

*

The bookstore was a throwback of forty years to a time before the large chains took over with their cafes and immense racks of magazines and music selections. Dusty books were stacked both vertically on the floor and horizontally on sagging wooden shelves.

The store was located on Piedmont Road across from a Cadillac dealership where dozens of shiny cars sat with windows glinting in the sun.

It took Jack a while to complete his purchase. A white-haired old gentleman, dressed in a cardigan and bow tie, identified himself as the owner and apologized for not having located the book yet despite their earlier phone conversation. He was certain he'd seen it but wasn't quite sure where it was at the moment.

The problem was solved by the appearance of the owner's wife, who shook her head and proceeded up an unstable-looking circular iron staircase and returned five minutes later with the book in hand. The men exchanged a look and shrugged at each other. Jack thanked them and left the store.

Outside, white and red azaleas and dogwoods fronting shops along the street all got the same memo and had burst into bloom overnight. Despite having grown up in Atlanta like Beth, Jack was always slightly startled by the process. He'd just started walking toward his car when a voice behind him said, "'Scuse me, sir, is you Dr. Kale?"

Jack turned to see an emaciated black man holding a large manila envelope. He could have been anywhere from thirty to fifty and was missing a number of teeth. Like most crack addicts, he shuffled from foot to foot, unable to stand still for any length of time. Jack stared at him and didn't answer immediately.

"Dude said to give this to you," the man said, holding out the envelope.

"What dude?"

"Don't know. Just some guy who come up to me and axed if I could help him."

"How'd you know who I was or that I'd be here?"

"Didn't. Dude told me what you was wearin' and that you'd be comin' outta that store soon."

Jack's heart began to race. The killer was someplace near. He took the envelope and tore it open. Inside were two eight-by-ten color photographs. One showed an operating table lined with ancient-looking instruments, one of which was a bone saw; the other showed Beth lying on a narrow cot in a dimly lit room. Her eyes were closed.

"Where's the man who gave this to you?" Jack said.

"Don't know. I was across the street when he come up and axed me if I wanted to make some money. I said sure, 'cause I ain't ate in two days. He say you probably throw some my way, too. Didn't see where he went."

Jack thought the last part was a lie but didn't care. He took ten dollars out of his wallet and handed it to the man.

"What's your name?"

"Devon. Devon Jefferson, sir. I used to play bass over to Blues Island in Little Five Points back in the day. You ever been there? Man, that was one sweet little club—"

"How long ago did he give you this?"

"Not real long."

"Five minutes? Ten Minutes? Take a guess, Devon. This is important."

Devon rubbed his chin and thought for a moment. "Fifteen, maybe twenty minutes. Somethin' like that."

"Show me where you met him," Jack said.

"I don't wanna make no trouble. No, sir."

Jack grabbed the front of his shirt so suddenly the man gasped. He pulled Devon to him.

"Listen closely. I'm a police officer and you're about to have more trouble than you ever thought possible. Unless you want to spend the next ten years in Reidsville for obstructing justice, walk with me across the street and show me where you met this man. There's twenty dollars in it for you."

"I . . . I . . . I'm tellin' you, I don't remember. That man had bad eyes. I don't wanna see him no more."

"A hundred dollars," Jack said, tightening his grip and lifting Devon onto his toes.

"Mister, please."

Releasing one hand, Jack took out his cell phone and pretended to call his office.

"This is Lieutenant Kale. I want a squad car at the corner of Piedmont and Pharr Road right away. I've got a suspect in the Jordan murders with me."

"Murder!" Devon wailed. "The man said you was a doctor." He was crying now and shaking all over. "I swear to Jesus I ain't murdered nobody. I just been tryin' to help."

"Hold on," Jack said to the phone. "What'll it be, Devon?"

"It was about a hunerd feet from that big car lot. That's where we was. Then he walked into that building there," Devon said, pointing.

Jack was disgusted with himself for bullying the man. But if there was a chance at finding the killer and saving Beth, that was all that mattered.

"Show me."

With one hand under Devon's arm, they crossed Piedmont Road dodging traffic.

"Right here," Devon said. "This where he come up to me. I ain't done nuthin' wrong, man. Just mindin' my own bidness."

"Tell me what he looked like. You said he had bad eyes."

"They was real dark, almost black like a shark. Didn't blink none."

"What color hair did he have?"

"Wh . . . what?"

"Hair, hair. What color hair did he have? Think, Devon."

"It was light. Not blonde, but darker with some brown mixed in."

"What about height? Taller or shorter than me?"

"Shorter. Heavier, too, I think."

"You're doing great," Jack said. "How old was he?"

"Maybe thirty, forty. Somethin' like that."

As they were talking, a police cruiser turned onto Pharr Road. Pulling Devon with him into the street, Jack waved to get the driver's attention. The car slowed and made a U-turn.

"Oh, man, why you arrestin' me? I'm helpin' like you axed."

"You're not under arrest, but I need you stay here for a while."

The car pulled up to the curb beside them and a cop got out.

"Everything okay?"

"I'm Jack Kale with RHD," Jack said, showing the cop his lieutenant's badge. "This man may have seen a killer we're after. Toss me your cuffs."

Devon looked like he was about to pass out. Jack locked one cuff to his wrist and secured the other around the pole of a street sign.

"You want me to call for backup?" the cop asked.

"Absolutely. What's your name?"

"Pilcher, sir."

"Listen, Pilcher, the last report we had indicated the killer was driving a late-model, brown Toyota Avalon. He may or may not still be in it. Before that, he was driving a black van. He's killed three people, kidnapped four others. This man is extremely dangerous."

"Got it," Pilcher said.

"According to Devon here, he might have gone into that office building across the street. I want him. We also need him alive. He's in his thirties or early forties, dirty-blond or light-brown hair, and a little shorter and wider than I am."

"Not much to go on," Pilcher pointed out.

"Best we have at the moment," Jack said.

"Any idea what he was wearing?"

They both turned to Devon.

"I don't know, man. I wasn't payin' no attention."

"Dark or light clothes?" Jack said.

"I—"

"Close your eyes and see him in your mind—you were a musician, right? Musicians are good with details." Jack didn't know if musicians were or weren't good with details, but he figured an appeal to Devon's pride might get him to focus. From the description thus far, he was reasonably certain the man Devon had seen wasn't the killer but rather the second man at Beth's house. Hair and eye color might change, not height.

Devon squeezed his eyes shut and concentrated, his forehead creasing with the effort. Several seconds passed before he said, "Blue jeans and a dark sweater. Black high-tops, like the kind Michael wore."

"Michael Jackson?" Pilcher asked.

"Jordan, man," Devon said, looking at Pilcher like he'd fallen off a turnip truck.

"Anything else?" Jack asked. "Jewelry on his hand? A watch maybe?"

Devon shook his head.

"Let's go. You stay put," Jack told Devon.

"Where I gonna go? Can't take the pole wit' me."

Good point.

Jack and Pilcher crossed the street to the office building. It was four stories and wider than it was tall.

Jack said, "I'll start at the top floor and work my way down. You try the shops and restaurants along the street. It's only been about twenty minutes since he was here, so we might have a shot at finding him."

"Will do, Lieutenant."

"Here's my card. My cell number's at the bottom. Call me immediately if you see anyone who fits the description."

"Backup should be here any minute. You want me to call traffic control and ask them to start checking the street cameras? We might catch a break and spot the car or maybe get a picture of your guy with the mutt back there."

"Good idea. But don't call him a mutt. He's just a scared little man. I intimidated the hell out of him. He's trying to help us."

Pilcher began to reply but then thought better of it and simply nodded. He started for the nearest shop while Jack headed for the front door.

According to the lobby directory, about twenty different businesses occupied the premises. Jack spotted a set of stairs near the exit and jogged toward them, the sense of urgency building as he went. Taking the steps two at a time, he practically sprinted to the fourth floor. He waited a moment to regain his breath and then started knocking on doors along the corridor.

No one saw anything and no one fit the description except for an accountant on the second floor who'd arrived at eight o'clock and hadn't left the office that morning. His secretary confirmed it.

As Jack returned to the ground floor, he caught a glimpse of a man in jeans and a dark sweater walking toward the garage through the glass doors. Without hesitation, he broke into a run.

By the time he exited the building and reached the garage entrance, there was no one to be seen. Gun drawn, he went in and started checking the floors.

Unlike the first two levels, the roof of the parking deck was open. He heard no engines start and saw nobody. The suspect had vanished. Jack rested his arms on the wall and looked down. No traffic was moving on Pharr Road. The police had reacted quickly. He walked to a stairwell in the corner and took the stairs to the bottom.

The street was now filled with cop cars and cops going door to door. Jack crossed to where Childers and Spruell were. Devon was sitting in the back of their cruiser still handcuffed, looking miserable. Jack handed Childers the envelope Devon had given him and explained what happened.

"So you were in the neighborhood and this man just came up to you out of the blue," Spruell said.

"If that's what you heard, you weren't listening very well," Jack said.

"Tell us again."

"I don't think I will. Your partner can fill you in later."

"How'd he know you were here?" Spruell asked, ignoring his jibe.

"The only explanation that makes sense is that I was tailed. The description doesn't fit with what we know of the killer. That means it was the second man at Detective Sturgis's house."

Childers agreed that made sense. Spruell shook his head and stayed quiet. His skepticism came through loud and clear.

"How about taking those cuffs off him?" Jack said, motioning to the cruiser with his chin.

"Departmental policy, Mr. Kale," Spruell informed him. "He's a material witness and we're taking him downtown to meet our sketch artist. You understand about department policy, right?"

Jack bit back a reply. He turned to Dave Childers and said, "Uncuff him. He's been trying to help us."

Childers searched Jack's face for a moment and then nodded to his partner.

Muttering under his breath, Spruell leaned into the back seat and removed the cuffs.

"Just trying to do things by the book," he said to Jack when he straightened out.

"That's fine, Detective."

"It's probably that you FBI types have your own way of doing things," Spruell said. "Am I right or am I right?"

Jack took a deep breath. He'd screwed up with the reporter and he knew it. Probably the whole Atlanta PD knew it. Whatever the other concerns, the only thing that mattered was getting Beth home safely. He was sick with worry over her. For a moment, he considered trying to smooth things over and promptly dismissed the idea. He didn't like James Lee Spruell, and he didn't have the energy to see who was the alpha male on the block. He moved closer to Spruell and spoke quietly so the other man had to lean in to hear what he was saying.

"It's fine to take him to the sketch artist, but treat him with respect. When he's through, I want you to give him this hundred dollars, then call St. Mary's Parish and see if they have a spot in their drug program for him."

"Listen—"

"I want *you* to do it. No one else. If I find out you didn't, I'll come and see you and we're going to have a major problem. Do you understand me?"

Jack and Spruell locked eyes. Whatever the younger detective saw in Jack's face hadn't been there a moment ago. He nodded and crossed the street to speak with one of the uniforms.

Dave Childers said, "He's still young."

"That what you call it?"

"You want copies of these photos for the book?"

"No," Jack said. "I've seen them."

Chapter 67

On Monday morning, Jack found himself sitting in Lieutenant Fancher's office.

The shades were drawn, giving the room a cave-like feel. Apparently, the lieutenant didn't care for the world looking in on her. He felt the same way.

"Glad we could get together, Jack. How are you doing?"

Jack lifted his shoulders. "Day by day."

"I understand. I was planning to call you later."

"To tell me I'm out of a job?"

"'Fraid so. The deputy chief said to thank you and we'll take it from here."

Jack nodded. He was expecting this.

"I'm sorry," Fancher added.

"Me, too," Jack said. "Maybe it's for the best. I'll clear out my desk."

"There's no hurry," Fancher said. "You've done fine work. I want you to know we all appreciate it."

"Not fine enough," Jack said.

"Don't be too hard on yourself. We'll get the bastard. If there's anything I can do, let me know, okay?"

"I will, Lieutenant."

A silence followed.

There really wasn't much more to say. Neither knew the other well enough for personal remarks beyond the usual condolences. It soon became obvious Fancher was one of those people who dislikes lulls in the conversation. She arranged the papers in front of her in a stack.

"I was just going over Beth's case expenses when you came in," she said, just to have something to say.

"Expenses?"

"Oh, just the usual stuff—gas, requisition requests for a car, that sort of thing."

Jack searched his memory. He couldn't remember having gone many places with Beth that would raise an eyebrow. Out of curiosity, he asked Fancher about it.

The lieutenant informed him, "The last was a trip to Mayfield the day she disappeared. Since the budget cuts, I have to account for every dime we spend these days. That's where my nickname comes from."

"You have a nickname?"

"Penny Pincher. The guys don't think I know."

Jack smiled, got up, and shook her hand.

"A privilege working with you, Lieutenant," he said.

"Same here," Fancher said.

He was halfway to the door when he stopped and turned back. "How many trips to Mayfield did Beth make?"

"Three," Fancher said.

"Really?"

"One by herself the day after she caught the case, one with Dan Pappas, and one over the last couple of days before she was abducted," Fancher said, reading from her notes.

Jack thanked her and promised to say good-bye before he left. He walked directly back to Beth's desk, sat down, and picked up the murder book. All her case notes were there including the ones he and Pappas had added the other day. There was no mention of any additional trips to Mayfield or why she went.

Pappas was sitting in front of his keyboard using the one-finger method to enter something on his computer. He stopped typing when he saw Jack.

"I spoke with the eminent Charles Raymond an hour ago and asked him about the list he put together," he said. "He told me he was just responding to Beth's request. Then I mentioned we might come back out to do some rechecking. He wasn't happy about that."

"Why not?"

"Said it would disrupt the harmony of their environment."

Jack blinked. "Seriously?"

Pappas held up his right hand in a Boy Scout oath.

"Did Beth ever mention going back to Mayfield on her own?"

Pappas frowned. "Not that I recall."

"According to Penny Fancher, she checked out a cruiser and drove there again in the last week."

"Don't make sense. She'da told me."

"I guess," Jack said. "You have any further thoughts on why she wanted that employee list again?"

"Double-checking?"

"The more I think about it, the more I think it's possible she hit on something."

"And decided to fly solo?" Pappas said. "Wouldn't be real smart in a case like this. Against policy, too."

"But not out of the question. She's fairly competitive and was embarrassed about making the wrong call on that personal trainer we pulled in for questioning."

"Happens to everybody. It's part of the job."

"Sure. But what if she wanted to make sure of her facts before going out on a limb again?"

"It's possible," Pappas said. "If she really was backtracking, then I've got an idea about what two of the letters on her list might mean. *L* for left and *R* for right. The killer's left handed so maybe she was trying to eliminate the men who aren't."

"I like it," Jack said.

"Yeah, but I'm still drawing a blank on the *E* and *S*."

Jack sat down across from Pappas, picked up a pencil, and began to tap a rhythm on the desk. Two minutes ticked by before his head came up.

"Physical characteristics," he muttered. "I think she was trying to pull all the matching physical characteristics together. *E* for eye color and *S* for shoe size. Remember we picked up a size twelve print at the farm with the first victims?"

They looked at each other for several seconds before Pappas nodded. Jack reached for the phone.

Chapter 68

"**D**r. Charles Raymond, please. This is Detective Kale calling." He figured that was still the truth for the next few hours.

The secretary informed him, "I'm sorry, Detective. Dr. Raymond's out of the office today. Can I help you?"

Jack motioned for Pappas to pick up his extension.

He said, "Detective Pappas is also on the line. According to our records, Elizabeth Sturgis visited Mayfield in the last week. We're curious why she was out there."

"I believe she was reviewing our security tapes."

The men exchanged glances across their desks. Pappas turned his palms up.

"Do you know what she was interested in?"

"I'm sorry, I don't."

"How about the period of time she was checking?" Pappas asked.

"I don't know that either. Tony Gillam is in charge of security. Would you like me to put you through to him?"

"No," Jack said. "I'm on the way. Please tell Mr. Gillam I'd like to meet with him. I'll be there shortly."

As soon as they disconnected, Jack informed Pappas that Penny Fancher had given him the axe.

"I heard," Pappas said. "She told me when I came in. You really think Beth might have found something?"

"I do. Something that set the killer off. Why else target her? You and Beth were in the background."

"Okay. But what'd she find?"

"No idea. Whatever it was, it required a visit she didn't tell either of us about."

Pappas stood and put his sport jacket on, then said, "You ain't cleared out your desk yet, right?"

"No."

"Then it ain't official. Let's go."

"Dan, you don't need to come with me."

"Yeah," Pappas said. "I do."

They broke the speed limit and managed the trip in twenty minutes. They went directly to Elaine Hilton, Charles Raymond's secretary. She led them through the halls to the security office. Tony Gillam was waiting.

He was around thirty-five, middle height, and medium build with sandy-brown hair. Gillam was dressed in a supervisor's uniform consisting of black pants and a white shirt with epaulettes. The single gold bar on his collar indicated he was a lieutenant.

It was the first time Jack had been to Mayfield. During the ride, he speculated what his reaction would be knowing that Pell was also in the building. He was mildly surprised to find there was none at all.

Pappas said, "Did the lady tell you why we're here?"

"Something about the videos Detective Sturgis was looking at. I was real sorry to hear about her."

Pappas thanked him and asked specifically what Beth wanted to see.

Gillam informed them, "I have no idea. I asked if I could help, but she said no. She just wanted me to set her up in front of a monitor."

"Exactly what's on them?" Jack asked.

Gillam shrugged. "Nothing much. Just personnel going in and out of Pell's cell. Pretty boring stuff, really."

"What period of time was she interested in?" Jack asked.

"The last two months."

"You keep a log of your tapes?" Pappas asked.

"Sure. Everything's time and date stamped," Gillam said. "They go back a full year. After that, we recycle them. And they're not tapes. We record onto DVDs. Each one lasts a full month."

"Great," Pappas said. "We'd like to take a look at whatever she did."

"No problem. What can I do to help?"

"We'll let you know," Pappas said. "Right now, we don't have a clue what we're looking for."

"Understood."

"Can you show us how to operate the equipment?"

"It's pretty simple. But I gotta tell you, even reviewing one month is gonna take a little time."

"We have a little time," Jack said.

Gillam nodded, went to a shelf over his desk, retrieved a plastic case containing a single DVD, and then brought in two chairs from an adjacent office for Jack and Pappas. He sat down behind them.

"I can identify our people, unless you guys want privacy," Gillam said.

"Nah. You're welcome to stay," Pappas said.

There was no sound on the DVD, which began on March 1st, approximately one month before the murders in Jordan. The first visitor to Howard Pell's cell was a guard carrying a breakfast tray at six thirty in the morning. He slipped it through a slot at the bottom of the door. Another guard came by later and took it away at nine o'clock.

"The first one is Felix Grazanka," Gillam said. "He's in today if you want to speak with him. The guard who took the tray is Ryan Thomas. Ryan works from seven thirty in the morning until three in the afternoon. You'll see him come by twice more to check on Pell. We do body counts every four hours. The nurses show up with the meds between six and eight o'clock at night."

Pappas nodded and continued to watch. Jack stayed silent.

Nothing of interest happened the first week. The meals and medicines arrived on schedule as Gillam said. The process was repeated again the following day. He was right about it being tedious. After a while, Jack began to look forward to seeing the guards and nurses just to break the monotony. At two o'clock in the afternoon, Pappas got up, stretched, and went to the bathroom. Jack remained where he was, his eyes glued to the screen. Gillam stayed with him. Days passed on the security disc. On Wednesday of the following week, Pell's routine changed with the arrival of a man Jack hadn't seen before.

"That's Dr. Cairo," Gillam said. "He does counseling with the inmates."

"Cairo?" Jack said, consulting Beth's list.

"DNA test cleared him," Pappas said.

Jack nodded and then asked, "What about Dr. Raymond?"

"He's been up a couple of times. More when I first got here. Mostly, he handles administrative stuff now."

They watched Howard Pell place his hands through an opening in the middle of his cell door so the guard could cuff him. When that was done, he stepped back into the room and Dr. Cairo entered.

"Can I get you guys a cup of coffee or something?" Gillam asked.

"I'm fine," Pappas said.

"No, but thank you," Jack told him.

A male nurse showed up at 7:48 PM with that day's medication. "Who's that?" Jack asked.

"Ron Curry. He's at Ellenwood Regional in Savannah now," Gillam said.

Jack nodded and made a note in the little book he carried. They continued to watch. The only time Pell was allowed out of his cell was for a one-hour break. He was taken to what Gillam described as their recreation yard, a triangular cement enclosure with forty-foot-high walls topped by razor wire. While he was out there, Pell walked the yard's perimeter. Occasionally, he did a few push-ups or sat in the corner against a wall with his face turned up to the sun.

On seeing his old nemesis, Jack had no reaction. Not hate. Not anxiety. Nothing. Strange. He was certain Beth was correct. Somehow, Pell was at the bottom of the murders.

*

At the end of the second week on the DVDs, something odd happened. Once again, the guards came for Pell and led him out to an enclosed recreation area, different from the one the general population used. Pell went through his walking routine for approximately fifty minutes and then came to a halt directly beneath the security camera. He stared up at it, smiled, and then mouthed the words, "Hello, Jack."

"Sonofabitch," Pappas said, sitting back in his chair.

"He knew we'd be watching," Jack said.

"Sick fucker," Pappas said.

He looked at Tony Gillam, who responded by raising his shoulders. "I don't review this stuff unless there's a problem."

"Are we looking at the original disc?" Jack asked.

"It's an exact copy," Gillam said. "Detective Sturgis asked me to make it for her, but she never picked it up. There's another one for the next month after this."

"Where are the originals?" Jack asked.

"In the security locker."

"May I see them?"

"Why? They're identical. I made the dupes myself."

"Just curious."

Gillam turned his palms up. "You're the boss."

"Before you get them, can we run the originals side by side with the copies you made on the two monitors here?"

"Sure," Gillam said. "But would you mind if we continue in the morning? It's after six. If I'm late again, my wife'll kill me."

Jack was willing to stay there all night but didn't have a choice. "That's fine," he said. "We're just trying to cover all the bases, not give you a hard time, Tony."

"I feel bad. I'd let you stay but the hospital regs won't allow it without a supervisor present."

"Does nine o'clock tomorrow suit you?"

"No problem. Thanks, man."

"Will Dr. Cairo be in then?" Jack asked.

"I think so," Gillam said. "I'm not real sure of his schedule. You want me to check with personnel?"

"Are they still open?"

"Shit. They closed an hour ago," Gillam said. "Sorry. If it's important, I can call Danita at home. She knows that stuff off the top of her head."

"Danita?"

"Danita Ritchey. She's in charge," Gillam said.

"It can wait until the morning," Jack said.

Everyone stood and headed for the door.

In the hallway, Pappas said, "I have a question about the nurse. Tell me his name again."

"Ron Curry," Gillam said.

"You said he's at Ellenwood. Why'd he leave?"

"Ron was a contract employee. He's with some company that has a deal with the state. Bill Tomlinson replaced him."

Pappas said, "I don't recall seeing Curry's name on the employee list."

"Probably an oversight. He was already gone when Ms. Sturgis made her request. Their employer sends us the fingerprint and DNA cards. I turn them over to Danita. She forwards them to the Georgia Bureau of Investigation. If there was a match, I guess they'd have told you, right?"

"Right," Pappas said. "Just curious."

293

Chapter 69

When they were in the car, Pappas commented, "Those tapes weren't worth much."

"DVDs," Jack said.

"Whatever."

Jack was silent for a moment, then said, "I want to know more about Ron Curry. Everyone here provided DNA samples, right?"

"Far as I know."

"And everything came back negative."

"True."

"I buy Gillam's explanation that Curry was already gone when Beth asked for the employee list again. But it can't hurt to be sure."

"I'll call the hospital in Savannah and get his records," Pappas said.

*

The world gradually came into focus. Beth's eyes fluttered as she emerged from the haze of drugs clouding her mind. She was lying on a cot in a room with bare brick walls and a cell door. The memory of a crowbar coming down on her collarbone returned. Tentatively, she explored it with her fingers and winced. Probably broken. The skin around the bruise was a mixture of black and yellow. Her arm also had a sizable mark just below the shoulder. Even the slightest movement sent waves of pain shooting through her body.

How long have I been here?

She had no sense of time, but from the discoloration of her skin at the bruise, she guessed several days had passed since her abduction.

The Soul Eater's attack came back to her in a series of vignettes. Peekachu lying dead in the middle of the room. Cold gray eyes behind

294

a ski mask. The bar coming down. A jolt of electricity passing through her body.

Beth sat upright, placed her feet on the floor, and stood. She had to wait for the room to stop spinning. When she felt sufficiently stable, she made her way to the door. It was locked. No surprise there. The bars weren't of a type you'd expect to find in a jail, but were sufficient for their purpose. She turned and took stock of the room she was in. Apart from the cot, the only furniture was a series of wooden shelves that lined one wall. They were divided diagonally. Most were empty except for a few bottles of wine. Next to the cot was a bucket and a bottle of water.

The room contained no windows, and the only way out appeared to be through the door. With nothing left to learn, she turned her attention to the rooms beyond the cell door. Her eyes settled on a large table. To the right of the table was a staircase with dusty steps. Beth returned to the table again. Her first thought was that it was an operating table, but the drain down the center made no sense. Underneath it was a square bucket.

It finally dawned on her what she was looking at. This was no operating table but rather a mortician's table, similar to the one the medical examiner used when cutting a subject open. Oddly, the instruments lining the table's edge were not the gleaming modern type. They were ancient. The chest and jars sitting along the facing wall confirmed her worst fears, though not as badly as the contents of the adjoining room to the left. Several bodies wrapped in linen cloth from head to foot lay side by side in wooden coffins. Standing upright in the corner was an empty sarcophagus.

"Houston, we have a problem," Beth whispered.

*

The following morning, they returned to Mayfield. Tony Gillam had set up one monitor to play the original disc and one to run the copy he'd made. Jack and Pappas began the process again. The discs appeared to be identical right down to the time clock ticking off seconds at the bottom right hand corner of the screen. Gillam hung in with them, answering questions when one came up.

When they reached the section where Curry arrived with Pell's medication, Jack asked him to rerun it. He and Pappas looked from screen to screen. They saw nothing unusual. Despite Gillam's initial enthusiasm, even he was getting bored. He left the room and returned with three cans of Coke. They continued to watch. The disc was now starting the month of April.

The second week was equally tedious with one exception. On the morning of the fourth day, Dr. Charles Raymond walked off the elevator at the end of the hall accompanied by Beth and Pappas. They went to Pell's cell and looked in it for approximately two minutes.

"Forgot we'd be on camera," Pappas said.

Jack merely nodded. Seeing Beth jarred him.

"You okay?" Pappas asked.

"Yeah," Jack said. He pressed the play button again and continued studying the disc.

Dr. Cairo showed up later in the week for another therapy session. Food trays went. Nurses brought medicine.

"Always thought working in Homicide would be exciting," Gillam said, stifling a yawn.

"More perspiration than inspiration," Pappas told him.

Jack had no comment. He stuck his legs out, folded his arms across his chest, and leaned back in the chair. His neck was stiff, and he was sore from sitting so long. Something was bothering him. Something he had seen. But he couldn't put his finger on it. Gillam was in the process of telling his wife that he'd be home on time when his hand slipped. He dropped his phone. The noise caused everyone to jump.

"Shit," he said. "Sorry."

"It's okay," Jack said. "Did you ever find out if Dr. Cairo would be in today?" he asked.

"Oh, right," Gillam said. "The doc's probably seeing patients now. You want me to page him?"

"We'll stop by his office on the way out," Jack said.

They said good-bye to Gillam. He called ahead to one of his coworkers and had the elevator waiting for them. As soon as they got off, Pappas checked his phone and listened to a voice mail message from Nolvia Borjas asking him to call the office.

The secretary answered and informed him, "A fax came in for you from Ellenwood Regional's personnel department. They don't have anyone named Ron Curry employed there."

Chapter 70

Instead of going to Alton Cairo's office, they detoured to Mayfield's personnel supervisor and met Danita Ritchey, a diminutive woman in her late sixties with curly gray hair. Dressed conservatively in a beige business suit, she had an intelligent face and bright-blue eyes and wore glasses that dangled from a chain around her neck. She reminded Jack of his fifth-grade teacher.

Pappas asked her, "Were you familiar with a contract nurse who worked here a couple of weeks ago named Ron Curry?"

"I didn't know him personally," Danita Ritchey said. "But I ran into him a few times in the cafeteria and such."

"Gillam told us he was transferred."

"That's right. I believe he's in Savannah now."

"That was two days after the first body was found," Pappas informed Jack.

"Would you have any contact information on him?" Jack asked.

"He worked for Southern States Medical. Their business card is in my desk. Would you like it?"

"Please," Jack said.

Pappas used his cell phone to call and reached Southern States' office manager.

"This is Detective Pappas with the Atlanta Police. Do you have a Ronald Curry working there?"

"We did," the manager said.

"He quit?"

"Leave of absence," the manager said. "Some family problems came up about a week ago. Ron had to take a little time off to deal with them. Is something wrong?"

297

"Not at all," Pappas said. "We're doing a routine investigation involving all employees who worked at Mayfield. Nothing to worry about."

"I understand. Is there anything I can do for you?"

"If you have a file on Mr. Curry and perhaps a photo, could you fax them to me? I'm at Mayfield right now."

"No problem. It won't take a minute."

Danita Ritchey wrote her e-mail address down on a piece of paper and handed it to him. Pappas winked at her and read it off to the manager. In under a minute, a chime sounded on her computer. She opened the e-mail program and stared at the screen, her mouth slightly open.

"What's wrong?" Pappas asked.

"There must be some mistake," she said.

"Like what?"

Without answering, Danita Ritchey pushed back from her desk, walked across the room to a file cabinet, opened it, and removed a green folder. She turned it around so Pappas and Jack could see. The photo in the file looked nothing like the one on her screen.

*

Pappas was on the phone with Jordan's sheriff.

"I'm tellin' you, Blaylock, it ain't the same guy. Not even close. I need you to get out to his house and, whoever this man is, pick him up for questioning."

"You're saying this man switched identities with the real Curry?"

"I don't know what he did. But something ain't kosher. Before we go off the deep end, let's see what he has to say. Maybe the photos got mixed up somehow. According to his employer, Ronald Curry lives at 471 Cochran Street."

"I'll have Avilles swing by and pick him up."

"You tell that kid to be careful. If he's the one we're looking for, you need to handle him like a viper."

There was a pause. Max Blaylock said, "Maybe I'd better go myself."

Pappas and Jack fidgeted for twenty frustrating minutes until the sheriff called back.

"I'm out at the house. You need to get out here. This is bad."

"Talk to me," Pappas said.

"There's a woman and a teenage girl lying dead in their bedrooms with their throats cut. Both of them have fingers missing. I suspect the real Curry's lying in the garage with a pick axe in his head."

"Shit."

"I called the medical examiner. The place is a fuckin' blood bath."
Blaylock's voice sounded shaky.

"What about the imposter?"

"No sign of him," the sheriff said.

Chapter 71

In the master bedroom of a house on Cochran Street, three men stood looking at the form of a forty-year-old woman in a green housedress. The smell of death from her decomposing body was nearly overpowering. Her daughter lay dead in the next room. The woman's throat had been cut from ear to ear, severing her carotid artery. Same with the daughter. Jack noted the wounds were precise and appeared to be the work of a scalpel or a very sharp knife.

In looking at the mother's body and her position in the hallway, it was obvious she hadn't gone easily. All the furniture had been knocked over. He knew for a certainty she died trying to protect her daughter. Sensing the desperation she must have felt, his own throat began to constrict. In addition to the slash across her throat, there were a number of stab wounds to her chest. In the garage, the scene was equally as gruesome. The axe that killed the real Ron Curry was still embedded in his head. He died on the spot, struck from behind.

"Mother of God," Pappas said under his breath.

They returned to the house where Jack dropped down to one knee and studied Loreen Curry's hands. They had shrunken in as the blood drained and rigor mortis took hold. Even after rigor let go, they were still retracted into claws. Horrible.

"What are you looking for?" Max Blaylock asked.

"Do you have a pen knife, Sheriff?"

Blaylock produced one and handed it to Jack.

"Thank you. Would you check in the kitchen and see if you can find a small plastic bag? And maybe some tape—masking tape, if possible."

The sheriff did as asked and returned with everything. Jack placed the paper under the woman's hand and very carefully unpryed two of her fingers and began to scrape under her nails. When he was through, he sealed the evidence in the bag, labeled it, and signed his name.

Hopefully, death had come quickly. Max Blaylock's face had lost much of its color.

"I've been sheriff here for fourteen years. In all that time, we had one murder. Now we have five in the space of a few weeks. This is something out of a bad dream."

Pappas nodded slowly. Jack remained absorbed in the scene, studying the details. There wasn't much either could say.

Blaylock continued, "I put a BOLO out on the imposter."

Jack nodded absently and asked the sheriff if one of his deputies could run the bag into Atlanta and ask Ben Furman to do a DNA test against the skin they'd found under Donna Camp's nails.

"Not a problem," Blaylock said.

"What a goddamn cluster fuck," Pappas said. He turned to Jack and asked, "See anything else?"

Jack shook his head slowly, then said, "I want to go back to Mayfield and look at those discs again."

"We just spent two freakin' days looking at them," Pappas said. "What's up?"

"How did Tony Gillam strike you?"

The detective was clearly surprised by the question and Jack's change of direction. "Gillam? Nice guy. Helpful."

"Very," Jack said.

"Kid seemed like a straight shooter to me. What are you gettin' at?"

"He stayed with us the entire time we were there."

"So?"

"You remember him asking if he could get us coffee?"

"Sure. He did that a couple of times. He also brought us Cokes. I thought it was a nice gesture. What's wrong with that?"

"By itself, nothing," Jack said. "If I recall, the only time he got up was to get the soft drinks or when we all broke to eat."

"And that's a problem?"

"I've been thinking about it. Gillam seemed nervous to me. You recall him dropping his phone?"

Pappas took a deep breath. "Anyone can drop a phone, Jack. Why are you making such a big deal about him?"

"Tell me what else you noticed," Jack said.

Pappas glanced at Max Blaylock, who shrugged, and then said, "He had a habit of rubbing his leg. People do that. My kid does that. You figure that makes him nervous?"

"I do."

"About what? Something on the discs?"

"That's my guess," Jack said.

"None of it involved him," Pappas said.

"It didn't hit me until a moment ago," Jack said. "Gillam was trying to distract us."

"You want to tell me why or should I just guess?" Pappas said.

Jack took his notebook out and consulted it. "Each time Alton Cairo showed up, our phony Nurse Curry was with him, or he got there first to bring Pell's medication."

"Yeah."

"And each time they did, Gillam chose that moment to ask us a question, tell us he was going for the drinks, or dropped his phone."

Pappas considered that for a moment, then said, "You think he was trying to cover something the imposter was doing?"

"It's possible. That's why I want to see the discs again," Jack said. "There's something there we missed."

"Beth thought the killer and Pell were working together. Maybe that's how he was passing his messages."

Jack raised his eyebrows. Pappas raised his.

Max Blaylock informed them, "I'm getting too old for this shit."

Chapter 72

When they returned to Mayfield, they were told by Danita Ritchey that Tony Gillam had left for the day. While they were talking, Childers and Spruell arrived. If the detectives were surprised to see them, neither said anything. Spruell, however, was annoyed and made no attempt to hide it.

"I understood you were off the case," Childers said.

"My last day," Jack said.

Childers seemed satisfied with the answer. He said, "Jimmy and I thought we'd follow up on why Sturgis was out here. The LT told us you asked about her trips."

When neither man responded, Spruell turned to Dan Pappas and said, "You want to tell us what you're doing back here?"

"I got issues," Pappas said.

"What are you talking about?"

"Issues. There's all kinds of psychiatrists running around this place. Thought I'd speak to one."

"Don't crack wise with me, Pappas. Sturgis was your partner, which means you're off the case, too. You know that. It's policy, man. I want your notes and anything else you and Kale have gathered."

"We'll get to that, Jimmy," Childers said. "Obviously, we didn't expect to run into to you guys. Something going on we should know about?"

Pappas told him what they had seen at the real Ron Curry's house and the scrapings Jack took but didn't mention the security videos. When he was through, Childers turned to Danita Ritchey and said, "Ma'am, would you provide us with your file on Mr. Curry, please? It may take us a while to separate fact from fiction, but whatever you've got in there could be helpful."

The supervisor looked at Dan Pappas. He nodded. She stood but apparently wasn't moving fast enough to suit James Spruell.

"While we're young, okay, lady?" Spruell said.

Ms. Ritchey stopped, faced him, and clasped her hands in front of her.

"A little courtesy would be appreciated, young man."

Spruell rolled his eyes and muttered something under his breath. Then louder, "Fine. I'm asking you nicely. Would you please get the friggin' file? We're dealing with multiple murders and have a lot of ground to cover."

One eyebrow on Danita Ritchey's face arched. She stayed where she was.

Spruell finally had enough. "Lady, do you understand why I'm here?"

"Years of inbreeding, I suspect," Danita Ritchey said.

Spruell opened his mouth. Closed it. His face reddened.

Pappas decided to study the laces on his shoes. Jack made sure to keep his expression neutral. Even deferential Childers was having trouble keeping a straight face. He chose the role of peacemaker.

"Ma'am, we would really appreciate your help."

She gave him a curt nod and continued to the file cabinet. Spruell informed his partner he would wait in the car and left.

Jack watched him go and commented, "Nothing changes."

Childers asked, "You plan to stay around?"

"If I can."

"I'm okay with it. Jimmy's another matter. You need to tread lightly with him."

"Sure."

"How about we get together at the North Precinct tomorrow. You can tell me what you know."

"I'll bring Pappas along, assuming we can resolve his issues," Jack said.

Childers smiled. "Ten o'clock?"

"Fine."

"Remember the address?"

"I'll find it."

Childers said, "We'd better take a look at the new murder scene. Sounds pretty bad from what you've told me."

"It is, Dave," Pappas said. "Take a breath mask if you have one."

Childers grimaced and then his expression turned serious. "Listen, I want you both to know how sorry I am about Elizabeth Sturgis. But that doesn't mean you can go after the killer yourselves. I'll run interference with Jimmy. He's just—"

"An asshole," Pappas said.

"I was about to say excitable," Childers said.

"Interesting way to put it," Pappas said.

"All right, he's an asshole," Childers said. "He's also a solid cop. The thing is, we're coming into this way behind the curve, which means we have a shitload of catching up to do. You guys willing to share?"

"Not a problem," Pappas said. "Glad to work with you."

"How about you, Jack?"

"Same here."

"Fine. They tell me you were out here earlier. What brings you back?"

Jack hesitated before answering. After a moment, he made the decision to cooperate. He had a good feeling about Childers and liked his even-keel attitude. Childers had been the same way during the original Scarecrow investigation: thorough, quiet, not excitable. He explained they were checking the people going in and out of Pell's cell on Mayfield's security videos and wanted to do some follow-up.

"See anything worthwhile?"

"The imposter was with Pell a number of times."

"You think that's important?" Childers asked.

"It might be," Jack said. "Dr. Cairo was also with him to do therapy sessions. I was hoping to speak with him and see if he noticed anything out of the ordinary about the man."

Childers nodded. "Sounds like this guy may be our killer. He got to the real Curry, James Bonded his way in here, then took out a whole family to cover his tracks."

"Reasonable theory," Jack said. "Assuming the person we saw on the disc is the bad guy, Pell could have used the meetings to coach him."

"That works," Childers said. "But there's a lot of ifs." He paused, thought for a moment, and then continued, "Jack, if Pell is involved, Jimmy'll want you to step away."

"Everybody has wants," Jack said. "Do we have a deal or not?"

Once again, the hardness he'd seen emerge in Jack Kale when they were in Atlanta appeared. It was an interesting change.

"We do. Asshole or not, he has a point. Officially, you're a civilian now. I'm willing to take your help because I need it. We don't catch this prick, more people are gonna die. What happened in the past with Pell is ancient history. You come into contact with the killer, you need to call us. You understand what I'm saying?"

Jack knew. "Got it."

"The chief won't tolerate vigilantism."

"I hear you," Jack said.

"I'm telling you, if you get crossways with Jimmy, he won't hesitate to make out an obstruction case."

Jack and Pappas remained quiet.

Childers waited for a response and got none. Just two men staring back at him, impassive. He tried to understand what they were feeling. Not so much different from what his mind-set would be if the situation was reversed. He looked from one to the other, took a deep breath, let it out, and turned to leave.

"You're right," he said over his shoulder. "Nothing changes."

Chapter 73

Dr. Alton Cairo, wearing a dark-brown Harris Tweed sport jacket, a blue Oxford shirt, and black slacks, met with them in the cafeteria. He was tall, in his early forties, and looked to be in reasonably good condition. His hair was longish, brown, and tied in the back to form a small pony tail of about three inches. He sat across from them drinking a cup of tea and answering their questions calmly. A pair of reading glasses with gold frames poked out of his jacket pocket.

The cafeteria was filled with square Formica tables that seated four people and brightly colored molded plastic chairs.

Jack was working on his third cup of coffee. It was okay; it was the caffeine jolt he was craving. Pappas was struggling with a small container of orange juice that had become problematic to open because it was soggy.

Cairo informed them, "I try to see Howard Pell at least once a week if my schedule permits. We've made some progress over the years, but it's largely a waste of time."

"Why's that?" Pappas asked.

"Because he's a classic sociopath. Howard's unquestionably bright. No doubt about that. Possibly too bright for his own good. That gets in the way. It's more important for him to fence verbally with you than to try to get better. I'm sure Dr. Kale will tell you that unless a patient wants to improve, therapy is a waste of time."

Pappas said, "The security video showed you going to see him twice a week toward the end of March."

Cairo ran a manicured hand through his hair and consulted his notes. "I believe I saw him three times the week of March 24th."

"How come?" Pappas asked.

"I can't discuss the details of a patient's treatment, but I can tell you that he was very agitated. That was the reason for my visits."

"Agitated about what?"

"It was just after the story about those murders in Jordan broke."

"He jealous someone was using his methods?" Pappas asked.

Cairo smiled without humor. "Hardly. I think Howard was upset the spotlight was being focused on him again. Dr. Raymond ordered his medication increased. I agreed."

"Where is Raymond?" Jack said.

"Oh, I suppose he'll be around sooner or later," Cairo said.

"Patients?" Jack asked.

"Golf game."

"Did he have much interaction with Howard Pell?" Jack said.

"Not to my knowledge," Cairo said.

"Detective Sturgis's notes indicate he considers himself something of an expert on Pell. Even volunteered to consult with our department," Jack said.

"I'm sure that was his opinion," Cairo said with a smile.

"You don't share it?"

Cairo shrugged elaborately. "I shouldn't say anymore. He's still my superior—factually speaking."

Dr. Cairo apparently had a sense of humor. Having met Raymond, Jack was inclined to agree.

"How about Ron Curry?" Pappas said. "You have much contact with him?"

"Ms. Sturgis asked me the same question. At the time I was non-committal, but I've thought about it and would have to say Ron struck me as a bit of an odd duck."

"How so?"

"I didn't know the man that well," Cairo said. "He wasn't here very long. I suppose it was his way of staring that made people uncomfortable. A number of staff members commented on it."

"That's it?" Pappas said. "He stared?"

"He wasn't given to socializing. Ate by himself and was very much a loner. I mean, he did his job. There were no complaints along those lines that I am aware of. These are just my observations, mind you."

Pappas took out the e-mail he received from Ellenwood and showed the photo to him.

"Who is that?" Cairo asked.

"The real Ronald Curry. The man you were working with was an imposter and might be the man we—"

Cairo was jolted at the news. "Are you serious?"

"'Fraid so," Pappas said. "Ms. Ritchey reacted the same way. We think he might be the man we're looking for."

"I can't believe this. I've been working next to a murderer?"

"He's just a suspect right now," Pappas said. "I know this is upsetting. Any info you can give us might be helpful."

"Christ almighty," Cairo said. He took a sip of his tea and then asked, "What do you want to know?"

"You ever see Pell pass him anything while they were together?"

"No. That's strictly prohibited. Guards can't take anything from an inmate."

"What about private conversations?"

"None when I was there. That doesn't mean they didn't talk when I wasn't around."

"Sure."

They spoke for another twenty minutes. Pappas asked the questions while Jack observed, as they had worked out earlier. The news had clearly shaken Cairo. Nevertheless, he appeared sincere in wanting to help, and his responses seemed candid. In the end, they promised to keep him updated, thanked him for his time, and said good-bye. Cairo left to see his patients, muttering to himself on the way out.

Before heading to the security office, they decided to fortify themselves with more coffee and a bag or two of chips. They were in the process of paying when Dr. Cairo came hurrying back through the door.

"I just remembered something," he said, catching his breath. "Your imposter and I were talking one day, and he mentioned he was having some work done on his house in Atlanta."

"Atlanta?" Pappas said. "That's a helluva commute."

"That's what I said. He told me he had just inherited it. From his grandmother, I think."

"He say where the house was?" Pappas asked.

Cairo thought for a moment and then said, "I'm afraid not. He did mention the traffic on Ponce de Leon Avenue has been getting worse and worse over the years. That's in Atlanta, right?"

Pappas smiled. "Yes, sir. I believe it is."

Chapter 74

The evening security officer was a man named Jerry Banks. He listened to their request to view the videos again. Banks thought about this for a moment and then asked, "This the case where the lady detective was kidnapped?"

"Yeah," Pappas said. "She's my partner."

"Oh, man," Banks said. "I'm sorry."

"Appreciate it."

"I never met her, but Tony said she's real nice. Follow me and I'll set you up in his office."

"I understand he had to leave early," Pappas said, as they started to walk.

"Yeah. Something came up with his kid."

Jack was content to remain in the background. Pappas was doing a good job. The big detective was a bright guy and could switch between blunt and subtle when he needed to. Anyone who underestimated him would be making a mistake.

Jack knew the portion of the disc he wanted to see again but had no idea what he was looking for. The sense that something was wrong continued to gnaw at him. It was another hour before he knew what it was.

As they sat in front of the monitors, Jack watched Alton Cairo approach Pell's cell door. Once the imposter had secured the handcuffs, Pell stepped back to allow Cairo to enter the room. Curry, or whoever he was, left and returned about fifty minutes later to remove the handcuffs.

"Freeze the picture, Dan," Jack said.

Pappas pressed the pause button. At the same time, Jack hit the button that controlled his screen where the master disc was running.

"There," Jack said, pointing at the screen on the right.

"There what?" Pappas asked.

"See it?"

Pappas looked from one monitor to the other several times, then shook his head. "They both look the same."

"They're not."

"Kale, I'm too tired and too hungry to play games, and my ass hurts from sitting here. Just tell me what I'm not seeing."

"Look at the nurse's back pocket on the left monitor."

"Yeah."

"See the outline?"

"Looks like . . . a book. You can see the top edge sticking out."

"Now look at Cairo. He goes into the room carrying what I presume is Pell's file, a tape recorder, and a pad to take notes. But on the way out—"

"Right there," Pappas said, pointing. "Between the file and the note-pad. They're not lying flat anymore. Sonofabitch is covering the book."

When they compared the original to the copy, they finally saw what happened. It wasn't much. No more than the blink of an eye. But the copy contained a small skip. No doubt about it. None at all. Several frames had been deleted.

Jack said, "The first time Cairo and the fake went to the cell, Gillam asked if we wanted coffee. On their next visit, he dropped his phone."

"And I bent down to pick it up for him," Pappas said.

"The noise pulled me away from the screen, too," Jack said.

"That's all it took. Gillam altered Beth's copy."

"Why? What the hell's with that book?"

"Good question," Jack said. "Let's ask him."

Chapter 75

They obtained Tony Gillam's address from Danita Ritchey and then called Max Blaylock. He had just finished at the new murder scene and sounded tired. Not surprising. It was horrific. Enough to drain anyone. He gave them directions and said he would meet them there.

The Gillams lived in a modest home in the middle of a subdivision just outside of Jordan. There was no community tennis court. No swimming pool. Just nicely maintained houses with neat lawns.

It was still light out when they arrived at seven o'clock. People were home for the evening preparing dinner. Kids were doing homework. A few were playing in their backyards. Max Blaylock's car was parked at the curb. The sheriff was leaning against the front fender waiting for them. A Ford Explorer and a Toyota Camry were in the driveway.

"Did you call Childers and Spruell?" Pappas asked.

"Completely slipped my mind to call 'em," Blaylock said. "Must be gettin' old."

Pappas smiled and informed him, "We ran a history on Gillam on the way over. He's clean. According to Ms. Ritchey, he's been working at Mayfield for eight years. You have any contact with him?"

Blaylock shook his head. "He phoned in a report about an abandoned car off Highway 92 a year ago, but that's about it. Maybe there was a glitch on the video you saw. He seems like a solid citizen to me."

"There wasn't," Jack said.

"You sure?" Blaylock said.

Jack stared at the sheriff.

"Yeah, I guess you are. How do you want to play this?"

"Here's the plan," Jack said. "We walk up and ring the doorbell."

"Right," Blaylock said.

"That's it," Jack said.

Pappas and Blaylock looked at each other. Finally, Pappas said, "Well, it's an easy plan to remember."

Pappas rang the front doorbell and waited.

When Tony Gillam opened the door, he didn't seem surprised to see them.

"Tony, I'm Max Blaylock. You know these other gentlemen. Mind if we come in for a minute?"

Gillam had changed into jeans and a T-shirt and was wearing a pair of old moccasins. He asked no questions. He simply nodded and led them to the family den. The room had inexpensive laminate paneling and a small fireplace. Over the mantel was a medium-size flat-screen television. The carpeting was tan and worn. Two cabinets topped by wooden shelves flanked the fireplace. Opposite it was a blue couch and two oversize leather club chairs. No one sat down.

Blaylock said, "Do you know why we're here, Tony?"

Gillam turned his palms up and tried to give the impression he was confused.

"We'd like to know why you altered the copy of the security disc you made for Beth Sturgis," Jack said.

"I didn't alter anything," Gillam said. "There must be some mistake."

"No mistake," Jack said. "You tried to distract us by asking about coffee when the imposter showed up with Dr. Cairo. After the coffee, you dropped your phone. We've examined the discs. They don't match."

"That's ridiculous. I was there with you the whole time. I was trying to help," Gillam said.

Pappas said, "Look, you're in charge of Mayfield's security. You had to have seen the file Southern States Memorial sent over. The photo doesn't look anything like him."

"I barely knew the man," Gillam said. "Why would I screw around with his file? That's crazy. I haven't done anything wrong."

Pappas informed him, "Two other detectives are involved in the case now. Sooner or later, they're gonna put it together. Lying to us is one thing. Don't get yourself in deeper. We need your help, kid."

"Do I need a lawyer?"

"I don't know," Pappas said. "Do you?"

Gillam was doing his best to come across as sincere, Jack thought, but he tended to answer their questions with questions of his own, a probable sign of deception.

"If there's a problem, let us help you, son," Sheriff Blaylock said.

"I don't have a problem," Gillam insisted. "I'm calling my lawyer."

Blaylock turned to Jack and shook his head. It was obvious to all of them Gillam was lying. Jack observed him, noting a slight sheen of sweat had broken out on his forehead. He and Gillam made eye contact, and as they did, one piece of the puzzle finally fell into place. A small one.

"Where's your wife, Tony?"

"My wife?"

"You know, the lady you're married to," Jack said pointing to a photo of them sitting on one of the cabinets.

"She's out right now," Gillam said.

"That's odd. Your carport has room for two vehicles," Jack said. "Looks like both are here."

"A friend picked her up to go shopping."

"I see. What friend?"

"Just someone from work. I never met her."

"She have a cell phone?" Pappas asked.

"Sure."

"Give her a call," Pappas suggested. "Make sure everything's copacetic."

"I don't need to call her. She's fine. And I've had just about enough of this. I'd like you all to leave now."

The color had risen in Gillam's face, and the calm he was trying to project was beginning to show cracks. You could tell it from the rising timbre of his voice. Max Blaylock saw it as well. His hand was now marginally closer to his gun.

No one spoke for several seconds. The sheriff decided to give it one more try.

"Tony, you'll need to come with us to my office. If it was my wife, I'd call and let her know so she doesn't come home to an empty house. Women worry about things like that."

Gillam stood there silently.

"How about that cell phone number?" Pappas asked.

Gillam shook his head in the negative.

Max Blaylock took a deep breath. "Tony Gillam, you are under arrest for tampering with evidence in a criminal investigation, obstruction of justice, and the destruction of government property."

He spun Gillam around and snapped the cuffs on his wrists as he read him his Miranda rights. Gillam put up no resistance. He appeared drained.

While the sheriff was patting him down for weapons, he came across Gillam's cell phone. He examined it and found a button on the keypad that brought up the address book. The first number on the list simply said, "Moira." Blaylock looked at Gillam as he dialed it.

A sharp trilling sound came from the bedroom.

Pappas shook his head, went in, and returned carrying a phone in a pink case.

"Looks like your wife forgot this," he said.

Chapter 76

The man in the ski mask came slowly down the steps carrying a medium brown cardboard box. He placed it on the floor at the side of the operating table. His eyes remained fixed on Beth, who stood watching him from behind her cell door.

"I apologize for your accommodations and meeting the way we did," he said.

Beth stared at him.

"You're still upset," the Soul Eater said. "I understand. Really, I do."

"Go to hell."

"There's no need to be rude, Beth. Believe it or not, I've grown quite fond of you."

"Is that so?"

"It is. Truly. Not to worry, though, I imagine Clever Jack will be along to rescue you in due course."

"Too bad for you then," Beth said.

"Not really," the Soul Eater said. "His fate, and unfortunately yours, are both sealed. I want you to know I've been extremely fair. All he needs to do is put the clues together. You nearly managed and that wasn't easy. Congratulations."

"I didn't *nearly* manage to figure out who you are," Beth said. "I did. It was right there on the videos."

"Ah, the security tapes. We were concerned about them. I figured as much when I saw your notes and the e-mail. No such thing as a perfect crime, eh?"

"You look ridiculous in that ski mask," Beth said. "Why don't you take it off?"

316

Ridiculous? Everyone was so rude to him lately. First that coarse woman at Underground Atlanta and now Beth.

"I don't know," he said.

"If you plan on killing me, what's the point in hiding your face?"

She had a point. What difference did it make if she saw him? He doubted that she'd guessed who he was, but it might be fun to see her reaction. He reached up, pulled the mask off, and said, "Boo."

Beth shook her head and looked bored.

Disappointed, the Soul Eater waited a moment longer. When nothing more was forthcoming, he supplemented his last comment. "So you figured out who I was and didn't bother to tell anyone. That, my dear, is ridiculous."

"Willing to bet your life on it?"

Her question brought him up short. She was bluffing. Had to be. Otherwise, the cops would have stormed the place by now. No, his plan was intact. Jack would work out the puzzle and come for her, which was exactly what they wanted. Howard was rarely wrong about such things. Revenge was a powerful motivator. That, and the rather predictable desire to protect the female of the species.

"Nice try, Beth. Really," he said. "You're an extremely resourceful and interesting woman."

"Your funeral," Beth said with a shrug. "You have a chance to get away. I'd take it if I were you."

"Thank you. But I have no worries on that score."

Beth inquired, "You know what a green light means?"

"Green light?"

"It's police slang for a kill order. Basically, shoot first and ask questions later. When the cops arrive, they'll blow you away without a second thought. Either that or I'll kill you myself when I get out."

"And you plan to do that how?" the Soul Eater asked.

"Come closer," Beth said. "And I'll whisper in your ear."

The killer frowned and studied her face. Even in the basement's dim light, her eyes were as hard as two emeralds. The way she was looking at him actually made him nervous. By rights, it should be the other way around. How much did she know? Hard to say exactly. Perhaps it would be better to put a bullet in her head and have done with it. No, no, no, stick with the plan. He and Howard had worked everything out in detail months earlier. Neither Clever Jack nor the woman would survive. That much was certain.

"Trying to provoke me won't work," he said.

"Why not?"

Annoyed, the Soul Eater flicked a dismissive hand at her and turned his attention to whatever was in the cardboard box.

"Question," Beth said. "Does your jaw still hurt from where Donna Camp kicked you?"

He looked at her and started to reply but then stopped. She really was fascinating, much more so than his normal victims, but engaging in a verbal fencing match was silly. He decided to change the subject.

"I know you can't understand why I'm doing this," he said.

A few seconds ticked by as she digested his statement.

"It may come as a shock," Beth said, "but I don't have to."

"What do you mean?"

"Leave me out of it. Explain the way your sick little brain works to your lawyer or maybe a priest."

"Honestly, Beth, that's a very provincial attitude. Don't you think?"

He wants to talk. This is what she was supposed to do. But the truth was, she really didn't care. It was enough to know a dog is rabid to understand the danger it posed to everyone around. She considered trying to form a bond. Some kidnapping victims who made an attachment managed to stop themselves from becoming dehumanized by their captors and thus harder to kill. She rejected the idea just as quickly as her anger and frustration boiled over. Considering the bodies in the next room, whatever he was looking for wasn't a friend.

"Provincial or not, tell it to someone else," Beth said, knowing her words would have the opposite effect.

"The odd thing," said the Soul Eater, ignoring her, "is that I come from a perfectly normal middle-class family. My mother wasn't promiscuous. My father wasn't a drunk. He didn't beat me. I wasn't raped as a child or shunned by my friends. No one ran over my puppy. In short, there were no traumatic events that changed the way I looked at the world. I thought studying psychology would give me some insight into why, ah . . . I do what I do. Apparently, it didn't. So I sought out Howard, the quintessential sociopath. It took me two years to secure a position at Mayfield."

"So?"

The Soul Eater grew pensive and folded his arms across his chest. He glanced around the room, not focusing on anything in particular. "I mean, it's strange, isn't it? Nothing at all happened, yet I turned out this way."

"Disease exists," Beth said. "Explanations about its origins are interesting, but they don't change the fact that it's here."

"Disease," he repeated quietly. "No, I suppose not." He took a slow breath and then paused again to line up a scalpel on the operating table. "Why don't you have something to drink? There are a few good Pinot Noirs in there. Maybe even a Cabernet."

"No, thank you," Beth said.

"It may make dealing with what happens later . . . easier." He shrugged. "Your choice. Try to make yourself comfortable. It won't be long now."

With that, he glanced at the four bodies lying silently in their coffins, then smiled to himself at some private joke. And without another word, he turned and climbed back up the stairs.

*

After the door closed, Beth listened to the sound of his retreating footsteps. When she was sure he was gone, she returned to the cot and lifted a corner of the mattress. The makeshift rope she'd fashioned from strips of cloth was there. She attached her shoe to one end of it for weight and moved back to the cell door, sticking her arm through. A surge of pain from her broken collarbone shot through her body. She clenched her teeth, ignored it, and fixed her eyes on the operating instruments. If she could just get one, she might be able to pick the lock. Certainly defend herself when he came for her. And come he would. There was no doubt in her mind on that score. The man was quite insane.

What would Jack do under the circumstances? Probably build a bomb with the wine bottles.

She had no idea how to make a bomb, but she did remember a game she used to play as a child with her sister. Dropping one end of the rope so the shoe was at the bottom, Beth began to swing it back and forth. Not unlike her childhood game at all. Only this time it was for life and death.

Chapter 77

The sheriff's office was located in the basement of the courthouse. It contained a total of three cells, only two of which had ever been in use at the same time, according to Max Blaylock. A small lobby separated their work area from the public. Beyond that was Blaylock's office. While the town of Jordan only employed two deputies, he explained, the third desk was for a part-time clerk who came in on weekends to file and do typing. Avilles and Barbara Tucker, who Jack had met at the Donneley farm, looked up when they brought Tony Gillam in.

Avilles informed the sheriff, "I called Detective Childers like you asked and let him know you were bringing in a suspect. He said he'll be here as soon as they finish at the Curry house. He didn't sound happy."

"Tough business," Blaylock said without sincerity.

"His partner doesn't want us to question the suspect unless they're present."

"Is that so?"

"Just what he said, Max."

"Did he say please?"

"No, sir, he didn't."

"Then it don't count."

Blaylock turned to Tony Gillam and tried again to convince him to cooperate.

"Son, you can do yourself a lot of good. Why don't you level with us and tell us why you screwed around with them security discs?"

Gillam's face was pale. He just shook his head as he had before and offered no response.

Jack didn't think he would change his mind. On the ride in, he and Pappas had discussed what Gillam had to gain by his actions. Neither thought he was the killer. He was too short and he was right-handed. The fact that his DNA didn't match the samples from the killer meant nothing, since he was in charge of forwarding the samples to the GBI for processing. It would have been an easy matter to switch his own out for someone else's.

"You think Curry bought him off?" Pappas asked.

"It's possible," Jack said. "Guess we'll know more after we examine his accounts. He certainly wasn't living like a king."

"You really believe they were working together?"

Jack shook his head. "This isn't very scientific, but Gillam feels wrong to me. He isn't someone I'd pick for a crazed killer."

"Me either."

There was no doubt Gillam and whoever had taken Ron Curry's place were linked together. No doubt at all. A lot would depend on what Ben Furman came up with—and Tony Gillam, assuming he could be convinced to cooperate. He took the copy of the newspaper article he'd made out of his briefcase and studied the image of Albert Lemon for a full minute. He could have kicked himself for not seeing it sooner. He had the first half of his answer. Jack shook his head and leaned across the desk and asked Barbara Tucker if he could borrow her computer. When he was done, he asked the sheriff if he could have a few minutes alone with Gillam.

Blaylock shrugged and motioned for him to go ahead.

Folding the newspaper article lengthwise, he placed it in the breast pocket of his jacket and headed back to the cells.

Minus his belt and shoelaces, Tony Gillam was sitting on the cot in his cell, head down, elbows on his knees. He glanced up at the sound of a key turning in the lock. Jack nodded his thanks to the deputy, entered the cell, and sat on a small metal bench directly across from him.

"I don't have anything to say, Dr. Kale."

"I know. And I think I know why. You don't need to say anything, Tony. Just listen . . . and look." Jack opened the newspaper article and placed it on the cot next to Gillam. "This is an artist's rendition of Albert Lemon, Atlanta's first serial killer. Take a close look at the face. You've seen it before."

Gillam started to reply, but Jack held up his hand. "It might be more accurate to say it looks familiar to you. It did to me, too, until I made the connection a little while ago."

Gillam examined the illustration again. It took a moment before the realization dawned on him. His eyes widened.

"I thought so," Jack said. "Your wife's name is Moira, isn't it?"

Unable to pull his eyes away from the drawing, Gillam nodded.

"How long has she been missing, Tony?"

Gillam's answer also made sense and coincided with the fake Ron Curry's arrival at Meadbrook. It simply confirmed the conclusion Jack had already reached.

"We don't have much time, so I'm going to be blunt with you. There's a chance that your Moira is still alive. I know you've been clinging to that hope, but I have to tell you I don't think she is. I'm terribly sorry to say it, but that's the truth. Neither Albert Lemon nor Howard Pell ever returned any of their victims. The copycat's following the path they laid out. Do you understand what I'm saying?"

When Gillam finally pulled his eyes away from the article and looked at Jack, they were red. "Yes." The answer came out as a whisper.

"And you went along with them hoping to save her life."

"They sent me her finger."

The words struck at Jack's stomach, and he closed his eyes for a moment.

"I hope I'm wrong, truly I do. And I hope we can find some way to save her. The bottom line is that Beth Sturgis is alive, at least I pray she is. Like you, I keep going back and forth believing and not believing. If there's even the slightest chance to help either of them, I need your help.

"A jury may understand a desperate husband trying to save his wife. I promise you, if push comes to shove, I'll testify to that. Right now, you have an opportunity to help me save Beth's life. If you're the kind of man I believe you are, you'll take it. Say no, and I'll walk out of here and it will be the last time we speak."

Jack waited.

"What is it you want?"

"Tell me everything you know about these people. Don't leave anything out, Tony."

Gillam related the phone call he received the night his wife didn't come home. That was followed by a visit to his house the following morning by a man bearing an article of her clothing and her cell phone. They were threatening to send Moira back in pieces if he didn't cooperate. Their plan was simple: work with them for several days and allow the imposter to take the real Ron Curry's place and falsify the security records and tapes.

"You believed they wanted to break Howard Pell out of Mayfield?" Jack said.

"Right."

"Is that it?"

"On the second night, I followed him, thinking he would lead me to my wife. But he didn't. He went to the Curry house and changed cars, then went to a motel. The room was registered to someone named Mathias Lemon. The name meant nothing to me until a few minutes ago. I went back for my gun, but I screwed up. He was gone by the time I returned."

"And you never thought to call the police?"

"I received her finger the next morning. Do you understand that?"

Fifteen minutes later, Jack returned to the lobby, where Dave Childers, James Spruell, Pappas, and the sheriff were waiting.

"Did you get your confession, Kale?" Spruell asked.

"No."

"I didn't think so. Even if you did, it wouldn't be worth spit. The sheriff told us Gillam already invoked Miranda. You had no right to speak with him."

Jack nodded slowly. Spruell turned away in disgust.

Childers asked, "Has he lawyered up yet?"

"He mentioned a lawyer at his house but never specifically asked for one," Blaylock said.

"But you did Mirandize him?" Spruell said.

"Of course."

"Was it videotaped?" Spruell asked.

"Nothing fancy here, Detective. I just read him his rights."

"The reason we do things fancy, Sheriff, is we don't want to screw up an arrest. Did you at least have him sign the Miranda card?"

"Nope. We all heard him answer."

Spruell shrugged. "I guess it is what it is. Look, I'm not trying to be a jerk, Sheriff. We simply don't want a killer walking on a technicality."

"He's not the killer," Jack said. "Alton Cairo is."

Everyone turned to him at the same time.

"The doctor?" Max Blaylock said, surprised.

"Gillam altered the security disc to protect his wife. He also never sent the imposter's security file to the GBI for a background check."

"What makes you say that, Jack?" Childers asked.

"Because he told me."

Childers and Spruell looked at each other, then the older detective asked, "But why alter the disc?"

"Gillam was forced into it on the promise they would return his wife. He needed to cover what's really going on between Howard Pell, Cairo, and the man calling himself Ron Curry, though that isn't his real name. It is Mathias Lemon."

"Bullshit," Spruell said. "You're basing this on a two-second slice of video and the outline of a book. Talk about a thin case."

"It happened more than once," Jack said. "Cairo had a good explanation for his recent increase in visits, but that doesn't fly for a number of reasons. First, Dan told me Pell was an iceberg when they met. He appeared self-contained, calm, and not at all in crisis as Cairo represented. Next, he said Dr. Raymond increased the medication Pell was taking, but there's no evidence on the video Raymond ever saw him during this time. The only place Pell went when he left his cell was to their recreation area. Even a doctor who's not terribly hands-on would want to see a patient before increasing his medical dosage. He'd certainly do some follow-up because antianxiety meds are tricky and have serious side effects if they're not managed correctly."

"I'm not convinced," Spruell said.

"I'm not surprised," Jack said.

"That's all you have, Kale? Pell looked calm and Raymond didn't hold his hand?"

"There's a reason Charles Raymond didn't hold his hand," Jack said. "The same reason nobody in Mayfield does. They're afraid of him. The people there exercise a great deal of caution around Dr. Pell. During interviews, he's handcuffed and shackled to a chair. Visitors are warned not to get too close to him."

"So?" Spruell said.

"So what was Alton Cairo doing going into the cell of an insane killer alone two or three times a week? Cairo is left-handed and six foot two, which fits with what Donna Camp and the Dorseys told us. I'd say Lemon is about five foot eight and fairly wide in the body. Actually, he looks a lot like his grandfather, Albert."

A look of shock appeared on each of the faces in the room one at a time. Jack placed the security file photo of Mathias Lemon next to the artist's rendition of his grandfather. He then explained how Tony Gillam had followed him to the motel and discovered his real name, though it meant nothing to him at the time.

Max Blaylock recovered first and said, "Maybe you boys should leave my prisoner where he is and go have a talk with Dr. Cairo."

An unspoken communication passed between Childers and Spruell. They started for the door. Pappas and Jack were about to follow them out when James Spruell stopped and informed Jack, "We spoke with Lieutenant Fancher again. According to her, your status at the Atlanta Police Department is now officially over, which makes you a civilian again. Go back to teaching, Kale."

"I'm sorry, Jack," Childers said. He looked embarrassed. "I'll keep you in the loop, civilian or not. Detective Pappas is welcome to join us."

"You go on," Pappas said. "I'm his ride."

"Understood," Childers said.

"Before you leave," Pappas said, "One of you geniuses ought to tell Tony Gillam there's a good chance his wife won't be coming home—ever."

Chapter 78

There wasn't much talk on the ride back to Atlanta. Pappas dropped Jack off at his car and said good-bye. They promised to stay in touch.

The light on his answering machine was blinking. Jack ignored it, fed Marta, then played the message.

"Jack, this is Penny Fancher. I just received a call from Dave Childers. They went to Cairo's home and found the place empty. It's possible he's headed your way. Call us immediately if you notice anything out of the ordinary."

He's not headed this way, Jack thought. He already knew where Cairo was going.

Jack clipped on Marta's leash and went outside. As they moved through Brookwood's streets, his thoughts turned inward. He was consumed by guilt. He had failed Beth. There was no denying it. He should have figured out the game Pell and Cairo were playing sooner. Based on the DNA, he also knew where Mathias Lemon fit in now. If he was right, too bad for Mathias now that their use for him was over.

Please, God, let her be alive.

The first signs of a panic attack appeared as he turned the corner onto his street. He recognized the pain building in his chest and the shortness of breath immediately.

Not now. Anytime but now.

Just as he'd rehearsed with Shottner, Jack shut his eyes and imagined he was sitting on a quiet beach. To his right was a calm ocean, the water indigo. To his left, clusters of vegetation, grasses, sea grape, and palm trees. The sound of waves dying against the shore reached him. He knew this beach. Knew the familiar clouds. The sand was so bright, it was almost painful to look at. He'd been to this place many times in his mind.

In the distance, he became aware of a solitary figure slowly walking toward him in a white dress. As the waves rolled in to the shore, water splashed across her ankles. The dress reached the middle of her calves. He couldn't see her face, but there was no mistaking her shape. Beth Sturgis came to him out of the light and placed her hand gently against his cheek.

"I'm so sorry," he whispered.

"Shh," Beth said. There was no accusation in her face. No recrimination in tone. She looked beautiful. Serene. Her green eyes met his.

"I failed," Jack said.

"You didn't."

Tears began to well up in Jack's eyes. "I should have been there to protect you."

"My job. My choices. I knew the danger when I took it, Jack. Don't you see that? We made a difference."

Her words had little effect on him. The pressure in his chest worsened.

"We never danced," he said. "I would have liked that. I would have tried."

Beth reached out and brushed the hair off his forehead. She smiled. "I know."

The thought of her alone with the killer was overwhelming, sapping the strength from his limbs. In that instant, he knew she was dead. The pain of her loss engulfed him so completely, he was certain his heart would break. He dropped to the ground. Felt the warm, powdery sand between his fingers. Overhead, a tern glided soundlessly across the water's surface.

Beth stroked his head.

"It's not over," she said. "You still have a job to do. It's who you are. What you've always been. Everyone matters, Jack."

He tried to answer, but the words caught in his throat. Unable to move, he watched her turn and walk back up the beach. Sunlight merged with the white sand and the water's glare until it was impossible to distinguish one from the other. The air tasted of salt.

Beth's figure receded farther and farther until she was gone. A minute passed and then another. Jack found himself down on his hands and knees. Marta was licking his face and trying to move him with her head. The street was deserted. Silent.

Slowly, gradually, the pressure in his chest eased. His heart rate returned to normal.

I'm losing it. She's not dead. Can't be.

Jack pushed himself up and wiped his eyes. The mind was a marvelous, complex thing. If he gave up, gave in to the killer's game, there was no hope. None at all. He had to believe there was still a chance. She'd been there. Spoken to him. Comforted him. He could still feel her fingers on his face. He closed his eyes, breathed in the heavy night air, and started for home.

"I still have a job to do."

Chapter 79

The phone was ringing as Jack came through the door. He lifted the receiver and heard a man's voice whisper, "Ah, Clever Jack. I'm so glad I caught you. Did you get my note?"

"No."

"Check your e-mail. You might learn something."

Jack went to his computer and opened his e-mail. There, at the top of his inbox, was another message from the deceased Betsy Ann Tinsley.

"Are you alone?"

"No. There are cops everywhere. I'm at the police station. Your call was forwarded."

"I doubt that. I think you're home. Click the link in the e-mail. It will start a live feed."

"And?"

"I'll do the commentary. There's something I'd like you to see, a special presentation as it were."

Jack didn't reply.

"You're a sick fuck, Cairo. Has anyone ever told you that?"

"How do you know this isn't Mr. Curry?" Cairo said and laughed a little.

"It's not," Jack said. "You can stop whispering. You're beginning to bore me. The game's over."

"Oh, not by a long shot," Cairo said. "Congratulations on figuring it out. We knew you would, of course. Have you opened it yet?"

Jack clicked the link. After a short delay, a browser opened and a picture appeared on the screen of a table with four rings attached to it. A naked man was shackled to the rings, arms and legs spread wide into the shape of an X. He recognized Mathias Lemon from his file photo. Poor schmuck. The camera was steady, mounted high. Shooting down from the front. On a tripod, Jack guessed.

There was no sound, but it was obvious Lemon was screaming. His head thrashed from side to side. His mouth was open. The tendons in his neck stood out like cords, knotting convulsively.

Alton Cairo said, "Tell me what you see."

"Your partner, Mathias Lemon, Albert's grandson."

Cairo hesitated. "You surprise me, Jack. May I ask how you knew?"

"Tony Gillam followed him to the motel he was staying at, hoping to retrieve his wife. He was registered under his own name."

Cairo looked at Mathias and shook his head. "Well, the choice in partners was somewhat limited."

"You have a funny way of treating your partners, Doctor."

"Soon to be our ex-partner, I'm afraid."

"Who's our?"

"I suspect you know the answer to that."

"You and Pell make a great pair. Two raving lunatics."

The camera continued to record as Cairo stepped into the frame. Jack watched as Cairo set the phone down. He glanced back at the lens and smiled. In his hand was a scalpel.

"Howard is no lunatic," Cairo said over the speaker. "He's a genius and far more insightful than you'll ever be."

"Bully for him."

Cairo moved to Lemon's side. His eyes were fixed on the knife. His head was turning violently from side to side. Jack could hear his screams in the background. Hysterical.

Cairo placed the tip of the scalpel about four inches below the man's navel and cut upward. Lemon's entire body jerked as a line of blood appeared. He continued to scream.

Cairo then switched to Lemon's rib cage and cut horizontally. His actions were sure and precise as a surgeon. Pell had done a good job coaching him. Blood flowed from the incision. A second cut was made above the navel across Lemon's stomach completing a large H shape on his torso.

"You're still there," Cairo said. "I can hear you breathing. Another panic attack on the way?"

Jack didn't answer.

"Yes, we know all about them. And we know all about your daughter, too. Morgan, isn't it?"

Jack said nothing.

"Come, come, Jack. I've given you what you need to solve the puzzle. Don't tell me you're squeamish. This is what you did to Howard. Does it bring back any memories? He thought you might like to see how it should have been done. In a little while we'll see how Ms. Sturgis handles the procedure. Surely you're not afraid to look."

Cairo reached down and took both flaps of skin on Mathias Lemon's stomach and pulled them back, exposing his intestines. All the while, he continued to scream and thrash his head from side to side.

Jack knew what was coming next.

Cairo's hands lifted out the man's intestines, then laid them on his chest. The camera picked up the horror on Lemon's face as he looked down and saw what was being done to him.

"You remember this part, don't you?"

Jack said nothing.

"You left Howard to die out there in the woods at the bottom of Cloudland Canyon."

"You're insane."

"Am I?"

"Certifiable."

"We'll see. I have a much more interesting fate planned for you and Ms. Sturgis. Now please pay attention. Normally, after the organs are removed, we store them in Canopic jars along with items the deceased valued in life. Then everything is placed in this chest."

Cairo bent lower and studied Lemon's face for a moment, then said, "Still with us, Mathias? Well, it won't be much longer."

He patted Mathias's hand and then inserted a cannula into the femoral artery of his inner thigh. Attached to the needle was a long tube. Blood began to flow down the tube into a pail under the table.

Cairo continued his narrative. "As you know, the records from the early Egyptian dynasties are very spotty. I've been studying them for years. It's something of a passion with me. Unfortunately, they didn't leave us a how-to manual on the mummification process. What we do know is sketchy and largely based on conjecture. Nevertheless, over time, I've made significant progress.

"Once the fluids are completely drained, I'll attend to the heart, liver, brain, and such. Did you know they used to remove the brain through the nose using a hook? 'Fraid I haven't mastered that part yet."

"There's a special place in hell for people like you," Jack said.

Cairo ignored the comment and continued, "The really interesting part," he said, "is the wrapping process. I don't think Mathias Lemon will mind if I begin." He picked up a roll of linen, cut off several long strips, and started to individually wrap the fingers of Lemon's hand.

Jack didn't need to see anymore. Using mouse and the arrows at the bottom of the screen, he killed the feed. The last image he saw was Cairo's smiling face. Behind him, Lemon had stopped moving.

"Still watching, Jack?"

"Fuck you."

"Such talk from a professional man. Surely you can do better than that."

"Count on it," Jack said, and killed the video feed.

Chapter 80

After the call ended, Jack shut his computer, went into the kitchen, and splashed some cold water on his face. He'd seen worse. What he was feeling went far beyond anger or frustration. It was hate, pure and simple. He leaned down and rinsed the bile from his mouth with tap water.

Jack went into his bedroom and dressed in black jeans, black shirt, and solid leather shoes with rubber soles. A 9 mm HK and an illegal switchblade he'd owned for years made up the balance of his outfit. He said good-bye to Marta and went in search of the monster.

Whatever else Cairo might be, he was not stupid. The information he fed them about "Curry" having to make repairs to the house he inherited coupled with his gratuitous comments about the traffic on Ponce de Leon Avenue getting worse and worse and his reference to Beth still being alive was an invitation.

If I can't come to you, come to me.

When Jack borrowed the deputy's computer, he'd accessed the Fulton County Clerk's online records for properties sold in the Old Fourth Ward. He knew the streets. What he was searching for were any homes sold in the last year. He found what he was looking for in fewer than thirty minutes. A second search pulled up the newspaper article he found at the library. A copy of the article was lying on the seat next to him.

Working day and night, investigators from Atlanta's police force tracked down lead after lead in their pursuit of Albert Lemon. The indignation of the city's residents had risen to rage with the discovery of the mutilated body of nine-year-old Charlotte Sewell. The girl's legs had been amputated. She died of shock and blood loss. Other injuries were inflicted by the madman too horrible to recount on these pages.

As good fortune had it, a tip provided by a responsible citizen of the Fourth Ward alerted detectives to the fact that Lemon might be living someplace on Linwood Avenue near Cleburne Avenue. An intensive search was undertaken wherein it was found that Lemon's maternal grandmother, deceased ten years earlier, had in fact owned property in the neighborhood. Police cautiously approached the house only to find it apparently abandoned, shuttered, and locked.

They were about to give up when Detective William P. Denney observed a trash receptacle that contained food items of a recent nature. Upon attempting to enter the killer's lair, the officers found the house had been booby-trapped with explosive devices.

A terrible fire resulted, taking the lives of three of our finest along with the killer who was burnt to death.

Lemon was last seen on the roof before it collapsed in the blaze. At least two witnesses to the event confirmed the madman's last words were "Death was only the beginning" and that he would one day return.

The city can now breathe a sigh of relief as it begins to heal.

*

None of the locations Jack found online bore Cairo's name. That would have been too obvious. Out of curiosity, he checked under Howard Pell's name. Nothing there either. He finally found what he was looking for in an executor's deed. Marshall Pell, as executor for the estate of Amanda Pell Pittman, deceased, had sold a home on Leland Avenue to a Three G Investment Group some ten months earlier. The time frame fit. Marshall was Howard Pell's brother.

Jack had no idea who the Three G Investment Group was. Didn't matter. The other pieces of property owned by the estate were sold the following month to different buyers. According to the deed descriptions, one was a lot with nothing on it. The other was a barber shop. He eliminated both as possibilities.

In the Old Fourth Ward, he found a business closed for the evening about two blocks from the Leland Avenue address. Jack parked his car and started back. An approach on foot was preferable to announcing his arrival in a vehicle.

The buildings he passed were uniformly stooped shouldered. Age and a declining economy had sapped the strength from the frames that held them up. There was no grass, no trees. Not even weeds bothered to push their way up through cracks in the asphalt.

Over time, the neighborhood had changed from middle-class white to poor minorities, eventually making a full circle back to families and young singles. Atlanta had simply grown away from it, pushing northeast and northwest along the I-75 and I-85 corridors.

Some attempts had been made to transform the area, all of which had fallen short. Inevitably, investors put their money into things that would have appealed to them had they lived there. The initial influx of trendy boutiques, lingerie, and novelty shops came and went. What remained were fading signs in damaged doorways. He spotted the house he was looking for on the next block.

His phone vibrated in his pocket. The caller ID said the call was restricted. He assumed it was Cairo again. Like a lot of psychotics, the man enjoyed the sound of his own voice. Pell had been the same way at the end.

"Did you enjoy the show?" Cairo asked.

"Not really."

"Ah, well, I'm sorry. I do have a surprise for you. A farewell gift, as it were. I'm going to give you your own mummy. I suspect the beautiful Ms. Sturgis looks quite good in white."

Jack didn't reply.

He turned a corner and continued past a group of adolescent teens hanging around the entrance of a midrise building. Half of them were smoking. The girls wore ridiculously short skirts and too much makeup. The boys were trying to look hard. No one paid him any attention. He was used to it.

"Still there?" Cairo asked.

"Mm-hm."

"Still think you can find me?"

"Without a doubt."

"Where are you now?"

"Standing in front of your door."

There was a momentary pause and then the curtain of a window on the second floor moved slightly. Jack smiled.

"You're lying," Cairo said.

"You never know."

"Yes, I do. Just like I know you lied about Howard killing your partner. You shot her, Jack. You and no one else."

Jack said nothing.

Concealed in the shadows of an alley, he studied the house. It was old, probably close to seventy-five years. Three stories high with a French-style Mansard roof. A small safety apron bounded by wrought iron grillwork about two feet in height ran around the roof's perimeter. Next to the house was a clapboard building in pretty bad shape. It was one story higher than the home he was interested in—that at least was a break.

"Still with me, Jack?"

"Still here. So you and Howard are a team."

"Indeed."

Jack nodded. "Where in the world did you find Lemon's grandson?"

"I didn't. If you must know, he found me. Mathias was my patient. He came to me very concerned that some of his grandfather's characteristics were beginning to emerge in him. Odd the way genetics works. I merely encouraged him to . . . ah, be himself."

"You manipulated him."

"We call it therapy, Jack. You should know that. Fortunately, the man served his purpose despite being something of a buffoon."

"A buffoon you picked to set the charges in the tunnel and break into the dam's computer system at Lake Lanier. Howard isn't very tolerant of people who make mistakes."

"Mathias was a tool. Some tools, as you know, work better than others."

"You think Pell will accept that explanation?"

The last statement finally got a rise. "Howard and I are extremely close . . ."

Cairo finally realized he was talking too much and caught himself.

"Very good," he said slowly. "You live up to your name, Clever Jack."

"Why don't we meet?" Jack said. "Then you can tell me all about how you're going to break him out of Mayfield."

"You'll learn soon enough. Medical advances are happening all the time. I told that to Beth. Psychiatry is no different. Once Howard's found to be sane, he's a free man."

"Interesting," Jack said. "What about a trade? Myself for Beth Sturgis. You let her go, and I'll deliver myself to you. No word to the cops. Pell'll have his revenge. Everyone will be happy."

A long time passed before Cairo responded. "You surprise me. I'll call you back."

*

Beth Sturgis was sick to her stomach. From the cell door she witnessed the horrific operation in disbelief and shock.

When it was over, Cairo turned to her and said, "As I said earlier, your savior is on the way to rescue you."

Beth said nothing.

"He's really not as smart as I gave him credit for. Either that or he completely failed to see my little joke."

"Joke?"

"Cairo, mummy, hieroglyphics, get it?" He pointed to the form of a female wrapped in linen bandages resting in her sarcophagus. "The late Mrs. Gillam. Elegant, isn't she?"

Beth shook her head.

"No? Oh, well. If you'll excuse me, I have a few more things to attend to."

He was at the top of the stairs when he heard the bottle break.

"Sorry to disappoint you," Beth called out, "but I don't look good in white."

The Soul Eater turned and ran down the steps to Beth's cell. She was sitting on the bed smiling at him, her arms covered in blood.

"No, no, no, no, *no!*" Cairo yelled.

He began to fumble for the keys in his pocket as Beth's head lolled to one side. A moment later she collapsed onto the bed.

Cairo threw the door open and raced into the room. The stupid woman was spoiling everything. A matched pair, that's what Howard said. A matched set.

"Selfish, selfish, selfish," he muttered reaching for her left hand and blinked. The wrist wasn't cut, just smeared with blood. Confused, Cairo looked at her face. Beth's eyes were open staring at him. He didn't see the broken bottle neck coming until it was too late.

Beth's free hand swung around in an arc slashing at his jugular vein. Blood exploded from the wound. Cairo lurched backward, his hand going to his neck in an attempt to stem the flow. Beth struck again, downward this time, jamming the glass shard into his thigh.

The Soul Eater let out a howl, staggering backward in disbelief and rage.

Avoiding his lunge, she ducked under his arm and made a dash for the steps.

*

Jack crossed to the building. It had been abandoned some time ago and now provided illegal shelter to several of the city's homeless population. Three of them lay in sleeping bags on the floor beneath blankets and newspapers. Trash, bottles of wine, and malt liquor littered the lobby entrance. He carefully stepped over them and went up to the roof.

From the street he had estimated the gap between the house and building was no more than eight feet. It looked considerably wider now. A short distance away he could see a stream of headlights moving along Ponce de Leon Avenue. Farther to the south, the Bank of America Building with its erector-shaped top lit up the night.

Jack backed up a few steps to give himself a running start and leaped to the opposite roof. He landed harder than he thought and was carried forward by his own momentum. But for the decorative iron railing, he would have pitched over the edge. He shook his head and moved to the nearest dormer and pried the window open. Nobody locks windows four stories up. From the street, he thought the dormer might be part of an attic. He was wrong. It was a storage room. He withdrew the penlight from his sock, turned it on, and looked around. The room contained a variety of cardboard boxes stacked neatly along the sloping walls. A playpen, a bassinet, and various items of dated furniture were there. Dusty. Forgotten.

The only door opened onto an uncarpeted landing with a staircase. Jack used the sides of the steps to lessen the danger of creaks and silently descended to the next floor where he found three more rooms. They were filled with furniture and covered by drop cloths. The house smelled as if no one had opened a window for a long time. If Cairo held true to form, he and what was left of Mathias Lemon were somewhere in the basement. There was every chance Beth would be there, too.

Why hadn't he called? What if she was dead? What would he do when he and Cairo came face to face? Let history repeat itself?

The heat began building in his chest, urging him to abandon stealth and charge headlong into the basement. That would be a mistake. His mind was his best weapon. Use it. Howard Pell and Cairo were still playing the game. Try as he might, it was nearly impossible to stay focused. If Beth was still alive, she needed him, particularly after seeing that video. Spending the rest of his life without her was simply unacceptable. The urgency to do something continued to grow to the point where he wanted to scream. With an effort he didn't believe himself capable, Jack regained control. His fingers closed around the handle of his gun.

You want me, Cairo? I'm coming.

*

Beth slammed the door behind her to find she was on the first floor of a house. Directly ahead was a living room with heavy Spanish-style furniture dating from the 1940s and a large fireplace with ornate plaque above it. The Inquisition's summer home. Classical music was coming from a pair of speakers against the wall. She didn't need music; she needed a weapon.

What little light there was came through an opening in the drapes. She could hear Cairo on the steps. No time to search for a weapon. Get out. Call for backup.

The front door was at the far end of the hall. She was nearly to it when the basement door burst open. Alton Cairo stood there silhouetted, holding a bandage to the side of his neck. In his left hand was a scalpel.

Keeping her eyes on him, Beth backed slowly away, bumped into the wall, and reached for the light switch. If only she could find something to fight with. An involuntary gasp escaped her lips when a hand closed over hers.

"Not a good idea," Jack said, coming down the last step. He was holding a gun and had it trained on Cairo.

"Jack! How—?"

Jack raised a finger and pointed upward. Suspended from the ceiling were a series of balloons with a thin wire running between them. She followed it to the light switch. The smell of gasoline was now apparent, filling her nostrils.

"Turn that on and the whole place'll go up. The house is rigged to catch fire in case the police close in. Sorry it took me so long—you're bleeding."

"I'm okay. It looks worse than it is. How did you find me?"

"I picked up where you left off and followed your trail of bread crumbs. Once we figured out the late Mr. Lemon and Dr. Death here were working together, it wasn't hard. With Pell's help, Cairo's been working off a blueprint."

"What do you mean?"

Flashing blue lights were now coming through the opening in the drapes.

"Lucky Jack," Cairo sneered.

"More like observant Jack. Drop the knife and keep your hands where I can see them."

Cairo did as he was told.

Jack continued, "Lemon's grandson, Mathias, probably murdered or was an accessory to murdering Ron Curry and his family in order to take his place at Mayfield. He's no longer with us. Cairo just operated on him."

"I saw."

Jack nodded. "When I was at the library, I came across a reference to a book called *Terror in the Dark*. It's a study on serial killers. Unfortunately, they didn't have it. After some searching, I located a copy at an old bookstore not too far from my house. It gives a good account of how Lemon rigged his home to catch fire.

"It was obvious to me back then that Pell was modeling off Albert Lemon. Cairo in turn patterned himself after Pell. Each one was trying to put his own stamp on the killings. I suspect the tunnels we encountered are Cairo's version of catacombs. Essentially like the mazes in the pyramids that led to the burial chamber."

Beth shook her head.

"When we searched Pell's home, I was always bothered by two empty spaces on his bookshelves sitting side by side. What we did find was a notepad with random doodling and quotes from the book. There were pages and pages of them. Pell was completely obsessed. My guess is one was Lemon's diary, the other *Terror in the Dark*. Once I found the copy and began to read, I understood what they were doing. That led me to some newspaper articles that identified this neighborhood."

"Congratulations," Cairo said. "Unfortunately, you'll never touch Howard. He's beyond your reach."

"Perhaps," Jack said. "Your phone call puts him right back in the mix. Fortunately, cell phone calls can be traced and monitored, in case you didn't know. Even that throwaway piece of crap you were using."

"The courts have already said he's not competent to stand trial."

"For the old crimes, maybe," Jack said. "We'll see about the new ones. Accessory to murder, conspiracy and all that."

"Why the clues?" Beth asked.

Cairo simply stared at her and then laughed to himself in a high pitched giggle.

"You know the answer," Jack said.

Beth glanced at him and thought for a moment. "Ego. He has a need to prove he's smarter than everyone else. But it's not a normal need. What do you call it?"

"Pathological."

"That's the reason for the game they were playing. Cairo told me he wondered why he turned out the way he is. I guess he was hoping a madman's diary would help him understand."

"You think it's over. I can assure you, it's not," Cairo said.

A silence ensued before Beth said, "He's right, Jack. They'll probably wind up as roommates."

Jack turned to look at her.

"Not much we can do. It's up to the courts now."

Beth was almost ready to agree until Moira Gillam and the other mummies in the basement flashed into her mind. Cairo was leaning against the door frame. The mummies were replaced by Betsy Ann Tinsley, Jerome Haffner, and Sandra Goldner, wearing her orange cocktail dress, all robbed of their lives by a monster. A monster who might be released on the public one day. The kind who took delight in killing defenseless animals and torturing people.

A long time ago, when she first joined the cops, she asked her father how he felt about shooting a man who had raped and murdered a ten-year-old girl in Charlotte. To her surprise, he was not emotional at all, nor was there any hesitation in his response. "There are certain lines you cross you don't get to come back from. I had no doubt when I pulled the trigger. To tell you the truth, I've never given him any thought since."

In that last moment, the Soul Eater may have understood what was going through her mind when she looked back at him. Certainly Jack did. His nod to her was almost imperceptible.

"You and the bitch haven't won anything," Cairo said.

As they turned to walk out the front door, Beth lifted her elbow and hit the light switch.

Chapter 81

It was early May. Dusk. Two figures stood on a little knoll in Chastain Park. Some distance away, electric lights burned over a baseball diamond, and boys were chasing grounders hit by a coach at home plate. Jack thought back to when he was young. He'd played on that field. It was a quieter, more predictable time, marked by greater civility and trust. The world had changed; the diamond remained a constant. Not really a bad time to sit in the backyard with someone you loved, sipping ice tea from tall glasses, and watching fireflies light up the night.

Beth had just finished spreading Peeka the cat's ashes on the sloping green lawn, the same place she'd found him years earlier as a starving kitten. Jack felt a pang for her loss, which melted away when she turned back and smiled at him. He'd never seen anything quite so beautiful. Marta sat close by watching her as well. Her tail rocked slightly when Beth waved.

The fire department had been able to contain the blaze at Cairo's house but couldn't save the structure. Just as well. The chamber of horrors had sunk back into the abyss from which it came. Perhaps fire would cleanse the city and give it a chance to heal.

Now that the ordeal was over, Georgia Tech wanted him back, but it didn't feel quite the same. He'd have to give it some thought. But not just then. Beth reached the crest of the knoll and without a word slipped her hand into his, then rested her head on his shoulder. From their vantage point he could see Atlanta's skyline in the distance. Most of the lights were on. Overhead, the first evening star appeared, bright against a deepening blue sky. Somewhere in the dark a scent of honeysuckle floated back to him. It was a beautiful time of year and Atlanta was a beautiful city. He didn't know a better one. There were probably more beautiful cities, but he didn't know them.

Marta finally nudged their hands with her nose. He looked down at her and then at Beth. She nodded. And together they walked down the hill and out into the vulnerable night.

Acknowledgments

This book wouldn't have been possible without the help and support of my dearest friend, Jane Mashburn, a gem of a person if there ever was one. Thanks also to Gary Peel, who patiently sat there and listened to the numerous scenes and passages I inflicted on him without ever once trying to flee.

Since this is my first book, it's difficult to speak with any authority on the craft of writing or the publishing industry. I can, however, point out some things that quickly became obvious to me as the novel progressed.

First, if there are better or more helpful agents out there than Jane Dystel, Miriam Goderich, and the people at Dystel Goderich Literary Management, I don't know who they are. At no point could I have asked for more. From the very beginning, they believed in the book and never gave up. Their efforts were not simply confined to finding it a home but in helping me develop as a writer through their suggestions and comments.

It would be disingenuous to claim this book was authored by me alone. In candor, it is the product of Matt Martz's insight and direction as my editor along with editors Maddie Caldwell and Nike Power—yes, that really is her name—all of whom dug in and helped me see what I could not. Their patience, advice, and nurturing is not to be believed. Any writer, let alone someone new to the profession, should be willing to walk over hot coals to have them on their side. Three editors for the price of one? Not a bad deal at all. They made the process of putting the final version together a wonderful experience. Each turned out to be part muse, part psychologist, and all friend. I simply can't imagine being luckier than I was to have such a fine group of professionals on my side.

My appreciation and gratitude also goes to Andy Ruggirello, Crooked Lane art director, for the great work in creating such a nifty cover, and to Alex Celia for his meticulous copy editing. A tip of the hat also goes to Jennifer Canzone, for her design of the book itself. Thanks as well to the amazing Sarah Poppe for all her help and assistance and to Butch Morgan for his impromptu proofreading.

Lastly, and most importantly, to those who have read, or will read, *Once Shadows Fall*, I sincerely hope you will enjoy the story *we* crafted for you.